Just In Case

By the same Author

BOOKS:

NO OFFICIAL UMBRELLA: An Autobiography *(DCG Publications.)*
DOCTOR WHO & THE SPACE MUSEUM *(W.H.Allen /Virgin Publishing.)*
THE DOUBLE DECKERS *(Pan Books.)*
HILDEGARDE H AND HER FRIENDS - *Illustrated by Arnold Taraborrelli*
(Abydos Publishing.)
DEAD ON TIME: - The first Thornton King Adventure
(Raider Publishing International.)

PLAYS PUBLISHED:

BEAUTIFUL FOR EVER *(Samuel French, London.)*
THRILLER OF THE YEAR *(Samuel French, London.)*
RED IN THE MORNING *(Samuel French, New York.)*

PLAYS PRODUCED:

BEAUTIFUL FOR EVER	EARLY ONE MORNING
PETER PAN *(Book & Lyrics)*	THE 88
BAY RUM	GENERATIONS
RED IN THE MORNING	THRILLER OF THE YEAR
CHAMPAGNE CHARLIE	OH BROTHER!
TELL ME YOU LOVE ME	WOMEN AROUND

FILMS:

A KING'S STORY (Columbia Pictures.)
RIVER RIVALS *(Children's Film Foundation.)*
THE MAGNIFICENT SIX AND A HALF *(Children's Film Foundation.)*
BINDLE *(Tannsfeld Films/Rank.)*
A HARD LOOK AT SOFTWARE *(Rank Documentary.)*
CLAN FRAZER, CLAN MACPHERSON *(Mica Films Documentary.)*
BATHTIME *(AJT Productions Documentary.)*

TELEVISION:

DOCTOR WHO & THE SPACE MUSEUM *(BBC TV.)*
THE DOUBLE DECKERS *(20ᵗʰ Century Fox - Writer and Script Editor.)*

Just In Case

Another
Thornton King Adventure

Glyn Idris Jones

DCG
Publications

First Published in Greece 2009

© Glyn Jones 2007

The author's moral rights have been asserted

DCG Publications
www.dcgmediagroup.com

ISBN 978-960-98418-1-8

10 9 8 7 6 5 4 3 2 1

Typeset by
DCG Publications

Printed in England by
Lightening Source.

www.glynjones.net

CHAPTER 1

According to that musical prodigy Rossini, the most musical of all instruments is the Spanish guitar, and currently in a London pub that very same instrument was being mercilessly and most unmusically strummed by a skeletal youth sporting a wispy beard, and lank greasy blonde locks; a Baroque pearl ear-ring, elephant hair bracelet on one wrist and various strings of beads around his neck. His Zapata moustache and the fingers of his right hand, and most probably his lungs, were dark brown with nicotine stains from a heavy indulgence in Woodbines.

Thanks to London's traffic, clothes don't usually last longer than a day in that city before needing to be laundered but the young man's flares, decorated with butterfly transfers and patched at the knees, never mind his vest decorated with little shards of mirror, looked as though they hadn't been near a washing machine or a dry cleaner in months.

A full pint mug sat on the floor beside his bentwood chair on the slightly raised platform that was his stage, though why the guv'nor chose to indulge this particular musician was beyond anyone's comprehension, anyone that is who wasn't tone deaf or had even a rudimentary ear for music. The chilly weather and the guv'nor's soft heart could account for it. Busking for pennies in Tottenham Court Road tube station with icy winds blowing down the passageways and around the fundament meant frozen fingers and probably the onset of piles and a winter enduring cough.

Thornton had almost subconsciously taken in the young man's appearance as he sat with his own half pint of warm mild ale, hardly touched. Americans never could understand why the English like their beer warm, but then the English never had much taste for chilled American beer until Bud took a hold as something slightly more exotic than good old ale. Thornton had taken in the scene, not because he was listening to the noise passing for music, and there were no frozen fingers as an excuse, but because he was ruminating on what might be the best way to commit suicide. Strange, considering he had recently been a couple of times within inches of an early demise anyway. An image of Ntombi, gun in hand, flashed through his mind and he shuddered at the memory, dismissing it as quickly as it came. But when a man sits in a pokey, damp, dingy, dirty, cold-water office, its upkeep costing an arm and a leg: the telephone doesn't ring and no one knocks at the door; the only mail he get consists of threats and final demands and he goes home to an apartment in serious need of refurbishment due to a mishap with an exploding golf ball, there seems nothing else for it but to top oneself. The cost of replacing windows alone would be astronomical and a white Christmas would simply put the kybosh on any attempt at keeping down costs as far as heating was concerned.

After his involvement in the Princess Spitskaya affair, starting with the death of an international arms dealer in a chic and exclusive Soho restaurant and followed by further strange deaths culminating in the death of Spitskaya herself he should, as a private detective, have become a figure of some note on the world stage; well the British stage if nothing else. His story should have been plastered over every national front page from Argentina to Zaire. Hollywood studio heads should have been on bended knees hammering at the door offering a king's ransom and waving a five hundred page gilt-edged contract for the film rights; gilt-edged in their direction that is, because it didn't always mean much to the poor mutt appending his signature although the studio's lawyers made it look pretty impressive, which is what they were paid astronomical sums for.

Alas, a certain Detective Sergeant Venables, as he then was, now promoted to Detective Inspector, saw to it that, though Thornton couldn't be entirely ignored, he could be kept virtually muzzled and placed well in the background whilst he, Venables, was awarded the kudos for having single-handedly and at a stroke solved half a dozen murders. It was his photograph that was seen in every newspaper in the land, his story holding bold headlines and television news for days on end, and he had absolutely no doubt he would be in line for more promotion, possibly to chief constable, and on the New Year's honours list for an MBE at least.

What did his snotty spotty teenage children, who made no bones about the fact that they considered him, both as a parent and as a person, but particularly as a parent, pretty weird … *Yeah … like, well you know … ah … well … yeah … I mean … whatever …* think of their dad now? If truth were to be told, still not much. As far as they were concerned he was a plain middle-aged balding basket case and, having basked in reflected glory for a short while, they grew bored with the whole thing, attention span among the young, even those getting close to losing their teenage tag, being of strictly limited duration, and seemingly growing shorter with each passing year.

The episode had a totally opposite effect on Rita, the wife and mother. Now that her man was a hero in the eyes of the world, well in the eyes of little England anyway, after years of keeping her thread-veined, cellulite legs firmly crossed, after years of denial and refusal to indulge in "that messy act" as she had secretly called it, she was now rampant. What a change was there; not a falling off but a distinct hike. All distaste swept aside she had become, and there was only one word for it, voracious. Maybe there was a second word for it – insatiable. She had gone totally insane with the make-up, applying it extravagantly and with no finesse whatsoever, especially the lipstick that her husband most strongly objected to. Had he been aware of lipstick's origins, that many many years past, certain ladies of easy virtue on the shores of the Mediterranean had invented lipstick as an advertising aid for a particular sexual activity they specialised in and which they were particularly good at, he would have banned its use altogether. Venables considered it wholly deviant and unnatural, this particular sexual activity, not the lipstick. Sex was pleasurable of course. That is why people did it, but it was meant for the procreation of children, the continuance of the species and not merely to satisfy lust. As for the procreation, it was obviously highly successful considering the number of humans now inhabiting and polluting the planet. The make-up he decided was merely an expensive pandering to vanity and to be truthful, or so he thought, made his wife look an absolute tart but, with only hints and the occasional mild remonstrance, he let it go at that. Hints and remonstrance she totally ignored. They possibly didn't even register. For Rita the sluice gates of sensuality had opened, much to her husband's deep disgust. He found it a total turnoff. She wanted it anywhere, anytime, in any position or fashion, all of which to his mind was total perversion and left him as limp as an earthworm and running for cover, especially after he had come across some appalling visual aids concealed in one of her drawers and a catalogue of sex toys that were positively mind boggling. What was the world coming to? Where on earth had she got them from? He couldn't bring himself to ask. He didn't even want to acknowledge their existence. All his life he had fought vice and here it was manifesting itself under his very own roof, come home to roost ... as it were!

Thornton King of course knew nothing of Inspector Venables' marital problems and sexual hang-ups, but he did know he had been virtually written out of the script as far as the Spitskaya affair was concerned, well and truly bested by that tight-arsed pillar of establishment rectitude in the solving and resultant publicity of what one tabloid had headlined, A MODEL'S LOT IS NOT A HAPPY ONE, though not too many of its readership, classified by the advertising fraternity as C and D, would have got the allusion to Messrs Gilbert and Sullivan. And what of Miss Holly Day's participation in this caper? Well, she was not the kind of girl who courted publicity which was just as well as, being gainfully employed in Whitehall by Her Majesty's government in its secret highways and byways, it would not have gone down at all well with her pin-striped, bowler hatted, umbrella wielding, tea drinking, biscuit nibbling superiors.

'So tell me, Inspector, how did you come to suspect the Princess Spitskaya?'

'Oh, I was onto her from the start, mate.'

The questioning journalist, by name the Honourable Duncan Devonport-Fawcett, known to all as Taps ever since at primary school he was lumbered with the nickname by the son of an American diplomat, was a young man from a good home, good schools, a good university and for some time now had been the law correspondent on a superior and very expensive monthly glossy. For law read crime stories. This was a position the desperate editor had introduced in a rash effort to boost falling sales and, not realising he would have done far better to hire someone from Liverpool or Essex, took on board a youthful member of the upper class from the Home Counties who he mistakenly thought would pull in the punters of his generation. After all the magazine's advertising was top drawer: art galleries and antique dealers in Belgravia, bespoke tailors and shirt makers, estate agents dealing only with houses of six figures or more both at home and abroad, expensive perfumes, interior decorators who wore expensive perfumes, fashion houses whose designers wore expensive perfumes.

At the moment this said crime correspondent and member of the upper class wasn't too sure he wanted to be called "mate" by this non too appetising in appearance obviously lowlife policeman. He raised a questioning eyebrow, cleared his throat and adopted his

4

most upper class expression, which consisted mainly of adding to the raised eyebrow one raised side of his perfect Cupid's bow upper lip that had been much admired when he was in the cathedral choir, and looking down his aristocratic nose, but the policeman carried on regardless.

'The minute I walked into that grubby little restaurant …'

'Whoa there! Hold on just a minute! Did you say grubby?'

Indeed, the décor of *L'eminence Grise*, the Soho restaurant where it all happened consisted mainly of various shades of brown that hadn't been touched up in years, and there may have been a few grease spots where tables were right up against the wall, but grubby was pushing it a bit. The blue eyes seemed almost to protrude from their sockets and the eyebrow practically reached the blonde quiff wuthering above it like grass on a Yorkshire moor. The restaurant happened to be enjoying the patronage of the young Devonport-Fawcett ever since he had reported the events relating to the demise of that aforementioned Middle Eastern arms dealer, a Mr Shoggi, happily lunching in that establishment until he slumped forward and his face connected with his dessert. Had he been fat and unable to slump forward he would have died sitting upright or toppled off his chair sideways but, as it was, he went to meet his maker with cream all over his face. Now, as a result of this unseemly incident, the restaurant was booked solid for months, but a table was always available for Taps, since a write-up in his glossy periodical was advertising François, owner of *L'eminence Grise,* couldn't afford in a hundred years if he'd actually had to pay for it. This interview with Venables was a late follow-up that would ensure a continuation of Taps' "most favoured diner" status for some time to come, though the story might by now be losing some of its fascination and growing as cold as François's vichyssoise. It had already slipped from the front pages of the popular press in favour of one or two possible political scandals involving members of the government, a call girl or two, and some dodgy Russian diplomats.

'*L'eminence Grise* grubby? One of the finest French establishments in the whole of London, grubby? François a cordon bleu chef? A finer cuisine than even Paris could provide?' Taps just couldn't be emphatic enough but Venables refused to be impressed. He was definitely a meat and two veg man with lashings of thick brown gravy.

'There you go you see, French. Anyway, be that as it may, mate

...' there was a distinctly audible intake of breath from the crime correspondent ... 'the minute I walked in there and spotted her skulking in a corner...'

'Now just a moment,' Taps interrupted, looking up from his notebook. Taps was an ardent fan of early Hollywood movies and in early movies all news photographers carried enormous flash cameras and all newshounds carried notebooks. They also wore fedoras, so named after the play of that name by Victorian Sardou, but Taps liked to run his elegant fingers through his blonde locks and you just couldn't do that wearing a fedora. Besides which he didn't think a hat really suited him. He kept his old school boater for sentimental reasons though he never wore it. The rim was practically coming away from the crown and had dirty schoolboy finger marks and grass stains all over it. 'What were you doing there in the first place?' he asked. Obviously non too appetising in appearance low life policemen did not dine at establishments such as *L'eminence Grise*. They probably couldn't even afford the cover charge. A Fred's caff for sausage and mash or a bowl of jellied eels in the Kingsland Road would have been more in Venables' line was Taps' spot-on guess.

'I was called there, wasn't I? We received a nine nine nine, didn't we? A man had collapsed and died under highly suspicious circumstances, hadn't he?' Did the inspector have to turn every sentence into a question?

'What highly suspicious circumstances?' Asked Taps, coming up with another question of his own and making a perfectly logical suggestion. 'He could have simply died of a heart attack, an embolism, a brain haemorrhage.'

'Yes, well er ... excuse me one moment.' They were standing outside Vine Street Police station and Venables, who had an uncanny knack of avoiding awkward questions, especially ones he didn't quite understand, crossed over to have a quick word with a constable standing nearby and then returned to the journalist with 'Yes, well now, you were asking how I cottoned on to that phoney princess, well ...'

'No I wasn't, actually. I was asking what you were ...?'

'It was when she laughed, that's what did it.'

'She laughed. People lunching in a first class restaurant are not permitted to laugh, is that what you're saying? They must dine in absolute silence I suppose. Dining is a serious business. Conversation must be discreet. A smile is allowed but laughing could upset the digestive system as well as annoying other diners. Like people eating with their mouths open.'

'That's not what I was saying, not at all. What I meant was, there's this poor old sod, just kicked the bucket, and she had the gall to laugh, right out loud. I have absolutely no objection to her laughing prior to this untoward event but, well, I thought; this really isn't on, is it? I mean, there's a certain thing called respect isn't there? A death should be treated with the dignity it deserves shouldn't it?'

'I don't think death's at all dignified. I think it's rather yucky actually.' To tell the truth Taps had absolutely no experience of death not even from afar. His grandparents were still hale and hearty in their nineties and it would seem he came from a long living family 'But tell me, Inspector,' he continued, 'what was she laughing at?'

'Search me, mate.'

There he goes again with that mate business, the young journalist thought, deciding to move on and get this interview over with as quickly as possible but before he could open his mouth Venables continued. The policeman was enjoying himself immensely.

'If you ask me it was because of that idiot she was with. He probably tried to make a funny and she laughed to oblige.'

'What idiot might that have been?'

Venables realised he had slipped up. He'd inadvertently brought Thornton into the conversation and, even though the word "idiot" was left out of the eventual article, Thornton was now established, however nebulously, as having been a part of the Spitskaya affair.

'Mr Thornton King.' He said it as quickly as he could. There was no point trying to pretend he'd forgotten the man's name but he would have to be more circumspect as to how the interview went from hereon in, choose his words more carefully that is to say.

'He was with the princess's party?'

'The princess didn't have a party. She was there on her tod wasn't she? But this King fellow evidently knew her from previous and ...'

'Previous what?'

'What?'

'You said "previous". I asked, "previous what?"'

Venables looked totally confused. He was so used to using the word previous in terms of a suspect's form, previously committed crimes, previous convictions or not as the case might be, he didn't understand what Taps was getting at.

'Oh, never mind,' Taps went on, seeing the furrowed brow and the eyes that had shifted to one side and appeared to be staying there. Obviously the man, apart from any impression he had already given, was not of a very high intelligence. It was no wonder crime was on the increase. He must have solved the murders more by good luck than good judgment and with a heap of backup from forensics.

'There's been talk that the Spitskaya woman was a spy for the KGB, or whatever it's called, is that right?' Taps was a bit hazy about what was going on outside his own milieu. He wasn't even sure if it was still called the KGB, but a Russian link could be a really exciting twist. He wondered for a moment if his magazine would pay for him to go snooping around behind the iron curtain, real third man stuff. He mentally hummed the first line of the Harry Lime theme. There was also the chance it could be profitable if he could make contact with the Russian Mafia. On the other hand, after a moment's consideration, perhaps it wasn't that good an idea. He had heard things about the Russian Mafia and he wouldn't want to put himself in any danger. The Hon. Duncan Devonport-Fawcett was extremely circumspect as a crime correspondent. Anyway, Venables had turned down the corners of his mouth and lifted his shoulders in a "who knows" shrug so it probably wasn't worth following up.

'And I'm informed that Mr King was until recently employed by ... MI5 was it?' Damn it, he was picking up the policeman's mannerisms. Again there was a shrug from Venables whose eyes had returned to focus on Taps' face but were narrowing to slits. It was high time to get away from the Thornton King line. Either that or call off this interview right here and now, but he couldn't do that, he was revelling too much in a misguided sense of his own importance.

'And that he is now acting as a private detective.' Taps continued. He had to stop himself saying 'Isn't he?'

'A what!' Venables let out a sort of braying sound that, apart from setting Duncan's teeth on edge, could only be interpreted as "you've just got to be joking, mate."

******

Thornton remembered how he had reacted when listening to Holly reading him the finished article and even now he was still seething at the thought of Venables taking all the credit. It would be just like Holly to subscribe to that type of glossy periodical: all froth, expensive froth at that, and hardly any substance, nine tenths of it advertising or so it seemed. Her excuse was she was only interested in the fashion and home decorating pages. So who was this so-called law correspondent anyway, this Duncan Devonport-Fawcett? Sounded like a right burke from the shires.

He lifted his mug and took the meanest of mean little sips, barely enough beer to moisten his lips, hardly more than some of the froth from the top as he was going to have to make his half pint last. The itinerant musician was now, with alternative flat fingers and then bony knuckles, bashing the body of his guitar in what he fondly imagined to be Flamenco fashion. Thornton decided he was from a working class background. His father was a gas fitter and they lived in a council house in Ilford and he drove his parents mad practising the guitar for hours on end in his tiny back bedroom. One day, unable to stand it any longer, they would kill him and plead disturbed minds.

Having decided this would be a fitting fate for someone with so little talent, Thornton turned his attention elsewhere. It wasn't that there was a more interesting sight in the pub, it being a little too early for the regular lunchtime crowd, one o'clock not yet having struck, the hour the surrounding offices would disgorge most of their working population. There was only one of the gin-and-tonic regulars, mutton dressed as lamb though admittedly still highly colourful even if the colours were all wrong, seated on her usual stool at the bar; and a couple of men at a nearby banquette, one of whom Thornton seemed to recognise from elsewhere but he couldn't think where. For a moment he admired the man's suit, definitely Saville Row, no shortage of pennies there, and then went back to brooding on his imminent suicide. He had crossed one leg over the other but now, remembering a too obvious hole had appeared in the sole of his elegant shoe, he dropped his foot to the floor.

The suicide would have to be as painless as possible of course, that went without saying. What could it have been in the Japanese psyche that they had invented something as ghastly as sepukku? Images of a ranting Mishima on a roof top haranguing cadets came to mind. Renaissance England of course was noted for it, but at least you had it done to you, you didn't have to do it yourself and anyway, it wasn't of your own choosing being hung, drawn, and quartered. Guilty, or innocent like the queen's poor hapless Portuguese doctor, framed and confessing under torture, with luck you would be so near death when they cut you down you wouldn't really notice the nastiness going on around your midriff before your head finally came off. The executioners though, with all the practice they had, (possibly apprenticed as butchers) were evidently so adept at their trade that that was hardly likely. Bad enough having your "privities" (as they were so coyly termed) sliced off and, with the mob howling for your blood, it couldn't have been much fun watching your steaming bowels being removed and bubbling away on the barbecue before you passed on to the great beyond, no longer the life and soul of the party. It was no wonder the Japanese have a stout fellow standing by to deliver the mercy stroke. Or has the tradition of sepukku, like duelling, been outlawed?

He didn't fancy hanging, or throwing himself under a train, or drowning. The Romans, he believed, used to lie in a hot bath before they slit their wrists, either that or they fell upon their swords or got a pal to stick it in if they were of a military bent, but neither of those methods appealed to him either. What about poison then? Ghastly thought. He had read in a book on Greek medicinal plants though that hemlock causes a painless death. Was it Socrates who knocked back the hemlock? Anyway, where in the British Isles was he likely to find hemlock? It was a cert you couldn't get it on prescription or from a health food store. He would have to spend the afternoon in The British Library doing some research. Perhaps Kew Gardens could come up with the answer. Perhaps Kew Gardens had a hemlock plant he could nick a few leaves from presuming a pocket full of leaves would be enough. He wondered how many he would need.

The tart at the bar turned and gave him what any number of years earlier would have been a simply ravishing come hither smile that he ignored. He was in no financial position to provide follow up gin and tonics or in the mood for inane conversation that would eventually lead to suggestive innuendo and finally to a downright invitation. Disappointed in the lack of response, the lady in question turned back to the bar and waggled her empty glass in the barman's direction as signal for a refill. There was no point her trying to attract the attention of the two men on the banquette; they were too wrapped up in their conversation. For a moment Thornton wondered what they could be talking about and why did he seem to know the one man's face? It wasn't a particularly interesting face. It was the kind of face that could get lost in a crowd so why did he think he knew it? Judging by their earnest expressions and the pianissimo of their voices they were planning either a bank heist or a great train robbery, he wondered which it could be. Actually, he went on to think, they were probably discussing nothing more important than the possible winner of the two-thirty at Kempton Park.

There being no immediate answer to his musings, Thornton lost interest. He switched off his radar and turned to look at the street door of the bar with its fine, as yet unvandalised, Edwardian etched glass panes, just as it opened and, accompanied by a chilly gale, she swept in. It was quite an entrance. She had the knack of making an entrance. Had the bar been full there would have been a momentary hiatus in conversation as all eyes were turned in her direction. As it was there was only Thornton to take notice, the two men deep in conversation, the barman busily wiping glasses and the mutton dressed as lamb who gave one haughty glance and a "humph" before looking away and concentrating on something really interesting on the shelves behind the bar.

Holly, as usual, looked ravishing. To-day's theme was tartan including the feathered bonnet that, considering the current Highland type weather, was singularly appropriate. The cold had brought a glow to her cheeks and, as she removed the bonnet and shook her head, her hair tumbled down in a manner which would have made any man into women's crowning glory, even a hair fetishist in the minor league, go weak at the knees. Thornton got up to greet her with a smile and a peck on the cheek that brought a further sneer to the face of the tart at the bar who caught the action reflected in a mirror.

Holly hung her bonnet on the back of her chair and slipped off her shoulder bag, placing it on her lap as she sat down and started to remove her gloves.

'What's your poison?' Thornton asked. His mind was no longer on suicide but the expression, "What's your poison?" that came into vogue in the nineteenth century after the execution of the mass poisoner, Doctor William Palmer who even got rid of his own unwanted infants with poison on lumps of sugar, was one he used quite often, though he wasn't aware of how it had come about. The older generation seemed to use the expression quite a lot, which is probably where he picked it up; from his father or one of his father's friends like Colonel Montcliff, a military man of solid tradition likely to have a fit if the port didn't go around the table in the correct direction following the rising and setting of the sun.

'Well, as I'm chilled to the bone,' Holly responded, 'I am going to be thoroughly basic and go for a rum and blackcurrant, not even a Bacardi but a daaaaaark rum to warm the cockles of my heart if nothing else. By the way, have you any idea at all what the cockles of your heart might be?'

'No idea,' Thornton said, jingling the coins in his pocket and wondering if they would mount up to a daaaaaaark rum and blackcurrant.

'Probably Irish,' Holly said, 'and hurry back. I've got a surprise for you.'

'Why can't I have my surprise before I go?'

'Because I want my drink.'

With a resigned shrug, Thornton headed for the bar, moving to one end as far away from the tart as he could get. Although, with the advent of Holly, there was obviously no longer any point her trying to entice him into her parlour, things could change and he wasn't taking the risk. The barman, who was new and who had physically if not mentally passed adolescence but not the acne that went with it, (and the greasiness of his hair might possibly explain that), placed his half-smoked roll-up in an ashtray. Then, with his head turned to one side, giving a fairly good impression of a fish by blowing smoke rings as he moved, he advanced slowly over to where Thornton was waiting. Thornton wondered if this one would last. The turnover in barmen was pretty regular. There were standards to keep up after all. Having duly arrived at his destination the barman, whose name was Sean, stood stony faced and waited in turn. Thornton, who was aware of the young fellow's antecedents, was inclined to inform him that he *was* permitted to speak and did he know what heart cockles were, but eventually decided to break the stalemate by ordering.

'A rum and blackcurrant please,' he said with a smile and Sean, who hailed from County Sligo and should have had the traditional glorious gift of the gab, waited a moment as though considering whether he was capable of producing this. Then, rock faced, he dragged himself back the way he had come to fulfil the order. He picked up his cigarette and took a drag before turning up a glass and placing it beneath the correct optic. Thornton turned to look at Holly, pursed his mouth and shrugged. He knew what her comment would be the minute he got back to their table. "Thornton, I really don't know why you patronise this particular pub. It really is soooooo dingy." To which his reply would be simply, "It's my local. It's handy and they know me." To which she would say, "Do they grant you credit?" At which he would only grunt because there was a sign behind the bar that read Definitely No Credit and another which read Do not ask for credit as a refusal might offend, so the situation was perfectly obvious. No, though he may be a regular patron, the guv'nor did not extend him the credit for which he was, more often than not, in need.

The barman returned to place his order on the counter and Thornton discovered sufficient coins in his pocket to pay for it, at the same time giving facetious thanks that went right over Sean's head. He returned to the table just as Holly opened her mouth to say ...

'Thornton, I really don't...'

He raised a finger. She stopped. They both laughed and he sat down, placing her drink in front of her.

'Cheers!' she said, lifting the glass.

'Bottoms up.' He lifted his mug in response and took another delicate sip, which was no way to enjoy beer, but *c'est la vie* as the saying goes. 'The Cretans say *aspro pato* which means, "white bottom". That is knock it back in one and show the bottom of your glass.' For emphasis he gave the bottom of his mug a tap. Thornton had a couple of years before spent a glorious holiday on Crete, not much of which he remembered because of the strength of the local raki and the renowned hospitality of the islanders. 'Now, what's this surprise?' he concluded.

'You'll love it.'

'That's good.'

She took another sip of her drink. He waited.

'Well?'

'Patience, Thornton, is a virtue. Enjoy the suspense.'

'The suspense is killing me. Actually I hate surprises. But, as I am to wait for whatever denouement is forthcoming, tell me something, you see those two men over there?'

'Over where?'

A few more of the lunchtime crowd had entered to keep Sean on his toes so Thornton had to indicate with his eyes and a tilting of the head in the right direction as to which two men he meant.

'What about them?' She asked.

'The one in the fancy whistle ...'

13

'Whistle?'

'Whistle and flute, come on, Holly, you know your Cockney rhyming slang, the one in the fancy suit; I seem to know his face. Can you place him?'

'I can't see his face. Wait till he turns around,' and right on cue, as if he intuitively sensed he was being talked about, the man did turn around, and Holly buried her nose in her glass until he turned back to his companion.

'Yes,' Holly said, lowering her voice. 'His name is Joost something or other. Can't remember the surname offhand. It's something un-pronounceable, one of those peculiar Flemish names that end in a cx.'

'Like you know someone is Rumanian because his name ends in cu,' Thornton chimed in, 'or a Greek, opoulis, or a Cretan, akis.'

'Have you done?' Holly glowered, She had heard all this before. Thornton sometimes had a habit of repeating himself. She went quiet again so as not to be overheard and he followed suit. 'Anyway, as I said, he's a Belgian. Customs have been interested in him for a long time.'

'Why?' Thornton asked.

'He travels a lot.'

'So?'

'South Africa, Amsterdam, London, Sierra Leone, Amsterdam, London, what does that suggest?'

'Diamonds?'

'Diamonds. But they've never been able to pin anything on him. He certainly has never acted as a courier, but we've also been keeping tabs on him and you obviously remember his face from mug shots at the department though it's not a face that stands out, no peculiarities of any description, rather bland in fact, nondescript I'd call it. CIA are also interested in him I believe. He's a member of the Army of The Righteous.'

'Oh, yes! Of course. The cult that, like the Colorado beetle, came over from America. Only it didn't come from Colorado, it came from California where all good cults come from. Why were we and our American cousins keeping tabs then? Did we think this particular cult so dangerous? It seems pretty innocuous to me. A lot of gathering in fields, a lot of hugging, and kissing, possibly going a bit further amongst the more amorous or those on a high at the time, chanting at the moon, tambourine tapping, bongo bashing. Kids' stuff really, except for the ones going the full mile.'

'No, Thornton, any cult that perverts minds, especially young unformed minds, is dangerous. Kids stuff you say. Kids these days looking for something to latch on to are so easily taken in. Traditional religion in the west for the most part has lost its flavour. This man, Joost, is what in the cult is called an "International Elder." There are a number of them from various countries but there is a charismatic figure at the top here in England, "The Beloved Leader."'

'Beloved Leader! Come off it, Holly, you're pulling my leg.' Thornton was shaking with silent laughter. 'What is he, from China? Korea or somewhere?'

'We don't know who he, or she, is.'

'You mean it's an hermaphrodite?'

'No, I mean we know he's English but evidently he or she appears at gatherings robed and masked. It comes, it speaks, it holds the faithful spellbound and it goes. It's almost a phantom. There's special sound effects and lighting and the followers scream hysterically like at a rock concert and some even faint or go into a trance in response to the magic.'

'All religion needs magic. When the churches decided to remove half their magic, their flavour you could say, they lost half their congregation. King James might have been a somdomite as dear old Queensbury termed it, but at least he was responsible for a beautiful Bible as opposed to the banality of modern versions. Talk about dumbing down!'

'It's not a religion, Thornton, it's a cult.'

'All religions start as a cult. All religions start off with a charismatic figure, but after he has gone the schisms and the in-fighting break out as the various branches fight for status, superiority, power, wealth, making up all sorts of rules and regulations as they go along. In the end the original message is all but forgotten. Anyway, what are the beliefs, the objectives, of this Army of the Righteous? Are they another lunatic "we're going to conquer the world" bunch?'

'It's possible. Up to now it would seem, as you so rightly surmised, they're mainly interested in their cash flow. What we're concerned about is that at some time in the future these relatively harmless religious gatherings, tambourine tapping as you call it, will turn violent and the violence could spread, could be deliberately fostered and could be very damaging. The cult could grow into a full-blown terrorist organisation. If the cash flow suddenly dried up they might decide to take to protection rackets, drugs, looting, kidnapping, robbing banks. Who knows? Others have done it before them, others will do it after them. But I didn't come here to talk shop. Here's your surprise.'

She had dipped a hand into her bag, withdrawn it and now held it and its contents towards Thornton.

'Airline tickets?'

'That's right. You and I are going to The Riviera for a few days. We both need a break and it's a Christmas present from daddy.'

'Christmas present! Look, Oxford Street might be all lit up, Selfridges windows are a fairyland for the eyes of tiny tots of all ages, shopaholics have lost all sense of restraint and the tills might be ringing merrily on high while the plastic knows no bounds and this nation of shopkeepers, as I believe Napoleon called us, rubs its collective hands with glee, but Christmas itself is weeks away.'

'Christmas gets earlier every year; you know that. All right, call it a pre-Christmas present.'

'You mean when Christmas actually does come around there'll be another stocking filler?'

'Maybe, if daddy's feeling generous. I believe the bonuses are going to be extra generous this year.'

'Lucky daddy. Well this may come as news to you, Holly but, even with daddy's super surprise present, I really am in no position to go away and spend a few days on the French Riviera, a rather expensive stretch of real estate or so I have been led to believe. There are other expenses to think about such as hotel bills and spending money and I am absolutely skint. Your daaaaaaark rum and blackcurrant took my last ha'penny. All I have in my pocket now is a deep hole.'

'All taken care of. Daddy's present covers everything. Do you object to being a kept boy for a few days? Look. Thornton, you and I had a bet at the golf course ...'

'When the dear old colonel bought it. Poor Madge. It will be a long time before she gets over it, if she ever does.'

'She hasn't got that long to go, Thornton.'

'Ladies like Madge tend to live for ever. Still I'm sure it was the way old Montcliff would have liked to have gone.'

'What on earth can you mean by that?'

'Well, being a military man all his life, how many battles did he live to see and he never copped it once either from mortar, shell, bullet, bomb, mine, bayonet or grenade, so an explosion, even from a booby trap golf ball, was a fitting end don't you agree?'

'You mean like it was a fitting end for the admiral to be torpedoed in his bath. Torpedoed in probably the most sensitive part of his anatomy.'

'Can't be too sure of that. They're still trying to put the pieces together.'

'Well, the colonel had a lovely funeral. Last Post beautifully played by a bugler always brings tears to my eyes ... no, seriously, don't smile ... guard of honour blazing away, coffin covered in the union jack. As I was saying before you interrupted, we had a bet and I lost but you wouldn't let me honour my bet. Now if a gentleman always pays a debt of honour, so should a lady. Fair's fair, wouldn't you say? Equality and all that? Consider this a settlement as it were.'

'There is still the small matter of redecorating my flat to be taken care of.'

'You've only yourself to blame for that. Well, your Peter Pan syndrome anyway.'

'My what?'

'You were showing off like a small boy, bouncing that exploding golf ball down the passage.'

'I thought it was a dud!'

'And you know what thought did don't you?'

'No, what did thought do?'

'Thought he'd fallen out of bed and got out to take a look.'

'That's an Irish story.'

'Cornish, actually. My nanny was Cornish so I presume that's where it came from. Anyway, you were insured weren't you?'

'One good thing I did.'

'And have you put in a claim?'

'I have.'

'And has your insurance company accepted it, even as fictitious as you have no doubt made it?'

'I took inflation into account.'

'Well?'

'Well what?'

'Have they accepted it?'

'Not yet, but with a few minor quibbles it seems they will. After all, they did send an assessor around to view the damage. Funny little man he was. I don't think he really knew his arse from his elbow.'

'So you managed to pull the wool over his eyes. But, getting away from anatomy, there's nothing then for you to worry about on that score. I must admit I'm surprised. Insurance companies on the whole are world champion wrigglers. Anyway I have already had words with Harold ... '

'With who?'

'Your friend and mine, the dodgy second-hand car salesman and Jack-of-all-trades, by name, Harold Norris. By the way, it seems the police didn't pursue him over his illegal hiring out of a motor so you are quite safe in talking to him again. He's arranging for some of his boys to do the work while we're away.'

For a long moment Thornton stared at Holly in total amazement, then he burst out laughing, quite aloud this time.

'Miss Day? You are an absolute gem. There's no other word for it.' He raised his mug. 'Here's to you.'

The guitarist, having gone out the back, presumably for a pee, but more than likely for a proper smoke where the smell wouldn't travel, had slouched back and, having replenished his beer and smoked his umpteenth legitimate cigarette of the day, placed his pint pot beside his chair, picked up his instrument and started to strum, sort of a warm up. Thornton drained the rest of his mild at one go and got up.

'Let's get out of here,' he said. 'I don't think I'll use this pub again.' He had the fingers of one hand crossed behind his back. Habit is a terrible slave master.

'Why do Cretan names end with an akis?' Holly asked as they left.

******

The Venables' bijou semi-detached residence had faux leaded pane windows. The paintwork was white with nice maroon woodwork as diligently applied by Reg himself because one cannot trust professional painters who tend to do sneaky things to save money, like mix undercoat and topcoat together and make believe they applied them separately. Reg believed the minimum was two undercoats with plenty of drying time in between. That way the paint lasted longer. He always used the best quality brushes, not cheap ones that left hairs all over the fresh paint, and made sure he washed them out well after use with plenty of spirit. They were carefully stored with his tools and gardening stuff in the little lock up shed next to the cloches at the bottom of the garden; a place for everything and everything in its place, all the places neatly labelled.

Situated close to the Great West Way and directly under a Heathrow flight path, the house tended at first to be just that teensy bit noisy at times, leading to shredded nerve ends already fraught from domestic tension and, since the Spitskaya affair, sexual frustration: sexual frustration that is on Rita's part; Reg had long since grown accustomed to the noise and ignoring the other. They had sometimes thought of moving but moving was reputably, after birth, marriage, and death, the most traumatic of experiences, there being an abundance of horror stories about removal firms smashing or losing the most precious and irreplaceable possessions that no amount of insurance could ever replace. So they decided rather the devil they knew, installed double-glazing paid for on the never never, and stayed put. Just as Reg, until Rita's conversion, had got used to doing without marital fun and games, so they had in a way grown used to the overhead noise to the extent of sometimes going for hours not hearing it at all. It was the same as when someone enters a room and notices a particular smell that, once the nose has registered and got used to, tends to disappear or at least lessen.

The dimity front parlour was furnished with a dark brown leatherette three-piece suite they bought when they first moved in, Parker-Knoll chairs over the backs of which were those reminders of Victorian days, embroidered antimacassars though who these days plasters his hair with maccasar oil? In front of the lace curtained windows there was a gate leg occasional table on which stood a vase of plastic flowers, the vase having been won by Venables many years previously, showing off at a fun fair shooting range, trying to impress his incipient bride, one Rita Claiborne, and succeeding. She was obviously easily impressed. There were large monochrome prints under glass of *The Light Of The World*, *Love Locked Out*, a bit naughty that one and *Patience On A Monument*, inherited from Rita's grandparents, and framed photographs of the children at various stages in their development, starting with face down naked on a rug and ending with school leaving, after which interest on both sides had diminished and been finally lost.

'Oh, mum! Do we have to?' Was usually the plaintive cry until that point was reached.

'Yes!' Was invariably the answer until the ritual died a natural death.

Although seldom used, the room had always been kept pristine, especially for special occasions which were occasional if nothing else as neither the neighbours nor the far distant Claiborne clan or the Venables relatives ever thought to visit and, since Rita's transformation into a budding nympho, the knick-knacks on the mantelpiece, once lovingly polished every day, now stood neglected and gathering dust. Mostly they were in the form of *A Present From* ... or *A Souvenir From* ... and bore the municipal coat of arms of various coastal resorts around the British Isles; small china souvenirs purchased in antique shops, not highly collectible *Goss* alas, but still fond mementoes of long past boarding house holidays when the kiddies were little and baths were strictly rationed.

Rita had never been slatternly, either by nature or upbringing. She was always distinctly house-proud, possibly too much so, although not going so far as to polish the coals. It was the way she had been brought up and what else had there been for her, apart from the telly and an occasional *Mills & Boon?* But now the kitchen smelt greasy and dishes waiting to be washed were piled high on the drainer and in the sink.

The kids were absent at college so for the next few days while the parents were away would not be bringing in burgers, fish and chips, Chinese takeaways from *The Jailhouse Wok*, (the owner originally from Hong Kong was a Presley fan), or Indian from The *Taj Mahal*, with its subdued lighting, its dark red Regency stripe flock wallpaper and photographic prints of various Indian sights, including of course the famous building it was named after. Although they could wash up a couple of plates if they felt so inclined, they most probably wouldn't but would dip greasy fingers into wrapper, newspaper, polystyrene or aluminium container as the case might be, wipe their fingers on a kitchen towel and toss the remains of their feast into the bin, which they would then forget to take out until after the dustbin men had been and gone.

In the bathroom, heated in winter, and then only when in use, with an almost useless glass bar electric fire fixed high on the wall, a pull cord to turn it on and off, the temperature even with the bar switched on and glowing red was still that of a refrigerator. Goose bumps, erect nipples, and retracting organs were the order of the day when sitting on the loo or taking a bath. There were stains in the washbasin, hair in plugholes, and a tidemark around the bath. The plastic shower curtain with its decoration of seashells, sea horses and sprays of seaweed in shades of blue was fast developing a nasty looking green mould.

In the front bedroom two suitcases lay open on the pink and lilac nylon bedspread and various articles of clothing lay scattered about waiting to be packed. In front of the bay window, Rita was standing at her glass topped kidney shaped dressing table with its triptych of mirrors, its veneer beginning to crack, wondering what make-up she would need in the south of France. She was a bit spaced out at the moment, what with the excitement of the coming trip and the thought of the famous name duty-free perfume she'd be able to buy. *Chanel No 5* would be first choice.

Reg was in the breakfast room watching the news on television. It had been airing for some while but nothing of stratospheric importance to grab the attention had been reported and it was nearing the end. Much to his disappointment the Spitskaya story had not appeared. Never mind, he would soon be back on the goggle box, and in the papers. Perhaps there would be reporters at the airport eager for his story. It wasn't every day of the week a British policeman was invited to be guest of honour at an Interpol do. He wondered if it was too late to telephone ... what was his name? ... Ah, yes, Duncan, that was the chap, and give him an exclusive. The Honourable Duncan even: younger son of a lord. Humph! He would have to look up Debrett and find out something of the boy's family tree. He seemed a nice enough lad. Certainly came up with the goods as far as the article was concerned. There it was on the dining room table, and a copy lying prominently on his desk in his office at the station for anyone who passing by might be interested enough to pause in and take a look-see.

Reg rose from his chair, leaned forward and, having gathered the following day would be overcast with light northerly winds and a faint drizzle, nothing bad enough to close airports or cancel flights, switched off the telly. A box of Swan Vestas and his pipe, already containing tobacco and half smoked, lay in a Bombay brass ashtray on top of the cabinet. He picked up the pipe, thumbed down the half smoked tobacco, wiped the ash from his thumb on his sleeve, relit the pipe and took a deep pull. It was a mistake. He should have given the pipe a good shakeout first. The stem was full of tar and the foul tasting stuff was now in his mouth. He fished in his pocket, came out with a grubby handkerchief and, sticking out his tongue, gave it a good hard wipe all round, inspected the damage, gave the hankie a mouthful of spit, inspected it, and put it back in his pocket. Rita was always going on about how his clothes stank of tobacco and this would really give her something to moan about. Take her mind off you know what for a while if that were possible. He chuckled to himself and wondered if he should go over his speech once more. He had written it with the aid of constable Roper and, just as he wasn't too sure of that young man's sexual orientation, neither was he too sure of the young man's syntax. Any policeman who, in an accident report, referred to a vehicle's fender as being "hurt" just had to be suspect. No, never mind, he would go and sit on the lavvy and practice the speech. Best to know it almost off by heart so as not to refer too often to his notes. He was led to believe that was the Churchillian thing to do.

Half an hour later Rita vigorously rattled the handle of the bathroom door and demanded to know what her husband was doing in there. She tried to peer through the frosted glass but with no result, which of course is what frosted glass is all about. She used to try peering in when her son Robin, still at a tender age, was in there; quite sure he was either smoking or playing with himself. She never caught him at either though sometimes she also went into the garden to see if any smoke was coming out the open window.

'Don't bother me,' was Reg's response to the rattle. 'I'm practicing my speech.'

'Well do you have to do it in there?' She demanded, following up the rattle with a knock on the door. 'There's other people need to use the bathroom you know. Selfish, that's what you are, and thoughtless.' She had a sudden change of thought. 'Reg, have you been, like, you know, constipated of late? I thought you must have been having a heart attack at least. You had me worried there. Men die sitting on the lavvy, you know, straining. Their hearts can't take it and they're found there, dead.'

'Don't talk rubbish, woman, and go away. Have you finished the packing? We leave early you know. What time's the taxi coming?'

'I can't go away, Reg, I need to use the bathroom!' There was now real urgency in her voice and she was about to hammer on the door with clenched fist when there was the sound of the bolt being withdrawn and the door swung open.

'Never any peace in this ruddy house,' he growled as he headed for the stairs.

'Have you flushed?' She asked.

'What for? I didn't do anything, did I?'

Rita slipped into the bathroom and locked the door, pulled the cord to turn on the heater and headed for the toilet. The seat for once was already down, and warm. She noticed as she went to sit that the paint was beginning to wear. Reg would no doubt soon say something like "I think I ought to do something about the toilet seat," produce a pot of white paint, a can of white spirit, his overalls already paint spotted but laundered, plenty of old rags and his best brushes and set to work. Rita raised her skirt, slipped off her knickers and sat down with a sigh of contentment. She lifted the lid of the pink painted, slightly rickety, cane laundry basket beside the pedestal. Reg and the kids never bothered to look in there. They usually left their dirty clothes on the bedroom or bathroom floor; sometimes even on the landing depending on how much of a hurry they were in. She took out a saucy magazine and settled down for her own happy half hour.

At the bottom of the stairs Reg noticed the two suitcases placed behind the front door: hers was blue, Rita was fond of blue, and his was beige with wide red and brown stripes all around the middle. You couldn't mistake it. Easy to pick out as it appeared and came around on the carousel. Then he went into the breakfast room to make sure everything was in order, a final check; tickets, money, traveller's cheques and passports laid out neatly on the chenille tablecloth. He couldn't resist another glance at Duncan's article.

Passport to fame and fortune, he thought. One day he would write a book on his experiences in the force. It would be a revelation. He looked at his watch. It was time for bed. Tomorrow was another day.

CHAPTER 2

Thornton had a persistent ringing in his ears and it seemed it wasn't going to stop. He groaned, turned over, stretched, and then curled himself into the foetal position. The ringing continued unabated. He uncurled; put out an arm from beneath the warmth of the duvet to reach for the telephone, lifted the receiver to his ear and, with eyes still shut, grunted as telephone, arm, and head all disappeared beneath the duvet. For some reason weather conditions in the bedroom seems to be more arctic than usual.

'Wakey wakey! Time for uppies!'

Bright cheerful sing-song voices at the fart of the first sparrow were not conducive to Thornton's getting up in a bright and cheerful mood and he grunted again.

'Come on, Thornton,' Holly persisted, still full of joviality, 'It's time. Now throw back the duvet, sit up nicely, swing your legs off the bed, put your feet firmly on the floor and open your eyes.'

Thornton reluctantly did as he was bid, all except for opening his eyes. He was shivering.

'Done it?' she queried. He grunted once more, the grunt presumably meant to affirm he'd followed her instructions. 'There now, that wasn't really so difficult, was it?' Another grunt. 'Now, Thornton, switch on the bedside lamp and I really do want you to open your eyes, replace the receiver, stand up, go to the bathroom to do what's necessary, then to the kitchen to put on the kettle for a nice cup of extra strong wake up and greet the day style coffee. You are under no circumstances to sit down on the bed again, is that understood?' Grunt. 'If you sit down again you will roll over, put your head on the pillows, pull up the duvet and be asleep within seconds even with the light on so please be a good boy,' the please was heavily accentuated, 'and do as you're told. We're due at the airport in two hours time. I'll call again in five minutes to make sure you're awake.' Grunt. 'Oh, and Thornton, don't forget to wash behind the ears.' The phone went dead.

The room was in pitch darkness. After a few moments of fumbling he found the light switch on the bedside lamp, nearly sending the lamp toppling sideways and saving it just in time. Why on earth did people have to catch planes at what he thought of as all hours of the bloody night? It was totally uncivilised. Planes should only take off from midday so that you didn't have to get up early and it wouldn't matter if they reached their destination all hours of the night because arriving somewhere in the middle of the night was okay. After all, you didn't think twice about leaving a party in the early hours so why not an airport? You could tumble straight into bed after a wearisome journey, especially if jet lag was involved. He remembered flying to New York and his generous hosts taking him out to dinner in the Village and wondering why like the dormouse in *Alice In Wonderland* he kept falling asleep at the table, not realising that, with the time difference, they were feeding the animal at gone three in the morning. Still, here he was getting a trip to the French Riviera for a welcome break, all expenses paid, and he really shouldn't complain. One of these days he would have to meet Holly's daddy and thank him personally for his generosity. He wondered if Holly had informed him how his largesse was actually being spent.

He opened the door and stepped out of the bedroom and hardly had time to register the passage light was already switched on when he nearly suffered a coronary being suddenly and unexpectedly faced by two total strangers. If he weren't made of such stern masculine stuff he might even have screamed such was the shock he experienced. As it was he almost had to be scraped off the ceiling.

'Morning, guv'nor.' It was another cheery voice, though not quite as melodious as the first that morning. 'Thornton is it?'

A naked and shivering Thornton could do no more than nod. Then, as he took the men in, his rapid heart rate slowed down somewhat. The elder, the one who had greeted him, was wearing a pair of grubby, paint and cement stained, once white overalls, and carrying a large canvas bag of tools. The younger, who couldn't have been more than sixteen or seventeen at most, was wearing a belt of tools around his skinny hips, carrying a lunch pail and, after a downward glance couldn't help but come up smiling, though he did have the grace to try and hide it.

'How did you …?' Thornton squeaked, and then, regaining his normal voice, 'how did you get in?' he asked.

'Easy peasy,' the elder said. 'Whoever fixed that up for you,' he indicated the temporary front door Thornton had ordered, the original having totally disintegrated in the bomb blast, 'didn't make much of a job of it I can tell ya.'

'You are?' Thornton enquired now beginning to feel desperately in need of relieving himself. Although they were obviously Harold's boys, he needed to reassure himself before they went any further.

'Oh, yeh. I'm Ron an' this is my assistant, Ted. There'll be anuvver one along in a minute. That'll be Dave (he pronounced it *Dive*) an' 'e's always late. Be late for 'is own bleeding funeral an' all.' He looked around. 'Yeh, well I wonder where's best to start then.'

'Isn't it a bit early?'

'Oh, no, mate. Maybe just a few minutes afore our reg'lar time but Miss Day said as to make sure we got 'ere early like before you left see? So as to how you could let us in. No need though was there? Considering.' He sucked in his breath, scratched the silver stubble on his chin and shook his head. 'Pretty shoddy workmanship that, I can tell ya.' His horny right thumb jerked towards the temporary door they had left wide open hence the freezing conditions there being no heating in the public areas of the building.

Thornton was by now practically hopping from one foot to the other, or would have been except such a manoeuvre might very well have opened the floodgates.

'Yes, well, look, I've just got up and, well you know how it is first thing in the morning, I'm desperate for a pee, so if you'll excuse me …?'

'Sure, mate. You go right ahead. Do what you 'as to.' It was Ron's turn to glance down. Men can never resist making comparisons. 'Yeh, an' we'll just mosey 'round then, take a butcher's like, size up the job as it were.' He cast a sideways glance at Ted but Ted was looking at the ceiling and biting his cheek. 'See what needs doin''.

But Thornton didn't hear the last part. Ron could go on rabbiting as much as he wanted, Thornton was already in front of the pedestal. He heaved a sigh of relief and listened to his stream hitting the porcelain, glancing down a couple of times just to make sure he was aiming in the right direction. It was inevitable a few drops would dribble on the floor. It always did no mater how careful he was. He presumed it was the shake off that did it. He started to wonder about Harold's boys, whether they really knew what they were doing or whether they were just a couple of oddjob cowboys and he would return from France only to find his apartment in an even bigger mess than when he left. He was glad he hadn't been sporting a morning water stiff when he met them. That really would have been embarrassing.

Having shaken himself off, he washed his hands, glanced at his unshaven face in the mirror, lifted his upper lip to examine his teeth and shuddered, slipped on a bathrobe so as to avoid any further sniggers and headed for the kitchen to find the kettle already on and to be greeted affably by Ron with, 'Find it all right did you, Thorn? Ha ha ha. Where do you keep your tea then?'

'Shit!' Thornton said.

'Wha'?' Ron and Ted looked at each other, both frowning. Was Thornton going to insult their working class status?

'I forgot to get the tea,' Thornton said.

This was even worse. Holly had rightly conjectured that Harold's boys would hardly go for Earl Grey, Lapsang Souchong, Jasmine, Jackson's of Piccadilly's Breakfast Tea or even Assam, and he had been ordered to get in a goodly supply of Tetley's teabags. No British workman could start the day or last more than an hour without a good strong cup of tea with milk and plenty of sugar.

'I'm sorry,' he apologised. 'Do you think you could wait till the shops open and Fred or ... Dive ... that's it, Dave, could possibly go and get some? Shop's just around the corner. I'll reimburse you later. Now I really have to get ready for Holly to pick me up so, if you don't mind, I'll just leave you to it.'

The phone rang. He crossed into the lounge and picked up the receiver. 'I'm awake,' he barked.

'Oh, good,' she responded sweetly. 'Are you all packed and ready to go?'

He glanced towards where his suitcase stood, a beige suitcase with wide red and brown stripes around the middle. A whole stack of them had been on offer at *Peter Jones*, thirty percent off, and he hadn't been able resist it even though at the time he had no intentions of actually going anywhere. 'I'm packed and I'll be ready in a jiff.' He assured her.

'Good. I'll hoot when I arrive.'

******

'Why did we have to leave so early?' Thornton asked.

'Traffic,' was the terse reply.

'It's not rush hour yet, not for another ...' he looked at his watch

... 'whenever ... and, even if it were, we're going against the flow.'

'Once passed Hammersmith maybe, but you never know what it will be like before then.'

For a time they moved along roads almost clear of traffic, Thornton feeling quite smug, but once they hit the Balls Pond Road and Islington they were forced to slow down and Holly glanced at her passenger without actually having to say, "Told you so."

The silence continued as she negotiated her way into the top end of a jam-packed Greys Inn Road, smiling sweetly at a male white van driver who had been determined not to let her through but eventually, with an inch to spare, gave way when he realised she was just as determined as he and they stopped ahead of him at the red light, waiting to turn left and head passed King's Cross for the Marylebone Road.

'Whose car?' Thornton asked, as he peered at the walnut dashboard and realised his back was practically forcing its way through the well-upholstered seat and his feet were going through the floor, not just because of the near miss but because he was wondering whether the white van driver would get out of his white van and tap on Holly's window, all steamed up (the driver not the window) and ready for a barney. Road rage, this vicious phenomenon growing at a pace with the ever-growing volume of traffic, was already not far below the surface.

'It's daddy's car. Who else's would it be?'

'What's he going to do without it for the next few days?'

'Use one of the others,' she replied.

'Humph!' Thornton was definitely not an early morning person, not even luxuriating in a top of the range limousine, property of a big time banker. Why oh why had he never thought of making banking his business? Because he was hopeless when it came both to mathematics and to money that's why. In his mind's eye he could see all those newspaper headlines announcing the bloated salaries of headhunted high-flying executives and captains of industry, not all of whom were equal to their responsibilities, but chutzpah and a big mouth will get you a long way in this world; free shares, dividends, and those yearly bonus cheques, any one of which would be worth more than he would probably earn in his entire lifetime, and the golden handshakes even for the proven incompetents. The world was going stark raving mad and it was likely to get worse.

Next to being a banker or a captain of industry then maybe he should have been a criminal, a romantic one of course, a Raffles stealing fabulous jewels from the boudoirs of rich ladies, preferably beautiful, or engaged in the legal profession. Lawyers did not come cheap and as for barristers, well! Less said there the better as, apart from any other business, some legal beagle would always be required to make sure those executives and captains of industry had novella sized watertight contracts that assured them money for old rope. Insurance? Hmn, maybe, a bit risky though. You can only wriggle so much. Stockbroker? Worth thinking about. Or perhaps politics would be a suitable alternative, not so much for the salary but for the perks, the expenses, all those company directorships, speaking engagements, public appearances, freebees like holidays on someone's yacht or tropical island, chance of a bit on the side, not corruption, not really, just using influence. Being a private eye just wasn't paying its way anymore, especially since divorce had been made that much easier. 'It's green,' he said, referring not to his obvious envy at other people's fortunes but to the traffic lights, 'and Holly ...'

'Hmn?' As the car moved noiselessly forward.

'I hate to bring this up but, if you do that again and the next time it's not a near miss, there will most certainly be a miss, because we will miss our plane while you have to pull over and exchange insurance details, etcetera with t'other driver who, being a man, even if not a white van one this time noted for their devil may care attitude to road safety, will be in a foul mood and cursing all women drivers. That will no doubt get your gander up, or should that be goose? There will then be a slanging match. I will have to step in to try and calm things down and all that will take time. Therefore, Q.E.D., we will miss our plane. You haven't heard a word I've said.'

'What's that, Thornton? Sorry, no actually, I'm concentrating on my driving.'

'I'll turn on the radio,' Thornton said, 'the weather forecast could be interesting.'

******

1969 was quite a year. It was the year that Richard Nixon was inaugurated as President of the United States, travelled to Midway Island to talk with the South Vietnamese president, and it was the year Ho Chi Minh died. The French and the English, having decided to like each other for a little while, or at least tolerate each other, things never having been easy between them ever since the Battle of Agincourt, had shaken hands for co-operation's sake, spent a zillion producing a supersonic airplane and in April, to much acclaim, *Concorde* with its unique droop snoop made its maiden test flight.

Sectarian battles flared up in Ulster again and the Irish Republican Army formed no-go areas and set up checkpoints around the Bogside and Creggan. Her Majesty Queen Elizabeth II invested Prince Charles as Prince of Wales and high-grade crude oil was found in the North Sea.

Agatha Christie's play *The Mousetrap* notched up 7000 performances, entered its 18th year and looked to endure a further eighteen if not more. Samuel Beckett won the Nobel Prize for literature, nobody could quite understand why, and *Oh Calcutta* opened in New York. Noel Coward, when asked if he thought he would like to see nude dancing on stage, evidently replied, or so the story goes, "Not really. When the music stopped, not everything would." Duke Ellington celebrated his 70th birthday and President Nixon presented him with the *Medal of Freedom*. Mick Jagger and *The Stones* just kept rolling along. Woodstock attracted more than 300,000 people and millions of people all over America voiced their disapproval of the Vietnam War. Inflation, (as Thornton knew to his cost) was becoming a worldwide problem. The price of coffee seemed to rise not by the day but by the hour.

The thirty-five year old Kray twins, who for some years had terrorised London's East End, finally got their comeuppance and were given life sentences for murder. A London woman gave birth to quintuplets after fertility drug treatment.

It was the year America notched up a sensational triumph when Neil Armstrong, Michael Collins and Buzz Aldrin flew to the moon in Apollo 11: Armstrong took a small step and mankind took a giant one.

It was the year Thornton King and Holly Day got mixed up with a crazy Russian princess and her school of female assassins, the year that was the apex of Reg Venables' career in the Metropolitan Police Force, and the year a new terminal was opened at Heathrow where a South African jewel thief by the name of Jakob Mynhardt flew in from West Africa with uncut diamonds worth a million pounds or more and walked nonchalantly and safely through the *Nothing To Declare* exit, even pausing in full view of customs to make sure his suitcase wasn't slipping off the trolley, surely not something a guilty man would stop to do. Smiling to himself he headed for the concourse. If the watching customs official was onto that trick he took no notice and, with luck on his side, Jakob was not going to be one of those occasional travellers pulled over at random for inspection. Everything had gone and was going according to plan.

******

The Portuguese called it Sierra Leone, which means *Lion Mountains*. In the 18th century, before the British parliament brought about abolition, it was notorious as a centre of the slave trade but in fact had always possessed something far more valuable going for it if only the indigenous tribes or the Creoles, as the freed slaves returning were called, had realised it earlier – diamonds, diamonds, and even more diamonds. Probably it was just as well they didn't realise the treasure under their feet or the British who took it over as a Crown Colony early in the 19th century and, towards the end, turned it into a protectorate, might never have left. If nothing else Freetown was very useful as a naval base. However, one day someone picked up this earth encrusted pebble that sparkled a little bit in the sun, dusted it off, held it up and said, in his own language of course, any one of sixteen, "Hey, you guys, what do you reckon this could be?" It didn't take long to find out and once the diamonds were discovered it became imperative to keep a constant guard on this wealth so from that moment on anyone caught smuggling could be sure of only one thing – death.

In the eight years since gaining independence the country had suffered under no fewer than four governments and would soon, like some other African countries that had gained their independence, become a one-party state, in other words a dictatorship. It was still in a state of flux and deep unrest, particularly from the army and from the moment Jakob Mynhardt took possession of those diamonds he knew he was taking his life in his hands, even with the connivance of a very important, very corrupt, very greedy member of the government who expected, by aiding and abetting this South African maverick, to see a healthy increase in one of his numerous tax haven bank accounts, already swollen with guilt-ridden handouts.

But it was only when Jakob had been escorted through the bush and arrived safely at the Liberian border with the diamonds in a knapsack on his back that he realised he was actually still breathing. He had been between a rock and a hard place any number of times in his life but this was the first occasion he had felt such intense fear. Almost by the second he imagined this long journey through the bush would come to a sudden and violent end, the quietness of the night suddenly erupting with gunshots and the cries of startled creatures and himself left there riddled with bullets.

They met soon after dark in a room at the back of *The Automatic Fish Grill Restaurant*, no more than a shack really with its rusting tin roof, bare scrubbed tables, benches, and dull and dented tin utensils and it was here Jakob was handed his precious parcel. There was no need to warn him of the consequences of any double-cross.

The Jeep was waiting for him in the narrow lane that ran behind the building. Two men were already seated in it, both in fatigues. They did not even turn to look at him as he climbed in. No one would question a foreigner being driven by two soldiers, one of whom was carrying enough military hardware to supply a regiment. It would be automatically assumed he was under arrest and probably being driven into the bush to be disposed of.

They travelled in the Jeep almost to the Liberian border. The two men passed the occasional comment in Krio, a language Jakob did not know, so he stayed silent the whole way. His right hand was never far away from his hip, at times the tip of his forefinger stroking the butt of his thirty-two-calibre Smith and Wesson, up and down, up and down, though should the man in the back with all the various bits of hardware at his disposal choose, or been instructed, to blow Jakob away there was really nothing he could do about it. He didn't have eyes in the back of his neck though every now and then he could feel the prickle start there and travel down his spine.

The Jeep was stopped and Jakob turned to look enquiringly at the driver.

'From here we walk,' the man said, jumping out, his companion following him. Without even looking to see if Jakob was following they set off through the bush. These guys must have been from the area, they knew exactly where they were going. It was almost an hour's walk before they stopped and the first man merely pointed in the direction Jakob should go.

Silently he shook hands with his escort and watched them return the way they had come, disappearing into the darkness. For a brief moment he felt sorry for them, knowing they would probably not even have the time to rue their part in the escapade or live long enough to spend their expected payoff. A bullet is oft times the reward for those who live with too much knowledge, but there were no true pangs of guilt and this sentimental feeling didn't last very long. Business was business after all.

Jakob, scion of an Afrikaner family, never married, though he might have sired offspring he knew not of, was now passed his seventieth year. His forbears were Voortrekkers who fled from British rule in the Cape Colony, once the Cape of Good Hope, and trekked north in their oxen drawn wagons to pastures new, fought against the Zulu at The Battle of Blood River, fought the British at Paardeberg and Magersfontein, and Jakob had also been a soldier, thrown into battle against Rommel's Afrika Korps at El Alemein. In fact the family had been involved in so much fighting it was a wonder there were any of them left, but there were, and the newest generation of nephews were still at it. Clad in South African army uniform they were having a go at SWAPO in what was the former German colony of South West Africa. Not all of them though, a couple of young Mynhardts had trekked further north and east to fight for Mr Smith.

Jakob stood in the dark for a while, listening intently, but heard nothing suspicious so set off in the direction indicated. He was a small man, dark of complexion and wiry, not an ounce of fat on him and despite his age as sprightly as a March hare, except when it behove him to become a fragile pathetic geriatric who wouldn't, couldn't, possibly undertake anything mean or despicable, let alone anything illegal or criminal, a helpless harmless little old man who wouldn't hurt a fly. He climbed aboard the Jeep waiting for him on the Liberian side, driven by another important individual, an army colonel, if possible even more avaricious and corrupt than his Sierra Leoneian counterpart. Jakob greeted him affably and shot him dead, his reasoning being that the colonel would have done the same to him at the earliest opportunity and Jakob knew how lucky he was the man hadn't already made the attempt. For a second or two the colonel's eyes remained fixed on Jakob's face as though, despite the neat round hole in the middle of his forehead, they still had the ability to see. Then his body slumped forward and, with a little extra help from Jakob, it rolled overboard. It wouldn't be discovered for months, if at all. In the meantime before the flies and the ants got to it, which wouldn't take long, it would provide nourishing meals for any carnivores happening to pass by. Jakob jumped into the driving seat, started the engine, switched on his lights, and checked the fuel gauge. It registered half, not enough to get him to his destination. He had more than two hundred miles to travel. He put the Jeep into gear and started off down the rutted track, keeping a sharp eye out for and carefully avoiding the dongas. A broken axle was the last thing he needed. He would stop off at the Lebanese store to fill the tank and have a bowl of pilaff before continuing on his way toward Caesar Beach and his hotel. Once through the bush and on passed rubber plantations he would hit better roads and be able to move at a pace. He would dump the Jeep a couple of miles from his destination get rid of his gun and walk the rest of the way.

He loved the bush at night. With no light pollution the sky was a million bright stars twinkling like diamonds set in black velvet, now and again a shooting star darted across what to all appearances seemed such a short distance before it died out. Except for the occasional cry of an animal a silence that could be almost physically felt lay over the bush and every now and again a pair of eyes were reflected in his headlights to disappear into the foliage at the side of the road. Once Africa is in the blood it is there forever. No matter how long he was away, every time Jakob returned it was as though there had been nothing in between.

When World War II ended, unable to settle into a nine to five job, he went into the safari, big game hunting business until his conscience started to nag and he packed it in. He could no longer stomach the sickening sight of beautiful creatures like the leopard or even ugly ones like the rhino or buffalo being killed by idiots in the name of so-called sport. True the buffalo was an evil brute but then so is mankind when he has a mind to it, which is pretty often and, in Africa, Jakob found his wartime experience and his bush craft suddenly paying dividends as he hired himself out as a mercenary and personally took part in man's inhumanity to man in various parts of the continent.

When he decided he had ridden his luck long enough he returned to South Africa and for a while staggered from one dead-end job to another until finally, with no visible means of support, he turned his talents to what, with practice, he was to become best at – thieving. Not petty thieving, but big time thieving, mostly as a loner but occasionally with a partner or partners in a number of countries and, after many years of dedication to his vocation, it was culminating in this Sierra Leone venture that without any doubt he just knew would now run smoothly to completion.

He drove passed smallholdings, dark and silent in the night except for the ubiquitous barking dogs; *The MacDonald Place, The Leroy Place, The Simpson Place* and the one he liked best which just read "*Gods Little Acre*" but gave no name for the inhabitants. Perhaps, as it was His very own, God did actually live there.

It was well into the morning by the time Jakob reached the hotel. Making sure no one was around to see what he was up to, and locking the door against an unwanted entry, he emptied the diamonds into a suitcase that had been fitted with what he believed was an undetectable false bottom, throwing his clothes willy-nilly on top. There wasn't much and some of it was soiled so any light-fingered gent at Monrovia or *Thief Row* would find nothing worth taking and probably be put off anyway by the cheesy odour of unwashed socks. Jakob hadn't changed them for a week or so. He left the suitcase open on the bed. He didn't want it damaged by being broken into and itchy fingers would soon discover it wasn't worth investigating. It was well labelled: front, back, top, bottom, and sides. There should be no mistake like having it go to the wrong destination and it would be easy to spot on the carousel: beige with wide red and brown stripes around the middle.

He left his room, paid his bill and repaired to the dining room for a hearty late breakfast. His knapsack he kept with him. It was cabin baggage and, anyway, he wanted to keep it from possible prying eyes. He had a long wait in Monrovia before his flight. After breakfast he would spend the day lazing down by the lagoon, or on the beach, watching the giant Atlantic breakers crashing onto the sand. He wouldn't attempt to swim. The beach at the water's edge sloped away far too steeply and the waves were much too high and receded with frightening force. All he needed was to be dumped and suffer a heart attack. He flip-flopped his way across the burning sand to the shade of a beach umbrella. The hot sun, the sound of the sea, made him sleepy as he lay musing on his future and every so often indulging in a little refreshment from the beach bar. In slightly less than twenty four hours he would be in England.

******

As she stood by the parlour window waiting for the taxi to

put in an appearance, Rita was beside herself with almost childish expectation: excitement, tinged with deep apprehension. She had never flown before and her imagination was working at full throttle. What if she were to suffer from motion sickness and couldn't find the paper bag in time? What if there was no paper bag! Oh, perish the thought! Would she be sick all down her new outfit bought especially for the occasion? How embarrassing! How expensive! Reg would never forgive her. Where was Reg? What *was* that wretched man doing? The cab would arrive any minute now.

She could never travel in the back of a car without feeling queasy, would the motion of flying be worse? Specially built black cabs with their high suspension were somehow all right but with minicabs being ordinary cars she had to sit in the front with the driver no matter how short the journey. This, on more than one occasion, had lead to a misunderstanding that, with her newfound persona could have led to a gratifying outcome, but at that time she had always pretended not to notice what was happening. On a couple of occasions when playing the innocent didn't work, she had to fight for her honour or inform the molester she was the wife of a senior policeman and that usually did the trick. The roving hand returned to where it should be, on the steering wheel. She wasn't a young woman but a mother of two almost grownup children and she couldn't understand what the taxi drivers saw in her in the first place though, she supposed, there was no reason why they shouldn't be interested in a more mature woman. Why couldn't the more mature woman be just as sexy and attractive as a youngster, as a skinny model with absolutely no flesh on her at all? What on earth did men find attractive in that? Making love to a bag of bones a man could do himself a lot of damage.

Her thoughts went back to the upcoming flight. What if the plane were to crash in the English Channel? They had to fly over the English Channel to get to the coast of France and, if the plane went down, heavens forbid, she couldn't swim. Never did take to the water, not even on seaside holidays. Reg was the same although sometimes he did roll up his trouser legs and paddle at the water's edge.

What if the pilot had a heart attack or something and blacked out? She had heard, she couldn't remember where she had heard it but she had heard it, that take-off and landing were the most dangerous moments. She would just have to close her eyes, cross her fingers and pray. Right now what she could do is go over to the sideboard and take out the Christmas brandy to give herself a little Dutch courage. Following up the thought with the deed, that's exactly what she did, unscrewing the cap with a shaky hand and taking a hefty swig which left her whooping, gasping for breath, and clutching the back of the furniture. Calming down somewhat, she hoped Reg hadn't heard her. What had happened to Reg? She cast a glance at the ceiling. He'd been in the bathroom an awful long time. He hadn't discovered her magazines had he? Oh, where is that taxi? Why doesn't it come? We'll miss our plane. But the taxi wasn't coming because it still had more than half an hour to go before it was due. She took another swig at the brandy bottle, a little more discreetly this time, and felt marginally better so replaced the cap and returned the bottle to the sideboard from whence it had come. Maybe she had better call Reg down. She sashayed towards the hall rather like a boat in a moderate swell so as to call up the stairs and there she noticed the two suitcases standing behind the front door and that brought on another panic attack. Had she packed properly? Had she included everything necessary? What if she had omitted something terribly important? No, that couldn't be. Reg was taking responsibility for the essentials like passport, tickets, money … Oh! What *was* that wretched man doing?

He was sitting on the loo going over his speech and it was getting better and better. It was also getting longer as he couldn't resist putting in another succinct phrase here and there. He thought it might even have some literary merit. Maybe he could get it published in the Police Gazette.

******

The car safely parked and locked, Thornton and Holly were making their way towards *European Departures* when the automatic doors of *Arrivals* slid open and they were almost rammed sideways on by a trolley on which was placed a beige suitcase with red and brown stripes around the middle.

'Ach! Sorry, man.' Jakob apologised, pulling back.

'Snap!' Thornton replied.

'Hey?' was the bemused response.

'Same suitcase,' Thornton said, pointing and cutting words to a minimum, well to begin with anyway because he then went on to add, 'bet you bought that in the Peter Jones sale.'

'No, man, what are you talking about? As a matter if fact if you must know I bought it in West Africa. Excuse me, hey?' as he manoeuvred to go by.

'West Africa, huh? Whereabouts? I was there myself a couple of years ago.'

'Thornton …' came a warning growl from Holly who sensed a long conversation about to take off. Thornton was a great one for chatting to strangers.

'Liberia,' Jakob said. If this guy knew West Africa he thought it best not to say anything about Sierra Leone.

'Oh, yes?' Thornton beamed. 'What's it like now? Old Talbot still ruling the roost in his safari suit?'

'Thornton! We have a plane to catch.'

'You folks off on vakansie? … Oh, sorry … off on holiday then?' Jakob, usually taciturn and unforthcoming, didn't know why but suddenly he felt he would like someone to talk to. He hadn't had any kind of conversation for a long while and everyone, with the exception of hermits, monks who have taken a vow of silence, and miserable gits who never open their mouths except to snarl, need to talk every once in a while. The problem with his way of life was, when you ran out of small talk, things could get a bit dicey as strangers tended to probe into your private life.

'Just a quick break,' Thornton replied airily, as befits someone used to taking frequent short breaks. Holly had folded her arms and was tapping a dainty foot on the pavement: not a good sign.

'So where is it you're going then?'

'Beaulieu-sur-Mer, South of France. Lovely place.' He said this with conviction even though he had never been there, never even seen a postcard for that matter. 'It's on the Riviera. Staying at The Metropole. Classy. We fly into Nice.'

'We won't be flying anywhere Thornton if we don't check in.'

'Oh, plenty of time for that, Holly,' glancing at his watch. 'Bags of time in fact. I told you the traffic wouldn't be heavy.'

'THORNTON!'

One or two passing heads turned in sudden alarm before moving on.

'Oh, all right. Well, nice to have met you. If you see anyone else with a Peter Jones suitcase, don't get them mixed up, you never know what you may find.' And, with a merry laugh, he followed an already briskly departing Holly, her heels clicking gaily on the paving. Jakob shouted after them.

'Mister! Where did you say you were going?'

'Beaulieu-sur-Mer!' Thornton shouted back, turning his head before moving on.

'And what was the name of your hotel?'

'The Metropole!' Thornton shouted, even louder as he was now that much further away.

Jakob watched them turn and disappear into the terminal. He noted the cold grey drizzly London weather with distaste, he noted the cold grey faces of the passers by and he stepped backwards into the warmth of the building he had just left and there he stood, still shivering. He had no winter clothes and that had been a mistake but in the heat of tropical Africa he hadn't given it a thought. A light shirt, khaki pants and a bush jacket would do little to keep out the damp London cold, let alone a cutting wind.

He stood a long while, leaning on his trolley and meditating while people passed by unnoticed and unnoticing. There was a very big question to ask and answer and the question was simply – WHAT THE HELL DID HE THINK HE WAS DOING? Was he crazy? Was he out of his mind? At the risk of his life he had stolen from a Central African Republic goodness knows how many carats worth of diamonds to deliver to an organisation he really knew nothing about. It was in exchange for quite a healthy sum that was true, but nothing like the stones' true worth. What was he? A courier, a hired hand, a mule, no more. He could negotiate for the lot himself and live more than comfortably, live off the fat of the land in fact as the saying goes, for the years remaining to him and the organisation could go ... Here he paused in his thinking. Maybe he was crazy. The organisation, if it were what he thought it to be, would hunt him down and that would be that, a nasty end for Jakob Mynhardt, but not if he really disappeared, hey; really, really, really disappeared. True the world was a small place and getting smaller by the day and the organisation would have tentacles everywhere but how about Barbados for starters? How about Venezuela? How about Tasmania? How about Chile? How about Alaska? No, not Alaska, too damn cold, Alaska. He shivered visibly just thinking about it, but there were plenty of places where he could hide out. He could have plastic surgery, change his name, he'd done it before on a number of occasions, not the surgery, the change of name, to which half a dozen passports in his knapsack could testify and, like a meerkat disappearing down a hole, that's the last they would see of him. Yirrah, man! Was that the answer? Was he in cloud cuckoo land or what?

'Beaulieu-sur-Mer,' he murmured to himself, 'Hotel Metropole.' The words sounded magical, so inviting he repeated them, a trifle louder this time and a young man passing by, first of all gave the old man an uneasy glance and moved on before deciding to play the good Samaritan and turning back.

'Excuse me, sir, do you need help? Are you lost?'

Jakob focused on the young man's face, he smiled, and shook his head.

'No, young man,' he said, 'I am not lost. I know exactly where I am and I know exactly where I am going but thank you all the same, thank you very much, for enquiring.'

The young man smiled in turn, nodded, and moved on, feeling very pleased with himself at his day's good deed.

Jakob had a rendezvous in central London with his contact, the Belgian, Joost. They knew each other well from previous transactions. It was through Joost that the organisation had approached him and the handover was to take place in the booking hall of the Piccadilly Circus underground in the evening rush hour when, in the crush of hurrying bodies, something like the handing over of a suitcase and receipt of a packet would go unnoticed. Should Joost for some reason not be able to make it and another be sent in his place, Jakob had forwarded a description of the case in which the diamonds were being carried so that the replacement, who also had a verbal description of the carrier, would be sure to approach the right man with the passwords, "Right makes might," to which Jakob would reply, "And wealth." It was the kind of cloak and dagger stuff some juvenile minds revel in. Other approaches by a stranger such as "Have you got a light?" or "Do you have the time?" could be interpreted as something entirely different, especially around Piccadilly. How the South African spent his time until the evening rush hour was up to him. Whatever he decided on, it was going to be a long day.

Jakob Mynhardt headed once more for the outside world but once through the doors instead of going for a taxi, or even a bus to take him into town, he did a ninety degree turn and, heading into the wind, following in the footsteps of his new acquaintances, made for *Departures*. It was fate that he had bumped into them and Jakob was a great believer in fate.

******

The taxi was ten minutes late arriving so that was not a good start, especially as the cabbie heralded his arrival by keeping his hand on the horn far too long causing various front room net curtains to twitch. Rita, already fraught from nervous tension, lack of sleep, the swigs at the brandy bottle, the long early morning wait and now hunger pains settling in because earlier she had not felt like breakfast, sat in the back, handbag clutched to her stomach and watched anxiously as the luggage was stowed next to the driver. That having been done, Reg got in beside her, slammed his door and the cab set off for Heathrow. Reg was in a bad mood due to the driver's impatient horn blowing and tardiness in arriving. Rita was quite alarmed at the amount already registered on the meter and her alarm grew by the minute as she watched the instrument clicking away and the fare mounting. They had hardly even reached the end of their, admittedly quite long, street. Taxis were getting to be more and more of a luxury. She gave Reg a nudge with her elbow and made a small motion of her head in the direction of the meter.

He followed her look and then turned to her and shrugged. 'It's all on expenses,' he assured her for the umpteenth time.

She had already complained about the new suitcase and his hiring an evening suit from Moss Bros. Why couldn't he have borrowed one from one of his East End or Shepherds Bush contacts? She hadn't complained though about her visit to the salon for a swish new hairdo that actually didn't suit her in the least, but then Mister Roy had such a persuasive way about him, especially in the use of his expressive hands, what woman could resist his blandishments? He never seemed to look at you directly. His eyes were always just slightly off to the side, or below, or above as though captivated by something on the far side of the salon, but then for a brief moment they would focus on your face and the smile that went with the look created such a frisson it was almost the cause of palpitations which was probably why his salon was so popular. She delicately touched the side of her head, putting a hair back in place and looked down at her smart new two-piece costume from C&A, now partly hidden beneath her mock fur coat, previously from the same source. She deemed the outfit a necessity for her arrival in France. For a moment there was silence as the taxi bowled along, not yet hitting main road traffic, and then, 'Did you shut the bathroom window, Reg?'

He assured her he had shut the bathroom window.

'And locked it?'

'And locked it.'

'Burglars are very good at getting in through bathroom windows you know, no matter how small or high up.'

'Is that a fact? I didn't know that. As a policeman of many years standing and experience you would have thought I would have known something like that. You would have thought it would have been one of the very first things they taught me in college, but don't you worry.' He gave her a hasty pat on the knee and hurriedly withdrew his hand before she could make a grab for it. 'The bathroom window is securely fastened.'

'It's because they're usually at the back of the house I suppose,' she said more to herself or the world in general as she was gazing out the window, 'bathrooms I mean, so they can't be seen from the road,' and then to Reg, 'What about the dining room?'

'What about the dining room?'

'The windows! The windows! Are they locked?'

'Considering they've been closed and locked since the cold weather set in which is quite some time now, I would suggest the dining room windows are most securely fastened.' The supercilious edge to his voice went over her head.

'The kitchen.'

'Look, Rita! Do you mind? Are we going to go through the whole flaming house?' He was obviously losing patience.

'I just wanted to make sure, that's all. After all, you wouldn't like to come back and find we'd been burgled, would you? How would you explain to your colleagues at the station that you were just a teensy-weensy bit careless and, despite our neighbourhood watch, less crime conscious than you ought to have been, hmn?'

He grunted and, deciding that remark wasn't worth a response, for a while silence returned.

'Did you turn off the gas?'

He blew.

'I turned off the flaming gas! I cancelled the flaming milk! And the flaming papers! I told the Bensons we would be away for a few days. I told Ewan Jones next door; that is, I told his missus. He was at choir practice, where else? You know Ewan. If he didn't believe he had a voice like Harry Secombe on a good day he wouldn't believe he was a Welshman born and bred. If you was to ask me, he sounds more like Spike Milligan on a really bad day. Anyway, I did everything I was supposed to do. Are you satisfied now?'

The driver glanced in his rear view mirror and chortled to himself. Silence descended once more.

'Have you got the tickets?'

The driver, desperately trying hard not to laugh, was slightly distracted and forced to quickly swerve to avoid the milkman's float parked at the kerb as well as the milkman just offloading a crate, narrowly avoiding an oncoming car which mounted the opposite pavement and stopped just short of a lamp post. Rita shrieked and clutched at Reg's arm as he was thrown against her. Reg shuddered and hastily straightened up.

'He should get a flaming ticket for driving without due care and attention,' Reg said threateningly. Turning to look out the back window he saw the car driver get out and stand looking after them, shaking his fist. On the other side of the road the milkman was doing the same.

'Sorry about that, guv'nor,' the driver apologised. 'Still, no harm done. Thought you was in an 'urry to get to the airport, you know.'

'I'm not in a hurry to get to the next world,' Venables snarled. 'Just watch what you're doing will you?'

'Righto, guv',' and he slowed to a snail's pace just to prove how awkward he could be.

Reg turned to look at his wife. 'Did you empty the fridge?' he asked. She blushed scarlet.

******

Jakob stood studying the departures board. He had no wish to use one of his credit cards, none of them genuine, so before re-entering the building he had checked his cash, American dollars and English pounds, and quite a bundle he had on him, enough to fly to Australia and back let alone the south of France. The next flight to Nice was KLM. That must be the one those kids would be flying on. To a seventy year old they were still kids, especially the girl. Couldn't be more than what? Twenty? Twenty two maybe? He wasn't very good at guessing girls' ages, especially nowadays when they all seemed to grow up so fast and so sophisticated. Not like the old days, no sir, not at all. She was very attractive though. Did he catch her name at all? He didn't believe he had. This musing brought him up to the KLM information desk where his presence attracted the attention of another attractive girl who favoured him with her switched on well trained smile. The name badge on her uniform read Blodwen Hughes and the we'll keep a welcome in the valleys lilt to her voice was a dead giveaway.

'Good morning,' Jakob greeted her, smiling in turn. 'The KLM flight to Nice, is it full?'

The girl's smile seemed fixed in position as she moved away to check and then looked up at the dishevelled little man standing on the other side of her desk. He hadn't shaved for a couple of days and the sweatband around the brim of his hat was most unbecoming as were, she couldn't help but notice though she would never have dreamt of remarking on it, the dark stained armpits.

'I'm afraid so, sir,' she said, a distinct coolness in her voice. 'Economy is fully booked, as is business class.' The enquiry having been dealt with she was about to move away when she was brought up short.

'Oh, I don't want economy, miss, or business,' the man said. 'I want first class.'

She looked at him for a long moment and coughed discreetly behind a delicate hand, at the same time fiddling with the silver bracelet on her wrist, wondering if she should call for assistance. The man was obviously mad. About to ask how he intended to pay for a first class ticket which was equivalent to buying a section of the plane for the privilege of being offered a glass of champagne and spreading your legs as opposed to having your knees under your chin and somebody else's knees constantly prodding the back of your seat, she was suddenly flabbergasted as, like a magician pulling a rabbit out of a hat, a wad of notes was produced and placed on the desk in front of her. Could it be counterfeit? Blodwen felt just the teeniest twinge of anxiety.

Almost as if he read her mind, he said, 'It is real, young lady, and honestly come by I can assure you.' The first part was true; the second part a little lie, which at the moment couldn't come amiss. Well, in fact, it was a complete lie. The money was part of the haul from at least three different robberies, which was hardly what he could tell her. 'Now, I would like a first class ticket to Nice on the next plane please.'

The ticket was produced with no further ado. She was about to go into the automatic spiel of flight number, departure time, etcetera but he didn't seem to want to hear it.

'Thank you very much,' he said, the essence of courtesy. 'Now, may I ask for a special service?'

'If it's at all possible, sir, we are only too happy to do anything we can for you.'

'Good. First of all can I have some labels please, tie on ones and sticky.'

She produced them. 'Is that sufficient? Would you like more?'

'Thank you, no. These should be enough. Now, I have only one suitcase, this one you see here' He lifted it off the floor and put it down again. 'And my knapsack. Strange thing for an old man to have, isn't it?'

She smiled weakly. The man may be eccentric but he just had to be a millionaire, a multi-millionaire even, and therefore should be treated with the utmost respect.

'That will go in the cabin with me. The case of course is much too big and will go in the hold. Now, would it be at all possible for it to be sent straight to my hotel rather than me having to hang about waiting for it to arrive on the carousel in Nice? I'm sure you know how long that can take and the pushing and shoving that goes on, a regular rugger scrum, hey?' As a Welsh girl she knew all about rugger scrums. 'Well I am an old man and rather frail as you can see and I'm afraid I am travelling this time without my usual assistance.'

'I think that can be arranged through your hotel, sir, which will have transport to and from the airport.'

'Good. Thank you. The hotel is the Metropole in Beaulieu-sur-Mer' ... she was duly impressed ... 'the case will not be locked, so should the French customs wish to inspect it, they are quite at liberty to do so.'

'But, sir! Isn't that dangerous? I mean, even if you're insured ...' she trailed off, not really knowing quite what to say.

'There's nothing much in there that cannot be easily replaced but I would like it to reach my hotel safely so that I don't have the bother of having to go out and buy new things, if you know what I mean.' He winked broadly with a big grin. She didn't know what he meant. He wasn't too sure he knew himself. It just seemed a saucy thing for a seventy year old to say to an attractive young lady as they both perhaps had a mental picture of his purchasing new underwear, probably bearing suggestive or even quite blatant mottoes. 'Now, I will go and label my suitcase and bring it back to you in a moment.' With which he wandered off to find a convenient seat but returned to say, 'I couldn't possibly borrow a pen could I?' There was no doubt about it, he just had to be a multi-millionaire and she would take a bet the pen worth a few pennies would never be returned.

******

There had been an accident on the Great West Road and traffic was reduced almost to a standstill reducing Rita almost to tears.

'They'll go without us!' she wailed, as she noticed in the distance a plane taking off. It appeared to be going up at a very steep angle. She hoped that was what it was meant to do or was the pilot having a funny turn?

'They won't go without us,' Reg reassured her. He looked at his watch. 'We've plenty of time yet. Lucky you had the foresight to order the taxi that much earlier than necessary, just to be on the safe side. Be prepared as the Boy Scouts say, always be prepared for the unexpected. Yes.' He took his pipe from a jacket pocket and tamped down the tobacco in the bowl. Rita pointed out the sign that said the driver would be grateful if his passengers refrained from smoking. Reg sniffed huffily and put away his pipe.

'You should give it up anyway,' Rita admonished him for the umpteenth time. 'I hear you coughing away in the mornings when you get up.'

'Ah, we're moving again,' he said before she could add that the stink was disgusting.

Unfortunately the taxi hadn't advanced more than a few yards when it stopped again.

'Oh dear, oh dear!' Reg muttered and, as extreme irritation took over, his Baptist vows about swearing were forgotten. 'Bloody traffic!' He said.

They passed the scene of the accident that seemed to involve half a dozen cars.

'Oh, I do hope no one was seriously injured,' Rita said, biting her lip.

'Serve them right if they were,' Reg contradicted her. 'Driving too fast and too close by the looks of it; tail-gating, that's obviously what caused that little pile-up.' He gave a cheery wave to a policeman standing next to his motorcycle and the policeman immediately stepped out and held up his hand for the taxi to stop.

The driver had seen the gesture in his rear view mirror 'Oh, cor blimey, guv'nor, now what've you been an' gorn an' done?' Reg couldn't be sure if this was a Cockney put on or whether the man actually did speak like that.

The cop walked around to the front of the taxi and inspected the tyres, giving the one on the passenger side a good hard kick. He then walked down the length of the vehicle and reached the rear door just as Reg wound down the window and said, 'Excuse me, mate.'

The policeman froze. He stood and stared through the window at Reg's smiling face but said nothing. He seemed to loom very large or maybe that was because Reg was forced to look up at him.

'It's just that we've got a plane to catch and ... '

'May I enquire, sir, what was the purpose of your wave?'

'Just a friendly greeting, that's all,' Reg said.

'Really? And just what was your purpose in giving me a friendly greeting?'

The policeman appeared to grow even bigger with big hands and a big jaw. He rolled his tongue back and forth across the front of his lower teeth, forcing out his lip, and then stuck the end in one cheek, moving it up, down and around as he waited for an answer.

'As one policeman to another, that's all,' Reg said, still smiling. The cop thought about this for a few moments.

'Really,' he said. 'You are a policeman, are you? Presumably you have identification on you to substantiate that claim?'

'Don't you know who I am?'

'Let me see now ...' He stroked his chin and pushed out his lips. He seemed to have a thing about his mouth. Rita was beginning to think him rather sexy in a sort of cavemanish way. 'Let me see now, how about ... Sherlock Holmes? How about Inspector Clouseau? Maybe your name is Poirot? Perhaps we have Miss Marples seated right next to you there.' He was obviously a fan of detective novels or television. Rita giggled. The taxi driver sat passively behind his wheel staring straight ahead. The traffic was beginning to speed up. His meter was ticking over; his cab had its MOT and was in perfect condition. What did he have to worry about?

'I am Detective Inspector Venables,' Reg said.

'Who?'

Who? Who! Reg thought. Had he heard aright? Did this fellow

47

not read a newspaper? Was it only detective stories he watched on television? Did he not watch the television news? Did he not listen to the talk around every station in the United Kingdom? Was the man a complete ignoramus?

'Detective Inspector Venables,' the taxi driver chipped in.

The cop leaned back to look sideways at the driver.

'And who asked you to stick your spoke in?' He said.

'I'm just confirming the man is who he says he is and if we don't get a shifty on they really are going to miss their plane.'

It was at this point that the cop's presence was requested elsewhere.

'We'll let it go at that,' he said as he moved off and waved them on.

'I've got his number.' Reg growled, now in a thoroughly bad mood. 'As soon as we get back I intend having a word or two with his superiors.'

******

Jakob was busy disposing of old labels, writing out, sticking and tying on new ones when a cheery voice interrupted his concentration.

'Hello there!'

He looked up to see Thornton and Holly, who had just checked in, standing in front of him.

'What are you doing here? Thought you were on your way out. Just in transit were you? Went out the wrong exit?'

'Ach, no, man,' Jakob replied, 'as a matter of fact I was going to stop off in London but I took one look at England's terrible weather and I thought of you two going to have a truly wonderful time on the French Riviera and guess what, hey? I decided on the very spot to do the same. So here I am just now busy relabelling my luggage ready for the off.'

'Jolly good,' Thornton said. 'Guess we'll see you around then. Oh, by the way, my name is Thornton, Thornton King and this is Holly.'

'Delighted to meet you,' Jakob said, smiling at Holly. 'Are you travelling first class?'

'Afraid not. It's steerage for us.' Thornton laughed, 'Thanks to...' He had decided to give up the pretence and was about to mention Holly's daddy and the Christmas present when a swift little sideways kick against his Achilles tendon stopped him. 'Yes, it's economy for

48

us, old chum. You're going first are you?' Jakob nodded. 'What did you say your name was?'

'Actually I didn't, Mister King, but it's Jakob Mynhardt.'

'South African, huh? Can tell by the accent.'

'Of course.'

'What part?'

'Ach, man, I come from a little dorp in the Transkei you would never have heard of, six houses and a trading store. Well, it is maybe more than that now. I haven't been back there for a goodly while you know. Listen: as you are not travelling first class and we won't be seeing each other on the plane, perhaps you will permit me to offer you a drink before we leave? They'll be free on the plane of course. On second thoughts, free for me that is. I'll meet you just now as soon as I've finished doing this.'

'Very kind of you, Mister ... Mister ...'

'Mynhardt.'

'Yes, Mynhardt. Get yourself checked in and you'll find us in the Duty-Free shop.' With which they moved on. Jakob watched their departing backs for a while. That Thornton chap was a bit of a card, he thought. Was that the English expression? Miss Holly though never seemed to say a word. Strange. He went back to his labelling and, finally satisfied, took his case back to the girl at the KLM information desk.

'Check in is over there, sir,' she said, pointing, 'But don't worry, I will make sure the necessary arrangements for your luggage will be made. Have a good flight.' At which she turned her smile and her attention to another customer and Jakob walked over to the check-in counter. She didn't think to ask him for her pen.

******

Reg was first out of the cab followed by a slightly shaky Rita. It had all been too much for her and the adventure had hardly started. She wrapped her coat tightly around her and kept a firm grip on her handbag as though any passer-by might suddenly attempt to snatch it away. The luggage was deposited on the pavement and Reg took out his wallet to pay the fare.

'I'm not giving you a tip,' he said, eyes narrowed in emphasis, 'except a verbal one. I've got your number, matey and if I ever hear of you driving like that again I'll have your guts for garters. You're a

49

bleeding menace, you are.'

The verbal tip the driver would have liked to have given Reg was not vocalised and was a suggested action Reg would have found difficult if not downright physically impossible to accomplish anyway. The man could have at least thanked him for intervening with that bolshie motorcycle cop. Still scowling, he picked up what was probably a more amenable fare and drove away with murder on his mind. Reg picked up the suitcases and, followed by his subdued missus, entered the terminal.

******

Thornton and Holly had grown tired of the Duty Free. Holly had bought some film for her new Pentax; Thornton a bottle of *Famous Grouse*, his favourite whisky, and that was the sole sum of their shopping. As there was now the usual wait before they boarded their plane they were seated at the bar and, Jakob not yet appearing to stand them that proffered drink, they had ordered for themselves, a bucks fizz for Thornton, a Dubonnet and soda for Holly. She thought that would get her in a sort of French mood.

'Funny little chap,' Thornton said.

'I didn't like him.'

'Yes, I noticed you weren't very forthcoming. In fact you didn't put two words together. Why didn't you like him?'

'Something about him bothered me. He reeks of violence.'

'Reeks?' Thornton laughed. 'What a funny word, Holly. Someone reeks of sweat or booze, reeks of tobacco or garlic, but violence?'

'All right then, there was an air of violence around him.'

'Something like an aura you mean. I didn't know you were psychic, Holly? He struck me as being quite an inoffensive little man.'

'All right then, let us just say there seems to be, as you put it, an aura of violence around him.'

'Woman's intuition, right? Rather than psychic.'

'Maybe. What were you going to add when he asked how we were travelling?'

'Was I going to add something?'

'Thanks to … you said. Thanks to what?'

'Your generous daddy of course.'

'Hmn. Thornton I'm sorry I couldn't satisfy your ego by having

50

us fly first class. Daddy's generosity didn't stretch that far. As a matter of fact I did have a first class ticket but I got the travel agent to change it so you could join me. I'm surprised she managed to do it. Airlines are buggers for not wanting to change bookings once made. It's like drawing teeth without an anaesthetic. Maybe daddy's name helped. Anyway, the fistful of change gives us heaps more spending money so look on the bright side'

'That was very kind of you, Holly.'

'Wasn't it? At least you'll be pampered in a first class hotel to make up for your disappointment. Cheers!' Holly lifted her glass and took a sip of her Dubonnet soda, Thornton his bucks fizz.

'Bottoms up,' he responded, 'and, oh, good grief! Will you take a look at who's here?'

Holly turned to look and nearly choked on her drink. Reg and Rita Venables had made their entrance.

******

In the men's toilet, his hat and knapsack placed next to the basin, Jakob was rinsing the soap from his face when he heard the voice.

'Hullo, old chum. Going somewhere?'

He went cold, took a deep slow breath and, eventually looking up saw, reflected in the mirror, Joost and his sidekick standing not too far off. Straightening up, with water still dripping from his face, he turned to face them.

'You were supposed to meet me at Piccadilly Circus this evening,' he said.

'That's right. But you're not anywhere near Piccadilly are you? And it doesn't look like you intend to be anywhere near Piccadilly. You're at Heathrow airport, old chum, and I guess about to take a flight to somewhere else. Now I wonder where that might be. Doing a runner were you? It never pays to be too greedy, Jakob,' Joost shook his head and tut-tutted, 'you of all people should know that. Greed gets a person into an awful lot of trouble. I had a feeling in my water something of this sort might be on the cards and I was right, so I've come to collect our investment. Where is it?'

Jakob didn't move, didn't utter a sound.

'Don't mess me about, Jakob. You're a loser on this one, pal, and you know it. Playing for time will get you nowhere. Now, are you going to be a good boy and tell me, or aren't you? Be sensible, Jakob, just tell me where the diamonds are and we'll say no more.' A flick-knife had appeared in Joost's hand, blade out, and another in the hand of his companion who stood with his back fast against the door to prevent any possible entry.

Jakob smiled and then laughed, shaking his head. 'Killing me is going to give you the information you want?'

'Oh, we're not going to kill you,' Joost said, smiling back, his voice hardly above a whisper. 'We're going to take you somewhere where, after a while, you'll be wishing we had killed you. Now, for the last time, please, let's be sensible about this, let's be civilised. The alternative is too painful to think about. Now for the last time, where are they?' He suddenly frowned. Something was happening which at first he couldn't understand.

It had been a long adventurous life but Jakob was suddenly very very tired. He had had enough. He felt no apprehension, no pain but his eyes, still open and apparently still looking at Joost were in fact no longer seeing anything as he dropped to his knees, rolled over and lay still. Then his eyes, glazed over, never closed.

CHAPTER 3

Joost's sidekick was named Cyril, a name hardly likely to command any kind of respect with the criminal fraternity, quite the opposite in fact, so had been shortened to Cy thus hopefully avoiding sniggers and innuendo and, when this didn't work, Cy knew quite well how to punish disrespect. He now stood looking down at the body on the floor and, 'Shit!' he said. 'What do we do now?'

Joost closed his knife and slipped it back into the pocket from whence it had come. Cy did likewise. Joost turned Jakob onto his back and, taking him under the arms, was about to drag him to a cubicle but changed his mind in case Jakob's heels left marks on the polished floor.

'Take his feet,' he ordered and Cy duly bent down so that together they carried the corpse into a cubicle and sat it on the seat.

'Anyone coming in?'

Cy leaned backwards to look out, looked back, and shook his head.

'Good. Help me get his trousers off, and his underpants. I'll hold him up. You pull them down.'

This being accomplished they sat the body back on the seat and Joost ordered Cy to fetch the hat and knapsack while he started to go through pockets, finding ticket, passport, money. He took everything he could except for a cheap ballpoint pen and, when Cy returned, he placed the hat on Jakob's head and, keeping hold of the knapsack, backed out and closed the door behind him. From the outside there was no way of locking it unfortunately but hopefully it would be some time before the corpse was discovered. They could consider themselves extremely fortunate no one had entered what was normally a busy location and they weren't going to hang around longer than was necessary.

Once outside they quickly crossed the hall to get as far away as possible from the vicinity of the toilet. The moment they stopped, Joost first of all looked at the ticket and then, Cy doing his best to shield his confederate from prying eyes, he rummaged in the knapsack and flipped through the passports he found there.

Discovering a South African one in which the rather old photograph could possibly, at a push, be mistaken for himself, his face after all was decidedly unmemorable, he decided to use it, hoping that the French immigration official in Nice wouldn't be too zealous in examining passports. Maybe if he could position himself in front of a really beautiful girl, the official would be so taken up in ogling her, he would get through without a second glance or, hopefully, there would be such a crush they would be trying to get people through as quickly as possible. Anyhow he was prepared to risk it. He slung the rucksack over his shoulder.

'Listen, Cy, the luggage will already be on the plane. There's no way we can get at it here so I'm going to have to take Jakob's place. Head back to London and, just in case anything else goes wrong, report what has happened and tell them to get a couple of our guys to stand by in Nice to pick up that case. You know what it's supposed to look like so give them a description. Got that?'

Cy nodded.

'Well go on then. What are you waiting for?'

'Car keys.' Cy held out his hand.

'Have you got a licence?'

'Got half a dozen.'

'Okay then.' He handed over the keys. 'Here you go.'

The first call for his flight was being announced.

'And there you go,' Cy said. 'Have a good trip.'

******

'Well bless my soul.' Venables said genially, 'who would have thought it? Fancy meeting you two, here of all places.'

'Fancy,' Thornton said, getting up in acknowledgement of Rita's presence and looking in her direction. Venables got the message.

'Oh, you've not met the lady wife, have you? Rita, this is Mister Thornton King: King, this is my wife, Rita, and this is Miss Holly Day: the wife, Rita.' It was like a litany that hadn't as yet had a response.

'Pleased to meet you,' Rita simpered in Thornton's direction, holding out a set of chubby fingers and totally ignoring Holly.

'How do you do?' Thornton replied, taking the chubby fingers in his hand and wondering why she was perspiring. He withdrew as soon as he could and turned to Reg. 'And where may you both

54

be off to?'

'Well …' was it an optical illusion or did Venables actually grow in stature, just an inch or so? 'As a matter of fact, Thornton, I suppose I could call you Thornton now, after all we're old acquaintances, are we not?' He uttered what Thornton supposed was a comradely laugh though it could have been something akin to a death rattle. 'As a matter of fact, Thornton, we're just on our way to Nice, South of France.' He made it sound as if they were walking there. 'There's an Interpol convention and'… he cleared his throat … 'I have been invited as a guest of honour. Can you believe that? You will know the reason why of course.' He didn't think in the circumstances it would be circumspect to actually mention the name Spitskaya, a case of international interest. 'I may be mistaken in this but I believe I am the only British policeman ever to be so honoured.'

'Isn't that wonderful?' Rita simpered again, still in Thornton's direction. It appeared she couldn't take her eyes off him which, in fact, was the case. He was wondering if she really thought that shade of lipstick suited her. As for her hairstyle, good God! Who talked her into that?

'Oh, yes,' he replied, 'simply wonderful.' He turned back to Reg. 'Congratulations,' he said, seething inside.

'And where may you two be off to then?' Venables queried.

'Same place,' Thornton said and was delighted at the sudden look of apprehension on Reg's face.

'Thornton, hadn't we better board?' Holly butted in as the second flight announcement was made. She got to her feet and smiled down sweetly at Rita. But Thornton wasn't ready to move just yet. There was a bit of knife twisting to take place first.

'The fact is, sergeant … '

'Inspector. Inspector.' The tone was quietly admonishing.

'Oh, yes, of course, I had forgotten. Congratulations again. The fact is, Inspector, Holly and I both really need a break after all we went through recently assisting the police with their enquiries.'

'Thornton!' Holly took Thornton by the arm and literally started to drag him away.

'We're on the same plane then?' Venables asked. 'Travelling first class are you?'

'I'm afraid not.' It was Holly who answered.

'That's a shame.' Reg was immediately his previous ebullient self. 'Won't see you for a drink then. What a pity.'

'Holly,' Thornton protested as he was being forcibly removed, 'I wonder what happened to, what was his name? Jakob? My heart?'

'Mynhardt,' she corrected him.

'We never did get that promised drink.'

The Venables watched the pair go and, as soon as they were out of earshot Reg turned to his wife, 'Rita,' he hissed, 'I've got to have a slash before we board.'

'Oh, no!' she almost shrieked, looking around with an anxious apologetic smile in case someone had overheard. 'You'll be ages, Reg, and we'll miss the plane.'

'No, I won't be long. It's an emergency. If I don't go now I won't be able to sit in the plane till take off time and not be allowed to use the loo, especially if there's a delay. It's like you're not supposed to use the toilet while the train is standing at the station. It's the same with planes standing at the airport. You wait here. I'll be back in two shakes.'

'No more than three and don't talk to any strangers you meet,' Rita added coquettishly, momentarily forgetting her anxiety, but fortunately Reg didn't hear it as, not waiting for any further objection, he had gone off at a fair old trot.

With a bursting bladder, he fairly slammed back the door, it was just as well no one was coming the other way, threw himself into the toilet and headed for the urinals, passing the closed door of the cubicle as he went. Maybe the door slamming, maybe the speed at which he was travelling caused it, maybe it had just got to the point, or maybe it was the vibrations from an overhead plane but, whatever the reason, as he stood relieving himself, a certain cubicle door swung slowly open to reveal the seated Jakob. Having emptied his bladder, shivered, and heaved his sigh of relief, Reg zipped up and moved across to the line of washbasins. It was then that he saw it reflected in the mirror and, for a long moment, he stood frozen before slowly turning around. He couldn't believe it. It was impossible. This had to be a bad dream. He had a flaming plane to catch. Already there had been the last call. He was due to attend the most important function of his life and here he was in a public lavatory faced with a man obviously dead as the dodo. What was he to do? 'Ignore it,' he said to himself, 'just ignore it.'

"You're a police officer," his conscience chipped in, "it's your duty to report it."

'He could still be alive,' he murmured, biting a fingernail, and then suddenly heard Rita's voice. "Men die sitting on the lavvy you know, straining. Their hearts can't take it and they're found there, dead." If the poor sod had suffered a coronary and really was dead then there was nothing he could do about it anyway, was there? So he had better make up his mind fast before someone else entered the toilet and he had to admit to being a sodding policeman. That would definitely have kept him there a very long time. He made up his mind and fled. He attempted to quieten his conscience by concluding the guy was probably a pervert anyway, indulging in some filthy disgusting practice in a public toilet, hoping someone would join him or at least be a voyeur and enjoy watching, so serve him right. But all the excuses in the world could not salve his feelings of guilt, and his dereliction of duty would haunt him for a long time to come.

*****

Marcel Malherbe was an International Elder for the Army of the Righteous in Marseilles. It was a title he didn't bandy about but of which he was secretly quite proud. Although he wasn't too sure what the position entailed he felt sure the rewards would ultimately be substantial. He was enjoying an aperitif in his favourite seedy café when he was called to the phone and, after listening to someone named Cy calling from London, he put down the phone, tossed a few coins on the counter and went out to pick up, in an even seedier café, a couple of the brethren, albeit on a temporary basis; the Neapolitan, Nino and the *pied noir*, Alphonse. The three were soon on their way in Marcel's battered old Peugeot to the Coté D'Azur International Airport to meet a KLM flight from Heathrow and, they hoped, a man with a suitcase full of diamonds.

*****

The Honourable Duncan Devonport-Fawcett, known as Taps, played with his champagne flute and regarded the passing scene. Heir to an hereditary, if somewhat bankrupt earldom, if his elder brother kicked the bucket before him and went to the family mausoleum without having produced issue, which certainly looked like being the case because, if ever he did get married Taps had decided, it would be simply for the look of the thing and to cover his tracks or to go into politics rather than take his seat on the Tory benches in the upper house.

It was not that Taps wanted his brother to suffer an early demise. Perish the thought. No, gay or straight, well as straight that is as a bent straight can be, he loved his brother like a brother but the fact of the matter couldn't be disputed, his brother was, and Taps was quite certain of this, a very strange beast with very strange tastes none of which would lead to his having any issue. Taps knew all about his brother's sexual peccadilloes because Gerrard, which was the elder bother's name, had confided to him one night whilst in his cups he did actually like women, don't you know? Have no doubts about that at all, old chap. Oh, yes! Most certainly. It was what he liked the women to do to him, that was the macabre bit and Taps was quite sure Gerrard, if he would only admit it, really ought to be on the other side of the fence where he would be much happier. He would probably be blacklisted from his clubs though and his clubs were Gerrard's life, especially the food so reminiscent of school dinners. Gerrard's highly colourful sex life had nothing to do with having been consistently thrashed at their public school though it could just have been something to do with matron who Taps was terrified of and who Gerrard seemed inordinately fond of, as she was for him, too much so one would have guessed for a rosy cheeked schoolboy no matter how prematurely mature as far as certain anatomical aspects were concerned; rampant, she noticed, even during a nasty bout of scarlet fever.

It was up to Taps, so Taps believed, to recoup the lost fortunes of the earldom and its various lordships that hadn't been sold off to nobility orientated Americans, mostly from Florida. There was no doubt that Taps was quite capable of producing issue but the heiress he had hoped for hadn't as yet materialised. He thought of his ancient parents whom he loved eking out their days in that draughty crumbling castle with the generations of family portraits, the ragged heraldic banners, the rattling radiators and rattling suits of armour and was even more determined to do something about it. The coronet might be tarnished, the ermine motheaten but they were still better than nothing at all. At this moment though he was not thinking particularly of his parents in their draughty crumbling castle and the pursuit of an heiress, he was merely interested in the female members of the population of Nice, though at this time of the year they were hardly walking about in the next to nothing. Still, in comparison to frosty England, the evening was balmy and he

58

could sit and appreciate what was visible, partially visible, and use his imagination as to the rest, and Taps had quite a vivid imagination where the female form was concerned.

He had settled into his suite at *Le Meridien* on the promenade des Anglais, unpacked, taken a shower, admired his pale, slender, almost hairless naked body in a full length mirror, front and as much of the back as he could manage, admired the Med from his balcony and, having dressed casual but smart; loafers, cream slacks and pale blue angora pullover, he moved on to *Le Chantecler* for a meal fit for a king. Now he lingered over his vintage Moët and toyed with the idea of visiting the casino. Thoughts of that establishment brought to mind an article he had recently read in his magazine about La Belle Otero, the famous, or infamous, depending on one's point of view, (Reg Venables would most definitely plump for the latter), Spanish chanteuse, dancer, and courtesan of La Belle Époque. At the age of ninety one, penniless and existing on state handouts, and after having earned incredible fortunes and a collection of the most fabulous jewels, more through her talents in the bedroom than on the stage where a New York critic said of her, "We have watched Otero sing and heard her dance" she lost it all at roulette. The fabulous jewels had gone via the pawnbrokers, she was living in one room in a seedy pension here in Nice; surrounded by a few tatty souvenirs of her one time notoriety when she died while cooking a rabbit stew. Her lovers had included The Czar, who gave her a set of black pearls that once belonged to The Princess Eugenie, the Emperor of Japan who gave her an island in the Pacific, King Leopold of the Belgians who squandered a goodly portion of his Congolese wealth on her, any number of minor royalty and American multi-millionaires and Edward the Seventh when Prince of Wales who took her to dinner at *Rules*. Hardly anyone attended her funeral, though the presence of a Rolls Royce with a faded coat of arms painted on the door panels was noted. What did that incredible woman have that drove men mad, some to bankruptcy, some even to committing suicide over her? Included amongst the latter was a nineteen year old penniless student who she noticed hanging around outside her Paris apartment day after day until one day she opened a window and a crooked finger invited him into her boudoir for an afternoon of ecstasy after which he hanged himself. L'apres-midi d'un faune, poor lad, or was it rather like the female spider who eats her mate once she's been satisfied? Whatever it was she possessed, and Taps heaved a sigh, the girls he saw passing by right now obviously didn't have it and never would. It's a wonder, he thought, that the young student could rise to the occasion on that once in a lifetime afternoon. If it had been he, Taps, he would probably have been so overawed after all that build up and high expectation he would more than likely have proved totally useless. Then on the other hand, maybe the young man didn't rise to the occasion either and that's why he topped himself. He returned to thinking of Otero's misfortune at the wheel and decided it might be prudent to leave casino visits to his last night.

How careful, he wondered, ought he to be, or rather how far could he go, with his employer's money, seeing as to how the magazine was paying all expenses? Tomorrow would be his first working day as he covered the Interpol jamboree. The place would be swarming with journalists from all over the world but he should be able to get a couple of interesting interviews. His accompanying photographer, a dour bearded Scot who went by the name of Hamish McKinnon, had gone off exploring, much to Duncan's relief who felt constantly apprehensive in the Scot's company as though under some kind of unnamed threat. The bearded bugaboo would probably return to the hotel in the early hours roaring drunk and belting out Scottish folk songs at the top of his voice. He was the boss's choice, not Taps'. It would have been much more fun if Duncan had got the freelance photographer he wanted, one Adrian Spangle. Adrian was a little over the top and could get one into a heap of trouble by being too bold in the wrong place at the wrong time but he was always fun to be with. He had however snootily turned down the offered commission saying he only did fashion, darling, though at a push, he might consider art and antiques. As policemen, even on the French Riviera, didn't fall into any of those categories, their uniforms didn't do a thing for him, Adrian was out which was a shame. Although not of Adrian's persuasion, Taps would have found life much more congenial in his flamboyant airy fairy company than in that of the hairy scary Scot who even kept a skean dhu in his sock, probably slept with it under his pillow. "Well you never know when you might need it," was his reasoning, "Cameras are expensive items and a great temptation to would-be thieves."

In his turn Hamish didn't particularly like Taps. As far as he was concerned, he told anyone who would listen, the man was an effete Sassenach and it was why he had gone wandering off to explore on his own. The less he had to do with that upper class toffee nosed twat the better. For his part, Taps couldn't understand why Hamish had ever taken up photography as a career, not that his photographs weren't highly professional, even in some instances artistic, especially moody shots of his beloved Scotland but Taps couldn't help thinking that, instead of taking their photographs, Hamish would have been better off roaring around the Highlands slaying those dozy looking long haired cattle with a claymore.

******

Thornton and Holly had stowed their cabin bags in the overhead lockers and settled into their seats, Thornton with his knees practically under his chin, Holly hoping she wouldn't get someone gross on her other side who would take up the whole of the arm rest and more than likely part of her space as far as the ribs and, what is more, as the journey progressed, get rather niffy under the armpits. What she got was a fidgeting midget who nearly drove her mad. As seasoned fliers they had fastened their seat belts and waited for take-off. With every seat on the plane booked, apart from first class, it had taken some little time for people to get themselves sorted out, not totally in a spirit of bonhomie and of course there had to be some dork who had gone to the wrong gate and was late. Thornton took the in-flight magazine from the pocket in front of him and Holly opened the book she had removed from her bag.

'What are you reading?' he asked.

She turned the cover towards him trying very hard to keep a straight face.

"North of Timbuktu," he read, "Now a magnificent spine-tingling film from the studios of the Gigantic Picture Corporation. Cord Wainer as you have never seen him before, starring in this heart stopping thunderous all adventure movie."

'What! Oh, my God! I don't believe it! Holly! How can you be reading this trash? Just because it mentions Cord Wainer.' He took the book from her and studied the cover with disgust.

'Not at all, it's a jolly exciting read.'

'As you've never seen him before. Yuk! He was exactly the same in every picture he made, vomit making, and fortunately we will never see him any different because we will never see him again. Magnificent? Who are you kidding? Spine-chilling? Spine-churning more like it. Thunderous? About as thunderous as a wet fart.'

'Thornton!' She took back the book and opened it at her bookmark. 'You're just jealous.'

'Well wake me when we get to Nice,' he growled. He replaced his in-flight magazine and settled down lower in his seat. He hadn't thought to bring a book.

'Don't you want breakfast?'

'All right, wake me for breakfast, whatever it may be.' He laid back his head and closed his eyes. 'God, I hate flying!' he growled and had fallen asleep almost before take-off.

******

In first class a beaming Rita, as befits a VIP, was taking in her surroundings as she delicately sipped her champagne. There were a few empty seats and Reg had left her to have a conversation with what seemed a very nice fella by the name of Jakob Mynhardt. They had met whilst standing at the rear of the plane waiting to use the overworked toilets. Obviously nerves were working overtime on Reg's bladder. Quite naturally on their seated return and in the course of their conversation, Reg couldn't resist telling his new acquaintance all about the Interpol convention and how he, Detective Inspector Reg Venables, had been especially invited to make this speech. Even as he was chatting away though, he couldn't help but notice that Jakob Mynhardt seemed to be just a little bit on the jittery side. Maybe, Reg surmised, he was nervous about flying.

'And what do you do for a living?' Reg enquired and added politely, 'if I may ask?'

'I'm into property,' Joost replied, neglecting to state it was other people's property he was into.

'Hmn ...' was the response. 'Pretty lucrative I suppose, property.'

******

Apart from the breakfast that, in Thornton's opinion, was worse than Cord's performance in *North Of Timbuktu,* not that he had seen it or intended seeing it, it was merely supposition; and as he used his fork to play with what passed for scrambled egg, he thought how he was always baffled by the smallness of the bones when chicken was on the menu – designer chickens he decided, especially bred for airline meals. He went back to sleep.

The rest of the flight passed off smoothly, which couldn't be said for the drama being unfolded at Heathrow Airport. There an hysterical cleaner, having entered the gent's toilet to inspect and maintain, discovered the body of Jakob Mynhardt and was currently under sedation while an investigation by a police inspector into the unknown man's death was underway.

Other users of the toilet had come and gone for legitimate, one or two for not so legitimate, reasons but all had ignored the man seated on the loo in an open cubicle, some out of embarrassment, some out of a sense of decency, some because they just didn't want to get involved though they would all, once outside, whisper to whomsoever they were with, "Hey, you're never going to believe this but there's a guy sitting in there with his trousers round his ankles and the door wide open. What do you think he's up to?" not realising he would never be up to anything ever again.

Now the toilet was sealed off with police tape and a guard by the door whilst inside, the doctor, having been called in, finished his cursory examination, stood up and backed out of the cubicle.

'Yes, well seems to me like a common or garden coronary, nothing suspicious there.'

The inspector, a man of florid complexion and shortish temper, who had been standing by waiting for the doc's conclusions, inspected the fingernails of one hand and wondered how a coronary could be common or garden, but only said the usual thing a policeman says in the circumstances.

'Can you give a time of death?' Why he personally should want this piece of information was anybody's guess but it sounded good and professional and Constable Roper could jot it down in his notebook.

Constable Roper, who had been seconded to Heathrow and had so far loved every minute of it with a boyish enthusiasm for aircraft and anything connected with them; his bedroom at home after all was full of models of World War Two planes; British, German, American and Japanese, looked at his superior and speculated as to whether or not he watched too many movies, or maybe he was a fan of Sherlock Holmes.

'Not exactly of course ...' they all say that, Roper thought ... 'but certainly not very long,' the doctor concluded. "How long's a piece of string?" Roper asked himself. He was keeping his mind busy because he had never actually seen a dead man before and was a wee bit concerned he might be asked to move in closer, not only that but might actually be asked to touch and would make a fool of himself. He waggled ten stiff fingers, wriggled his toes, and felt a sort of cold chill run up his spine at the very idea. He knew, as a policeman, this was bound to happen sooner or later but he wished it could have been later. The only good thing about this corpse was there didn't appear to be anything truly horrific about it.

'Thank you, Doc,' the inspector said. The doctor didn't like being called doc. It smacked of a Hollywood animated cartoon.

'Yes, well, you won't have any more need of me and a p.m. will confirm it. Ambulance should be here soon so I'll bid you good-day.'

"This one's also seen too many movies," Roper thought as the doctor left him alone with the inspector and the corpse.

'Yes, well, what do you suggest we do now, Roper?' the inspector asked.

'Wait for the photographer,' Roper said quick as a flash. He too had watched a lot of movies.

'Hmn…' The inspector moved in close and started to go through Jakob's pockets and there were a lot of pockets. 'Empty,' he said. 'Empty empty empty empty, empty, every pocket empty. Nothing suspicious did the doc say?'

He removed a cheap pen from a breast pocket of the jacket and tapped it against the palm of his hand three or four times while he mused, then he slipped the pen into his own breast pocket. 'How do we identify this geyser, sitting here with his trousers down and nothing on him to say who he is, where he came from, or where he intended to go, that's what I'd like to know?'

'Fingerprints?' Roper volunteered. The inspector gave him a steely look. Roper blushed. The inspector lifted Jakob's shirt front.

'One thing we do know for sure, he wasn't Jewish. Then, as he lifted the shirt higher, "Ullo 'ullo 'ullo! An' what do we have here then?'

Roper hoped that, one day when he was made inspector, he wouldn't be so crass as to talk in such clichés.

'Take a butcher's at this, young Roper, tell me what you make of it?'

Roper stepped gingerly forward and inspected Jakob's stomach and chest. 'Scars,' he said.

'Yes, yes,' the inspector agreed with some signs of impatience, 'I can see that they're scars but what kind of bloody scars, that's the question? Looks to me like this gentleman's been in the wars. Doesn't it look like that to you?'

'Bullet wounds you mean?'

'Quick on the uptake, that's what you are, young Roper. That's exactly what I mean. What kind of hanky panky do you suppose he's been up to then?'

'None necessarily. He could have got the wounds in World War Two. He's the right age for it and they look pretty old to me.'

'You're an expert on bullet wounds I take it?'

Roper blushed and decided to keep his mouth shut unless directly ordered to open it. Meanwhile the inspector, somewhat deflated by this observation on Roper's part, took the pen out of his pocket to poke in his ear and remove some wax which he inspected before rubbing it off with a finger. It was then that he noticed the initials on the pen. At the same time the outer door opened and the policeman on guard looked in to say, 'Ambulance is here, sir.'

The inspector nodded. 'Send them in,' he ordered. 'And Roper, I want you to go to all the KLM desks and question the staff as to whether or not any of them might have recently given or lent this pen to a passenger. Got that?'

And Roper, only too happy to leave the scene, took the pen, said, 'Yes, sir,' and skedaddled, just as the ambulance men arrived with a stretcher.

'He's in there,' the inspector jerked a thumb towards the cubicle and moved away to give the ambulance men room to manoeuvre. They lifted Jakob off the seat, pulled up his trousers, not out of modesty but because it would make it easier to manhandle him and, laying him out on the stretcher, placed his fallen hat on his chest, covered him with a white sheet and were about to move him out when they were ordered to stop.

'Half a mo'. Hang about while we try and figure out who this geyser is,' the inspector informed them. 'There may be a possible witness.'

The men looked at each other and without saying a word, turned away and produced cigarettes which, despite the no-smoking signs, they proceeded to light; retiring to the row of basins to have something to lean on and somewhere to flick their ash.

The inspector wandered back into the cubicle for another look around in case he had missed something and there was definitely something he had missed. That is something should have been there and it wasn't. He called one of the men over and jerked his index finger downwards towards the bowl.

'What do you make of that then?' he asked.

'Make of what?' the man replied, looking into the empty bowl.

'Use your imagination, sonny,' the inspector coaxed. The ambulance man was a bit long in the tooth to be called sonny but it was just the inspector's way. 'A man sits on the toilet for a purpose, doesn't he? And it isn't to die. Now what do you suppose is the purpose of that purpose?' He could be a bit verbose when carried away and on a short fuse 'And, if he had used the toilet for that singular purpose, then where is it?'

'Where's what?' The ambulance man looked totally confused.

'The SHIT, man! The SHIT! Where is it?'

The ambulance man turned to look at his companion, looked back again, looked into the empty bowl, looked up at the inspector and said, 'Maybe he flushed.'

The inspector scratched his forehead and nodded, saying softly almost to himself though definitely meant for the ambulance man's ears, 'So the man is already a busted flush but he manages to flush anyway even though he's turned up, or about to turn up, his toes. Do me a favour. The answer is, there never was any in the first place and, to my mind, that is highly suspicious, that is.'

'Yeah,' the ambulance man agreed, 'I suppose it is.' He looked at his companion again, raised his eyebrows and shrugged. 'Look, how long are we going to be here? We *are* on call you know.'

'I told you, until a witness comes along, one I am expecting any moment, one who can identify this ...' He pointed to the body under its sheet.

******

Well on their way to the south of France, Reg, like Thornton, had fallen asleep, fortunately without dropping his head on his new companion's shoulder which would have been embarrassing to say the least. Rita, bored with looking out the window with nothing to see but cloud tops was wondering if they were going to fly over the Alps and how long would it be before they appeared, those beautiful snowy white peaks she had seen in so many pictures, and would they poke their majestic heads up through the clouds? Romantic novels constantly stimulated Rita's imagination. She turned her attention to the cabin, caught Joost's eye as he glanced up from the courtesy *Financial Times* and, quickly making sure Reg was fast asleep, she gave the stranger a wide though ever so slightly coy smile which was reciprocated, though not so coy. Joost folded up his paper and left his seat to slip into an empty one next to hers. Rita was thrilled. She had absolutely no intention of joining the mile high club which she had read all about, certainly not with Reg sitting there, but Reg was hardly good company, no company at all in fact and this seemed quite an attractive man with whom to be whiling away the time.

'Lovely day isn't it?' was her opening gambit. The English always start with the weather. It's traditional. 'I mean now we've left dreary old England. Wasn't England just so dreary this morning? Now we're here above the clouds and can see the sun. Aren't the clouds so lovely and fleecy? That was quite a whoosh when the plane took off wasn't it? Gosh!' She had gone slightly girlish, 'It really took my breath away.' She laid a hand on her chest just below the throat, fingers spread wide hoping he would notice the swell of her bosom, which was still, or so she fondly imagined, alluring. After all, even after suckling two kids, and Robin was a right little biter, they had not dropped even a centimetre. She had used more lanolin on her nipples than a dairy farmer used on his cow's udders and that was a fact. 'I never expected it to be like that, did you? Oh, no, of course not. You will have done a lot of flying, won't you? An old hand as it were so you would be used to it. Are you travelling on business?'

'What makes you think that?' Joost was already beginning to regret his impulsive move in changing seats. The regret would grow bitter.

Rita pointed to the paper he had discarded on the seat he had left and he regarded it somewhat with longing.

'*The Financial Times,*' she said as though it was a paper she read every day.

'No, I am not travelling on business.' He turned his attention back to her. 'Well actually only in a round about sort of way, but I like to follow the prices, particularly commodities.'

Rita didn't realise he had mentally gone back to his newspaper or really understand what he meant by commodities but she pursed her lips and nodded knowingly.

'How about you?' he asked. 'You and your husband,' now he glanced in Reg's direction and quickly looked away. Reg's mouth had fallen open and Rita was obviously embarrassed by it. 'I take it you are attending this police convention.'

'That's right, Reg, that's my husband,' she cast another quick glance in his direction to note with satisfaction his mouth had closed again as he turned on his side, 'is to give a speech. He's ... '

'Yes, so he told me.'

'... been working on it ever so hard.'

'You must be very proud of him. I know all about this so-called modelling school affair. It was very clever of him to crack the case.'

'Yes, it was, wasn't it?'

'The old girl, Russian wasn't she? The one who ran the scam? She was killed by one of her servants I believe. Papers were full of it for days even in Belgium.'

'Oh, is that where you're from? Belgium?

'Yes. Where is it you'll be staying exactly, for this convention?'

'Oh, I forget.'

'Beaulieu-sur-Mer would it be?'

'That's right. How did you know?'

'Reg told me.'

'My name's Rita by the way.' Still with her left hand on her chest she passed him her right with a crossover so that, when he took it, his knuckles brushed her left arm. She shivered.

'Joost Broecx. How do you do?' Had he lost concentration and forgotten who he should be?

His name didn't really matter. Being so strange it had either not registered, she hadn't heard it or, by the time they had shaken hands, she had already forgotten it.

******

Full of self importance whilst on police business, Roper strutted like a bantam cock across the departures hall and stopped dead: there being no KLM flight for a while the desks stood empty and in semi-darkness. He looked around; saw there was a girl at the information desk and trotted across to her. She was busy with a customer.

'Excuse me, Miss,' Roper said. She glanced briefly in his direction and then ignored him. He waited a moment then cleared his throat and repeated himself. This time she did turn to actually look in his direction.

'I'll be with you in a moment,' she said, somewhat terse and certainly not granting him the gracious regulation company smile but ungraciously turning her back on him.

But Roper wasn't having that. 'Sorry, Miss,' he said, 'urgent police business. I need to talk to you now.'

Forcing a leaflet on her customer and with an exaggerated smile and an apology she moved around to where Roper stood.

'What is it?' she hissed somewhat irritably. 'Can't you see I'm attending to a customer?'

'Have you seen this before?' he asked, holding out the pen.

'Of course I have. I've seen hundreds of them. Now if you don't mind …' She was about to turn away again.

'No, Miss, what I mean is, could this be yours? Could you recently have given or lent this pen to a passenger?'

The young lady took the pen and laid it on her counter.

'Yes,' was the answer. 'I said to myself at the time, he'll never bring it back, I said. That's the trouble with millionaires…'

'Millionaires?'

'That's how they get to be millionaires you know. You mark my words, it's take, take, take and never give back. There now, very nice I must say for the police to return it to me but haven't they got better things to do with their time than return cheap pens? Like catch burglars or harass drivers or something? Now, if you'll excuse me …' She was turning back to her customer once more.

Roper's eyes took on a steely glint, as Mickey Spillane would have had it, or as steely as his youth, eyes of cornflower blue and peaches and cream complexion untouched by safety razor would admit. He was definitely a late developer. This girl was too narky for her own good and was due for a comeuppance or conversely, taken down a peg or two.

'Excuse me, Miss …' His voice too had acquired a more mature edge … 'but I would like you to accompany me if you don't mind.'

She had turned back. 'Accompany you?' She squeaked. 'Accompany you to where might I enquire?'

'To the gents toilet, over there.' He pointed in the right direction.

'What!' She hadn't intended to shriek quite so loud and looked hastily around to see who had noticed. Her customer for one - youngish but prematurely bald: skinny but with an unfortunate paunch; heavy horn-rimmed pebble glasses, dead ringer casting for a serial molester of the young in the back rows of cinemas - was obviously intrigued by what was going on but pretended to be wholly absorbed in his leaflet.

'To assist the police with their enquiries,' Roper hastily added.

'Enquiries into what?' she demanded to know. 'In the gents? Funny place to hold enquiries don't you think?'

The customer ran the end of a pink tongue across his upper lip. He probably thought it an excellent place for the holding of enquiries.

'How do I know you're who you say you are? How do I know you're even a policeman? You don't look like a policeman. You look like someone pretending to be a policeman. You could be one of ... them!'

Roper wasn't sure exactly what she meant by "them". Baby-faced serial killer maybe? 'Miss, if you don't come with me this instant and stop prevar ... prevar ... pre... stalling you're going to be in very serious trouble.' He was truly piqued by her disparaging remarks.

'Don't you threaten me, young man. Is this a practical joke? Someone's put you up to this haven't they?' She looked around to see who it could possibly have been. 'It's that Denise,' she said. 'Where's she hiding? She's always playing tricks on people, really nasty ones sometimes. One day someone's...'

Roper, feeling his authority ebbing away by the second, decided there was nothing for it but to put her in the picture. He had thought the sight of the corpse without warning would have been the comeuppance he had hoped for but this young lady was proving to be a difficult witness before she had even witnessed anything.

'It's called obstructing the police in the execution of their duty, miss, and it's a very serious offence that can land you in jail.'

'Gwan!' she said, giggling. 'Pull the other one.'

'We happen to be investigating a suspicious death, miss.' This brought her open-mouthed to a standstill. 'And we need you to identify the body.'

The mouth opened even wider. So did that of the customer who cast a hurried glance in the direction of the toilet door and back again to Constable Roper. No pretence now of not listening in to the conversation.

'We believe whoever gave the body ...' He liked the reaction he got on the repetition of the word body; she had gone quite white although the mouth had snapped shut ... 'whoever gave the recently deceased that pen, and I'll have it back if you don't mind, it's evidence ...' She held it out and he took it. '... is in a position to make a positive identification' (he was getting the jargon off pat) 'so, as you have already admitted to lending that pen to a passenger a short while ago ...' He peered at her name badge ... 'I would kindly request, Miss Hughes, that you come with me to the gents toilet where the body is lying and waiting for you to take a gander at it.' The jargon had gone out the window but she got the message.

'I can't just leave like that,' she squealed. 'I'm on duty. Someone needs to be here at all times.'

'Then find someone to replace you on a temporary basis. Miss.' He was his old self again. 'It shouldn't take more'n a moment.'

'Is it very nasty?' She whispered. 'The body I mean.'

Roper suddenly realised she was a very pretty girl, small and dark with large brown eyes. He had the feeling she probably came from Cardiff and, although her father might have been Welsh, her mother was something totally other which was what gave her that alluring Gypsy appearance and he felt a twinge of remorse at his behaviour. There really was no need for truculence. Members of the public should be treated with due respect and understanding at all times. Even criminals were human, up to a point.

'You'll be all right,' he reassured her. 'You've only got to look at his face, that's all, and it's just like he's lying there asleep, honest.'

'But I'll know he's ... you know ... I'll know he's not just, well, you know ... asleep.' She sucked in her lower lip behind her top teeth, very nice pearly teeth they were too, thought young constable Roper, and then she submitted to his wishes. 'Well, all right then,' she said, as though she really had a choice. 'Oh, here's someone who can take my place for a while.'

A young man, not that much older than Roper, smartly dressed in blazer and slacks, was passing by and stopped as she called out. 'Mike!' He turned back. 'Oh, Mike, could you possibly hold the fort for me for a short while? I have to go with this young man to sort something out.' She turned back to her customer still pretending to go through his leaflet but whose ears were now waggling so hard it was a wonder they weren't dropping off. 'I'm so sorry, sir, to neglect you like this. If you'll excuse me just a moment ...' she trailed off as she joined Roper.

'Do you think you'll be long?' Mike asked.

'No, not really,' Roper said. 'It won't take any time at all.' He was rewarded with a genuine dazzling smile from Mike, not an automatic company smile at all. It never took much to make Roper blush and he blushed for all the world to see. Blodwen thought he was rather sweet for a policeman. Mike thought so too though, in his case, it was the uniform that clinched it.

The ambulance men and the inspector were leaning against the washbasins enjoying their smokes when Roper returned with Blodwen who, immediately on seeing the corpse, felt her knees grow weak but, coming as she did from a long line of hardy Welsh miners used to singing *Bread Of Heaven* at full belt, she pulled herself together to face her ordeal.

'This is Miss Hughes,' Roper said. 'She informs me she was the person who lent the pen to ... to ...,' unable to think of an identity for the unknown other than corpse or body or deceased which he was now reluctant to use in front of Miss Hughes he lamely waved a somewhat limp hand in the direction of the late Jakob Mynhardt.

The inspector opened a tap, held his cigarette under the running water, dropped the soggy mess into the basin and walked over to the paper dispenser to wipe his hands before returning to where Roper and Blodwen were standing.

'Miss who?'

'Hughes,' Roper said, 'Blodwen Hughes.' He smiled at her and the smile was, albeit a little on the weak side, returned.

'Well then, Miss Hughes, you know what you are here for, yes?' She nodded. 'All right, Roper.'

'All right, what, sir?'

'Show the lady.'

'Oh.' Gingerly after a moments hesitation Roper stepped up to the stretcher and lifted a corner of the sheet. Blodwen looked.

'Have you seen this man before?' The inspector asked. 'Is this the one you lent your pen to?'

Unable to speak, Blodwen nodded and looked away. Roper dropped the sheet and stepped back. He had a sudden desperate desire to put his arms around Miss Hughes but he was standing on one side of the corpse, she was on the other and he thought it might look a bit odd if he walked around to fulfil his wish, besides which it could be considered as sexual harassment and he would be up on a disciplinary charge.

'Do you know his name?' the inspector asked.

'I don't remember it offhand.' Blodwen had found her voice, squeaky but clear. 'It's a foreign sounding name. I remember he was travelling to Nice and, if we go back to my desk, I can look up his details. His flight has departed of course, right on schedule.' She was keeping her eyes averted from the sheet-draped object. This was not

72

how she had planned her itinerary for the day.

'Right,' the inspector said. 'Then let's do that' He turned to the ambulance men, 'Okay, you can get him out of here.'

The wash basin now held three soggy cigarette ends.

Once outside, a curious crowd of sensation seekers faced the trio. Obviously Blodwen's customer had spread the word and a number of policemen on guard, the first one having had to call for back up, were having a hard time keeping the mob at bay. Only the sighting of a television camera in a public place could have been the cause of so many gathered together in so short a time for so little purpose. When the police tape was removed and the ambulance men emerged with the stretcher, the gawping crowd parted like the red sea before Moses and, having had their day made by this unexpected event, dispersed, chatting to newly acquired friends who had shared the experience.

'Here you are,' Blodwen said, back at her post, 'His name was Jakob Mynhardt. South African passport, number L331398.'

An open-mouthed Mike, taking in what was going on around him but casting sideways glances of longing was standing close to Roper. Never would there be a better opportunity for opening up a conversation and launching the start of a beautiful friendship but it was not to be because Blodwen continued with a piece of information that had them all agog.

'There's strange,' she said, 'He's on the plane.'

'What?' The inspector roared. 'What are you talking about, girl? That's impossible. He's over there, look! That's not a bloody mirage. You've just identified him, dead as a bloody doornail, and he's being taken away out to an ambulance, from which he will be transferred to a mortuary fridge before being transferred once more, this time to a slab in order to be cut up to ascertain cause of death.' Blodwen felt her legs grow weak again, did the inspector have to be quite so explicit? 'Could you have made a mistake?' he asked.

Blodwen shook her head and emphatically denied any possibility of error as far as identification was concerned, but then how could he possibly be on the plane?

'Perhaps he's a ghost.' The inspector said facetiously.

'Whoever or whatever he is,' and she gave this rude policeman her most scornful look, 'you can check it out for yourself.' And she handed him the manifest, which proved without a shadow of doubt - Jakob Mynhardt was on that plane, and well on his way to Nice.

******

In fact Jakob Mynhardt, aka Joost Broecx, was at that very moment desperately seeking an excuse for leaving his recently found companion who was still giving his ears a right old bashing. She had got on to the subject of selfish ungrateful kids (her own) and the modern generation, (everybody else's), a favourite topic of conversation with many of middle age and above but hardly original; it went with the territory of each and every older generation as Arthur Miller might have put it, even ancient Greek philosophers were known to moan and speak disparagingly and despairingly of the younger generation but Joost, not having kids of his own and not being particularly interested in kids, was bored stiff and there was no sign of Reg waking up and taking his missus off his hands. She went off the subject of children and segued easily into health, her own in particular and her martyrdom to travel sickness. It was at this point that Joost decided, excuse or no excuse, it would be expedient to move, so he moved. He left Rita wondering what she had said to upset him.

CHAPTER 4

From the dismal depressing grey of London, Joost was the first to step out of the plane into glorious almost blinding sunshine. Screwing up his eyelids to counteract the dazzle and ignoring the stewardess's standard smile and politely murmured adieu, hoping he would travel with them again, all issued through moist, pale pink, Bridget Bardot lips, he cast a beady eye around the landscape. It seemed to be swarming with les flic and more than usual activity but, as on the plane he had been made only too well aware by Reg of the forthcoming Interpol jamboree and knees-up, it didn't bother him in the least, not at first that is. Later he noticed the slightly quizzical look and surreptitious signal passed on by the immigration officer as his passport, Jakob's passport rather, was stamped; but as it was handed back to him with a smile and Joost could not make out for whom the signal was intended, perhaps it was only his imagination. If not, he was used to living on the edge, the die was cast and there was little if anything he could do now except hope he could still get away with it.

He had intended using Rita as a possible cover when passing through immigration. Surely, if she opened her mouth, she would be enough to distract anybody but he found he simply couldn't go through with it. Unhurriedly he continued on his way and, first class luggage already off the plane and coming through, he lifted from the carousel a beige suitcase with red and brown stripes around the middle. He had time only to register that, apart from the airline's destination and flight number tag around the handle, the case seemed devoid of any owner information. This was because there was also string knotted around the handle, to which was attached a small section of label by its ring reinforcements, the rest of the label obviously having been ripped off in transit. Careless baggage handlers, he thought, but had no time to take another step or ponder further as the heavy hand of the law was laid upon his shoulder and he accepted the fact that his plan had miscarried and he was well and truly nicked. Obviously Jakob's corpse had been discovered too soon and, worse luck, fairly quickly identified, but how? He had left nothing on the body that could have lead to identification so quickly. Or had he?

'Shit!' he muttered, trying desperately to mentally retrace events that led him to this point. His story would need to be a good one to wriggle out of the mess he was surely in.

'Commént?' queried the man holding Joost's right elbow in a discreet but firm grip.

'Deed you say somtheeng?' queried the man holding his left elbow ditto the man on the right. This one on the left, who had no need for a razor to remove the bum fluff from his cheeks, (policemen on both sides of the channel seemed to be getting younger every year), looked suspiciously like the young Alain Delon and had the kind of accent youthful method actors aspire to when transposed from New York workshop to Hollywood and cast as French thugs from Marseilles.

In this instance, and despite Marcel driving in true Gallic fashion, the real thugs from Marseilles, only one of whom was actually French, were late on arrival at the airport because it is a fairly hefty stretch between that great Mediterranean port and the city of Nice, and they were not even in time to see Joost being led away, suitcase and all. So they stayed where they could see the passengers exiting and keep a sharp lookout for anyone carrying a beige suitcase with red and brown stripes around the middle. They didn't have too long to wait before inspector Reg Venables and his lady wife emerged, and the inspector was carrying such a case.

******

Thornton and Holly, ceaselessly jostled by those with less patience than themselves, everyone of whom seemed to have either very large feet or extremely sharp elbows, stood by the carousel craning their necks to look over and between collected heads when a gap appeared for what was coming through the slashed curtain and, when Holly's case appeared, she proved her elbows, let alone her heels, could be as sharp as anyone else's as she lunged forward quite unladylike to retrieve it. 'Sorry,' she said. 'Sorry,' being not in the least bit sorry; merely getting some of her own back. "We learn our manners from the company we keep," she thought, and her apologies were musically chirpy and insincere.

Thornton on the other hand stood scowling and, on Holly's

return from the melee, remarked that his suitcase, if it appeared at all, would inevitably be the last one, as it seems it invariably was. On some previous occasions, long after all other baggage had been collected and taken away by happy travellers, his suitcase would appear through the slashed plastic in solitary majestic splendour like a prima donna taking her solo curtain call. Now and again though he had noticed strange and wonderful objects, like a lacrosse stick or an elephant's foot umbrella stand, were left going around and around and were still there unclaimed and forlorn looking when the carousel stopped and the lights went out. In this instance the carousel stopped empty, the overhead lights went out and not only had they waited an eternity, Thornton still hadn't collected his case. The crowd of passengers had dispersed, only too happy to be away, and in the gloom of the empty hall all was silence.

'Oh, dear,' Holly said, very quietly, waiting for the volcano to explode; which it did, in no uncertain terms. It was not a good start.

******

Reg put down the suitcases and was busily examining his guide book whilst Rita, having never before been abroad, gazed in wonder around her.

A suave, handsome, young gentleman of what she presumed to be Latin appearance and nattily though casually dressed, passed by and, accompanied by a suggestive wink, blew her a kiss and ran his tongue across his upper lip at which Rita quivered and blushed with delight and her gaze went with him as he continued on his way.

A few yards further on he turned his head and gave her so delightful a smile, had she been a Nineteenth Century maiden in a Nineteenth Century novel, she would have swooned on the spot. She was still all of a tremble from her first experience of flying. The trembling certainly had absolutely nothing to do with that awful Belgium man who came onto her and then so rudely left. She never wanted to see *him* again. No, she was recovering from her alarm when the plane touched down and her embarrassing scream as the wheels hit the tarmac and the brakes were applied with a force she hadn't expected.

'The pilot likes to know his wheels have touched the ground,' Reg informed her.

'Well you could have warned me.' She squealed 'Touched the

ground? They practically dug a trench!'

So the attentions of the young charmer, no matter how insincere, brought forth a deep sigh and a happy smile to her face. Simultaneous to this mini romance, Marcel accosted Reg to ask for a light for his Gauloise, and Reg happily obliged, wishing he could say something in French when he was politely thanked with a "merci beaucoup," but nothing came to mind, even his schoolboy French letting him down. Still, being a typical Englishman who didn't want to make a fool of himself, the only way to make Johnny foreigner understand is to speak English very slowly and very loudly. In the meantime, the pied noir, Alphonse, had lifted the beige suitcase with the red and brown stripes down the middle and made off with it in the opposite direction to Antonino the Neapolitan, and Marcel, having taken an inordinately long time to light his cigarette despite the total absence of any breeze, also finally departed in yet a third direction. All this was witnessed by Taps who, standing unnoticed not too far away, evidently thought it a great piece of copy for his magazine. English policeman invited as a guest of honour by Interpol on his very first moments in the south of France loses his luggage to a bunch of obviously well experienced thieves, the kind of incident Taps would no doubt refer to as a scoop.

******

The room was small and barely furnished: a desk on which stood a telephone, a grimy overflowing ashtray, and wire in and out trays; a couple of hardwood chairs, a metal filing cabinet, badly scratched and the corners of its drawers somehow dented, a waste paper bin used, it seemed, mainly for aiming paper aeroplanes at.

Inspector Leroux lounged in the chair behind the desk, a second man leaned against the filing cabinet, the beige suitcase at his feet, and a third man stood by the door. All three happily dragged on their cigarettes filling the room with pungent smoke, drank their coffee from chipped mugs and ignored the man seated miserably in front of the desk, looking down at his feet, deep in thought, going around in circles that were getting him nowhere. Eventually Inspector Leroux decided to acknowledge his existence.

'Sooooo ...' he said in a slow drawl as he leaned forward and poked the butt of his cigarette around the ashtray with nicotine stained fingers trying to find somewhere to stub it out. Embarrassingly his English was going to turn out to be almost perfect, the result of having once been a student in Bournemouth where he played football, smoked pot, seduced some of the local girls (no pregnancies fortunately) fought pitched battles with the local xenophobic yobs and learnt the language. He could have spoken in French had he known Joost was Belgian but he wasn't as yet aware of that, presuming from the passport, the man was passing himself off as Afrikaans. Besides, he prided himself on his English and liked to practice it anyway. He picked up the passport lying on the desk, opened it and for a while studied it for the third or fourth time, flipping the pages, turning it this way and that as though it would suddenly, like a Jack in the box, release some weird and wonderful secret. 'Sooooo ...' he said again, 'Ja ... kop ... Myn ... hardt.' He sniffed through one nostril, twisting his nose to the side and had another peek at the photograph before looking up at Joost who had raised his eyes from the study of his shoes. 'You didn't really think you would get away with this.' He chuckled, taking in his colleagues to share the ridiculousness of it. It wasn't a question; it was a statement of fact. They smiled dutifully.

Joost shrugged.

'So tell me, who is this Jakob Mynhardt whose identity you appear to have stolen?'

Joost shrugged again. The policeman pushed out his lips and scratched an eyebrow, cleared his throat, and tried again. 'All right then, let us try a different tack, what is your name, your real name?' As Joost had plenty of cash thanks to Jakob he had thoughtfully cleared out his own pockets of any possible identification. There was silence as Leroux sat regarding him. 'You might as well come clean you know,' the policeman advised. He liked that "come clean" bit; it showed how familiar he was with the jargon. 'We'll find out sooner or later anyway.'

'Joost Broecx.'

'Pardon? Speak a little louder if you please.'

'Joost Broecx.'

'Belgian?'

Joost nodded.

'And may I enquire, M'sieur Broecx, as to why you have come from London to Nice, travelling with a false passport?'

'Holiday.'

'Oh, really?' There was no change in Leroux's expression but for a while he seemed disinclined to ask any more questions. Joost fidgeted restlessly. Finally the policeman looked towards the second man and, moving the ashtray and wire baskets to one side in order to make room for it, requested the suitcase be brought over to the desk where it was turned this way and that, given the once over in the same manner as the passport before Leroux held out his hand, resting it on the lid of the case with his palm upwards in Joost's direction, and waggled his fingers in a give gesture. Joost looked a trifle baffled.

'Key,' the policeman said, not wanting to waste any more words.

'Don't have it,' Joost replied.

'I would advise you not to play games with me,' the inspector growled, a note of warning for the first time creeping into his voice. He was almost tempted to give up on the English and start in in French.

'It's not my suitcase,' Joost said.

'Really? Really?' Inspector Leroux looked firstly at the policeman against the filing cabinet and then the one against the door, his look showing quite clearly that he was expected to believe dinosaurs still roamed the earth. He turned back to Joost. 'Then why did you claim it and why were you prepared to leave the building with it?'

'I thought it was mine but, as you can see, the label has been ripped off.'

'Yes.' Leroux fiddled with the remains between forefinger and thumb. 'It's not by any chance in one of your pockets.'

"Fraid not. You can search me if you like. You can search me for the key as well if you like.'

'I think we will take your word for it, though I might add, at this very moment a search is under way elsewhere, how do you say it? With a fine toothcomb, for the missing label. So we will know sooner or later whose suitcase this is. In the meantime...' He took from his pocket what looked like a Swiss army knife, the kind with various blades, one of which Boy Scouts are told is for taking stones out of horses' hooves, something they would hardly be likely to be tested on but one never knows. The blade he opened however, whatever its purpose normally, was inserted in the suitcase's first lock that flicked open with a little metallic click, then the second and 'Voila!' Leroux said, smiling at Joost like a magician who has just performed a successful trick. 'Now let's see what we will find.'

Joost suddenly felt an urgent desire to urinate. There was no way they weren't going to rip this case wide open and for certain they would discover the diamonds. The game was up for sure. He decided there was no point in asking if he could use the toilet. It would only delay the inevitable. He would try to control his bladder. He decided it was all psychological anyway and returned to inspecting his shoes. Leroux had started to whistle softly to himself, an almost tuneless whistle, hardly the standard of a siffleur but a whistle nevertheless. He was thoroughly enjoying himself.

First out of the case was an evening suit. He turned the jacket inside out and inspected the label, *Moss Brothers of Covent Garden*. 'Hmn…' he went and held it out to the second man. 'Go through that,' he ordered. The policeman took the suit and started to go through the pockets. Finding them empty he ran his hands down the sleeves, over the lining before putting the jacket and trousers on the desk and shaking his head.

The second man had been handed a pair of patent leather black shoes, shiny as glass, but these were also returned to the desk with a shake of the head. In the meantime Leroux had gone through the rest of the contents, which consisted of nothing but various garments, mostly it seemed originating from *Marks and Spencers*, but now came the crunch; was there a false compartment anywhere? Joost looked up from his own shoes and watched like a hypnotised hen as Leroux's experienced hands moved over the inside of the lid, over the sides, the back, and finally the bottom of the case. There was nothing. The least he had expected to find was a cache of drugs but there was nothing.

Joost, totally bemused, now really did need to pee and asked permission to do so. "Where are the diamonds? Where are the diamonds?" He kept asking himself as he was escorted from the room while Leroux pondered on why his suspect would be travelling on an obviously false passport and trying to leave the airport carrying a case that held absolutely nothing incriminating. It was then that the rest of the torn off label was brought to him on which was written *Detective Inspector Reginald Venables. CID. Hotel Metropole, Beaulieu sur Mer.*

Inspector Leroux fitted the two pieces together and reached for the telephone.

******

Hotrodding it back to Marseilles the jubilant gang of three felt like singing out loud and Nino, being a Neapolitan did so, as Marcel drove with cavalier abandon and the other two cradled between them what they firmly believed was a suitcase full of diamonds.

'What a stupid rosbif to have let the case out of his hands for even a second,' Marcel chortled with delight, 'and Nino, you certainly did a good job distracting the wife. She really fell for your charms.' Nino, who had stopped singing to listen to this, grunted with satisfaction at the praise and fondled his charms just to make sure they would be there if and when needed.

******

To say that Reg Venables was out of sorts would be to put it mildly. He was furious with himself.

'To think I would fall for one of the oldest con tricks in the business,' he growled, 'with all my years of experience as a copper. I'm going to look a right burke aren't I? Gordon Bennett! I hope no one at home ever gets to hear how it happened.'

'I told you you should have put more labels on that case,' Rita said.

'Damn it all, woman!' Reg was almost at exploding point. 'The case hasn't been lost, it was stolen! Stolen from right under our very noses!'

Rita wasn't really taking much notice. It wasn't because she was feeling car sick or unsympathetic but because she was dreaming of the Adonis who had winked so suggestively and blown her a kiss, who turned as he went and smiled so engagingly, who ... She brought herself up short, didn't think she ought to be imagining things like this, not sitting in the taxi next to her Reg and with what he was going through and all. Did he say something?

'Did you say something, dear?' she asked.

'What's the matter with you, woman?' he retorted. 'You gone mutt and Jeff or something? I was saying ...'

But before he could repeat what he had been saying, they both suddenly lurched forward in their seats as the taxi driver hit the horn and simultaneously the brakes, with a squeal of tyres narrowly avoiding a head-on collision with a car coming the other way and passing on a blind bend.

'My God!' Venables yelled. 'These Frenchies drive worse than ours do and that's saying something. They're all the same these Continentals!' The near miss had put him in an even filthier mood if that were possible. 'This whole thing is going to turn out an absolute disaster. I just know it. We should be there soon.' He looked at his watch purely as a reflex action. 'That is unless he's going all round the houses to bump up the fare. Wouldn't put it passed him.' He pulled at the watch's bracelet, letting it snap back against his wrist. 'I'm only surprised this wasn't half-inched,' he said, referring to the watch itself. 'Can't trust bloody foreigners, not as far as you can throw them.'

Rita, who had taken in this last bit, forbore to inform him that at the moment he was the foreigner.

'I've still got my speech thank goodness,' he indicated his cabin bag nestling between his legs, 'but how can I go to the dinner when I don't have a dinner jacket? It's a black tie affair naturally.'

'What's that, dear?' She had been lost in thought again.

'What on earth's the matter with you, woman? You haven't heard a word I've said.'

'Yes I have, dear,' which wasn't a complete lie because she had heard some words, but she was still holding in her mind's eye the picture of Nino running his tongue over his upper lip. What if he were to do that to a breast? As Rita was not wearing a bra, she had always found them terribly uncomfortable and didn't feel it would be amiss in France where anything goes, or so she believed, the very thought of Nino's tongue and what it could do had her nipples practically piercing her blouse and unable to suppress her emotions any longer she couldn't help but utter a little squeal which brought her back to reality.

'You're behaving very strangely,' Reg said, eyeing her suspiciously.

'It's all the excitement,' Rita replied never having said a truer word and mentally hoping she would see Nino again. Little did she realise how soon her wish would be granted. She wondered what his name might be, something terribly romantic no doubt.

******

Thornton was somewhat mollified, having been assured the airline could not be more concerned over his predicament and his case would almost certainly turn up soon but, if not and in the meantime, there was a very chic menswear shop not too distant where he could purchase everything he needed and the airline would pick up the tab.

Having finished his shopping, something he normally loathed especially if he had to act the contortionist, trying on a pair of pants in one of those tiny cabinets that pass as a changing room where you couldn't swing a six day old kitten let alone a fully grown cat or try on a pair of trousers without the possibility of slipping a vertebra, he was now seated in the taxi next to Holly wondering somewhat guiltily if he had overdone it. After all, articles in *tres chic* menswear shops in a tourist town in the south of France weren't exactly inexpensive and he had run up quite a hefty bill, certainly one he would have thought twice about at home, even using his Barclaycard and living on Micawberish expectations.

'Did you get everything you need?' Holly enquired, sweet-talking.

'Hmn, think so … shirts, pullovers, jacket, slacks, shoes, socks, handkerchiefs. Didn't bother with ties. My God, Holly! Did you see the prices they're asking for a tatty piece of silk?' Even on a freebee he had baulked at that.

Holly smiled to herself. When Thornton mounted one of his hobbyhorses there was no point in even talking to him.

'Restaurants that demand ties,' he continued, 'can usually supply one anyway if the lost case doesn't turn up though, I'm going to need another one to hold all this stuff.'

******

At the reception desk in the Hotel Metropole there was considerable consternation. The head receptionist and his assistants together with the head porter and his underlings, stood around a suitcase eyeing it as though it were some strange and incomprehensible phenomenon. It was abundantly labelled with the name of the hotel but what was causing the head receptionist and consequently everyone else to be truly foxed was that nobody by the name of Jakob Mynhardt was booked in as a guest.

'I wonder what is the best thing we can do,' the head receptionist said. They all lifted their gaze from the suitcase to look at him but no one came up with any suggestion. 'Well,' he continued, 'I don't think we can just send it back to the airport. It is after all clearly marked,

"Hotel Metropole" so someone is expecting to collect it here. I'm sure that someone has been, how shall I put it, a little bit absent-minded? And will come looking for his case sooner or later saying he addressed it to the wrong hotel or he meant to register, something like that though I must say it won't do him any good as we are full up anyway. Still, in the meantime I guess it is our responsibility, so ...' with an imperious wave of his hand he dismissed them all and went back to his register... 'put it in a store room,' he ordered.

And that is where the beige case with the wide red and brown stripes around the middle went and was instantly forgotten.

*****

Reg and Rita Venables were standing at the side of the road and Reg was now beside himself with impotent rage. All he wanted to do was get to their hotel. He crossed one leg over the other above the knee so that his foot was within reach and knocked the tobacco from his pipe against the heel of his shoe with such force he broke the stem; and it was his favourite pipe. He picked up the bowl from where it had fallen and for a long moment he stared at the pieces in his hands before hurling them from him narrowly missing Rita who took swift evasive action. Seeing the state he was in she was practically on the verge of tears.

'Don't be like that, Reg,' she said.

'Be like what?' he yelled. 'Be like what? That's a stupid remark to make, woman. Nothing is going right, is it? The whole thing is a disaster, a bloody flaming catastrophe!'

The driver who was on his knees replacing the wheel with the punctured tyre looked up at this crazy Englishman, shook his head and returned to tightening the bolt he was working on only to have his box spanner, not securely fixed, slip, and his knuckles meet hard metal as he lost balance and tipped forward. 'Merde alors!' he yelled, so loudly that Rita emitted her second shriek of the day. The driver waggled his hand in the air before blowing on his grazed skin. Reg looked down at him as if he were the mad one that, at the moment of course, he was.

'Serve the bugger right,' Reg said.

'Shhhh ... Reg ... he might speak English.'

'I don't flaming care if he speaks Esperanto.'

'You're not speaking Esperanto. You don't know any Esper ...'

'For heaven's sake, Rita! Will you belt up and stop spouting rubbish?'

'Sorry, Reg.' Rita pursed her lips. She was not going to give way, not on her first day in France.

'If the man maintained his cab the way it should have been this wouldn't have happened in the first place. First of all we have to go to the police station to report a stolen suitcase and that takes hours and hours.'

'Not hours, Reg.' Her pleading was really quite pathetic.

'And now here we are standing on the side of the flaming road breathing in fumes from flaming French road racers, and that's just the flaming lorries, and I have broken my best pipe.' He was on the verge of tears but her next remark put a stop to that.

'The view is lovely,' Rita said.

'Never mind the flaming view!' he yelled. 'Just look at those bloody tyres. Look at them! Down to the flaming thread they are. It's a bloody wonder we're still alive.'

CHAPTER 5

They hadn't been in the hotel more than ten minutes before Thornton's euphoric mood evaporated like steam from a rapidly cooling tub, or water gurgling away down the plughole. Facing them across his counter was the head receptionist whose name was Boyer and who had never forgiven his fond parents for having him baptised Charles. Like Cyrano with his nose, a less likely candidate for swanning it as a matinee idol would be hard to find and he had lived with the embarrassment of jesting wits all his life. At the moment however he was giving every appearance of being extremely embarrassed for quite another reason than his visage, and Holly was virtually biting her lower lip and not knowing quite where to look.

'I am very sorry, sir,' Charles looked up from the information to hand, 'but we have absolutely no record of any booking for a Mr Thornton King. Miss Day yes indeed, that we have. Mr King? No.' The announcement was followed by a "what can I do about it" Gallic shrug and a little moue accompanied by a raised eyebrow.

'Could you check again please?' Holly asked. Charles shook his head. He had checked with everybody and with everything there was to check. 'You must have one teensy-weensy spare room surely,' Holly pleaded, putting on the little girl act she hated but which sometimes did the trick. She was feeling so guilty it was giving her butterflies in the tummy which is all very well for a naughty little girl in the nursery faced with an irate nanny, or a thespian in the wings with first night nerves, but hardly credible in a sophisticated grown woman in a four star hotel on the French Riviera, but the reason for it was obvious, this was where the buck stopped. Of course it was one of daddy's secretaries who had made the original booking but Holly, busy busy busy, had neglected to make any further arrangements when Thornton was included.

'Not even a spare bed,' was the reply, 'unless Mr King would care to sleep on a lounger on the terrace. Look around you,' he added with a wave of his hand.

They had no need for that. The place was a veritable ants nest of activity.

'There are three conventions,' Charles continued by way of explanation, 'apart from any other visitors booked in and we are crammed to the rafters. And I am afraid all the hotels will be the same. I am sorry. There has obviously been a lack of communication somewhere down the line.'

Thornton was beginning to dislike this man. Was it possible he was actually enjoying the situation or was it his own fraught imagination? Besides which the Frenchman spoke English far too well. How was it Continentals seemed to speak English with such ease and the English usually couldn't manage more than a dozen words, if that, (as Reg Venables had already discovered), in a foreign tongue, or master an accent? Have you ever heard His Royal Highness speaking French?

'So what do you suggest we do about it?' Thornton asked.

The Gallic shrug came into operation once more before Charles turned away to greet new arrivals.

'Well well well, would you Adam and Eve it? Will you look who's here, Rita? Small world isn't it?'

Reg was still full of the clichés, probably even more than usual, the false bonhomie disguising the embarrassment he still felt at the thought that someone might find out how he lost his suitcase, and his illogical anger at all taxi drivers both French and British.

'Everything hunky-dory with you two? I must say you look a bit down in the dumps, Thornton. Something wrong is there?'

But before Thornton had time to answer there was a clearing of the throat, a discreet but quite audible cough from the man behind the counter and Reg turned scowling towards him.

'Venables,' he barked.

'Ah, yes, Mr Venables ... '

'No, no, not mister, it's Inspector, Detective Inspector Venables.'

'Oui, Inspecteur Venables.' He pronounced it "Ven*ah*bles". There is a message for you from Inspector Leroux in Nice. Your suitcase has been recovered.'

'WHAT?' Reg's reaction wasn't in the least bit discreet. It practically brought the place to a standstill. He looked around him, smiling apologetically and then re-addressed himself to Charles.

'They've found it already?' His voice was now hardly more than an incredulous whisper. He was almost awestruck at the super efficiency of the French police.

'Lost your suitcase, did you, inspector? Snap.'

'What?' He turned back to scowl at Thornton.

'I said, "snap". Mine hasn't even put in an appearance.'

'Really. That's too bad. I'm certainly glad mine's been recovered I can tell you. I have to give this speech tomorrow night you know and … '

There was another discreet cough from behind the counter. Charles and his assistants were very busy people. Reg turned back.

'Ah, yes. Have to register, right? Want my passport, right? Here you go.' He extracted it from his breast pocket and slid it over the counter. 'Wife's included,' he said. 'So are the flaming kids though they're not with us of course. High time they got passports of their own. They're old enough. Go off to India like the Beatles and hopefully stay there a while. Maybe do the Indian rope trick and disappear up their own…'

'Reg!' She turned to Holly and Thornton. 'He doesn't really mean it you know.'

'Of course I flaming well mean it.'

Again there was that discreet cough.

'What?'

Charles had looked up from writing and gave what passed for a smile, which translated, meant could he please finish with the Venables and get on with other things he had to do.

'What do I do about the suitcase then?' Reg asked.

Charles considered for a moment rattling the end of his pen between his upper and lower teeth, something he did in times of stress, but thought better of it in front of guests so twiddled it between his fingers instead. 'You go to the police station and pick it up,' he said, and then resumed his task of registering the Venables' as guests of The Metropole.

It was now Holly's turn to signal with a cough that she was still around and had unfinished business, causing Charles to look up again.

Reg though was not going to be diverted. If there was one aspect of his character everyone noted it was his single-mindedness even when he was dead wrong. 'Listen, mate,' he said, tapping the counter with a middle finger, not a gesture inclined to make friends and influence Charles Boyer, 'why can't they bring the suitcase here? Why do I have to go traipsing all the way back into Nice to collect it? I've spent enough time in that bloody station. A regular busman's holiday this is turning out to be an' all.'

Charles did not know what a busman's holiday was but presumed it was some quirky English ritual. 'It isn't so very far, Inspecteur Venahbles,' he said, turning away to collect a key from its cubbyhole and turning back to wordlessly hold it out to a passing bellboy, at the same time indicating Holly's case which the curly headed lad, by name Lucien, picked up, took the key and indicated to Holly by a teasing smile and a toss of the head that she was to move. But, before she could, Charles said with another half-hearted attempt at a smile of his own, 'The porter will show you to your room, Miss Day. I hope you will be most comfortable.' He was finding life difficult in the face of Reg Venables and feeling as harassed as that belligerent Englishman though to all appearances he was as cool as the proverbial cucumber.

Thornton had a suspicion that this might be the turn of the screw and bridled somewhat. He turned to Reg. 'I tell you what, Reg … may I call you Reg? Why don't you and I share a cab back to Nice? You to pick up your suitcase, me to look for a place to doss down.'

'You're not staying here?' Reg enquired, somewhat surprised, but no more surprised than Thornton had been.

"Fraid not. Seems to have been something of a cock-up. Someone neglected to book me in.' He was feeling dispirited, despicable, and mean and said it loud and clear but Holly, with her curly headed escort trailing behind her, his adolescent eyes fixed on her derriere, was halfway to the elevator and it would seem she didn't hear.

'Come on,' Thornton urged, 'Let's move.'

'Hang on a tick. Where's our Rita got to then?' Reg looked around but of Rita there was no sign. She had obviously had quite enough of her husband for the moment. 'Drat that woman. What's she want to go wandering off now for? One of these days she's going to do it once too often. Well best I go look for her I suppose before she gets herself into trouble.'

'I'll come with you,' Thornton volunteered. 'Suppose I might as well have a look around while I'm here. Have a gander at the luxury I was supposed to have enjoyed for the next few days.' He was beginning to sound really pathetic. They started to make their way through the throng when a voice called them back.

'Inspector Venables, if you please!'

They turned back to see Charles lean over his counter and with a sweeping wave of his arm indicate on the carpet Rita's suitcase and the evidence of Thornton's shopping.

'Keep an eye on it for us will you, mate? Have to go find the missus. Never know what she might be up to.' The pair turned away again and Charles, finally feeling the need for some kind of reaction to ease the tension, slapped his forehead with the flat of his hand and mumbled something quite filthy under his breath and obviously not very flattering to the English. He called over a second bellboy, a Sicilian by the name of Luigi, and ordered him to remove the offending baggage to somewhere where it wouldn't be in the way while he attended to his next guest.

Reg and Thornton weaved their way through the throng to eventually find themselves out on the terrace where they caught sight of and advanced on Rita chatting amicably to a young man whose back had a familiar look about it. Rita, seeing them coming, waggled her fingers in what was meant to be a cheery greeting and the young man turned to face them.

'Well bless my soul, will you look who's here?' Reg exclaimed.

'Bonjour, Inspector,' Duncan greeted Reg with a welcoming smile, 'Comment allez-vous?'

'And the same to you, mate,' Reg responded, 'with knobs on, ha ha ha! And what might have brought you to this neck of the woods?'

'Five hundred or so policemen, Inspector. I'm a journalist, Inspector, am I not? I write articles for my magazine, hopefully with some bite and innuendo, and that's not an Italian suppository as Max Miller would have said, ha ha ha.' But Reg and Rita didn't get the joke and it took a while for the penny to drop for Thornton by which time the joke had grown stale. 'There must be a thousand stories to report here at the moment,' Taps continued, 'like, to start off with, how did your suitcase get stolen?'

Reg's jaw practically hit the paving as he stared pop-eyed in disbelief at the young Duncan Devonport-Fawcett who smiled in return as if butter wouldn't melt in his mouth. Reg finally recovered his voice.

'How ... how ... how ... how did you fi ... fi ... fi ...know that?' Reg stuttered in alarm.

'Grapevine, jungle drums, Morse code, man with message in cleft stick, BBC news, official leak, Reuters, what does it matter how I know? What matters is the story, so tell.'

'Stolen?' Thornton queried, looking at Reg. 'Stolen! I thought you said you'd lost it.'

'Well I did lose it in a way, didn't I? If something is stolen you've lost it, haven't you?'

'And who might this be?' Taps asked, turning his attention with sudden interest to Thornton.

'Thornton King,' Thornton said before Reg could answer. He held out his hand, which Taps took and shook quite firmly much to Thornton's surprise. He really had expected it to be a bit like holding a wet fish.

'Ah yes,' Taps said, 'I've heard of you of course. You're the one who ...'

'And you are?' Thornton enquired in turn.

'Duncan Devonport-Fawcett,' was the reply, 'but just call me Taps, everyone does. Here ...' he held out a card ... 'the publication that employs me. I'm here to report on all the shindig and ballyhoo that's going on this week.'

'Nice work if you can get it,' Thornton said.

'Too right,' Taps agreed. Pity old Somerset Maugham kicked the bucket a few years back. Could have gone over to his villa ...' he pointed ... 'on Cap Ferrat over there and done an exclusive interview. Would have got ten brownie points for that.'

'Many a true word said in jest,' Reg snorted. 'You would have been done, mate, well and truly. You know what that old scribbler was don't you?' Reg had little time for poncey writers, either of novels or of journalists such as Taps and saw an opportunity of getting away from the subject of his stolen suitcase and onto one of his definite favourites – perversion! He also sounded as though he half wished Maugham were still alive to roger Taps till he squealed, whether from passion or pain Reg didn't care to think about. He had gone right off the Honourable Duncan Devonport-Fawcett for the moment and was about to continue with his righteous ranting when Rita, aware of what was coming, brought him up short.

'Oh, don't start on that, Reg, please! Not now! Just tell Duncan how ...'

'Taps.'

'Taps, how your case got stolen.'

'If you don't mind, that's police business. I have no wish to talk about it, not at the moment. As a matter of fact, so I have been informed, the police here have already recovered it ... '

'WHAT!' this was from both Rita and Taps.

'...and Thornton and myself are just on our way into Nice to collect same,' he continued. 'Well we were on our way before we had to come out here looking for you.' He glared accusingly at Rita. 'So, if you don't mind, you'll excuse us, Duncan, won't you?' Reg couldn't bring himself to say Taps. 'We'd best be on our way. Come along, Rita.' With which he turned and marched back into the hotel, Thornton and Rita following. Thornton, as a sort of afterthought, turned back and said to Taps, 'Nice to have met you.'

'And you,' Taps replied. 'Maybe we can get together for a drink sometime.'

Thornton nodded, stood for a moment as though he wanted to say something else, and then turned and disappeared into the hotel.

Much to Charles's consternation he suddenly saw a heavily scowling Reg making his determined way towards him with a sort of Groucho Marx lope and wished he were anywhere but where he was. However, he put on a brave smile and waited for the storm to break, as he was sure it would. Rita, following behind, didn't look at all happy and a thoughtful Thornton was bringing up the rear. Charles thought he would lessen the tension by holding out the passport, a bit like holding out a bone to pacify a dog, but Reg had stopped and was looking down at the carpet. Rita stretched out and took the passport, whispering a thank you. Charles took his handkerchief from his pocket and ostentatiously wiped the counter where Reg's finger had earlier assaulted it. Reg looked up from the carpet.

'Where's the stuff we asked you to keep an eye on?' He turned to Rita, saw the passport in her hand and took it off her to shove back into his pocket. 'That's probably gone and got half inched an' all, has it?' He turned back to face Charles who was busy clicking his fingers at the curly headed lad, Lucien, returning from seeing Holly to her room where he had graciously accepted a quite handsome tip, but only after he had ostentatiously held out his open hand. 'Have you seen Luigi?' Charles asked.

Reg, who hadn't of course understood what was said, glared at Charles and snarled, "Ere, mate! I was talking to you? I asked you a question.'

'And I am trying to find the answer,' Charles retorted, still the essence of politeness. 'I had a boy take it away and put it somewhere safe but since then I haven't seen the boy and I don't know where he is. I knew I shouldn't have employed him. He's a Sicilian, so unreliable, but that's my problem.' Seeing Reg open his mouth, he hurriedly added,

'But there is no problem with the luggage I can assure you. When he returns ... he has, I think, sneaked off somewhere for a sly smoke and will be severely reprimanded. As soon as he comes back he will take the suitcase up to your suite.'

The sound of the word "suite" sweetened Reg a little. A suite, hey? Well well well. He and Rita had never enjoyed the luxury of an actual suite before.

'And my shopping had better go up to Miss Day's room for the moment, Thornton chipped in from behind.

'Certainly, Mr King.'

'And, by the way,' Thornton continued, 'I don't seem to recall her registering.'

'That is no problem either,' Charles said. 'Indeed she should have done it but she can do it later. In the meantime ...' He lifted another key from its cubby-hole and handed it to Lucien with instructions to see Rita to the Venables' suite.

This time Lucien led the way. Rita's broader derriere evidently not being as inviting as Holly's, but Rita in her turn couldn't take her eyes off the slight curve of the tight little boy bubble butt in front of her. It was all she could do to control her knees and their sudden tendency to wobble. Lucien was on course for his second handsome tip, and this time without even having to hold out his hand for it and Rita felt a slight twinge of shame. The child was no older than her own teenage son and she had never before felt toy boys were up her alley, no matter what her magazines might recommend to jaded or neglected appetites.

Charles coughed to attract Reg's attention and, having got it, said, 'I took the liberty, inspector of ordering you a taxi to take you into Nice. The driver is waiting for you.' He gestured towards the front doors.

Reg turned to Thornton. 'Right, mate,' he said, 'shall we mosey into Nice then? I only hope it's not the driver we had coming out. Surprised we actually made it.' He turned back to face Charles. 'Does the driver know where he's taking me?' he asked.

Charles nodded in the affirmative and the pair set off once more.

'I wonder what my horror scope says for today,' Thornton grumbled as they went.

*****

94

Holly and Rita were sharing a girl's tea party. Rita wasn't too sure she approved of the actual tea (Earl Grey). It was not the full-bodied brew she was used to at home, one that could almost melt the teaspoon in the cup, but she thought the French patisserie were ever so good, smashing in fact. The way éclairs were disappearing into what Adrian Spangle would have referred to quite naturally as her "cakehole" or something a bit ruder, depending on the company, the mood, and the occasion, had Holly just a little concerned. Keep this up, she thought, and by the end of the visit it would be death not only by chocolate but by fresh double cream.

There could have been others invited to the table but it seemed they were all fraus, madames, or senoras and signoras. The first lot looked for the most part rather dour and standoffish, stiffly Prussian. The second lot played either very much the grand dame or the opposite extreme, flighty and skittish, though they were neither one nor the other, the third were far too loud and the fourth expansively operatic, so they had decided it was best for the moment to be tête-à-tête Anglais, a conservative all England affair.

Having opened the meeting with the usual preliminaries, such as who should be mother and what about this wonderful Mediterranean weather, they were ready to move on to any other business, like ...

'I wonder how Thornton is getting on,' Holly said. 'He wasn't exactly in the best of moods when he left. Not that I can blame him.' She felt an urgent need to unburden herself of some of her guilt but, on second thoughts, she didn't feel Rita was quite the right person to confide in. She would only blab to her Reg who would ho ho ho all the way back to Thornton; not that Thornton hadn't probably already guessed.

'Hmn ...' was the response from her companion as another unhealthy chunk of éclair disappeared. Unaware that Taps had witnessed the suitcase incident, she too was in need of the confessional, having inadvertently let it slip during their chat that Reg's case had been stolen. Well, letting it inadvertently slip is quite the wrong way to put it. She had been only too eager to blurt it out as a fascinating talking point with this charming young man. Where, she had thought, was the harm in that? If Reg was aware of her gaffe she would be in for quite an earful when he got back from Nice.

Having disposed of her mouthful of éclair, she took a delicate sip of her tea, pinkie raised, and replaced the cup on its saucer.

'And my Reg,' she said. 'He was in a really filthy temper. And I don't blame him either. He is absolutely scared stiff the story will get back to the station and he will be a laughing stock.'

'I don't see why getting back to the station should worry him when he's here in the middle of a positive beehive of international law enforcement and by now they probably all know about it.'

'Oh, dear! I hadn't thought of that. What happens if he gets up to make his speech and they can't control themselves and all burst out laughing? He's going to look such a fool. Oh dear! It doesn't bear thinking about.' Rita sounded really distressed.

'Oh, I hardly think that's likely to happen.' Holly felt she was now in need of an éclair herself but they had all gone. She reached out for a millefeuille but Rita's chubby fingers beat her to it.

'You never can tell. That Taps person might have already spread it around,' she said as the pastry approached her mouth but was stopped in mid air. 'Oh, dear! This is very naughty of me. I really shouldn't, should I?' She gazed at the pastry in her hand and then reluctantly returned it to the cake dish. Holly looked at it, sighed, and went right off the idea.

'Have another cup of tea,' she said, lifting the pot. There was a silence as Holly poured two cups, both women being obviously deep in thought.

'Thank you,' Rita said and took another decorous sip before putting down her cup and eyeing the millefeuille lying temptingly within reach. Eventually she dragged her eyes away and looked at Holly instead. 'I wonder where Reg can be,' she said, 'he's been away an awfully long time. Are you and ...' Not wanting to actually mention a name, she gently waggled the fingers of one hand to indicate Thornton. 'Are you ... you know?'

'No,' Holly replied. 'To put it in the vernacular, we're just good friends. At least we were good friends before today; hopefully we still are.'

'What's the vernacular?' Rita asked, reaching for the pastry.

******

One subject of their conversation was seated in the gloom of the *Café Apache*, at that time of the afternoon rather deserted, morosely nursing his grudge and a Jack Daniels on the rocks. Before leaving England he had persuaded Harold Norris to cash not too large a cheque so that he wasn't entirely reliant on Holly's generosity. He felt he had got the balance right but was nevertheless still surprised Harold actually agreed. The English currency was exchanged for French at Thomas Cooks and now here he was spending some of it.

Surveying the interior designed dinge; the black and white photographs of long dead French cabaret artistes and film stars, theatre posters, old blown up photos of Marseilles and ships with masts, badly painted murals involving out of proportion matelots, he took a sip of his whisky and stirred the ice with his index finger. He had finally found a room in a pensione whose homely comfort and the motherly welcome of Madame Violette he refused to acknowledge. A pensione, no matter how comfortable was not the same as a four star hotel and that's all there was to it. He didn't have his own bathroom for a start and if there was one thing he really hated it was having to share a bathroom. Share a bath with a friend, yes. Share a bathroom with total strangers? Definitely not. There could always be exceptions of course.

He supposed he ought to call Holly some time and tell her how he was fixed but it could wait a while longer. Hopefully, in the luxury of her four star room, she was feeling really bad. At the moment ingratitude was his middle name.

******

The second subject of their conversation was still at the police station and, if it were possible, bearing an even bigger grudge than was Thornton. After his stressful day he should have been relaxing back at the Metropole hours ago instead of which here he was.

It had all started off quite amicably, if you can call a kiss on both cheeks from a moustachioed French police officer amicable. It struck Reg as something men should in no circumstances indulge in. Who knows to where it could lead? Although he had noticed footballers seem to be doing it more and more often these days whenever one of them scored a goal, unfortunately and of necessity considering they were still on the pitch, in full view of the public, a terrible example to impressionable youngsters. It never happened in his younger days, footballers were more … well … manly and, if anyone had tried it on, they would probably have ended up with a mouthful of fives. What Matt Busby would have made of the trend he dreaded to think.

On introducing himself he had held out his hand to deliver a firm, Protestant English handshake and was completely taken aback by the French inspector's sudden and totally unexpected onslaught, so no one could possibly accuse him of inviting it, especially as the smell of garlic from the inspector's previous night's dinner (snails no doubt, or frog's legs, how disgusting) was still more than faintly in evidence.

Salutations being over, the suitcase was produced and identified together with its contents. As nothing incriminating had been found, and as it didn't seem to be important and would not be wanted as evidence, it was agreed Reg could take it away with him, especially when he explained in all modesty that he would need his evening suit in order to give his speech the following evening. Inspector Leroux was suitably impressed, as Reg had intended. It was then that he made his mistake, the reason for his being hours later still at the station.

'I really must congratulate you, inspector,' he enthused. 'You fellows are really on the ball. How did you manage to recover it so fast? I presume you have the villains banged up?'

'Banged up?' Inspector Leroux had visions of a stick of dynamite being thrust into an orifice and exploding. He had heard lurid stories of what went on in English police stations.

'Locked away.'

'Oh! Oh, yes. We have the villain banged up.'

'Pardon me? Maybe I didn't hear you right but did you say *the* villain?'

'Mais oui, there is only one villain. How many villains did you think?'

'Well two at least, more likely three.'

'Excuse me, Inspecteur Venahbles, but are we talking the same language here? You wanted to know how we managed to recover your suitcase so quickly? We caught the guy before he could leave the airport.'

'I don't understand.' Reg was quite naturally totally confused. 'What guy leaving the airport?'

'The guy with your suitcase naturellement!' Was this English inspector a little on the dumb side? Did he not understand his own language? 'The guy we have banged up in one of our cells.' Inspector Leroux it would seem, as well as practicing his new example of English slang, was growing a little impatient. If there was one thing he hated it was straightforward open and shut cases that, having been shut, later reopened to become tiresomely complicated. Like a surgeon sewing up his patient before ascertaining all the instruments were accounted for and then having to open him up again to probe around for one gone missing. It was even worse if, having gone to all that trouble, they had miscounted in the first place.

'But I left the airport with my suitcase, inspector. It was stolen outside, on the street, while I was looking through my guidebook. I left the airport with my wife and two suitcases, mine and hers. Mine is the one you see there, hers is a blue one, now presumably in our suite at the hotel Metropole in Beaulieu.'

Reg had risen from the chair he had previously occupied and Inspector Leroux surveyed him for some time before flapping his hand and saying, 'Sit down, Inspecteur Venahbles. Please, sit down and tell me how you think your suitcase was stolen.'

'It's not how I think it was stolen,' Reg contradicted his French counterpart a little tartly, as he sat down again. 'It's how I know it was stolen. As I said, I was looking through my guidebook when this chappie came up to me and asked if I had a light for his cigarette, which of course I had, and it was while I was lighting his cigarette that an accomplice must have nicked the case.'

'Nicked?'

'Stolen.'

'Ah.' As Reg continued, Leroux mentally said nicked a dozen times so he would remember it.

'Now there must also have been a third person because my wife, Rita, was standing close by and this third guy obviously distracted her in some fashion so she didn't see what was going on. Maybe he bent down to tie a shoelace or something. Reg Venables was such an innocent. 'If you don't believe that is what happened, question Rita. She will bear witness to it. Now you tell me all about your man leaving the airport with my suitcase.' Reg sat back and waited. Leroux, who had lit his own cigarette while listening to this, now offered one to Reg but it was politely declined with. 'If you don't mind, I'll have one of my own. A bit too strong for me yours are.' He took out his pack of Capstan Full Strength and lit up.

'Right,' Leroux started off, blowing out a cloud of smoke, 'we received an urgent telephone call from London where evidently a dead man was discovered in a gents toilet at Heathrow airport.'

He had only got as far as "gents toilet" when a startled Reg inhaled too much too quickly and started to give a good impression of a case of whooping cough.

Leroux regarded him for a while and then turned to agent Mathieu still leaning on the filing cabinet. 'Fetch a glass of water for the inspector,' he said. Mathieu disengaged himself from his metal support and left the room. By the time he returned with the requested glass the coughing fit was over; all that remained was a pair of streaming eyes dabbed at with a hankie, clean fortunately. Now Reg went cold, knowing full well what was coming next and his mind was racing. What if somebody had seen him leave the toilet and associated him with the man's demise? What if the same somebody could give his description to the police? No, he really had nothing to worry about. After all, the door to the closet could have been closed while he was having his slash and he wouldn't have known there was a dead man sitting in there. Inspector Leroux's voice brought him back to earth as he stubbed out his cigarette with a shaky hand.

'The man had no identification on him but fortunately one of the airline staff was able to identify him as a traveller purchasing a first class ticket on the very same flight you came in on. This was the man.' And Leroux held out Jakob's passport, open so Reg could see the photograph. 'I don't suppose you recall ever noticing this guy at the airport?' Reg shook his head. 'No, a long shot, it doesn't matter. We know who he was and we were on the qui vive for the passenger travelling on the dead man's ticket and carrying his passport. This man's name is Joost Broecx, a Belgian national currently banged up, as you put it, and about to be shipped back to London.' He made it sound rather like an import/export job. 'For questioning,' he added. 'Now presumably this man Broecx had the description of Jakob Mynhardt's suitcase and was supposed to pick it up here but he picked up the wrong one, yours, which is obviously the same or similar. The question then is, where is the one he *should* have picked up, the one that obviously has something very interesting, very valuable, inside it?'

'And obviously the three men who stole from me what I thought was my case, but which obviously I took by mistake just as this Belgian fellow took mine, presumably they now have it.'

There was a long silence. Leroux finished and stubbed out his cigarette, used the stub to toy momentarily with the stubs already filling the ashtray before picking it up and tipping the overflowing contents into the waste paper bin.

'Then Inspector Venables, I must ask a big favour of you, as one colleague to another. I would like you to go through our mug shots to see if you can identify the man whose cigarette you lit and, if he is not there, we can do an identikit or an artist's impression.'

And that was why Inspector Venables was still at the police station when he should have been taking it easy in a luxury suite in a four star hotel.

*****

Marcel and his two cronies sat in Marcel's flat and pondered their next move. Apart from sending out for more cigarettes, another bottle of whisky and a couple of baguettes, they'd been at it all day and got nowhere. Who was this Thornton King? Why was he carrying the suitcase? Who was the woman he was with? Was that his wife? He was supposed to be travelling alone. Why did he leave the airport without handing over the case? Where was he now and where were the diamonds? So many questions but no answers. Marcel had telephoned the Metropole only to be informed no one by the name of Thornton King was registered there. A refill of the glasses and some good North African kif only made them more befuddled. Somebody had made a huge cock-up somewhere and the Beloved Leader was not going to be at all pleased. It was up to them to do something about it and the first thing to do, it was decided, was find this Thornton King and, if his suitcase was clearly labelled Hotel Metropole, why wasn't he registered there?

Their quarry had moved on from the *Café Apache* and was now at the *Chat Noir* where he had been joined by an enormous, bearded, kilted Scot by the name of Hamish McKinnon who was somewhat at a loose end and, although they were not consuming whisky at the same rate as Marcel and friends, they were drinking enough to make Thornton slightly maudlin. Hamish, having been an imbiber of scotch from early days, had a stronger head for it.

'So where might you be staying now?' He asked.

'The Bates Motel,' Thornton answered.

'Awa wi ye! It canny be that bad.'

'This whole bloody trip has been a total disaster,' Thornton moaned.

'You've only been here since this morning.'

'And that's quite long enough. It's going to get worse. I can feel it in my water.'

'Have another wee dram. It'll make you feel better.'

'No, I think I've had enough. I suppose I really ought to give Holly a call, tell her where I am.'

'Mebbe ye better.'

******

'So tell me ...' Holly said, (they were still lingering over their tea. It would seem neither had the desire to go anywhere.) '...how did Reg's suitcase get stolen?'

'Well I'm not too sure really,' Rita replied cagily. 'I wasn't watching.'

'What weren't you watching?'

'What was going on I suppose you could say.'

'You mean something distracted you?'

'You could put it that way I suppose.'

'Something terribly interesting?'

'I suppose. I mean, Reg was just standing there, wasn't he?' She had now picked up her husband's speech patterns by the sound of it. 'He was looking at his guidebook and this French chappie just came up to him and asked him for a light.'

'Was there anybody else around? I don't mean just coming and going, passing by, I mean sort of, you know, sort of lurking, acting suspicious.'

'Could licking lips and blowing kisses be considered suspicious? That's what distracted me.'

'What?'

'This man. Oh, Holly! He...' She so very much wanted to share the experience of her encounter with the young Adonis but wasn't too sure she should, so pursed her lips in case an indiscretion should escape. But he was so handsome and he had winked at her, and smiled that gorgeous sexy come-hither smile, and she still could see his face and his shoulders and his chest and his long legs and his ...

'Was he terribly good-looking?' Holly asked, interrupting her before she could get there, at the same time looking into her empty teacup and wondering if they should order another pot.

Rita blushed like a lovesick schoolgirl. Holly raised an eyebrow.

'So he was there to distract you,' she said.

'Oh, no!' Rita exclaimed not wanting to believe it, 'I don't think so, not deliberately.' She thought about it for all of two seconds. 'No, I don't think that at all,' she added with emphasis and then, as though to change the subject, 'I wonder what could have happened to Reg. He's been ever such a long time.'

******

Reg had finally gone through the photo albums and come up with a blank and the artists couldn't do a likeness of the villain because Reg hadn't a clue as to what Marcel had looked like, not even as to whether or not he had facial hair. Was the moustache he remembered on the villain's face or on the taxi driver's, or both? All he could remember was that the cigarette he lit while his case was being stolen was, because of the smell, a Gauloise or a Gitanes, French anyway, and a fat lot of use that was considering the number of Frenchmen who smoke Gauloise and Gitanes.

'What about his hands?' Leroux prompted. 'Maybe he, how do you say it, covered?' He made a bowl of his own two hands.

'Cupped?'

'That's the word, cupped.' He scribbled the word cupped on his blotter. 'Maybe he cupped his hands around the cigarette, around your hands as you held the light. Maybe there was something unusual about his hands, like maybe there was a scar, was he wearing a ring or was he missing a finger, something like that?'

'I don't know. The smoke was getting in my eyes.'

Leroux took a very deep breath and looked at agent Mathieu again standing by the filing cabinet almost as if he were a semi-permanent fixture there. Mathieu shrugged and inspected his fingernails. This really was one helluva dumb English cop and the dumb English cop knew he was failing badly and just wished to get the hell out of there before matters got worse. It was because he was nervous of course, he told himself consolingly. He had never before been any nearer the continent than Bognor and this strange territory had unsettled him. He now knew how it felt to be interrogated.

Leroux rose from his chair, walked around the desk and stopped by Reg to pat him on the shoulder. 'Never mind, my friend,' he said patronisingly. 'You might think of something later in which case all you need do is telephone. In the meantime, take your suitcase, go to your hotel, have a good rest, and enjoy your stay. Oh, and good luck with your speech tomorrow night. Adieu.'

103

Reg got unsteadily to his feet. It had been a long day. He wondered if the two cheeks kissing ceremony was about to be repeated but obviously not as Leroux held out his hand. Reg took it and Mathieu, finally disengaging himself from the filing cabinet, escorted him from the premises.

******

It wasn't so much a case of in vino veritas as it was in whisky veritas that Thornton was, in the language of the period, letting it all hang out, and Hamish was certainly a sympathetic listener.

'So your suitcase never arrived, and your inspector ... '

'Not my insh ... insh ... '

'Inspector.'

'Him. No, never, never my insh ... insh ... '

'Venables had his case stolen but evidently the police have already recovered it, is that right?'

'I guesh so. That is ... the long and the short of it. Yes.'

'Hmn ... '

Thornton turned two bleary eyes on his companion. 'What are you ... thinking about?'

'Oh, nothing in particular. What does your suitcase look like?'

'It's brown ... no, cream ... I think. I got it at Peter Jones, thirty percent off. That was a bargain wasn't it? But my bargain has gone up in a puff of smoke. Poof! Just like that. ... Poof! ... and it has ... red and brown ... no, orange, I think ... stripes around its middle. And if I had red and brown stripes around my dimmle I'd need to see a doctor.' And he gave vent to a peal of laughter.

Why, Hamish thought to himself, do drunks always make feeble jokes they find so uproariously funny?

'So your two suitcases must look very much alike,' Hamish said.

'Oh, yes. Dead ringers they are, all three of them. Snap! I said to them. Snap!'

'Wait a minute, what do you mean by "all three"?'

'Exactly what I'm saying, all three.'

'Whose was the third one then?'

'His. Him. He ... funny little fella from somewhere. Africa, that's it. Promised us a drink and then disappeared, just like my suitcase. Poof!'

It really was time to go. For starters, Taps would be wondering what had happened to him, he was, after all, supposed to be taking pictures of something or somebody somewhere or other, and he felt a little responsible for the state Thornton was in and thought he ought to see him safely back to his pensione.

******

It seemed the girls were still finding it difficult to drag themselves away from their tea table although the cake plate had been empty and the teapot cold for a long while, and conversation seemed to have ground to a standstill. It was as if their table was a raft to which they clung in a sea of foreigners and Babel of tongues.

'I really ought to go and unpack,' Rita ventured halfheartedly after a while.

'Haven't you done it then?'

'No I haven't!' There was a hint of acerbity in her voice. 'Otherwise I wouldn't be saying I have to go and do it, now would I? Have you done yours?'

'No, actually, I haven't as yet.' In response there was the hint of an icy upper class accent in Holly's voice. Tensions seemed to be rising at the tea table. Where, oh, where could those men be?

There was no sign of them but the man who did unexpectedly turn up was Taps, bright and breezy as ever.

'Well bless my soul, will you look who's here?' It was almost a sneer from Rita in a fair imitation of her husband's manner and feeling she might be tempted to give away more secrets if she was nice to him because Taps really was quite a dishy young man. 'Turning up like a bad penny.'

'That's a fine greeting I must say.' He seated himself between them. 'Now why on earth would you say something like that? Any tea in that pot?'

'No. Are you staying in the hotel?' Holly asked.

'No, I'm staying in Nice as a matter of fact but this is where the action is, right?' He lifted the teapot lid, took a quick peek inside and replaced it.

'What action?' Holly said, looking about her. 'All I can see is a whole lot of people milling about, for the most part rather aimlessly by the looks of it.'

'Not at all,' Taps replied. 'All sorts of stories are circulating and I hope to catch a few before I leave. Where's Reg by the way? Not

105

back from the police station yet?'

'No,' Rita said, 'and I'm getting really worried.'

'Well worry no longer because, speak of the devil and who should turn up like that proverbial bad penny you mentioned a moment ago but, tara tara! Inspector Reg Venables CID.'

The girls turned from Taps to see a dispirited Reg slowly approaching their table.

'Reg, where have you been? I was getting that worried about you.'

'I don't suppose you've seen Thornton have you?' Holly sounded quite upset.

Reg lowered himself into a fourth chair and looked around the table as though he was about to burst into tears. 'By heck!' He said. 'I need a good stiff drink.'

******

Marcel put down the telephone receiver and returned on unsteady legs to the other two still seated at his kitchen table. All they had heard was his grunting and yessing and noing, pausing for a few seconds to jot something down and saying, 'Spell that,' and now they waited anxiously for what had transpired.

Marcel sat down and turned the whisky bottle upside down to pour himself another drink but the bottle was empty. He peeked down through the neck as though he thought it could be playing tricks on him and there might actually be some hooch left, but as that wasn't the case, he slammed the bottle down on the table with such a bang the other two visibly jumped.

'Well?' Nino asked.

Alphonse followed up with, 'Who was it?'

'That was this guy called Cy, phoning from London with a message for us from the leader.' Marcel couldn't bring himself to say "Beloved"; it was too stupid for words.

'What was the message?' This was Nino again.

'What he said was, "Pull your fingers out and find the diamonds or else." That was the message more or less.'

'Easier said than done,' Alphonse chipped in. 'Did he say how we were to pull our fingers out?'

'Quickly.'

'Oh, very funny. Didn't he even suggest how we go about it? No big ideas?'

'Yes. He suggested that, as Thornton King had the suitcase and, as the diamonds are no longer in the suitcase', they all turned to look at the suitcase, which lay on a day bed, its contents scattered about, 'then Thornton King must obviously have taken them and stashed them away somewhere, so ... get Thornton King.'

They sat ruminating on this for a while until Alphonse broke the silence. 'How? I mean, if we're to pull our fingers out so quickly, how?'

'Painfully,' Nino said and laughed.

'You think this is a matter for jokes?' An agitated Alphonse was trying to rise to his feet spoiling for a confrontation with Nino who held up his hands, placating, and Alphonse sat down again with a thump. 'We have to find this Thornton King and we haven't a clue where he is?'

'Even so,' Marcel said, 'we have been ordered to find him so find him we must.'

'And if we do find him and he won't talk?'

Marcel shrugged. 'He has a girl friend by the name of ... ' He took from his shirt pocket the crumpled piece of paper on which he had written with his stubby pencil, flattened the paper on the table and read, Holly Day.'

'Stupid name.' Nino said, 'and, looking at her, I'm not surprised she'd have a name like that.'

'You've seen her?' Alphonse said.

'Well of course I have, you imbecile. Wasn't I dancing around her while you snatched the suitcase?'

'That was the girl-friend?'

Nino shrugged. 'Who else could it have been? It takes all sorts. Every man to his own. For me, she's a dog but there you are. Mind you, I didn't think much to him either.'

'Anyway,' Marcel said, 'the point is, women are easier meat than men so, to find Mister King, all we have to do is let him know we have his woman and, voila! He comes running to us. Simple, my friends.'

******

They finally found the *Pensione Garibaldi*. Thornton remembered the name but he had forgotten the name of the street and no one from whom Hamish elicited directions seemed to have heard of it.

'Why would it be called after an Italian do you suppose?' Hamish enquired of his companion as they wandered along towards it. 'Are you sure that's its name?'

'Well it's not called *Dunroamin,*' Thornton replied with a giggle and then burst into song, "Roaming in the gloaming, by the bonnie banks of Clyde ... Roaming in the gloaming with my lassie by my side."'

'Fantastic,' Hamish said. 'You're nae going to be sick as well are you?'

'No,' Thornton said, 'I don't think I'm going to be sick but, as to your question about the I-talian, once upon a time this part of the world wasn't what it is now you know. Oh, no, not at all. The French kept on giving bits to the I-talians and the I-talians kept on giving bits back to the French and old Garibaldi was a terrific hero all over.'

'All over what?' It was Hamish's turn to make with the jokes.

'Lay me down, roll me over, and do it again,' Thornton sang. He stopped walking in order to think. 'Maybe it's the other way around, maybe it's, roll me over, lay me down, and do it again. Well, whichever way it is, as long as I get done what does it matter?'

CHAPTER 6

Thornton woke up to the sound of traffic and the smell of freshly percolated coffee permeating the building. Surprisingly, although he had only a hazy memory of what had gone on the evening before and his mouth, as he would have put it, tasted like the bottom of a budgie's cage, he did not have a hangover, but he was most certainly starving. As if in answer to his prayers there was a knock at the door. Thornton wasn't expecting a visitor.

'Who is it?' he called.

'C'est mois, Madame Violette.'

'Come in. I mean entrez!' He hoped he'd used the correct word. Being naked he kept the duvet up to his chin and felt almost ashamed of his clothes he could see lying scattered about.

And in she waddled, a plump but tiny, grey-haired, rosy-cheeked, smiling figure, everybody's mother except Whistler's, carrying a tray that looked much too big and much too heavy for her; laden with brioche, croissant, butter, fig and apricot conserve, and an enormous pot of coffee with cream jug and sugar bowl on the side. She had entered the room backwards having obviously pushed open the door with hip or rump and she now turned around to close it the same way.

'Bonjour, m'sieur!' She trilled. She reminded him for all the world like a Walt Disney bluebird in *Snow White*. 'You slept well I think.' It wasn't a question. It was a statement of fact. She placed the tray on the table in the centre of the room and stood beaming at him.

'Good morning, madame,' Thornton replied. 'I didn't know breakfast was included.'

'Oh, this was especially ordered for you this morning, m'sieur King, by Miss Holly Day.'

'Holly! Oh, God, Holly! I never called her. I don't think. Did I call her? No, I didn't. Then how did she know I was here?'

'That I do not know, m'sieur, but she is waiting for you downstairs.' Madame Violette didn't seem in too much of a hurry to move so Thornton coughed politely and said, 'Excuse me, madame, but I need to use the toilet.' For some reason the men working on his flat came to mind and he wondered how they might be getting on, in between tea breaks.

'Of course, m'sieur. You remember where is the bathroom, no?'

'Yes, I do, I do.' He was beginning to grow anxious and, if he didn't go now, by the time he got back, the coffee would be lukewarm and he hated lukewarm coffee.

'Then I leave you. Bon appetit, Enjoy your breakfast.' She was finally out of the room. Thornton threw back the covers, leapt out of bed and was busy looking for his underpants when the door opened and she reappeared. Apparently unphased by his nakedness she asked if she should send Holly up.

'Yes, do,' Thornton said, having found his briefs and holding them in front of him though, as she had already seen what he was trying to hide, why continue trying to hide it? Two days running he had been caught on the hop by total strangers. It was most undignified. He slipped into his pants, opened his door and looked both ways to make sure the coast was clear before he sped to the end of the corridor and the bathroom. The door was locked and there was the sound of splashing water. Rattling the door handle didn't stop it, in fact whoever was showering decided to burst into song and Thornton couldn't make out if it was a female tenor or a male contralto.

'Shit!' He said, hopping from one foot to the other, 'That's all I bloody well need. Is there another bathroom? Maybe there's another bathroom.' He looked wildly around. The situation was getting desperate but this was obviously the only bathroom there was.

'Try the next floor down.' It was Holly's cool voice that saved the day as he flew down the stairs and made the end of the corridor in the nick of time saying, 'Excuse me, m'amselle but this is an emergency,' as he brushed passed a hatchet faced young lady wrapped in a faded corduroy dressing gown and shower cap and carrying a plastic toilet bag, one who would obviously have occupied the bathroom for quite some considerable time. She was still waiting there when he came out. He gave her a weak smile, meant to be an apology, and received a stony glare and a slammed door in return. It's a wonder she didn't shatter the frosted panels. Much relieved, he moved in a more sedate fashion along the corridor until he came to the head of the stairs and, glancing down to the ground floor, he thought he saw someone recognisable just leaving. He stopped, thought about it, shook his head, shrugged, and raced up the stairs and into his room to say,

'Good morning, Holly! And how are you this bright and breezy morning? Would you care to join me for breakfast?'

'No thank you, Thornton, I had breakfast at the hotel.'

'And a jolly splendid one it was too I bet. You know, it's a funny thing, just now, I could swear I saw Taps leaving the building.'

'Delirium tremens and I am not surprised. I hear you had a skinful yesterday evening.'

'We did go over the top a little I suppose.'

'A little?'

'Anyway, who filled you in as to my comings and goings? And how did you know I was here?'

'Your new friend Hamish told me.'

'Hamish? He's been to the hotel?'

'No. He had the courtesy to telephone and apologise on your behalf.'

'I'll kill him. No I won't. He's rather large, isn't he? He'll more'n likely kill me.'

'Eat your breakfast.'

'Yes.'

He pulled out a chair and sat down at the table, indicating another chair for her as he picked up a knife to stab the butter.

'Come and sit down Holly. How's your room? Did you sleep well?'

'My room is lovely and, yes thank you, I slept very well and I woke up to look out at the shimmering silver and blue Mediterranean.'

'Isn't that nice? Weren't worried about me at all I hope.' He had sliced and buttered a croissant and was about to lather it with jam before closing it up again.

'Not in the least. I knew you'd have to work off your high dudgeon before becoming civilised and your old charming self again.' She smiled at him across the table, he now busy chewing a mouthful of croissant. 'Thornton, I really am terribly sorry about the mix up.'

'Think nothing of it,' he replied magnanimously through his mouthful, and swallowed before he went on with, 'would you like a cup of coffee? I'll have Madame Violette bring up another cup. Only I wouldn't know how to get in touch with her. You don't see a bell or anything around do you? Maybe I just holler down the stairs.' Holly shook her head to decline the offer of coffee and touched the corner of her mouth with her little finger to indicate he had a blob of apricot conserve trying to escape from his. He recaptured it with the tip of his tongue.

'Isn't this cute?' Holly said. 'We could be an old married couple.'

'Old? Speak for yourself. And I do believe I've heard you say that before. But seriously, Holly, don't apologise for the mix-up. Everything's for the best in this best of all possible worlds and I am sure that what seems like a gaffe must in reality have some reason behind it.'

'Philosophy so early? Is that what France does to you?'

'I think therefore I am ... pretty certain I saw Taps downstairs.'

'Imagination. It was probably another resident. And, if you did see him, what's the problem? He's a journalist. Journalists snoop around.'

'Yes, but why at the Pensione Garibaldi?'

Holly lifted both shoulders and pulled a *how would I know* face. 'Don't be so suspicious, Thornton,' she said, finally giving in and helping herself to a brioche. 'Now, what shall we do today?'

'You suggest.'

'I thought we might get a car and we could drive over to St Paul du Vence. There's the most fabulous restaurant there where we can have lunch. It's patronised by all the big French film stars, and not just French, British ones too, Jack Hawkins, David Niven, Moira Shearer, Anna Neagle.

'A bit passé wouldn't you say?'

'Diana Dors, Virginia McKenna. You might meet up with one of your favourites.'

'I have favourite film stars? Perish the thought. I hate to bring up the subject...'

'Then don't'

'But I never could understand why you were so keen on Cord Wainer.'

'You're not a woman.'

'How very true. But keen? You were absolutely besotted as I remember.'

'I was.'

'I seem to remember you had a paper frock with his picture on the front.'

'Dress.'

'What?'

'It wasn't a frock. It was a dress.'

Thornton was momentarily tempted to ask the difference but

decided to skip it.

'I had more than one in fact. I had a dozen. And it wasn't Cord Wainer's picture. It was Marlon Brando, if that's the one you're thinking of. And I had another with a dozen Hollywood stars on it altogether, John Wayne, Montgomery Clift, James Dean, Elizabeth Taylor, Shirley MacLean, and one with Andy Warhol's tomato cans.'

'Do you still have them?'

'They were meant to be worn for a day, Thornton, and then trashed. That was the whole point, but the fad didn't last more than a year because people suddenly began to think seriously about the environment and the damage being caused by the throwaway society so conscience was what really finished them off.'

'And electricity finished off good old Cord. Yes, an unexpected and untimely demise much deplored by his studio and the insurance company and mourned by millions of fantasising women and not a few fantasising men of which I obviously am not one. I'm reliably informed he started his career as a porn star, gay for pay I believe they call it. Poetic justice though, wouldn't you say?'

'What on earth is that supposed to mean?'

'I mean as an American and absolutely the world's worst actor that he should die in an electrified chair.'

'That is the most insensitive remark I've ever heard, Thornton King. No, it's worse, damn it! It's downright disgusting. Did you pull the wings off flies as a small boy? Don't answer that. Anyway, if you're not interested in film stars, there were artists who once frequented *La Colombe D'or*, that's the name of the restaurant, Picasso, Modigliani, to name but a few, and they left paintings there so that is interesting you have to admit.'

'Hate Picasso. Hate Modigliani.'

'You're a Philistine. Now, are we going to go to lunch or aren't we?'

'It's a great idea. How do you suggest I dress?'

Having taken another bite of her brioche and not wishing to answer with her mouth full, Holly pointed to the bagged evidence of Thornton's previous day's shopping spree where she had deposited it on the bed.'

'No sign of the original stuff turning up I suppose?' Thornton asked.

'Afraid not. So get yourself dressed and I'll meet you at Hertz. Madame Violette will point out the way. What make of car takes your fancy?'

'Something sporty, a Porsche maybe? Or maybe a Ferrari.'

'Only the best for our Thornton. I'll see what I can get.' She rose from the table and was about to go when Thornton stopped her.

'Holly … '

She turned back. Thornton smiled and delicately placed a little finger to the corner of his mouth.

******

Having received no further instructions from London, or from anywhere else for that matter, the three would be master gangsters who, it has to be said, would never rise above being a bunch of petty crooks and it was highly surprising none of them as yet had a record, or previous as Reg would have said, sat around Marcel's table desperately trying to come to some sort of a decision as to what course of action to take. Their thinking wasn't helped by the fact that, unlike Thornton, they were all suffering massive hangovers, most probably because whisky was not their normal tipple.

'Obviously,' Marcel said, though it wasn't at all obvious, 'obviously, we have to put the screws on this Thornton King.'

'Obviously,' Alphonse said. 'We've agreed on that, but first we have to find this Thornton King, n'est pas? Please contradict me if I'm wrong.'

'You're wrong,' said Nino.

'What?'

'We know where he is. He's in Beaulieu with this Holly woman, isn't he?'

'Oh, yes. I forgot.'

'No, he's not in Beaulieu. The hotel said he wasn't registered there.'

'There are other hotels in Beaulieu and where his woman is, there he is likely to be as well, or at least not so far away, right?'

'So we'd best head out for Beaulieu and find him.'

'Just like that, huh?' This was from Marcel. 'And what reason would we have for visiting a posh hotel like the Metropole if someone was to ask?'

They sat and thought about this for a while, Apart from the handsome Nino who took great pride in his appearance and whose shoplifted designer wardrobe was extensive and tasteful, the other two had to admit they were pretty scruffy sartorial specimens. Then Marcel came up with another question.

'And what do we do when we find him? We just walk up to him and say, "Good morning, Mr King, nice day." And then we push a gun in his ribs, maybe a knife, or give him the old cosh and carry him to the car, which is conveniently parked in the hotel car park in somebody else's space, and hope nobody has seen us doing it. Fat chance of that.'

'What do you suggest then, bigshot?'

Marcel cast a mean glance in Nino's direction then leaned forward, placed his elbows on the table and stroked his moustache with the index finger of his right hand.

'Well ...' he said, rolling his eyes toward the ceiling before lowering them to look at each of them in turn. 'I have been thinking about it and what I have come up with is this: if anyone was to ask what we are doing there, the answer is delivering something.'

'Like what for example?' Alphonse was obviously in sceptic mood and ready to raise objections.

'Like Mr King's suitcase naturally which we found dumped somewhere or other, I'll think of a good place where we could have found it. It's got Hotel Metropole labels all over it so that's why we've brought it. Maybe there could be a small reward for returning it, he he he!' He thought this a good joke though the others were not inclined to join in with his laughter. 'Anyway,' he continued, 'that's the plan. Any objections?'

For a while there was silence.

'There's an angel flying over the house,' Nino said.

'What?'

'That's what we say in Italy when there's a silence.'

They both sat regarding him for a while.

'I suppose he's just flown back again. Had himself a return ticket.' Alphonse laughed.

'Okay okay, let's get back to business,' Marcel ordered.

'Okay, okay! So we take back the case, so what? You haven't told us what we do next.' This was from Alphonse again. Marcel was getting just a little tired of Alphonse.

'Right, I'm coming to that. I stay in the car ...'

'What?'

'Why?'

'Isn't it obvious? I am the only one this King fellow can recognise.

It was my cigarette he lit. My face was as close to him as that.' He held a hand up to his nose. 'He didn't see either of you two. At least I don't think he saw you, not if you did the job properly. Now, while I wait in the car, you two ...'

'Ready for a quick getaway.'

'Ready for a quick ... Hey! What are you saying? You think I would run out on you if things went wrong?'

Alphonse gave a shrug and rummaged in a cigarette pack only to find it empty. Cursing under his breath he crumpled the pack and tossed it over his shoulder. Marcel glared but, as the place was a pit anyway, decided to say nothing. There was enough tension as it was. Instead he went on with his plan.

'You, Alphonse, will take the case into the hotel and spin them the line about finding it. While you are doing that Nino will look out for Miss Holly Day. I have decided, instead of tackling Mr King head on, it's better that what we do is, as we first thought, get to him through his woman.'

'How do I find her?' Nino asked.

Marcel ruminated on this for a while. He obviously hadn't given it that much thought.

'Ye-es ...' he said. Obviously Miss Day could be anywhere and anywhere meant not necessarily even in the hotel, not necessarily even in Beaulieu, not necessarily within a hundred kilometres of the place. She might have taken a trip into Monte Carlo or even crossed the border into Italy. Who knows? He heaved a deep sigh and interlaced his fingers on the tabletop and then holding the tips together almost as if he was about to pray. 'You will have to play it by ear, Nino.'

'I'd rather play it with my fingers. Ouch!' Nino cried, hastily withdrawing his hand, a fraction too late as a bottle came down on it.

'Another crack like that and you won't have any fingers to play with. This is a serious business we're on.'

'Yes, boss. Sorry, boss.'

'You're too damned cute for your own good, you Italian gigolo. You could die of it. You have to remember what's in it for us.'

'Yes, boss. Sorry, boss.'

Marcel glared at him.

'No, boss. I mean it boss.' Nino was all contrition as he rubbed his bruised knuckles.

'All right then, let's put that suitcase together again, fortunately it's not too badly damaged, and let's get going. And Nino, Mussolini might have acted the clown, doesn't mean to say you must be one.' He gave Nino a friendly slap across the cheek and smiled and Nino, his cheek stinging, knew exactly what that smile meant.

******

They had enjoyed a late late breakfast and were now out on the terrace, taking the air, enjoying the sun. That is, Rita was enjoying it. She had laid her copy of the *Daily Express* across her lap and, with eyes tight shut, had thrown her head back to catch the sun's rays full in the face, covered, as were her arms, with generous amounts of anti-sun lotion. Reg on the other hand, having forgotten to bring a hat or buy one, had knotted his handkerchief on his head to ward off those very same rays. What was good enough for Blackpool or Morecambe was good enough for Beaulieu. It was a wonder he hadn't rolled up his trouser legs and worn socks and suspenders, with his sandals; socks with clocks on, and braces to complete the ensemble or, despite the warmth, his favourite Fair Isle pullover. Reg's sartorial inclinations seem not to have advanced from his World War II demob suit. He was currently mouthing his speech to himself and growing more nervous by the minute. He had never made a speech before and was beginning to fervently wish he hadn't agreed to this one. He held his script in one shaky hand while he gestured even more shakily with the other.

There had been an almost imperceptible reaction from Charles Boyer when Rita ordered her newspaper. It wasn't the usual request. Newspapers normally asked for at the Metropole were *The Financial Times, The Times, The Telegraph,* and if millionaire Labour voters were in residence, possibly *The Guardian* to show a more liberal-minded if somewhat woolly mentality.

Reg looked up from his notes. 'I've got to go to the loo,' he said. 'Lend us your paper. I'll want something to read.'

'What about your speech?' Rita said, opening her eyes and raising her head from prone to vertical to squint at him beneath the shade of her hand.

'I've looked at that enough. I practically know it off by heart.' He got up and held out his own hand for the paper. She passed it to him.

'Nothing interesting in it,' she said.

117

Let's hope there's nothing interesting in the loo like a dead man with his trousers down, he thought as he turned and walked away.

Charles Boyer watched from the hotel entrance as the English apparition approached and shook his head sadly. What was the world coming to? It was crumbling before his very eyes. Any more guests of this calibre and it would destruct completely. Charles was, like most of the lower orders, a true blue snob. He didn't want the Empire back but he fervently wished the revolution had never happened. In his opinion the only good thing about that awful lot across the channel was they hadn't decapitated their royalty, not since his namesake the first anyway. He turned and went back inside unable to take any more.

It was a good half hour before Reg returned from the Venables suite to find no one at the table; but Rita's bag was still on her chair.

'Where the hell has she got to now?' he said out loud, looking around for some sign of her. He would have been very surprised had his question been answered.

******

Showered, shampooed, shaved, dressed, and smelling of Knize 5, his favourite, exclusive and very expensive gentleman's cologne available only in Jermyn Street, (it had been a present from Holly a couple of years before and he was making it last as long as possible, using it only for special occasions), Thornton stepped briskly out for his date with Holly and a Ferrari, or maybe a Maserati, a Lamborghini, an Alfa-Romeo even. He found her waiting for him leaning against a large black open top Mercedes.

'Where's our car then?' he asked.

She stepped away from the Mercedes and waved a hand towards it in the graceful but stiff-fingered manner of an air hostess indicating an emergency exit.

'This?'

'This.'

Thornton could hardly believe she was serious.

'Sorry, Thornton, there isn't a car to be had from any of the hire firms, not even for ready money. They're all out. It's because of these damn conventions.'

'Then where did you get this number from?'

'I called Charles at the hotel ...'

'Charles?'

'The head receptionist.'

'Oh, yes? The snooty geezer who threw me out into the cold cold snow.'

'Hardly cold, Thornton, hardly snow.'

'It's an expression.'

'Anyway, I explained our predicament and he said his brother-in-law had a car we could possibly use, and this is it.'

No more was said for a long while as Thornton surveyed what to a motor enthusiast would be a vintage model, to anyone else, an antique, and Holly watched Thornton as he went about his inspection.

'This,' he said, 'once belonged to a German general. He used to be driven in it, standing up with arm raised shouting "sieg heil seig heil seig heil!" and he abandoned it here when he fled before the advancing Allies.'

'Why would he abandon it if he were fleeing?'

'Couldn't afford the petrol anymore. It probably does about four miles to the gallon. I bet Charles's brother-in-law is charging you a small fortune for the use thereof. Have you tried to start it?'

'No, but Charles's brother-in-law drove it here so it must be all right, though I doubt it's insured.'

Thornton nodded. 'It will be like driving a tank,' he said. He was beginning to wonder about Holly. For a girl so together how could she have mismanaged this little escapade, firstly with the hotel booking, now with the car? Nice was quite the wrong place to choose with so much going on. Maybe it was daddy who made the decision. He figured that's how it must have been; but what next he wondered. 'So who's having first go, you or me?'

'You can have the honour,' she said. 'The key's already in the ignition.'

'Oh, good. It doesn't need a crank start then.'

'Have you done? If you don't want the bloody car, just say so! I've done my best and any more cracks from you and you can go boil your head! Got it?'

Thornton realised he had gone too far and Holly was now really upset. He had been at odds with the world ever since that wretched suitcase failed to materialise and it was high time he pulled himself together. He opened the passenger door.

'Would m'amselle please take her seat?'

'Humph!' Holly cast him a sideways glance and slid into the seat as Thornton closed the door before he walked around to the driver's side, still inspecting the car as he went. He got in and sat down to take a long look at the dashboard; try the brake pedal a few times, then the clutch, the gear stick, the accelerator. Holly watched it all until she had had enough.

'Why don't you make brrmm brrmm noises while you're about it?' She said.

Thornton started the car, put it into gear and lurched away from the sidewalk like a nervous novice taking his driving test for the first time, narrowly avoiding a battered old Peugeot going the opposite way, containing three men, and a woman with her head down who looked as if she had been slugged.

'White slave traders,' Thornton said as they now moved smoothly on, the old Mercedes, being a product of perfect German engineering, purring like a contented cat.

'That wasn't someone we know, was it?'

'Who?'

'That woman in the car.' Holly turned to look back but the Peugeot was long gone. 'I thought for a moment … Oh, never mind.' She turned to face front again. 'Let's go eat.'

******

Reg had made enquiries and searched everywhere in and around the hotel but there was no sign of Rita. He held her handbag in front of him as though it would somehow, like a mine detector or a gun dog, lead him to her but all it achieved was a succession of very strange looks.

Charles had suggested she might have gone for a stroll along the beach and Reg had walked for miles with no sign of her before returning to the hotel exhausted and with aching feet. He was no longer a young man and being an inspector didn't require too much in the way of strenuous exercise so he wasn't up to much cop where fitness was concerned. However he was deeply concerned about the disappearance of his wife, even though it was just like her to be so inconsiderate as to go off without a word when she knew how nervous he was, and that he had to make his speech that evening. On the other hand, why would she go off without her handbag? That was something Rita would never do. Something must have happened to her. Perhaps he ought to report her a missing person, but then she had only been gone ... how long was it? ... An hour? Two? He would just have to be patient, and calm, and not think the worst, and wait until the silly bitch reappeared, and then wouldn't she half get a mouthful. In the meantime he would go and have some lunch.

******

Hamish had spent his morning at the marina. He liked boats and there were any number of beauties to admire and photograph; from yachts that only billionaires could afford to own or charter, to the very latest in sleek speedboats, to craft more humble, but colourful and picturesque nevertheless and probably much loved.

Having taken all the pictures he felt like taking he sat a while longer soaking up the sun and then reluctantly got to his feet to go and find the Honourable Duncan. But where to find him was anyone's guess so he thought he would just follow his nose and see where it led him. It led him passed the *Chat Noir* where he stopped, thinking a wee dram before a late lunch would be most welcome. Hamish was not a wine drinker, not even with meals.

Daylight never seemed to enter places like the *Chat Noir* or the *Café Apache*, in fact it was actively discouraged and it took a moment or two for Hamish's eyes to grow accustomed to the gloom. When they did he noticed the only other occupants were two individuals at a small table who looked as though they had the weight of the world on their shoulders and who ignored his nod of greeting as he made his way to the bar, ordered his whisky and took it to a table within listening distance of the men's conversation.

Despite his Scottish accent, the much travelled Hamish was not what one might regard as a thoroughbred Scot. Although he had spent a great deal of his childhood and younger days with his paternal grandparents in Glasgow and was, like many an expatriate, inordinately proud of his Scottish heritage, he was actually born in Quebec and his mother was French so he had a bob or two when it came to the French language even if his accent was somewhat peculiar, a sort of amalgam of home and colonial.

Thanks to a nubile, peroxide blonde, baton twirling, cheer leading, cowboy boot wearing, small town dairy queen of some year or other, then resident in Boston, with whom he had a brief and fulfilling fling while she was vacationing at Niagara Falls, he moved to the states to be with her.

However, away from the romance of the falls, she lost interest in the romance with Hamish and married a small-time lawyer in her local burg who could give her security, children, and allow her to go to seed still living off the memory of past glory. So Hamish moved on to Washington where he had lived on and off for the past few years. Fortunately a Transatlantic accent never made its presence felt to create an overload.

It didn't take too long for his neighbours in the bar to realise they were being overheard and, with the mood they were in, they didn't take it kindly. After a brief glance at each other and a nod they rose to their feet and advanced on Hamish's table. He waited to make sure of their intentions before unsheathing his skin dhu and laying it on the table. They never saw where the lethal looking dagger had come from but it brought all movement to an immediate halt as they stood there not knowing quite what to do. It was Alphonse who broke the silence.

'You found our conversation interesting I hope.'

Hamish frowned, looking puzzled. 'I'm sorry,' he lied, 'but I don't speak French, laddie. Non parlais Francais.' As if to reinforce the lie he took a phrase book out of his camera bag and started to thumb through it, at the same time standing up to show he was at least six inches taller than either of them and twice as broad.

'Ah, you are Eengleesh?' Alphonse asked.

'Nae, lad, I'm a Scot.' He sat down again.

'What did he say?' Nino enquired.

'He's from Scotland,' Alphonse informed him.

'Yes?' Nino leaned forward to look over the tabletop and saw again the kilt that confirmed the truth of what the stranger had said, 'Yes. He is a Scot.' Then, with a Neapolitan English accent he added, 'Have a wee doch and doris on us,' without having the least idea of what he was talking about. It was a trifle he had learnt from relatives who kept a fish and chip shop in Edinburgh. Without turning around, he flicked finger and thumb of one hand over his shoulder, a gesture he had seen in gangster films that was meant to impress, and the barman scurried over to Hamish's table and generously refilled his shot glass.

'Okay, my friend,' Alphonse said, 'but make sure in future you do not listen to other people's conversations, even if you do not understand the language,' which seemed a somewhat incongruous remark, as Hamish frowned with non-comprehension, but which was obviously intended as a threat and with which they returned to their table.

It had in fact been quite an interesting conversation. Interspersed with a constant repetition of expletives the story appeared to be that they had made an almighty fuck-up, or at least that is what they believed, and if this was true they were in for a right old bollocking if nothing worse. Hamish had caught a few salient words: Beaulieu ... Metropole ... King ... Marcel ... wife ... and was hoping information would keep coming so, in a pause, he looked over to their table and raised his glass as some sort of encouraging sign.

'Cheers!' He said.

'A votre santé,' they replied almost in unison before glumly returning to their discussion though now sotto voce so Hamish could catch no more. Had Alphonse and Nino been of slightly more intelligence they would have been analysing recent events. As it was they were merely going around in circles reliving what they had just been through without coming to any definite conclusion as to the possible outcome, although they feared the worst. Marcel should never have got them to do it but, there you are, what is done is done.

They had set out from Marseilles once more for Beaulieu-sur-Mer and the Hotel Metropole, just the two of them in Marcel's Peugeot with orders to find out where Thornton was so they could inform him they had abducted his lady. Nino as usual was dressed to kill and even Alphonse for once looked fairly respectable. Marcel had seen to that. There was no way, he said, that they were going to walk into the Hotel Metropole looking like a couple of scruffs. He actually went so far as to lend Alphonse his favourite suit which proved how important was their mission. Luckily he and Alphonse were of a size. Nino complained most of the way. 'I am fucking fed up with all this fucking driving,' he moaned. 'Marseilles, Nice, Beauleiu, Beauleiu, Nice, Marseilles. It's a fucking long way. How many fucking times does he expect us to do it?'

'Just think of what we get in the end and stop your moaning,' Alphonse replied.

Despite the language indicating his state of mind, Nino was driving in a totally non-continental fashion; that is he was driving with due care, attention and, unbelievably for an Italian, consideration, which was partly what had put him in such a bad mood. Going so carefully would add half an hour, if not more, to their journey, but he had no wish to be pulled over by some zealous stupid cop although Marcel had provided him with quite a sizable amount of francs should that emergency arise.

Alphonse, on whom the onus lay to make the pitch, was seated next to him and mouthing whatever it was he thought he was going to say once they were there. Thornton's suitcase lay on the back seat.

Luigi was out the back of the hotel having a crafty smoke as the Peugeot drew up. He watched the two men get out. Alphonse collected the case and they set off for the hotel. Luigi was watching slit-eyed. He flicked away the remains of his cigarette in a great arc, blew out a cloud of smoke and placed himself in front of them.

'Bonjour, messieurs' he said, though addressing Nino in particular 'May I take the case?'

'Fuck off!' Nino snarled and then, remembering himself, 'I mean, no it's okay, kid, we'll take it.' He smiled and almost put out his hand to tousle the boy's hair in friendly fashion but thought better of it. Firstly it could be misconstrued and secondly it looked as though the lad had poured half a bottle of oil on it. Luigi stepped aside to let them go. They hadn't gone more than a couple of paces when he said:

'Nice case.'

Which stopped them dead in their tracks. They slowly turned around.

'And what exactly do you mean by "nice case?"' Alphonse said.

Luigi gave a shrug. 'There's another guy in the hotel got one exactly the same,' he said.

'Is that so? And who is this guy? What's his name?' It was now Alphonse's eyes that were narrowed to slits.

Luigi knew then he was definitely onto something. These guys might look like they were out of the top drawer with their fancy duds but they were just a couple of cheap crooks. He could tell by the accent if nothing else, especially as far as Nino was concerned whom he realised was Italian. What is more he could place his birthplace exactly - Naples. What is more he would say without fear of contradiction that Nino had spent a great deal of his misguided youth in the *Piazza Vittoria* with any number of other misguided youths. These two were up to something and whatever it was it had to do with that suitcase. Taking a slightly circular route he manoeuvred his way around them and sauntered towards the hotel.

'I don't know,' he said as he passed. 'He's a guest. He's here with his wife.' And he disappeared around the corner.

The two men stood looking at each other, both frowning. 'Wife? What's he mean, wife?' Alphonse queried. 'I thought she was supposed to be his girlfriend.'

Nino shrugged. 'Come on,' he said, 'let's go find out.'

They moved around to the main entrance and, once inside, approached the reception desk and Charles watched them with a wary eye every step of the way. He was as suspicious of the pair as Luigi had been. He didn't even ask if he could be of assistance as was his fashion but merely raised an eyebrow and waited. It would seem he didn't even register the suitcase.

'Bonjour, mon ami.' First mistake. Charles was most definitely not their ami, not even a nodding acquaintance as long as he could avoid it. There was no response to Alphonse's big friendly smile.

'We've brought this suitcase,' Alphonse continued. This elicited the first response from a stony faced receptionist.

'And why,' he enquired snootily, 'have you brought this suitcase?'

'It is labelled to a Mr Thornton King at this hotel.'

'Mr King is not registered here.'

'Oh?' Alphonse pretended surprise. 'Then why is his suitcase labelled Hotel Metropole?'

'Because, my friend ...' and Alphonse did not get the sarcasm ...'he thought he was going to be staying here but someone forgot to book him in. Now, if you will excuse me, I have other business to attend to.'

'So where is he then?' Nino burst in.

This was answered with a Gallic shrug and, 'I have no idea.'

'Maybe Miss Day knows. We can ask her.' Second mistake.

Charles, who had started to move away, turned back.

'Who?'

They both stared at him, realising that Nino had put his big foot in it. Then Alphonse decided to brazen it out.

'Miss Day, Miss Holly Day,' he said, but before Charles could question them further as to how they knew about Holly, Reg appeared from the lift and moved across to the front door. He was no longer carrying Rita's bag but he was carrying the air of a very sick bloodhound. Nino saw him and nudged Alphonse who grunted (the nudge having been between the ribs) and turned to look. Then he turned back to Charles.

'Aha!' he said, accusation in his voice, 'If Mr King is not in the hotel then tell me please, who might that be?' Mistake number three.

'Not that it is any business of yours …' Charles was now deeply suspicious of these characters …'but, if you really wish to know, that is the English police inspector by the name of Venahbles.'

'Police inspector?'

Nino had suddenly gone soprano and Charles noticed the reaction with satisfaction. He leaned forward and crooked his finger to bring their heads closer to him

'His wife seems to have gone missing.' He whispered. 'If she does not turn up soon we will have to inform our own police.' Then, leaning back and louder, 'The hotel is swarming with police …'

'Swarming?' Nino had not only gone soprano his voice had practically disappeared.

'… and one of our guests decides to disappear. What do you make of that?'

But neither of them was prepared to make anything of it.

'We thought there might be like, you know, a small reward for returning the suitcase but c'est la vie, if that is not to be … '

'Where did you get it?'

'What?'

'The suitcase, where did you get it?'

'Oh! Found it. Yes, very strange. Just lying there it was. And if it hadn't been for the labels … Yes. Well, I tell you what, we'll leave it here and Miss Day can take it to … yes ….well, is that okay? Good.' He waved a hand and they turned and left the hotel trying very hard to look the picture of composure and not to hurry. Nino was wondering if the English policeman had maybe recognised and could identify them but decided on the whole that was unlikely. Charles didn't try to call them back. They passed Luigi on their way out.

Now they had stopped off in Nice, delaying their return to a Marcel who was going to be beside himself with fury, and the *Chat Noir* seemed an ideal place to discuss their possible future, if they had one. With spirits at their lowest ebb they were spending some of the francs Marcel had given them buying up Dutch courage. Being hauled over on the way home for driving while under the influence wouldn't matter. The damage was done. They had given up the suitcase, almost got mixed up with the wrong guy, a police inspector of all things, still hadn't made contact with this mysterious Holly

Day and still didn't have an arsehole's clue as to where they could find Mister Thornton King. If only they had known it, they could have asked the Scot.

Charles saw Holly's key was in its place and decided he would tell her about the case when she returned to the hotel and, as the boy went by the counter, he indicated the suitcase and said: 'Take that to the store room.'

Without missing a step Luigi picked up the case and continued on his way. With thumb and forefinger of his other hand he was busily squeezing a pimple that had had the audacity to suddenly erupt on his cheek.

******

Thornton leaned back with a satisfied sigh. It had been a fabulous meal in fabulous surroundings. The cooking of Provence was, to his mind, without doubt the most satisfying, the most flavoursome, the most any gastronome could wish for. They had started with *Artichauts à la Barigoule*, followed by *Sole au Chablis*, *La Daube de Boeuf Provencale* all cooked to perfection and ending with a simple fresh grape tart. He just wished he hadn't eaten quite so much. It's all very well being a gourmand but being a glutton is quite another matter and it might be a case for Pepto-Bismol later. However he looked across at Holly who had been a little more abstemious simply by leaving portions on her plate, for Miss Manners as she put it, and said: 'Holly, what can I say? However did you find this fabulous place?'

'I didn't. Daddy brought me here, when I was younger of course.'

'I really must meet this daddy of yours sometime,' Thornton said, delicately swirling the cognac in his balloon. 'He is obviously the complete man of the world.'

'You wouldn't get on.'

'No? What makes you think that?'

'You are what he would call a layabout.'

'A layabout!' Thornton had taken a mouthful of cognac and nearly choked on it. 'A layabout! Well you would just have to disillusion him, Holly. I am without doubt one of the hardest working persons on this planet.'

'Really.'

'Yes, really. How can you doubt it?'

'How come you never manage to attract any clients?'

'Who says I don't?'

'I do.'

'Well that just shows you how wrong you are.'

'Does it? Name one.'

Thornton took another sip of his cognac and swirled it around his mouth with pursed lips.

'I thought so,' Holly said. 'Thornton, you really have to change your modus operandi.'

'I change them every day,' Thornton smirked.

'I'm being serious, Thornton, for your own good. You can't be so laissez faire for the rest of your life.'

'France has really got to you, hasn't it? I'm amazed how much French usage there is in the English language. When you come to think of it they're practically the same language, aren't they? They're pronounced differently, that's all. But you're quite right, Holly. It's just that there seems so little call for private investigators these days.'

'Thornton, we've been through all this before. You're just not going after the right people.'

'People are supposed to come to me, not me to them.'

'There you are. See what I mean?'

'Holly, let's not spoil a beautiful day. I'll think about it back home. Now is not the time.'

'With you, Thornton, it never is.'

******

Judging by the colour of his face, Marcel was about to have an apoplectic fit.

'You're telling me we've got the wrong woman?' he yelled, glaring ferociously at the others as though it were all their fault and he had nothing to do with it. 'And the wife of a policeman? Mon Dieu!' From glaring at them he turned his attention to the woman on the day bed, still out for the count. 'How much of that stuff did we give her?' he asked. It must have been a rhetorical question because he went on immediately with, 'So what the hell do we do now? Do we give her another dose before she comes round and then wait till dark, cart her out of here and drop her off somewhere?'

His question was answered by a groan from the couch as Rita opened her bloodshot eyes, sat up rather groggily and squinted across the room, which gradually came into focus. If it hadn't been for the presence of the beautiful Nino who she saw first she would most probably have let out a piercing scream but as it was she remained quiet as she surveyed the three men looking silently down at her.

'Where am I?' she asked at last with croaking voice and dry lips.

Marcel cleared his throat. 'I am sorry to tell you, madame, there has been a terrible mistake.'

'Oh, yes? And what might that be if I may ask?'

'Yes,' Alphonse was foolish enough to butt in. 'You see we wanted to have a word with…'

A stinging right-hander from Marcel cut him short and sent him flying almost to the opposite wall and now Rita did scream; and screamed and screamed and screamed.

In Marcel's neighbourhood screams were fairly common and unlikely to attract attention, but Rita's screech was so nerve racking Marcel was all for giving her the same treatment as he had administered to Alphonse, but it was Nino who put an end to it by sitting beside the distraught woman, putting his arm around her, and crooning sweet Italian nothings in her ear.

CHAPTER 7

Reg Venables was now more worried than he cared to admit. There was an empty feeling in his stomach that had nothing to do with the lack of food because he had earlier enjoyed, if that is the right word for it under the circumstances, a quite substantial lunch. Nothing with garlic he had stipulated and fortunately there were a number of dishes that suited his English taste.

It was fine for Rita to go off on her own back home or even here if it had been merely a matter of a little exploration and she hadn't roamed too far. He knew how easily she could lose her bearings but she had been gone far too long and it was quite obvious something had happened to her. It was also obvious he would never be able to make his speech that evening, not being worried to death about his wife, on top of being as nervous as a kitten. His hand holding his precious notes would tremble, he would lose his voice and, lifting his glass of water to wet his dry throat, he would spill it everywhere. He just knew he was going to make a complete ass of himself and wished heartily they had never come. From the very beginning, nothing had gone right. Nothing was going to go right. Even their luxurious suite was no compensation. Bloody French! What had they done with his missus?

It was time to report her a missing person. With this in mind he left off staring out sightlessly towards Cap Ferrat, turned and went into the hotel to ask Charles to call inspector Leroux only to find that was unnecessary. Leroux was already there, in evening suit, a row of medals on the breast of his jacket from his days in the military, ready for the night's events and chatting to some Spanish colleagues. They would have a lot to talk about, reminiscing over their respective North African colonies, the loss thereof and, nearer home, ETA, the Basque separatist movement. Leroux simply could not understand why anyone in Europe these days wanted to be separate when Europe had never been so united and would become even more so as time moved on but, there you are, there is no arguing with fanaticism, especially where nationalist sentiment or religious belief is concerned. He saw Reg and smiled in greeting.

'Ah, Inspector Venables!' he called, 'Good to see you. Ready to give your big speech? Let me introduce … '

But Reg was in no mood for introductions. 'Can I have a word with you?' he asked, almost pulling Leroux away by his sleeve, 'in private?'

'You're not getting cold feet?' Leroux chided as he moved, not realising the seriousness of the situation.

'No, it's not that,' Reg said. 'It's the wife, Rita. She's disappeared.'

'Pardon?'

'Rita, she's disappeared. I haven't seen her since late this morning. Nobody seems to have seen her. I've made enquiries every-where. Goodness only knows where she could be or what could have happened to her.'

'I don't think this part of the world is good for you, my friend,' Leroux said. Reg, right at this moment in time, as they say, could not have agreed more.

'First you lose your suitcase, now you lose your wife.'

'It's no joking matter!' Reg hissed. 'I tell you something terrible has happened!'

'Calm down, calm down, doucement, come and have a drink and let us talk about it.' He turned back to the Spaniards. 'Excuse us, please. It appears we have a bit of a crisis here.' The Spaniards nodded, eyeing Reg in the oddest fashion, or so he thought, and resumed their conversation among themselves.

'Now then, Inspector,' Leroux took Reg by the arm as they moved away, 'let us start at the beginning. Where did you last see your wife?'

'Oh, my God!' Reg exclaimed between gritted teeth, staring over Leroux's shoulder, 'Look who's here.'

Leroux turned to see Taps and Hamish approaching, Taps in cream tuxedo, and Hamish, everything Scottish, only lacking the bonnet and bagpipes. They reached the two policemen before the pair could disappear for their confab.

'Hello there!' Taps cried out in boyish fashion, or anyway, that was Reg's scornful opinion having read *Tom Brown's Schooldays* and a number of Henty novels when he was a youngster. He was in a mood quite naturally to criticise anything and everything. 'All ready for your big speech then?' Taps asked.

"Why in heaven's name does everyone keep on about that bloody speech?" He thought, forgetting that he had been proudly going on about it to everyone for days.

'I'm not making it now!' He almost yelled.

'Oh? Why is that?' Taps asked, genuinely surprised. 'I was really looking forward to it. You're going to disappoint an awful lot of people, Reg. I mean, wasn't it one of the reasons you were invited? I smell a good story here,' he said, turning to Hamish. 'Take a picture of Inspector Venables with this nice looking French officer. May I ask your name, sir?'

'Leroux. Inspector Gaston Leroux.' The nice looking inspector ran his index finger beneath one half of his moustache. Wouldn't do to have it photographed at half-mast.

Taps looked down to make a note of the name in his notebook, looked up and continued with: 'Seems I've heard that name somewhere before. You don't keep a phantom in your police station by any chance do you?'

'Old joke,' Leroux said coldly. 'So old it has, how do you English call it? Got whiskers on it.'

'Quite right too.' Taps was unabashed. 'And what, inspector Leroux, do you make of your colleague here chickening out of making his speech?'

Taps would have been in for a big surprise had Hamish not quickly stepped in between and taken a firm grip on Reg's wrist thus preventing a scandal and a severe case of grievous bodily harm and a possible cashiering.

'You poncey little arsehole!' Reg yelled, retrieving his arm and bringing the whole place to a tableau'd standstill. 'My wife has gone miss…' He brought himself up short but it was too late. The cat was out of the bag. Taps' eyes opened wide, Hamish's narrowed.

Thornton and Holly, who had just returned from their long day out, having driven for miles around the countryside after their delicious lunch, and who were now at the counter waiting for Holly's key which Charles held between them suspended in mid-air, turned to see what all the fuss was about, as did Luigi who was just about to sneak out for another cigarette and was stopped in his tracks. Even though his English was poor it was evident something highly dramatic was going on and he was not going to miss out on it.

******

The fog was gradually clearing as Rita sipped the water from the rather grubby plastic tumbler she had been handed and regarded her captors who were all regarding her back with hardly a thought between them as to what to do next. It was almost as though they were surveying an alien species that could turn out to be highly dangerous. She removed Nino's arm from around her waist. She was having none of that hanky-panky thank you very much, not after the way she had been treated and she didn't find the man at all sexy any more; quite the opposite in fact. As far as she was concerned, he was an oily lounge lizard, a gigolo, a pimp and a pander. That was the best way to describe him. It was a pity he wasn't in London. Her Reg would soon put a stop to his fun and games. How she could ever have thought him attractive in the first place she had no idea. She must have been mad. She sniffed and took another sip before she said something positive for the first time and that something was: 'My Reg will be awfully worried you know.' This was followed up separately by, 'How long have I been here? You do realise my husband is a high ranking police officer,' and 'what is all this about then?'

Rita would never have considered herself a particularly brave woman but these men, whoever they were, were spoiling her very first trip abroad and she deeply resented it. This was France after all, a civilised country, a country of culture like … like … she tried to think of cultural things and came up with what she always referred to as "The Eyeful Tower." Reg called it the "Awful Tower." For jingoist Reg, if it was French it stood to reason it was no good. Then there was the Arc de Triomphe and, naturally The Follies Bergere. There was that painter, what was his name? Degas? Who painted the girls at The Follies Bergere and of course there was van Gogh with his sunflowers who cut off his ear, daft git. What did he want to go and do a thing like that for? Wasn't there a palace with fifteen hundred rooms and not a single loo? Everyone did their you know what on the marble stairs. That wasn't the least bit civilised, or cultured. I mean! Anybody passing by could see you squatting there. The drug seemed to be having a secondary effect like the aftershocks of an earthquake. No, France was definitely not some out of the way exotic corner of the world like … like … she couldn't think of an out of the way exotic corner but Arabia came to her wandering mind. The fact that her life could be in danger hadn't bothered her one whit or, if it had passed through her mind, it was like being on an express train roaring through a station. She hadn't even been able to read the platform signs. She took a deep breath and tried to pull herself together.

'We are very sorry, madame,' Marcel said.

Nino tried putting his arm around her again and got his wrist slapped. He withdrew.

'But there has been a ... a ...sort of a ... '

'Cock up?' Rita ventured, much to Nino's astonishment. What was the world coming to? Any mother, sister or sweetheart in his corner of the woods who used language like that would get her face slapped pretty darn quick.

'Well, I suppose you could put it that way,' Marcel went on. 'You see the lady we really want to er ...to er ...talk to ...yes, talk to, is Miss Holly Day.'

'Holly? What on earth do you want to talk to her for? Well, if it's Holly you want I might as well be on my way then.' Despite the feeling of being on a ship in high seas, Rita made as if to scramble off the bed but Nino pulled her back down again and got his other wrist slapped.

'I'm afraid we can't let you do that,' Marcel said, 'not just yet. Maybe later.'

'How much later?'

'That depends.'

'On what?'

'Oh, merde! Stop asking so many questions.'

'Have you a telephone? Maybe I can call Reg so he won't be so worried.' She looked now as if she were about to burst into tears but Nino, unaware that it was mostly an act, wasn't about to have his wrists slapped a third time though he stayed seated next to her just in case she tried something; though he couldn't think what something that might be.

'No phone.'

'What do you mean, no phone? I can see it right there, in the hall.'

'I mean we cannot let you make a telephone call. Calls can be traced.'

'You're the men who stole the suitcase aren't you?'

Marcel shrugged and looked away. Confessing to anything even if obvious or proven is not the name of the game. Rita looked from one to the other.

'Have you got a beefsteak?' she asked.

Good God! Marcel thought, can these rosbifs not go a day without their favourite viand? 'I'm afraid not, madame.'

'It's not for me,' Rita said, 'it's for him,' pointing to Alphonse. 'He's going to have a beautiful shiner.'

'Shiner?'

'Black eye.'

'Oh. Well it won't be the first time ... or the last.'

'Anyway, talking of steaks, I am hungry. I haven't eaten since breakfast.'

'Nino, go out and get something for the lady to eat.'

'Like what?'

'Like use your nous.'

Nino shrugged and moved off. 'Don't blame me if she doesn't like it,' was his parting shot, pretty pathetic under the circumstances as he slammed the front door and clattered off down the stone stairway. Rita looked to her right, looked to her left, moved forward on the bed and looked behind her.

'Where's my bag?' she asked in some alarm. 'Where is it? I never go anywhere without my bag.'

'We didn't touch your bag,' Alphonse said.

'My Reg will go berserk, he will! Now he will know something's happened to me. Soon as he sees my bag... I should think he's already reported me a missing person.'

******

News of Rita's disappearance spread like a summer fire before the Mistral and, starting with a stiff cognac courtesy of Gaston Leroux, a distraught Reg was soon being comforted and reassured by his international colleagues. What comradeship, Reg thought, growing more and more maudlin. When brave lads stand shoulder to shoulder like this it really is most inspiring.

'Don't worry, my friend,' Gaston Leroux said, gripping Reg's arm in brotherly fashion, 'we will find her, I promise you, and she will be back in your arms tout de suite.'

That wasn't exactly what Reg had in mind but he did desperately want her back, the house simply wouldn't be the same without her, and he decided, as a tribute to her and his many fine colleagues, (how could he let them down now?) he would make his speech. Unfortunately his fine colleagues' sympathies were too often accompanied by something more substantial than mere sentiment and Reg didn't exactly have a head for the hard stuff so by the time dinner was served, let alone the time for after dinner speeches, he was simply in no condition to stand up, let alone speak.

The first thing Gaston did, after having sat Reg down and given him his cognac, was to march over to the counter and order Charles to hand him a phone so he could call the commissariat and set wheels in motion.

A little further away Taps too was on the phone, a public one in his case, presumably phoning in his story, it being too juicy to wait, but he was giving nothing away. He spoke very quietly and covered the mouthpiece with his free hand. Other journalists, no doubt feeling the same, queued up for their turn and the phone lines were red-hot.

Thornton and Holly waited by the counter (Holly had at last been handed her key) in order to have a few words with Leroux when he came off the phone. It was just as well because Leroux, having knocked back his own cognac in double quick time, had forgotten something terribly important. He put the receiver down on the counter and turned to go back to Reg when Holly stopped him.

'M'sieur Inspecteur ... '

'Excuse me, m'amselle, I am very busy. I must get a description of the missing lady.'

'Oh, we can give you that,' Holly assured him...

'Really?' He lifted the receiver again, redialled and, after a moment gave a gesture with his free hand, palm uppermost, meaning "Fire away," and Holly did so, giving a detailed description of the missing woman, which he relayed into the telephone as she spoke. Leroux, replacing the phone on its cradle, was most impressed. 'You're not a member of the police force are you, m'amselle? I don't think even her husband could have given me a better description, apart from some more personal details that is. I congratulate you on your observance.'

'No, I am not in the police force but I am in ... how shall I put this? ... Security.' She gave him one of her winning smiles and Gaston, for a moment fell in love, forgetting his dutiful wife who hated crowds and was at home supposedly lying in a darkened bedroom suffering a migraine but who in fact was sitting in front of the television. Wrapped in her favourite woolly dressing gown, her hair tamed with curlers and a net, her feet in comfy mules that were kind to her bunions, spooning vichyssoise into her mouth from an inherited antique porringer she was watching an old western dubbed hysterically into French. A cowboy had just slammed open the saloon doors and, spurs clanking, strode up to the counter, slapped down a hand and said, 'Hello, Jacqui!' in a heavy accent. 'Weeskee!'

Soon however, having allowed himself the sentiment for that brief moment, hardly an encounter because they weren't exactly alone, on a railway station, or even in England, for madame Leroux's husband it was back to business.

'And when did you last see Mrs Venables?' he asked.

'I saw her, that is I saw them both at breakfast this morning, before I went into Nice to meet with Mr King here.'

'Mr King?'

'Thornton King. Pleased to meet you.'

'Enchantè, m'sieur.' They shook hands. 'You too are in security?'

'In a way,' Thornton replied, assuming an air of modesty that proclaimed him to be nothing but the best, 'I'm a detective.' He omitted the word "private". She gave him a sideways glance. 'Holly and I used to work together, in the same department.'

'Is that so?' Gaston nodded his head. 'Well, tell me this, mister detective (did Thornton catch the hint of a jibe in that voice?) can you think of any reason why Mrs Venables should disappear?'

'None whatsoever, inspector.'

Leroux grunted, an *I thought as much* grunt. He turned to Holly. She shook her head.

'Ah well,' the inspector continued, 'we shall no doubt find out sooner or later.' He saluted and was about to turn away when, this time, it was Charles's voice that stopped him.

'Mr King, your suitcase has been returned. Shall I have it fetched?'

All three turned to look at the receptionist. It made him feel as though he had suddenly sprouted a second head.

There was a silence before Leroux nodded, 'Do so,' he said.

Charles clicked his finger and thumb at Luigi still standing by. It was a wonder the boy's ears hadn't developed cramp they had been exercising so vigorously. His brain had been working overtime as well, desperately trying to keep up and translate what his ears were hearing.

'Fetch Mr King's case,' Charles ordered.

Luigi was off as fast as Puck girdling the earth. Charles turned back to the threesome.

'Who brought my suitcase back?' Thornton asked.

'Two men. Said they found it.'

'Found it? Found it where?' This was from Leroux.

'They didn't actually say, Inspector. I didn't like the look of them I can tell you.'

'I take it from that you didn't know them, never saw them before.'

'Quite right, Inspector.'

'I am going to need a description,' Leroux said. 'These must be two of the men who stole that suitcase from inspector Venables.'

'Reg had my suitcase all the time?' Thornton asked incredulously.

'Not all the time. He had it till it was stolen off him. The big question at the moment is, why would the thieves bring it back?'

'They thought there might be a small reward. They also wanted to talk to Miss Day.'

'Talk to me?' Holly turned wide-eyed to Charles. 'What on earth for?'

'And here is the most stupid thing of all,' and Charles allowed himself a sly chortle, 'they thought Inspector Venables was you, Mr King.'

'What!'

'Curiouser and curiouser, said Alice.'

'I beg your pardon?'

'Oh, nothing, Inspector, it's an English saying.'

'Yes, but I am very interested in English sayings. From whence does it come?'

'From a book, inspector, *Alice In Wonderland* by Lewis Carroll.'

'Ah,' was all she got in reply, and then, 'Of course I have heard of that book and I shall now look out for it.'

'In the meantime,' Thornton said, 'you're meant to be looking out for a missing lady and a couple of crooks that stole my case.'

'Of course, of course.' Then to Charles, 'A description if you please.'

'Well, they were both well dressed I have to say, though in a slightly bizarre manner. Obviously no idea ...'

'Never mind their dress for the moment, clothes can be changed, what about their looks? What did they look like?'

Before Charles could launch into a description of their looks, Luigi returned with Thornton's case.

'Open it up,' Leroux ordered, 'see if anything's missing.'

Thornton hoisted the case up onto the counter, opened it and started to rummage which didn't please Charles one little bit. Guests passing by paused to wonder what was going on. Suitcases on a receptionist's counter in a first class hotel, open and being savagely ravished, was most de trop. Charles offered them a weak smile and they moved on, no doubt to discuss it on the way to bed.

'It's quite amazing,' Charles said, eyeing the case and wondering how much polishing and scratch remover his counter was going to need after such thoughtless misuse, 'there are three suitcases all alike, if not exactly the same.'

Thornton stopped his rummaging.

'What did you say?' This was from Leroux.

'Three suitcases...' Charles looked from one to the other, wondering why they were staring at him so hard. Now he really had developed two heads or a bad case of BO. He sincerely hoped it wasn't the latter. 'I just said how strange, that's all, that they ... all ... seem ... to be alike.'

'Where's the other one?' Leroux asked.

'Inspector Venables I presume he has it.'

'No no! The third one! Where is the third one?'

'Luigi? The other case like this. Bring it here please.'

Luigi nodded and trotted off once more.

'Who does it belong to, this third case?'

'Just a moment. I made a note of it when it arrived. Here ...' He flipped through a pad. 'No, not there. Another pad. I will fetch it.'

He stepped into the office and they silently and impatiently waited for him to return which eventually he did, riffling through another notebook.

'The case is covered in labels all addressed to this hotel. The owner certainly didn't want it to go astray ... but no one by the name of ... ah, here it is ... someone called Jakob Mynhardt.'

There was a simultaneous 'WHAT!' from all three facing the counter, which almost made Charles drop his pad.

'Are you certain that is the name?' Leroux asked.

'Quite certain. Look for yourself,' and Charles held the pad out towards the inspector. 'No one by that name is booked into the hotel which is why it was so strange his suitcase should be addressed to this establishment. I took the decision to put it away somewhere safe until such time as Mister Mynhardt himself appeared to collect it or the mystery was cleaned up.'

'Cleared up,' Thornton said, unable to stop himself making the correction though this was hardly the time for lessons in English because right now there was another mystery to clear up. Luigi should have been back with the suitcase but there was no sign of him. Charles slapped his hand down on the counter bell and, after a while, Lucien appeared and was ordered to go and find him. Lucien too disappeared. They waited. Leroux stroked his moustache and glanced at his watch. Charles moved further down the counter to attend other guests. Eventually Thornton, who thought the boys really should have been accompanied on so important a mission, lost patience and was all for going in search of them both when the errant pair returned, but without the suitcase. Charles, on seeing this, returned to the group.

'I no find it.' Luigi said.

His announcement was greeted by a stunned silence allowing the hum of conversation and laughter from the dining room to suddenly seem much louder and more intrusive than it actually was. Charles was the first to recover.

'What do you mean, you no find it?'

'What I say, you know? No case like that.' He pointed to Thornton's still on the counter, though Thornton was no longer interested in its contents. 'I look and I look. It not there.' Lucien nodded in agreement.

'You mean, it's disappeared?' Charles whispered.

'It disappear,' Luigi agreed, lifting his shoulders and opening both arms wide, palms upwards. 'It disappear. No there at all.'

'That's impossible.' Charles was aghast. That something left in the care of the hotel, even if by accident, should go missing was a disaster. 'It must be found.' He was almost wringing his hands.

'If someone has taken it walkies,' Thornton said, 'then in all probabilities I no think it will ever be found.'

CHAPTER 8

They were sitting around the table when Nino returned carrying a couple of round loaves and a covered bowl Rita eyed with suspicion.

'What's that? It's not snails is it?'

'No, it's not snails,' Marcel reassured her.

'It's never frog legs! I wouldn't dream of eating frogs' legs!' She could feel her stomach churning slightly at the very thought.

'It's not frogs' legs.'

'What is it then?' She peered into the bowl. It did not look too appetising. In her opinion there were too many bits and pieces of something or other unidentifiable floating around. 'It's not horse, is it?'

'No, madame, it is not horse.'

'Why won't you tell me what it is then? There's sheep's eyes in there, aren't there? Her imagination had gone through the stratosphere. The three men burst out laughing and for a while simply couldn't stop as Rita sat silently eyeing them. 'What's so funny?' she demanded to know as they calmed down.

'Madame,' Marcel said, wiping the tears from his eyes, 'Nomads, Bedouin, they are the one's who eat sheep's eyes in the desert. We are not Nomads and we are not in the desert.' He sniffed and wiped his nostrils with finger and thumb and then the back of his hand. 'It's bouillabaisse,' he informed her proudly.

'Oh, I couldn't possibly eat that!' she protested 'I really couldn't … What's in it then?'

'Fish. It's a fish stew.' Marcel had found a large much used wooden spoon and now gave the bouillabaisse a gentle stir. Rita wrinkled up her nose. There are ways of cooking fish and ways of cooking fish but stewing was not one of them.

'If you will excuse me,' she said, 'I think I will give it a miss.'

'But this is one of the … the …' He couldn't think of the word so he put the fingertips of one hand together and kissed them, the gesture accompanied by an appreciative 'Mmmmm!' continuing with, 'of the region. You don't even know what you are missing if you do not give it a try.'

'All the same, thank you very much. Anyway, that can be said of a great many things; about trying or not trying I mean. I will just have some bread if you don't mind.'

Nino picked up one of the loaves and broke off a hunk of bread that he passed to her. She looked at it with disgust.

'Don't you have knives?' she asked.

'Sure we do,' Nino replied, taking out his flick-knife and opening it, 'but what did God give us hands for?'

'To do a great many things,' she said, 'including some things too disgusting to mention in polite society which reminds me, I need to go to the loo.'

'It's through there,' Marcel said; nodding in the direction of a rather battered, paint peeling closed door.

'If you will excuse me then ...' Rita rose from the table and went out.

The men looked at each other, Marcel distributed some bowls, and they helped themselves to the bouillabaisse.

Rita found herself in an almost airless bedroom in one corner of which was a bidet, a wash-hand basin on rusting brackets and a toilet, above which was one small window with rotting frame and cracked panes opaque with years of grime, probably only ever washed away by rain. It was fairly high up. The door had a bolt she pushed home before surveying the room.

Marcel's apartment was in a very old building and obviously the conversion to include toilet facilities was rather makeshift, having little or nothing to do with hygienic considerations, modesty, privacy, or planning permission and probably installed by a fly by night cowboy as a rusting tin can behind the toilet was strategically placed to catch a steady drip. She crossed the room and stood looking at the bidet. The stains were rather off-putting. The toilet bowl was worse. For a woman as house proud as Rita, until fairly recently that is, these conditions were simply beyond the pale. She seriously wondered whether she would actually sit down or just sort of squat a couple of inches above. All thoughts of France being a civilised country had flown out that tiny window. She lowered the seat, slipped off her shoes, and climbed up to look out of it. All she could see were rooftops and, anyway, the window was so small, she would never have squeezed through. She got down.

When she returned she discovered the men had made short work of the fish stew and most of the bread and she was now really very hungry indeed. She picked up the piece of bread Nino had passed her and took a bite; then sat silently chewing.

'Would you like a drink?' Marcel asked.

'Yes please.' She had earlier emptied her tumbler of water. He selected another glass and poured her a drink from out of what looked like an earthenware flask.

'Cheerio!' Nino said, as she lifted the glass to her lips and took a mouthful, a great deal of which immediately left her mouth in the opposite direction, spraying the men and the table as she coughed, spluttered, and nearly choked to death. She eventually found her wheezing voice as the men were wiping themselves down.

'Good heavens!' she squeaked. 'Are you trying to poison me? What on earth is that filthy stuff?'

'It's calvados,' Marcel coldly informed her, still wiping down his shirtfront. 'Made from apples. It's a sort of apple brandy.'

'Well it certainly isn't cider and I find that strong enough.'

'It's made from the cider,' Marcel said.

'In which case they should leave well alone. It's horrible.'

Alphonse took her glass and swallowed the remains of the calvados in one gulp, then went across to the tap to get a refill of water. Returning to the table he placed the glass in front of her and smiled. He had rather a nice smile. It wasn't a sexy smile like Nino's used to be but it was warm and genuine. Rita was beginning to wonder whether or not she should be enjoying this adventure, this unique experience. There couldn't be too many middle aged suburban housewives in this situation. Or should she really be terribly afraid? She had heard all the stories about kidnappers and how their victims were seldom found alive if found at all, and she still couldn't really fathom out why she was there in the first place so she enquired, quite politely as to the reason.

'You're a mistake,' Marcel said.

Rita thought about this for a moment. 'Yes,' she said, 'I am. I was a mistake to my parents. I'm a mistake to my husband. I am most definitely a mistake to my kids.'

'Oh, no!' Nino objected. 'No mother can be a mistake to her children.'

'You're an Italian,' Alphonse chipped in. 'Not only that but you're a boy. Of course you love your mother because your mother has spoilt you rotten all your life. That's the Italian way.'

'The Mediterranean way,' Marcel said.

'Anyway,' Rita continued, 'if I am a mistake, perhaps it would be better if I just left, don't you think? I don't know who you are, I don't know where I am, and I'm not going to give anything away. In fact you have all been so nice to me I wouldn't dream of turning you in anyway, even though my husband's a policeman. So how about it?'

Marcel shook his head. 'Later,' was all he said.

******

The party in the dining room had not as yet wound down, there were still a few diehards keeping hotel staff from their beds although they had quietly and efficiently started to remove debris where possible without spoiling the enjoyment of those remaining.

The police had obviously enjoyed their evening as the food and wine stains on the linen evidenced. It was a pity Reg was unable to give his speech considering he had come all this way specifically for that purpose. Someone from the German delegation suggested that one of their number stand in for him but the motion wasn't seconded so the proposal was dropped.

Everywhere else in the building was pretty mute and almost deserted, the occasional apparition weaving its way along a corridor to disappear through a door. The ladies, with more sense than their men folk, were already either in bed or sitting in front of their dressing tables removing their make-up ready for it. There were those already having it of course, that is, if their partners weren't suffering from brewer's droop.

Reg was almost blotto in the Venables suite. His glorious mates hadn't actually put him to bed, just laid him on top of it. They hadn't even removed his shoes. He lay on his back wishing the room would stop heaving.

Thornton and Holly were seated at the bar enjoying a nightcap and musing over the day's events preparatory to Holly driving Thornton back to Nice. Holly had been abstemious and was in a fit state to drive. Thornton hadn't and wasn't.

'Let's recap,' Thornton said, 'and see what we come up with. We're off on a jolly jaunt to the south of France and we bump into this South African guy at Heathrow airport. Well, he bumps into us to be exact. He has just flown in from West Africa, Liberia he says. We figured London was the end of his journey because he appeared to be on his way out but the next thing we know he's back inside and booking a first class flight to Nice on the same plane as us. Did we give him the idea? I suggest that is the case because, if I remember correctly, he virtually said as much referring to England's lousy weather. He suggests he buys us a drink before take-off but never shows up. In fact that is the last we see of him but his suitcase, which looks exactly like mine, oh, and like Reg's too, turns up at the hotel here. Three suitcases all alike, is that a coincidence or isn't it? Well, be that as it may, it's a bit like that *find the lady* con trick sharps play in Oxford Street, you know, find the marble under one of three cups which, of course, after finding her the first time and collecting your winnings, you never do again so lose your all. It's amazing how many idiots think they can beat the system but then, as Barnum said, there's one born every minute. So we arrive in Nice. My suitcase apparently doesn't arrive but in fact has been accidentally picked up by Reg from whom it is stolen by three guys the moment he steps outside the airport. Meanwhile Reg's own suitcase has been picked up by someone inside the airport who the cops nab then and there. Reg gets his suitcase back from the cop shop, I get mine back, returned by two of the guys we assume stole it in the first place, but there is still no sign of Jakob. His suitcase sent to the Metropole has disappeared as has Rita, and no one knows where. Are we clear so far?'

Holly nodded.

'So what do you make of it?'

'Not much?'

'No ideas at all?'

'Not as yet.'

'The piece of information we really need to slot into this jigsaw is, who was the guy the cops arrested at the airport, and here right on cue is the very man to tell us. Inspector Leroux!' he called out as Leroux was making his way across the bar, presumably heading for the toilet. It had been a long evening. Fortunately he had a driver to take him back to Nice when it was finally over. He tacked in their direction.

'Inspector,' Thornton said, 'Holly and I have been going over things and there is something we really need to know.'

Inspector Leroux wasn't too sure he wanted to divulge any information until Holly favoured him with another of her smiles and he fell in love for a second time that evening.

'What is it you want to know, Mister King?'

'The name of the guy you picked up at the airport. The one who half inched Reg's suitcase.'

'Half inched?'

'Pinched, nicked, lifted, stole.'

Leroux nodded. 'Half inched,' he said, 'that is a most interesting one, most interesting. I will remember that one.' He turned as if to continue on his way.

'Inspector!'

He turned back.

'The man's name.'

Leroux shrugged. 'Oh, yes. He's a Belgian national,' he informed them, 'by the name of Joost Broecx.'

'Eureka!' Thornton almost yelled, giving Leroux quite a start so that he took a firm grip on himself. 'That's it! Diamonds! Jakob from West Africa and I'll hazard a bet, a fart to a fortune, Sierra Leone comes into the equation. The case is stuffed with bloody diamonds and that is what our boys are after.'

'Yes,' Holly agreed. 'But that still doesn't explain Rita's disappearance. What could she possibly have to do with it?'

'We are assuming that to be the case?' Thornton queried. 'That she has something to do with it? Not possible.'

'But I'm afraid we must assume that,' Leroux butted in, 'If not, she should have surfaced by now do you not think?' The word "surfaced" gave him another idea but he hastily put it from him. It was too horrible to contemplate. 'But now, if you'll excuse me, I have to ... what do the English say?'

'Well, once upon a time, before inflation, we used to say you have to spend a penny. Nowadays it's more like ten.' Holly said.

'You've got to have a slash,' Thornton added. 'Or you have to take a leak.'

'You need to see a man about a horse,' was Holly's contribution.

'You have to point Percy at the porcelain,' Thornton topped her.

'So many delightful expressions for one thing. English is such a remarkable language.'

'Yes, it is amazing isn't it?' Thornton said, not quite sure about the "delightful" bit. 'Do you know there are over two hundred euphemisms for a ... oh, well, forget it.'

The inspector was out of earshot anyway, weaving stiff-legged towards the door of what in earlier times was euphemistically referred to as the necessary house.

'Shall we go?' Holly asked. Thornton nodded, drained his glass, picked up his suitcase, they nodded goodnight to the barman and went out to the car. Holly got behind the wheel, started the engine and switched on the headlights while Thornton, who couldn't be bothered to open the boot, or the trunk as our American cousins would call it, tossed his suitcase on the rear seat before he opened the passenger door, slid in, slammed the door, and the great black Germanic beast nosed almost silently out of the car park.

******

The phone had been ringing a long time before Marcel plucked up enough courage to answer it. In fact they had sat around letting it ring a few times previously, deaf to its insistent call, knowing it would have to be answered sooner or later but preferring to put it off until later and later had arrived. It really couldn't be put off any longer. Now the other two, still seated at the table, Rita had been bundled off into the bedroom, could hear Cy on the other end of the line telling Marcel how many kinds of total incompetents they were in the vilest of language.

'You tell us what we should do then!' Marcel yelled back, having had a bellyful of this Englishman's insults, and immediately removed the receiver from his ear, holding it at a distance of at least a foot from his head as Cy's ranting came through loud and clear for all to hear before the phone suddenly went dead. There had been no offer of advice.

Marcel stood for a while tapping the receiver against the palm of his hand, controlling the urge to smash it against the wall or rip it from its moorings. He replaced it and moved slowly back into the room, obviously deep in thought. The other two waited; Alphonse leaning back in his chair, hands deep in his trouser pockets, Nino paring his fingernails with his flick knife. Moments passed. Somewhere on the rooftops cats were either doing what comes naturally to produce more unwanted kittens or having one hell of a punch up. Either way the noise was horrendous. The silence that followed was broken by the sound of a police car as it sped by, its horn blasting away, fading into the distance.

'They're looking for her,' Nino muttered.

'Of course they're looking for her,' Marcel responded. 'What do you expect? But they've got as much chance of finding her as we have of finding the diamonds unless we can get to this Thornton King person and make him talk. Talk, damn it! Talk! He is obviously the only one who knows where they are.' He slammed his fist down on the table. Alphonse for no particular reason, removed a hand from his pocket and righted a knocked over glass.

'What I would like to know,' Marcel went on, 'is how this Cy fellow in London got so quickly onto what has happened. Who told him? Hey? Answer me that. Who told him? To my way of thinking there is someone here passing on information.'

'Well it certainly isn't either of us,' Alphonse said, sitting up and removing his other hand from his pocket to lay both on the table as if to show they were clean. 'We haven't been out of your sight. Wait a minute, Nino went to fetch the food and he was rather a long time doing it don't you think?'

Nino looked up for the first time, sent his knife spinning high in the air before it fell with the haft neatly in his hand. 'If I was you, Alphonse, I would put my mind in gear before opening my big mouth. I happened to meet up with an old girl-friend and we chatted, okay? Not that I owe you a reason.'

'Okay, okay! Let's not fall out, not now. I guess this Beloved Leader person'- Marcel had managed at last to spit it out- 'has got spies everywhere and we're not likely to know who they are so let's put our heads together and decide what we are going to do next because, as they say, the shit is really about to hit the fan and I, for one, do not want to be in the way because it's going to be a big load of shit and an industrial size fan and if it doesn't blow the shit out it's going to suck us in.' He had to stop to draw breath.

'We use her,' Nino said softly, returning to his manicure.

'We what?'

'We use Mrs Rita Venables, the lady in the next room.'

'How?'

'Bait. You want to talk to Miss Holly Day don't you? You want her to lead you to, or tell you where to find this Thornton King, yes? Or, if she won't talk, we inform King that we have her and he had better come and collect which was the plan in the first place wasn't it? You know there is an old saying, set a thief to catch a thief? Well, in this case, I suggest we set a woman to catch a woman.'

Marcel was intrigued. He opened his hand to give Nino the carry-on. 'And how do you suggest we do that?' he asked, the essence of politeness.

'Well ...' Nino closed his knife and slipped it back into a pocket. He glanced towards the bedroom door and then leaned forward to talk quietly. He was certain he had put his own mind into gear and the result would be pretty impressive. 'We tell Mrs Venables that we have decided to let her go.'

'What?'

'Are you crazy?'

'Listen. We tell her we are letting her go because it was all a big mistake, you know? She's of no use to us. However, we need to make sure she doesn't do anything stupid like go straight to the police.'

'She'll go straight to the police, you idiot! What about her husband? He's a policeman.' This was from Alphonse.

'No problem.'

'What do you mean, no problem? Are you crazy? His wife gets kidnapped, she goes back to him, she tells him the whole story, and he is going to do nothing about it? Merde! I've never heard such a load of bullshit in my life.' Marcel glowered across the table, his hand closed tight again. 'Imbecile!'

'What do you suggest then, boss?'

There was silence.

'So are you going to let me finish?'

Silence.

'Good. So, we are going to drop her off somewhere and, because she won't know where she is, she has to be picked up by someone she knows and we, she, would like that someone to be Miss Holly Day.'

Marcel and Alphonse stared at Nino, turned to look at each other, turned back to him. Their faces showed quite plainly they still thought he was mad and this was, as Marcel said, a load of bullshit.

'Hopefully she will have forgotten we said we want to talk to that woman. She will ask why it can't be her husband who picks her up and we will say that would be a bad mistake because he has seen us more than once and could give a really good description to the French police. We realise she could do that as well but we trust her, have absolute faith that she wouldn't.'

'You reckon she's going to buy this crap?' Alphonse snorted.

'Why not? She's in no position to say no or to bargain and I think the state she's in she will believe anything. We have to be extra extra nice to her though from now on. Brain-washing, that's what it is called.'

'Why beat about the bush?' Alphonse asked. 'Why not ask for Thornton straight away?'

'Now who's crazy? Ask who? We don't know where he is, do we? And I shouldn't think she does. Why should she?' He jerked a thumb towards the bedroom door. 'He could be anywhere between here and Ventimiglia if he's decided to pay my home country a visit. So who are we going to ask, huh? Where are we going to ask? Miss Day is the only person who can give us the information. I think woman-to-woman would be better, don't you? Really?'

They ruminated on this for a few moments and then Marcel said, 'Okay, let's do it. We've got to do something and it's better than sitting here jerk … Yes. Well …where should we take her?'

'The farm.'

'The farm? The farm! Why the farm?

'Out in the country, dark, wild animals, kilometres from civilisation, nervous women, what could be better?'

'How do we contact this Holly?'

'You know that kid, Luigi? I reckon he will be happy to make some extra money. He's an Italian after all, a Sicilian if I've got it right. We give him a note with instructions to pass it on to Miss Day, secretly of course. He must be made aware no one else is to know or …' Nino put a forefinger to his temple.

'Merde! She won't take any notice of a note,' Marcel said scornfully.

'She will if there is also a phone call and she hears Rita's tearful voice.'

'Hmn …' Marcel shook his head, obviously still dubious.

'What's the big problem?' Nino asked.

'Firstly I do not like the idea of trusting that Sicilian kid and secondly I don't like the idea of two kidnapped women being in the same place at the same time. Something could go badly wrong. I mean this one doesn't seem to be too much of a problem but we don't know anything about this Holly dame. She could be big time trouble, you know? She could be one of these "I go to the gym every day and take karate type classes" kind of female.'

'Ah!' Nino was dismissive. 'There isn't a woman yet I can't handle.' He made a couple of short sharp chopping motions with both hands. It impressed no one.

'So we keep them apart.' Alphonse said. 'One here, one there.'

He shrugged. Such a simple solution. 'As for the Sicilian, leave him out of it. Just put a note in an envelope and leave it at the desk, then tell her it's there.'

Still blissfully unaware of the true nature of the situation, that now no one knew where the suitcase containing the diamonds was, except for the one who had removed it, it was so decided, and the next time Cy would have occasion to phone they would have Thornton King and they would have the diamonds and could metaphorically tell the Englishman to go swivel.

******

They sat opposite each other at a table by the window, partly hidden from the street by café curtains that hadn't seen a washing machine for many a day. The table was covered with a traditional red chequered cloth somewhat stained, in places somewhat holed by cigarette ends fallen from ashtrays. She was smoking a cheap cigarette and drinking red wine. He was drinking a German beer. The café was directly opposite the *Pensione Garibaldi* and he was in truth desperate to get out of this smoke filled place redolent of human presence almost as unwashed as the curtains and the tablecloth, but it was as yet too early to move.

'Do you want another drink?' he asked after she had drained her glass and set it down on the table. She shook her head. She was a little afraid of this man sitting opposite her no matter how charming he appeared to be.

'That's right,' he nodded, smiling. 'You need to keep a clear head because you have to get a really good look at him.'

'It's dark,' she said.

'But light enough,' he countered.

She stubbed out her cigarette and lit another. He watched for a moment.

'Monique, you smoke too much,' he said, gently admonishing.

'Nerves.' She shivered.

'What is there to be nervous about? Would he be the first man you've seduced?'

'This is different.'

'Different? From all the others? What is so different about it?'

'I don't know ... I don't know what you want him for.'

'What we want him for need not concern you. You're being paid to do just so much. Do it well. Earn your money. Who knows? You could even enjoy it and I'm sure it's more than you would make from a customer. Is customer the right word?'

She shrugged.

'A trick then. Anyway, if you smoke that much and smell like an ashtray he's not going to be interested and you lose out. Remember that.'

'What if he doesn't like me anyway?'

'Why shouldn't he?' The man surveyed her carefully. She had come well recommended and, even in the half light of the café he could see how beautiful she was. There was no doubt he would fall for it. The man found it hard to believe or understand why she had chosen the world's oldest profession to make a living, if it could genuinely be called a living and if it had been a choice and not a necessity. Was there some pimp who had a hold over her? Was she a nympho? A lesbian who just used men for their money? Did she have family to support? She was certainly a dark mystery.

'Unless he's gay,' he smiled at her across the table, 'and I have absolutely no reason to believe he is, he will fall for you hook, line, and sinker as the saying goes.'

She pouted. 'Hook line and sinker. What does that mean?'

'It means you will catch the big fish and I believe the big fish has arrived.'

The Mercedes had pulled up outside the *Garibaldi*.

The girl lifted the bottom of the curtain just enough to peer out and get a good look at Thornton as he stepped from the car. He stood there a while bidding Holly good-night and even remained there after the car had pulled away. He gave a last wave and turned to go into the pensione. Monique dropped the curtain.

'Well, will you recognise him if you see him again?' He corrected himself, 'When you see him again?'

She nodded, smiling. 'Now I will have that other drink,' she said.

'Of course.' He looked around and clicked his fingers to attract attention, waved her glass to indicate what was required, rose to his feet and dropped money on the table. 'But I'm afraid I'm leaving you to drink on your own. Good-night.'

He turned and left the café taking a fair amount of smoke out with him as he opened the door. He hadn't even finished his beer that, in truth, he found had grown too warm to be potable.

Once outside he stood a long while looking at the building

opposite and breathing in the fresher air. He was worried. There was no doubt his rooms had been broken into and someone had been going through his things. The drawer of his Louis Quatorze reproduction bureau was still locked but, as far as he could remember the order in which they had lain, the contents were not in the exact same position as he had left them, though nothing was taken. His cheques and cash were intact. Who could it have been? And why? Things were not going well, not at all well.

He who wills the end must will the means. So far the means at his disposal seemed to have been extremely rocky.

******

From a deep sleep and a fairly erotic dream as she briefly remembered it on coming around, Holly was woken by the ringing of the telephone. She groaned and switched on her bedside light to look at her watch. Three a.m. This was ridiculous. Someone had the wrong room or possibly Thornton couldn't sleep and wanted to chat. Perhaps though he was in some kind of fix so maybe she had better answer it. It obviously wasn't going to stop ringing until she did. She found and lifted the receiver to be met by a howl.

'Holleeeeeee?'

She jerked the receiver away from her ear and, when the howling stopped, put it back again, gingerly in case the howling was resumed.

'Yes?'

'It's me, Rita.'

'Rita! My God!' She threw back the bedclothes and shuffled her feet on the carpet trying to locate her slippers. 'What's happened? Are you all right? Where are you?'

'I don't knooooow!'

'What is that supposed to mean, you don't know?' The feet stopped shuffling.

'Come and fetch me please.'

'What?'

'Come and fetch me!'

Holly leaned forward and switched on her bedside lamp. 'Rita, do you know what time it is? You've been missing for hours. Your husband is going crazy with worry. The police are hunting high and low for you. Have you been doing something really silly? It doesn't look too good, does it? Someone just disappearing like that,

153

especially that someone being a policeman's wife when the place is literally swarming with policemen.'

Holly was deeply suspicious. This wasn't just idle chat on her part. She had the feeling that Rita was hiding something, that she had gone off for an assignation, got herself into water too deep for her and had been hiding out all this time, too ashamed to return to Reg's welcoming and forgiving arms. There was the sound of a sob on the other end of the line that seemed to confirm it.

'Rita, have you been…' she wanted to put this as delicately as possible '… Are you hurt? Have you been assaulted in any way?'

There was another howl on the other end followed by, 'Holleeeeee! Please! Just come and fetch me!'

'Rita! Answer me, damn it! Are you hurt?'

'No. I just want you to come and fetch me.'

'How can I come and fetch you if you don't know where you are?'

'Someone … someone will … bring you to me.'

Holly frowned, thinking about this. 'Rita … tell me in words of one syllable, if that's possible … what is going on?'

'I've been kidnapped!'

After the initial howling, this abrupt announcement with no more emotion, or so it seemed, than a statement like "I have been invited to the vicarage for tea" produced a long silence at Holly's end. If she hadn't been wide awake up to this point she was certainly wide awake now and her mind was racing. Favoured pets, pedigreed or mongrel, for which a large ransom could be screwed from a doting owner in London, Paris, or New York, especially New York, get kidnapped. There was even a famous racehorse kidnapped, maybe more than one. Champion greyhounds are liable to kidnapping. Unguarded children of wealthy and famous people get kidnapped; journalists in the world's trouble spots get kidnapped. Who on earth would want to kidnap Rita? Poor, plain, slightly silly, middle-aged Rita, was certainly no Persephone, no Helen of Troy, no Cleopatra, so it couldn't have a sexual motive. Though, on the other hand, why not? It takes all kinds with all kinds of taste. Money? Ridiculous; the lower middle class wife of a lower middle class policeman on a policeman's salary? Revenge by some villain Reg was responsible for having had put away? South London maybe but hardly south of France and Reg never in his life put away a villain that big, though one never knew with psychopaths, big or small. No, she had obviously been taken in mistake for someone else. Holly didn't realise how true this thought was. But who? An heiress? The wife of a politician? Who? Her thoughts were interrupted.

'Holly, are you still there?'

'I'm here.'

'Will you come and fetch me please? Someone will bring you to me.'

Alarm bells were suddenly ringing loud and clear.

'I don't understand, Rita. You're saying whoever it is kidnapped you is now letting you go?'

'Yes.'

'Why?'

'What do you mean, Holly?'

'Just that. Why?'

'They said I was a mistake.'

'Then why can't he ...?'

'They, Holly, I said they.'

'There's more than one.'

'Yes. If I say they it means there's more than one, all right?'

'Don't get shirty with me, Rita, just try and stay calm.'

'Calm? Calm!'

'How many are there?'

There was another short silence and then, 'Only three ... I think.'

'Only! You mean it's a gang?'

'I suppose so.'

'And you don't know where you are.'

'Nooooooo!'

'Well, are you in a town?'

'Yes.'

'In Nice?'

'Holly this is not twenty questions or a kiddie's game. All you have to do is come and fetch me and that's aaaaall, Holly!'

'All right, Rita, please try to stay calm.'

'Yes ... all right.' She wiped her nose with the back of her hand.

'Why can't they bring you back to the hotel and just drop you off? That is, if they are genuinely letting you go. I mean, they must have taken you from the hotel in the first place so why not just bring you back?'

The silence was again from Rita's end, longer this time. Was someone giving her instructions? Telling her what to say? Holly held on. Rita came back on line.

'Please, Holly! Tonight. There's a message for you at the desk.'

And the line went dead.

Holly sat a long while; receiver clutched in her hand, and stared at the bedroom door as though it would suddenly open like Aladdin's cave and some genie would appear with an answer to the riddle, and tell her what she was going to do about it. The situation was macabre, farcical to say the least. A gang of kidnappers take a middle aged nonentity, hold her for a few hours, make no ransom demands and then decide out of the goodness of their wicked hearts to let her go? Sheer nonsense. Something lay behind it and she couldn't for the life of her figure out what it could be. Sitting there, however, was not going to produce an answer. She looked at the phone nestling in her hand and wished she could get hold of Thornton but there was no bedside telephone in a pensione and, anyway, he had rather overdone the party spirit and would probably be out like a light and worse than useless if his personal light was switched on again. Regretfully she replaced the phone on its cradle.

The first step obviously was to go downstairs and find out what was in this note. Wrong, the first step was to decide what to wear to go traipsing about foreign soil in the middle of the night not knowing where one was heading or what one was heading into. No gun this trip. A girl didn't take a loaded pistol along on a Riviera holiday. No black sweater, no black trousers, no balaclava; the gear she had used for breaking into the Spitskaya School of modelling that fateful night. Everything she had brought this trip was fashionable, or simply bright and pretty. No, hang on a tick, the black cocktail dress! What? It might be the south of France but it was December and a flimsy sleeveless low cut cocktail dress at three in the morning? She'd freeze to death. Besides, it was fashionable and had been an extremely expensive purchase and she had hardly time to wear it. The robes in the bathroom were white so they were useless. Holly was almost wringing her hands, it seemed hopeless, and then inspiration struck. Rita would have something she could borrow.

Rita at tea had been boastfully unable to resist pointing out, both by number and position, their luxurious accommodation so Holly, now in negligee and slippers, knew exactly where she was heading. What if Reg was awake to challenge her? She would tell him the truth. She was going to fetch his wife. Then why wasn't she doing that instead of prowling around their suite in the early hours? She was looking to borrow something to go out in. Oh, dear! Truth or no truth, it did sound pretty lame. Knowing Reg, he would most likely assume he'd caught a cat burglar in the act and have the French police called to arrest her but, by the time she had thought all this, she had reached the door to the Venables' suite. She paused for a moment, to take a quick look up and down the lighted corridor making sure no one was about, and tried the handle. The door was unlocked. She pushed it open, slipped inside, closed the door behind her and stood in the semi-dark.

There was light coming from the open bedroom door. She stood listening for sounds of life. They came from the same room as the light, loud and clear, the heaviest snoring she had ever heard, not that she had that much acquaintance with male snoring, especially elderly male snoring. Whenever she had experienced young male snoring a quick jolt from an elbow soon put a stop to it. It was to the source of light and sound she needed to go. She only hoped the snoring would continue while she was there. It did. Reg was flat out on his back and dead to the world. The war cries of a hundred lagered-up football fans trashing the room wouldn't have woken him. Holly went first to the wardrobe but found nothing suitable there. She decided to try the bathroom before having to start opening drawers and was in luck. Rita had discarded a tracksuit there; heavy, warm and, above all, dark in colour, Rita's favourite navy blue. It carried the scent of *Chanel No 5.*

Carrying the tracksuit and ignoring Reg who was still snoring heavily she made sure the coast was clear before hurrying back to her own room. She would need one of her belts to keep the trousers from dropping to her ankles; the hip measurement was broad enough for two of her or more. Then, having made a quick change, slipped on a pair of canvas shoes and flapping about a little like a half-filled sack, she headed for reception.

The night porter eyed her warily as she approached and reached the counter.

'You have a message for me,' she said, totally blasé, as though she was used to picking up messages at gone three in the morning.

'Did you see the person who brought it?' She asked as he passed it over. The man shook his head.

'It wasn't handed to you direct?'

He shook his head again. 'No, m'amselle. I was in the office back there. I thought I heard a noise and it was here on the counter when I came out, but whoever left it had gone.'

'Thank you,' she said and turned away. He watched her rip open the envelope. The message read – *go to your car now and start engine. Other car will blink headlights two times and move. You must follow. Do not think to call police. All will be well.* That was it. She crumpled up the paper and envelope and shoved both in a trouser pocket and, watched by the night porter, left the hotel.

CHAPTER 9

The back of a chair placed at a forty five degree angle had been jammed beneath the door handle of the bedroom in Marcel's apartment, just in case Rita woke up and decided to make a nuisance of herself. There seemed little likelihood of that happening though as, after the day's traumas, she was flat out on the bed and snoring almost as heavily as her distant spouse. Now and again the snoring stopped just long enough for her to give a little whimper, probably reacting to a bad dream. She also gave a shiver, drew up her legs and crossed her arms tight as the room was quite chilly. In endeavouring to shut the window all she had succeeded in doing was pull the rusting screws from its rotten frame and send it crashing into, presumably, a courtyard below. She hoped it hadn't hit anybody or, if it had, it was one of her three obnoxious captors, especially that Italian gigolo who she would never forgive as long as she lived for making her have amorous feelings towards him. She hadn't heard anything apart from the crash so presumed no one was in the line of fire and it couldn't have hit the Italian gigolo anyway because he had been set to guard her and was probably doing lewd things to himself in the front room while thinking of her, the beast. So she lay there and shivered.

Remembering the state of the apartment, especially the bidet and the toilet, and feeling quite grubby enough as it was, she definitely had no wish to get beneath the blankets no matter how cold it got even though the morning's summery dress she was wearing to bask in the southern sunshine was hardly enough to keep out a cool evening breeze let alone the chill of an early December morning.

Good grief, she thought just before she fell asleep. It will soon be Christmas and she hadn't done a thing about it. She had visions of a crowded Oxford Street and thought fondly of their empty home beneath the Heathrow fly path. "I wonder if I will be home for Christmas or what?" She thought. She didn't like to specify or speculate on the *what*. That made her think of the kids and wonder what they were up to. No good, she could be sure of that with which, chill or no chill, she managed to fitfully doze off. It had been a long day.

Nino was stretched out on the daybed in the front room. He had slipped off his shoes and thrown an overcoat over his shoulders but he too was not going to get right into bed, just in case something untoward took place. He never really knew whether he was awake, half awake, asleep, half asleep, dreaming he was awake or dreaming he was asleep as the hours passed but, like a mother sleeping with her child, had there been the slightest unusual sound or movement, he would have been instantly on the alert.

******

The farm consisted of a collection of dilapidated buildings that included a barn, a cowshed, sty, a chicken run and a small cottage under a steep slate roof. A tall crooked chimney ran up the middle of one side wall. The windows were small squares seemingly deeply imbedded in the thick stone walls and the whole building appeared even more dilapidated than the rest.

Inherited and inhabited by Marcel's ancient parents, the land was no more than a few hectares of fairly arid soil next to a wood of cypress, fir, and pine and located some kilometres inland in a small valley. A few straggly vines were sufficient to produce enough very dry enamel rotting vin ordinaire for the household: a pear tree, an almond, and a lemon survived in the stony ground. Half a dozen gnarled and twisted ancient olives, a species that never required water no matter how hot and dry the summer, supplied an abundance of fruit both to eat and for oil. Corn in the summer, some for the table but mainly to be used as animal and bird feed, a small vegetable patch and a herb garden protected from the weather by giant rosemary bushes and, finally, a row of sweet scented lavender meant the household was almost self-sufficient.

The place was run, if that was the word for it, gradually being run down would probably be more to the point, by Marcel's older brother, Laurent, who had never and was never likely to fly the nest. His one and only talent seemed to be an ability to shoot the smallest creature at the greatest distance which, added to chicken, duck, goose, rabbit, pork and, on occasion, wild boar, did stretch the family cooking pot but left the little valley totally bereft of birdsong.

To put it mildly, Laurent did not possess quite as many marbles as his younger sibling, who sometimes seemed to be missing quite a few of his own anyway. It obviously ran in the family. Their younger sister, Lydie, no longer that slip of a girl much courted in the neighbourhood but now an attractive, (unlike her brothers who with advancing years seemed to want to emulate the olive trees) woman, was the only one with a normally functioning brain and had wisely opted out and married a man from the Morvan which was somewhere her family wouldn't particularly want to visit, not even to see grandchildren, so she was safely shot of them.

She did her filial duty keeping in touch by the occasional letter including snapshots. Fortunately the grandchildren she produced took after her and her husband and not after the Malherbe clan. Never was there a family more aptly named and had any of them threatened to descend on her, she would have found any excuse to keep them away, or emigrated before their arrival. She had visited her brother in Marseilles a couple of times simply because she had foolishly, at one time when he was in serious trouble, (he was her brother after all) lent him money and there seemed to be no indication of it ever being returned.

Nothing untoward or overly exciting ever happened on the Malherbe farm. The seasons came, the seasons went, each with the work they entailed. The folk grew older and the older they grew the more aches and pains were sent to try them. God willing, one day the aches and pains would pass and the parent, Laurent senior for one couldn't wait for that day. Great events, unless seen on their small black and white television set, if the reception was good and there was no power cut, passed them by. The latest they knew was that General de Gaulle had resigned as president of France, not long after he had insisted most emphatically that he was going to see out his term. Just like a politician, they thought, saying one thing, doing another and, shook their heads, never realising, how could they without being psychic? the miserable old thorn in England's side would be dead the following year and, much to everyone's surprise, the earth didn't stop revolving.

So it was a great surprise when early one December morning and while still dark not long before Christmas, two cars, a battered green Peugeot and an ancient but shiny well preserved Mercedes Benz pulled up in front of the house, a man they did not immediately recognise in the dark as the Mercedes' powerful headlights had half blinded them before being switched off, got out of each car and between them lifted out an unconscious young lady in a blue tracksuit ten sizes too large for her and holding her up between them advanced towards the house only to be stopped by Laurent the younger, who had heard them coming and stood levelling a twelve bore double-barrelled shotgun in their direction. Old the gun might be but, like the Merc, lovingly looked after down the years, cleaned and oiled, and still lethal, especially in the trigger happy hands of one who was not in possession of all his marbles and who was being pushed forward by two shivering in their nightdresses myopic and very nervous geriatrics.

A large, shaggy, flea-bitten hound by the name of Max, equally geriatric, should have incessantly barked a warning but, having been chained to his kennel, (a tea chest covered with a piece of tarpaulin to keep out the worst of the weather), for so long and with nothing to keep him interested he had given up on life and this exciting episode had really come too late; so he merely watched the proceedings through rheumy eyes and gave a pathetic couple of flicks with his tail that raised a little cloud of dust on his kennel floor. Laurent had decided he really ought to be put down but strangely, for one to whom animal life was as nothing, he couldn't bring himself to do it. He had got the dog as a pup and it was once his hunting companion after all and the closest creature he would ever call friend.

'Who are you?' Madame Malherbe squealed. 'Be careful! Don't come any closer or my son will shoot you.'

'Don't be silly, maman, it's me, Marcel.'

'Marcel? Is that you?'

'I've just said so, haven't I?'

'Who's the other one? The one with you? Stop there!' she shrieked. 'Don't come any closer! How do I know you're who you say you are? I can't see you properly.'

They stopped.

'She always was an idiot,' Marcel whispered to Alphonse, 'now she's gone right round the bloody twist.'

'What are you whispering about?' the old girl cried, 'and who is that other one? The one between you?'

'I tell you, if someone wanted to make a film today about the French revolution she would be a dead ringer for Madame Defarge.'

'She's your mother, you shouldn't talk about her like that.'

'Bullshit! I'm only stating a fact and this woman is getting heavier and heavier. I'm going to let go in a minute or have a heart attack.'

'It's your own fault,' Alphonse hissed. 'How much of that stuff did you give her? You're not a medical man. You don't know what you're doing. You could have killed her.'

'Will you shut up, just for one fucking minute?' He turned back to face the door. 'Listen you lot!' he shouted to his family still guarding their house. 'Are you going to let us in or are you not?'

'Not till you tell us who the woman is,' the old girl replied.

'Someone we kidnapped,' Marcel said.

There was the sound of laughter from monsieur Malherbe, the first sound he had made. He hadn't actually wanted to say anything because he didn't have his teeth in and this always embarrassed him in front of non-family members.

'That's good,' he said. 'That's rich that is. Kidnapped!' His voice had reverted to the piping treble of his pre-adolescence. 'You wake us up at this hour of the morning to make stupid jokes about kidnapping? What kind of a son are you?'

'It's not a joke. It's a fact and you would have to get up soon to milk the cow anyway.'

'We don't have a cow anymore. She died.'

'Goat?'

'Yes, we have goats.'

'Good. Can we come in now?'

'Yes, I suppose so. Laurent, mama, let them in.' The old man turned away and slouched back into the house to go and look for his teeth. He wasn't too sure where he had left them.

Laurent lowered the gun and smiled for the first time. He did have teeth in his mouth though they weren't exactly in tip-top condition.

'I knew you would come to no good, living in Marseilles.' Madame Malherbe had to have the last word.

******

Nino yawned, stretched, and lay for a moment wondering what had woken him. He threw off the overcoat and sat up, listening. There was no sound from the bedroom. Maybe it was a dream that woke him. Maybe it was a full bladder. That was the trouble with drinking so much before going to bed. You're up and down all night long; up and down, up and down.

He got off the bed and, in stockinged feet, made his slow and unsteady way to the wall and groped for the light switch, then padded over to the bedroom door, placed his ear against it and listened. Nothing. He didn't like that. Surely she would be making some sort of noise if she were asleep? He had heard the snores earlier on. What if there was something wrong with her? What if she had died? Would they face a murder rap? Manslaughter at least. Well who would be responsible? They could point the finger at Marcel. She would be found in his apartment after all. He didn't like these thoughts. They were giving him the willies. Nino was highly superstitious. Bad thoughts bring bad results.

Hmn ... Maybe it would be best to let sleeping dogs lie as the saying has it and he had called her a dog. He was a bit sorry about that now. In fact he had grown to quite like her. There are dogs and dogs and some dogs are likeable and some are lovable even. Though he wasn't on the whole a dog man himself this one was definitely quite likeable. He hoped she wouldn't be trouble. He would hate for anything to happen to her. He moved over to the table and searched among the debris for a pack that might contain a cigarette. There was none. In the ashtray he found the remains of one that still had a couple of draws in it. Carefully, it would be too easy to split the now bone-dry paper; he unfolded where it had been bent double on being stubbed out. He lit it and coughed as he inhaled the first drag. It was quite a violent cough; enough to bring tears to his eyes and it didn't immediately stop. He felt he was choking. He sat down abruptly in the nearest chair. Shit! That must surely have woken her.

The cigarette was stubbed out a second time. He wasn't going to risk another drag. After a few moments he calmed down and went to the sink for a mouthful of water, stood leaning against it, surveying the pile of dirty dishes, then he looked over his shoulder at the bedroom door on the other side of the room. Maybe he had just better check that all was well. On the other hand maybe he just ought to go back to sleep and forget all about it. He dithered for a while and then tiptoed back across the room. As he was in stockinged feet there was no need for him to tiptoe but somehow it was automatic. He listened again with ear against the door. There wasn't a sound.

Carefully he removed the back of the chair from beneath the door handle and put the chair gently to one side. Then he slowly opened the door. There was a slight creak, which made him wince and stop for a second but, on the whole, the manoeuvre was fairly silent.

He entered the room and crept silently up to the bed. He had left the door open so that a shaft of light from the front room shone down on her and he could see Rita was fast asleep. All was well. He turned to go back but thought, while he was there he might as well have that piss he had almost forgotten about but the pressure of which was now making itself urgently felt and there were too many dirty dishes to do it in the sink. He crossed over to the toilet, having decided if he aimed for the porcelain and avoided the water he would also avoid waking up the sleeping dog. There was just enough light to see by in that dingy corner of the room.

Rita opened her eyes wide and could not believe what she was seeing. The man had no shame. He was actually in her presence going to … going to … she couldn't even bring herself to think it. What she did think of doing, as he had his back to her, which was some small gesture towards common decency she supposed, was to get off the bed and creep silently out of the room while he concentrated on what he was doing. It was her turn to tiptoe and she had plenty of light to see by.

Reaching the front room she carefully closed the bedroom door and replaced the chair. She thought it must have been there previously because she had earlier rattled the door to mime she wanted a glass of water when Nino opened it. It had taken a couple of minutes for Nino to close the door, fetch the water, return to open the door and hold out the glass for her to take. The back of the chair was in his other hand and when he closed the door she realised where he had placed it. She had given the door a push just to make certain and it hadn't budged and it wasn't going to budge now, not if she had done it right.

She headed for the passage, the front door, and freedom and it was not until she was half way across the room she realised she had left her shoes in the bedroom. Oh, well, nothing for it, she would just have to go barefoot. She was halfway down the hall and right alongside it when the telephone rang. Rita let out a shriek that virtually rocked the building. It alerted Nino, just shaking himself off, to the fact that his prisoner had escaped. He ran for the door only to find he couldn't move it. Meanwhile Rita stood in the hall a quivering screaming mess. Eventually she pulled herself together enough to lift the receiver.

'Help!' she tried to yell but it only came out as a hoarse whisper that turned into a whimper.

'Hello? Hello? Who is that?' the voice on the other end politely enquired.

It took a moment or two for Rita to realise it was not a French voice.

'Hello?' she said. 'Help me please. I've been kidnapped.'

'Who are you?' the voice asked.

'Rita Venables. I'm the wife of Detective Inspector Reginald Venables. Oh, what does it matter whose wife I am? I'm ... I'm ... hello? Hello?' But the line had gone dead.

The rest of the building though seemed to have come to violent life. There was a hammering on the front door and a bashing on the bedroom door as Nino tried to break out. Rita dropped the phone and stood in the middle of the passage, her hands over her ears, the tears streaming down her face, heart thumping, a quivering jelly and not knowing what to do. Should she make for the front door? Who was out there? They were strangers. They could be dangerous. She was a stranger. She couldn't speak the language. They could molest her. Where was her Reg? Where were the police? Were they not out looking for her? Where was Holly who was supposed to have come to fetch her? Why had these men taken her and what was going to happen?

What happened was that the hammering on the front door continued unabated and Nino finally managed to break out of the bedroom, toss aside a now shattered chair and hurl himself in her direction, stubbing his toes on a table leg on his way and giving out a yell of pain that added to her blood curdling scream as she saw him performing a sort of anguished pirouette in her direction.

He hobbled towards her, flaming mad and desperately trying to calm himself down. It would not do to have murder on his mind, not after his earlier thoughts on the subject. She sat down in the middle of the passage defying him to move her and, when he leant down to take her arms, she hid them as much as she could behind her back. He tried lifting her by the elbows but she had become a dead weight. It was just as well he did not have his knife with him for threatening her with it would have raised even more screaming. Meanwhile the knocking on the front door continued together with the sound of voices.

He went to the door and opened it a crack to find half the residents of the block standing on the landing and the stairs. Nearly all were in their night attire. A couple had pulled trousers on over their pyjama bottoms. The French mostly had their wives with them. The immigrants made sure their wives, sisters and daughters remained safe and invisible inside their apartments and it was a large, hairy, and bellicose Algerian dockworker and small time smuggler of hash who now faced Nino, wanting to know on behalf of them all what the fuck was going on? He tried to peep into the hall but Nino's body prevented his getting a good view. There was a woman sitting on the floor, the Algerian could see that, but it did not really tell him much.

Nino had to think fast. His first reaction had been to tell the man to go to hell. Whatever was happening it had nothing to do with any of them, but then he thought it might be best if he were conciliatory and gave some sort of an explanation no matter how far fetched. He lifted his hands, palms out, making small pushing movements in order to quieten them down which, as they were all on tenterhooks as to what the ruckus was about, was quickly achieved. It could be blood was already spilled, not that that was a novelty in the area, but they didn't want to be woken in the early hours of the morning for sweet f.a.

Nino blew a kiss to one of his favourites who happened to be standing quite close, a gesture she appreciated but that was met by a low growl from the others meaning get on with it, so he pursed his lips and nodded, not realising just how like Mussolini he looked. He heard a loud sob from behind but it had given him time to think so he grinned and said, 'You remember Marcel's crazy sister don't you?'

They turned to look at each other. Some raised their eyebrows, one or two shrugged, others, after some coaching, nodded. The fearsome dockworker said: 'No.'

Nino stared at him, very hard, but the man was not going to back down.

'Of course you do,' Nino insisted. 'Lydie. You must remember her. Or maybe you weren't around when she came to visit. And you know why she came to visit don't you?'

A woman had poked her head around the door just long enough to get a glimpse of the pathetic bundle still flopped all over the passage floor.

'I remember Lydie,' she said. 'That's not Lydie.' She turned to face the mob. 'I remember Lydie because she came to borrow something off me, I can't remember what it was exactly… '

'If you can't remember what it was your memory isn't worth shit,' Nino said scornfully.

'Hey hey hey! Watch your language,' the hairy one growled. 'There are women and children here.'

Nino couldn't see any children, at least not those young enough to be clinging to mother's skirts, and those older would in all probabilities have a vocabulary far worse than his.

'I tell you, this is Marcel's crazy sister and she is here,' he dropped his voice to a whisper, glanced over his shoulder for a second and then faced front again and continued with, 'to try and collect the money Marcel owes her.'

'What money?' someone asked.

'Maybe she won the lottery someone suggested,' a remark which was greeted by a ripple of laughter.

'The money she lent him,' Nino said raising his voice again to ride the laughter. 'Twice she lent him money … '

'More fool her,' another voice chipped in.

'Exactly,' Nino said. 'That's why she's behaving like crazy because she knows she will never get it back.'

'Where is Marcel?' the dockworker asked. 'Why are you here in the flat with her?'

'Marcel had to visit his parents. His father is sick.'

'The whole family is sick.'

'I'll mention to Marcel you said that.'

The perpetrator of the remark hurriedly disappeared behind friendly shoulders.

Nino was saved from further questioning by the sound of an approaching police siren. Visits from the police were fairly rare in this non-too salubrious neighbourhood of Marseilles. Everyone stood stock-still to listen. It would pass them by. It could not possibly be coming to their building. No one could remember the last time a patrol car stopped at their building but this one did. Now who in hell called the cops? If the culprit was ever discovered, he or she would most certainly face social ostracism if nothing worse. Nobody in their right mind would dream of calling the cops.

There was a knocking on the downstairs door. Heads peered over the stairwell railings. An ancient crone on the ground floor who was obviously unable to mount the stairs and join in with the neighbours three floors up but had been craning her neck trying to catch what was happening and now had a definite and painful crick in it went to answer the knock. Nino stood by the slightly open apartment door wondering what kind of a story he was going to cook up to save his own skin. He could hear voices down below, but strain as he might, he couldn't make out what was being said. It was the dockworker, who saved his bacon by shouting down the well, 'It was nothing, a family row. It's all over now.' He turned back to smile at Nino as much as to say "You owe me" but Nino had disappeared and the door was shut. The crowd dispersed disappointed. On the ground floor the woman returned to her apartment and the police, probably much relieved that they were not required to interfere, left, closing the street door behind them.

Inside the apartment Nino stood looking down at the pathetic figure still sprawled on the floor. He knelt down and gently lifted her tear-stained face, took a hankie from his pocket and wiped her cheeks. He smiled at her, took her hands and gently helped her to her feet then he stood in front of her and shook his head from side to side, waggled a finger in front of her meaning naughty naughty and slid the same finger across his throat meaning don't do it again. Then, replacing the dangling receiver on its rest, he led her back to the bedroom, closed the door and heaving a sigh of relief, looked around for another chair and something to drink.

******

They were sitting in Marcel's car in the hotel car park, waiting and growing impatient. Marcel was tapping the steering wheel with the fingers of both hands.

'Where the hell is she?' he growled. 'She should have been here by now.' He tried to look at his watch (the clock on the dashboard hadn't worked for years) but in the dark it was impossible to see and he did not want to risk lighting a match.

Alphonse just sat. He was much more laid back and patient. She would be with them soon enough, he was sure of that.

'What if she's not in her room?' Marcel said. 'She wouldn't hear the phone.'

'Why shouldn't she be in her room? Whose room do you think she's in at this hour of the morning?' Alphonse turned to look at Marcel's profile as he stared out of the windscreen, straight ahead, waiting for Holly to appear. But it was not Holly who put in an appearance. A figure emerged from the shadow of the hotel and advanced warily towards the parked cars, obviously looking for something as the head turned from side to side.

Marcel who was about to risk lighting a cigarette thrust it hastily behind his ear and whispered. 'Can you see who that is?'

'Yes,' Alphonse answered, 'it's that Sicilian boy, what's his name?'

'Luigi?'

'That's the one.'

'What do you suppose he's up to?'

'No good, that's for sure, not at this hour of the morning. I reckon he's after breaking into cars.'

And that was certainly what it looked like. Luigi, in dark street clothes as opposed to his hotel uniform, had stopped by the Mercedes and now looked all around to make sure no one was about before he went any further. He was totally unaware of the two in the car watching his every move but, before the boy could make another one, something else disturbed him. He left the Merc and moved away to crouch down behind another car, this time a stately Bentley.

It wasn't only Marcel and Alphonse observing the boy's actions. A figure was standing in the shadows who saw it all but was himself unseen and never made a move.

Then Holly appeared and made her way to the Mercedes. She didn't look around to see which car was the one she was destined to follow but got into the Mercedes and started the engine. Immediately behind her the green Peugeot's headlights flicked twice and then switched on again as the car moved slowly passed her. Looking straight ahead she put the Mercedes into gear and followed.

Luigi came out from crouching behind the Bentley. In the Mercedes' headlights he had noted the Peugeot's number. He spat on the ground and bent down to pick up the piece of paper that had fallen from Holly's pocket. Still observed by the man in the shadows and muttering the number over and over in case he should forget it before he had time to write it down, he went back into the hotel. The man moved out of the shadows and headed for a car. He glanced at his watch. He would make a couple of phone calls when he got back to Nice and then drive on to Marseilles. He should be there by daybreak.

******

Nino woke up and squinted at his watch. Had he heard a knock at the front door or had he dreamt it? The room was still fairly dark and he couldn't make out the position of the hands so he got up and went to switch on the light. He saw it was just gone six and there was definitely a knock on the apartment door, not too loud but definitely there. Who would be knocking at this hour of the morning? He slipped the watch off his wrist and held it to his ear to listen in case it had stopped but it was ticking away quite happily. It was an old wind-up watch that he inherited from his grandfather and the tick though not loud was, if he listened really hard, just discernable. He slipped the watch back on his wrist and looked hard at the bedroom door. Everything seemed in order and he padded off down the passage to answer the knock. Once behind the door he paused for a moment. Should he open it or shouldn't he? Had it not been so early in the morning he would, as he was wont to put it, have put his brain into gear and thought to ask who it was. Instead, he assumed it was probably the others returning, unlocked and opened the door and was met by a straight right that not only laid him out for the count but sent him flying virtually the length of the passage. Assumptions can be dangerous.

******

Reg woke up and for a long while simply had no idea where he was. Gradually the fog cleared and he sat up only to fall back with a groan. His head was not his own or, at least, he wished it weren't. After a while he tried again; only this time instead of sitting up he rolled slowly off the bed, knees touching the floor first, and then leaned on the edge for a while as if in prayer before using it to hoist himself to unsteady feet and weave his way to the bathroom.

Having first performed the necessary, steadying himself with one hand against the wall, he moved over to the washbasin, peered at himself in the mirror and groaned again, if anything an even deeper groan than the one before. His eyes were red, his jowls were green and when he went to pick up his toothbrush because his mouth tasted simply foul, his hand trembled almost uncontrollably. Swearing he would never touch another drop of liquor in his life, he dropped the toothbrush: in his current state he would more than likely brush his gums instead of his teeth. Turning on the cold-water tap he filled a tumbler, eventually managing, without knocking out a tooth as the glass reached his mouth, to rinse out his mouth with what was left after the spillage.

He returned to the bedroom, plonked himself down on the bed, and dialled reception. Charles Boyer answered.

'Good morning, inspector. How may I help you?'

'Is there ...' Reg croaked, then cleared his throat. 'Is there any news of my wife?'

'I have not heard anything, inspector. Wait one moment.'

Reg waited. Charles was obviously asking around before coming back with, 'No, I am sorry, inspector, there is no news. Oh, one moment!' There was another pause and then, 'Inspector Venables, I am informed there has been a phone call to say she is at this moment on her way back to the hotel. I am sure you will be most relieved to hear it.'

'Thank you,' Reg said. 'Thank you so much.' He put down the phone and burst into tears.

******

Holly opened her eyes and lay quite still for a while before turning her head to survey her surroundings. She was in a room, a bedroom obviously as she was lying beneath a quilt on a double bed with a substantial but plain wooden headboard. There was the faint scent of lavender emanating from a sachet next to her pillow and from somewhere she could hear a cock crow.

The room had once been painted pink but damp stains had caused some of it to turn a pale brown in strange almost Rorschach type patterns. There were half a dozen assorted wooden chairs and a bedside cabinet. Nothing else. The door seemed flimsy enough; vertical hand-sawn wooden planks braced together, a latch and no lock. There was one small square window letting in a little early morning light.

The ceiling was low and flaky and a central light hung on an old-fashioned twin flex. The floor was stone with only a couple of small rag rugs as covering, one on each side of the bed. She could almost feel the chill rising off it. She stroked the quilt and admired the intricate pattern of roses on a black background. It was obviously hand stitched and definitely collectible. It was nineteenth century more than like and, as genuine folk art, it would probably go for quite a fair sum in any big city flea market. She snuggled down into its warmth and tried to recap on events. What could she remember?

She remembered reading the note at reception and leaving the hotel. She remembered getting into the car, starting it up and then … oh yes! The car with the flashing headlights, it was becoming clearer now. She followed the car out of the car park and stayed behind it as they drove through Nice and kept on going, through Cannes and kept on going. There was no traffic on the road at that time of the morning so there was no problem in keeping up with the green car ahead. She could see in her headlights there were two occupants and she had already memorised the number for possible future use. It was not until they turned off onto a minor road and headed inland that Holly suddenly had grave doubts as to exactly what was going on here. Rita had said she was in a town. They had passed through two. This did not smell good. In fact it smelled decidedly rattish.

They continued on for a couple of kilometres until they were passing through a copse and the Peugeot disappeared around a sharp bend. Holly stopped and switched of the engine and the lights, sat for a couple of seconds and then slipped out of the car, leaving the door open. She stepped over a ditch and disappeared into the trees at the side of the road.

It took a short while for Marcel and Alphonse to realise the Mercedes' headlights were no longer behind them. Marcel pulled up and they sat for a few more minutes waiting in case she might catch up but there was still no sign of her.

'What do you suppose she's doing?' Marcel finally broke the silence. Alphonse responded with a shrug. He had had a premonition that this one spelt trouble.

'We'd best go back and see,' Marcel suggested. Alphonse turned to look at his companion and then turned out front again. He was not going to hazard any suggestion as to their next course of action.

'Okay,' Marcel said. The road was a bit narrow for a three point turn so he put the car into reverse and they drove slowly back the way they had just come, once or twice nearly coming to grief in the ditch but finally in the rear view mirror sighting the Mercedes standing empty, the driver's door open, and no sign of Holly. Marcel stopped the car and nudged Alphonse who got out and cautiously approached the Mercedes. This was where he wished he had a gun, just to scare her a little. He didn't want to take out his knife. Accidents can too easily happen.

He walked around the car; stood looking into the dark beneath the trees but could see nothing. There wasn't a sound. The quiet was almost ominous. He looked towards the Peugeot and shrugged, raising both arms and shaking his head to indicate he hadn't a clue, then he returned for some reason to examining the Mercedes. That was when she pounced.

She had him in a half nelson flat over the bonnet when she felt the prick of the needle and knew no more.

CHAPTER 10

Thornton didn't know who it was who seemed to be forever barring him from using the bathroom on his own floor whenever he needed it but, having again made his way down the stairs to the floor below, he had beaten hatchet-face by about a half metre and was the subject of silently mouthed imprecations and Provençal curses as, clutching her tatty toilet bag, she turned away from the bathroom door. He studied himself in the mirror over the sink and started to lather up preparatory to shaving. But the operation was only half finished when he heard Madame Violette calling him as she started to climb the stairs.

'Meester Keeng! Meester Keeng!'

He backed away from the basin and, shaving brush in hand, opened the bathroom door and called back. 'I'm in here!'

'Telephon!' she called, grateful she didn't have to climb any higher and regaining her breath by stopping her ascent and, with one hand on her chest, leaning on the banisters. Thornton walked to the landing so that he could look down at her.

'Telephon for you,' she said looking up at him.

'Do you know who it is?' Thornton asked, thinking Holly would be the only person to call him at the Garibaldi. 'Is it Miss Day?'

'Non. It is a man.'

'Oh?' He stood irresolute for a moment and was about to suggest she ask whoever it was if he could call back in a few minutes when he heard the bathroom door slam and, turning to look, saw the shadow of hatchet face hang her robe on the hook behind the door.

'Damn!' he said.

'Comment?'

There was nothing for it but to go down to the phone and find out who it was.

'All right,' he called, 'I'm coming.' He looked at the shaving brush in his hand and, smilingly, shook his head. Hatchet face had beaten him to the draw. He started off down the stairs.

Thornton had tried using an electric shaver, a number of different makes in fact, but they always brought him out in a barber's rash, the painful consequence of having a delicate skin. With a safety razor and plenty of foam the result was always a cheek as smooth as a baby's bottom. Using an electric razor he could have continued shaving all the way down the stairs but, by the time he reached the phone, the foam had dried on his cheeks and he knew that was going to have a disastrous effect. Oh, the problems created by Miss Holly Day not booking him into that first class hotel. Still, the pensione was a lot more homely and comfortable than many an English boarding house he supposed so be grateful for small mercies. He picked up the phone.

'Hello?'

'Thornton, old chap. Hi!'

'And a hi to you?'

'Well, good morning if you'd rather, or bon matin even.'

'Who is this?'

'It's me, Taps.'

Thornton should have recognised the boyish enthusiasm if not the voice.

'Oh, yes, well hi again, Taps. What can I do for you?'

'You can meet me for a drink.'

'Taps, it's …' He looked at his wrist and remembered he had taken off his watch to go to the bathroom. He looked around but there was no clock in sight.

'What time is it?' he asked.

'It's just gone nine-thirty. You should have been up hours ago, Thornton, it's a beautiful day.' The boyish enthusiasm was still coming through loud and clear.

'Taps, give me one good reason why I should meet you for a drink at nine-thirty in the morning?'

'All right, breakfast then, say in an hour?'

'No. I'm supposed to make arrangements to meet Holly. Anyway, what is this sudden palsy-walsy act that you want me to have drinks with you on this bright and breezy morning? Is it your birthday or something?'

'Don't be like that, Thornton. If you really want to know it's to talk. I want to hear your side of the Spitskaya affair.'

'You WHAT?'

'Yes. You heard me right, old chum. I've heard Reg Venables' side of the story and somehow it doesn't quite ring true.'

'What are you talking about? You swallowed it wholesale and

176

you wrote it up wholesale. Holly read me the entire article. She wastes her money subscribing to your stupid and, if I may say so, very expensive and not worth the money magazine, and I promise you I nearly puked.'

'I'm not that bad a writer, Thornton.'

'No, unfortunately you're not. You're quite good actually.'

'Thank you.'

'It's the pretentiousness of the periodical that makes me want to puke. But anyway, your whole piece was a tissue of lies from beginning to end. Well, almost.'

'That is why I want to hear your side of the story.' Silence. 'Thornton? Thornton, are you still there?'

'I'm thinking.'

'Come on, Thornton, be a sport. We can resurrect the whole episode … '

'Episode? Is that what it's called?'

'All right, call it whatever you want to call it. Now are you going to meet me or not? We don't have all that much time. It's back to dreary old England soon you know.'

'How did you know where to find me?'

'Hamish told me.'

'Hamish?'

'I believe he tucked you up in bed the other night?'

'Hardly.'

'Well anyway, it was Hamish. So, do we have a date?'

Intrigued by the possibility of putting the record straight (he could just imagine old Reg's face if it were to happen) he decided to agree.

'All right, if that's how you want to put it. Maybe we can create an episode.'

'Good. About eleven then? I'll be at the *Place Rossetti*, as close to the church as I can find a table. You shouldn't miss me but if I see you looking lost, I'll wave.'

'Holler "cooee!" while you're about it,' Thornton said and put down the phone. Then thought, while he was there, he might as well call Holly. She should be awake by now. Madame Violette was standing behind him looking slightly quizzical.

'Excusez mois, madame.' Wearing only a pair of slacks, Thornton indicated his bare chest.

Madame Violette smiled broadly. 'C'est formidable!' she purred.

'Would it be all right if I were to make a call, madame?' he asked her.

'Be my guest,' she replied.

'I am your guest,' he said.

She shrieked with laughter and gave him a friendly punch on the arm. Thornton winced and rubbed it. She thought he was joking but she didn't know the power of her punch or the sharpness of her knuckles. Fortunately it was not the hand on which she wore her rings the size of knuckledusters. She turned and hobbled away still chuckling to herself.

Holly did not answer the phone. She could have been in the shower of course but eventually Charles came back on the line.

'I'm sorry, Mister King, Miss Day does not appear to be in her room. Would you like me to have her paged?'

'No, don't worry,' Thornton said, 'I'll try again later,' and he put down the phone.

He mooched moodily up the stairs wondering where Holly could be and why, after all this time, Taps suddenly wanted to hear his side of the story. He reached the second floor landing to find the bathroom door still closed but he marched towards it all the same and, as he reached the end of the corridor, the door opened and a flushed and triumphant hatchet face waltzed passed him smiling broadly. She probably uses carbolic and a scourer, Thornton thought entering a steam filled bathroom to finish his ablutions. He turned on the hot tap. The water was cold.

*****

Reg was waiting impatiently for her outside the hotel. He wished she would hurry up. He wanted his breakfast. He was shaved showered and shampooed, had even used a conditioner, something he normally wouldn't dream of doing, adding a couple of squirts of Rita's deodorant for good measure and never did a day dawn brighter than this one. He didn't see who it was who returned her to him because he was too busy watching her bedraggled figure as she approached and, as soon as she was within reach, he gathered her in his arms, something he had not done for a long time. There was the sound of clapping from behind and he turned to see the hotel staff, led by Charles Boyer, applauding madly.

He wasn't sure if Rita's sniffing was emotion at their reunion or because she was taken by surprise at getting a whiff of her own deodorant

******

Inspector Leroux eased himself into the chair behind his desk and took a sip of his first cup of office coffee. In an endeavour to clear a thick head he had already, before leaving home, drunk enough coffee to sink a battleship, but somehow there was never anything like that first sip in the office; strong, hot, and black, accompanied by the first long draw on a Gauloise. Out of respect for his wife he did not smoke at home. The apartment was small and despite wide-open windows, aerosol, and pot pourri the stale smell of cigarette smoke lingered and she complained of her bronchial condition and she was sure it contributed to her migraines.

Mathieu entered the office with a piece of paper in his hand.

'Morning chief,' bright as a button he greeted Leroux with easy familiarity.

'What's put you in such a good mood?' Leroux wanted to know.

'Something really weird has happened,' Mathieu said.

'So what's new? Something weird happens every day, every hour of my life.'

'No, this is really weird.'

'Oh, yes? They found the crew of the Marie Celeste.'

'What's the Marie Celeste?'

'Forget it. What has happened that's so weird?'

'There was a fracas in an apartment in Marseilles last night, in the early hours of this morning that is.'

'You call that weird? What's so weird about that? It would be weird if there weren't a fracas. In fact it would go down in the Guinness Book of Records. Have you ever seen that book, Mathieu?'

Mathieu shook his head.

'A quite remarkable publication.'

'No, the weird bit is that it was reported to the police.'

'Reported? You mean a citizen of Marseilles who had nothing to do with the fracas, as you put it, actually called the police to report it? That ... is weird.' He took another sip of his coffee and another draw of his Gauloise.

'No, that's not the really weird bit.'

'Then what is? Spit it out, man!'

179

'The phone call came from Nice.'

Leroux looked up at Mathieu as if the man had gone mal fini.'

'Let me get this straight. There is a fracas in an apartment in Marseilles, hundreds of kilometres away, and it is reported to the police by a telephone call from Nice? That's not weird, my friend, that's crazy. Was the caller psychic?'

'It's weird,' Mathieu said, 'but there it is.' He laid the piece of paper on the desk.

'It can be explained quite logically,' Leroux said. 'Someone in the building phoned the someone in Nice and got them to call the police in Marseilles. That way the informant in Marseilles would not be directly involved and there would be no come-back.'

'Really? I don't know how they did that because the call came from a public phone.'

'Hmph! Easily explained,' Leroux said. 'You know how devious the criminal mind can be. Whoever it was in Marseilles who telephoned the caller in Nice, at his home mark you, then told him to go to a public phone in order to call the police, just in case the call was traced, which it was.' Leroux was determined to get rid of this word *weird*. Weird would probably mean a lot of extra paper work. He failed lamentably because Mathieu went on, 'Not only that but what is even weirder is, it was followed up later by the same caller evidently wanting to know what had happened. The caller from Nice I mean.'

'Yes, of course, of course. What was his interest? I am presuming the caller was male?'

'Yes. What his interest was is anyone's guess but he wasn't French. That is, he spoke French evidently but with some sort of foreign accent.'

'And what was he told, on this second call?'

'That a patrol car had gone to the address but the men were informed the row was a domestic so they left it at that.'

'Much relieved I guess not to have to do anything. What was his response?'

'Who?'

'The caller of course! The caller!'

Mathieu shrugged. 'Evidently he rang off.'

'They didn't enquire who he was?'

This was met by another shrug. Leroux shook his head, pondering on what he had just heard.

'Who lives in that apartment?'

'Someone by the name of Marcel Malherbe.'

'Do we have anything on him?'

Mathieu shook his head.

'Marseilles thought you would be interested though, the call having come from Nice.'

'Yes, get on to them. Ask them to send somebody back to check. I don't like this at all. It's got something to do with the Venables woman I'm sure.'

'Not really,' Mathieu said. 'She's back.'

'Back? Back? Back where?'

'Back in Beaulieu at their hotel. Inspector Venables telephoned a moment ago to say so, just before you got in.'

'This gets crazier and crazier. Call Marseilles. I want to know all about that apartment.'

Mathieu nodded and left the office. Leroux lit another Gauloise. His coffee had gone cold.

******

As she had obviously been transported back into the nineteenth century, Holly thought there would be something under the bed she could use. She rolled to the side and flopped over to take an upside down peek. Yes, sure enough, there it was in all its glory, a china giant prettily decorated with flowers both outside and in, a design that would have done credit to Fragonard. She would not have to ask for the toilet and most probably have to straddle a Turkish one or plonk herself down on a wooden seat over a cesspit, neither of which appealed to her.

Having performed the necessary and shoved the pot back under the bed, she found her shoes and, slipping them on, made for the door, lifted the latch and, to her surprise found it unlocked. In fact, as she examined it, she found it had no lock either side. When she stepped into the next room she realised why. There was a strange looking beast seated at the table lovingly cleaning with a pull-thru one barrel of a double barrelled twelve bore shotgun. He looked up and gave her a somewhat shy black and white smile.

'Bonjour, m'amselle.' He growled.

Holly nodded and took a quick look around the room.

'Would m'amselle care for some breakfast? Some café crème

maybe? Maybe a frappé? Or a tisane?'

'I don't suppose by any chance you would have some English tea, would you?'

Laurent looked slightly baffled by this. Is a tisane not a tea?

'Black tea?' Holly ventured. 'I could die for a cup of real tea.'

Without a word Laurent laid down his shotgun, rose from the table and left the room. She heard him outside shouting for his mother, his voice growing fainter as he moved away. Going to the front door she saw him disappear into the barn. She noted the two cars parked close by, one behind the other and wondered if she should make a dash for it before the man returned. Loud voices proceeded from the depths of the barn and, before she could make a move, the man reappeared trailing an ancient crone who advanced on her with surprising speed. Holly stepped to one side as the woman approached and passed her without the slightest acknowledgement to disappear into the house. A grinning Laurent followed, nodding his head, which probably meant maman would see to it that Holly got her tea.

Holly was still outside all on her own. This was crazy, she thought. If I have been kidnapped, which seems to be the case, why have I the freedom of the place? Or that is how it would seem. No locks on doors? No guards? She only noticed Max in his kennel when he flicked his tail, raising the dust a little. Until he moved he could have been a pile of old carpet.

'Hello, boy,' she said, causing another wag to take place. 'My goodness, you are a mess, aren't you?' Max must have taken this as a compliment because the tail wagging became quite energetic. Holly decided she wouldn't stroke him, not because she was afraid but because she wasn't sure where she was going to wash her hands afterwards. Max watched her move on and the tail wagging stopped.

She strolled over to the cars. Ignoring the Peugeot she looked at the dashboard of the Mercedes. Naturally the key was missing. She could maybe take a walk up the track behind the cars and set out to do just that when she remembered why she was there, or the reason she thought she was there – Rita!

She turned and went back to the house.

******

Thornton reached the *Place Rossetti* and stood in front of the

182

church looking around at the packed square. Every table appeared occupied but sure enough Taps was seated at one close by and waved a languid arm in Thornton's direction. The private investigator assumed a Hollywood saunter as he went to join the young journalist who was going to turn him into a household name and bring in multi-millionaire clients urgently seeking his expertise and, what is more, paying handsomely for it.

Taps, who was already sitting with a cappuccino in front of him, didn't bother to rise but, with the same languid arm, indicated the chair next to him. He had rather beautiful hands and he knew it; long graceful fingers Michelangelo would like to have sketched and Rodin to have sculptured. Thornton sat.

'What will you have?' Taps asked.

'What's that you've got there?' Thornton enquired, eyeing the cup that appeared to be nothing but froth, rather like the rag Taps worked for, he thought.

'Cappuccino.'

'Why are you drinking Italian type coffee in a French town?'

'Because I feel like an Italian type coffee. Do you want me to go over the border for it? Any more questions?'

'Not really.' There was a menu on the table but Thornton ignored it. 'I'll have the same,' he said.

Taps indicated his cup to a nearby waiter by pointing down at it with a forefinger and then gave the man twos-up. He enjoyed doing that sort of thing knowing, if the waiter were au fait with his French history, he would be extremely offended by the gesture. Evidently he wasn't because he smiled, nodded and gave twos-up back. He most likely wasn't even French.

'You know where that gesture came from do you, Thornton? The rest of the world gives one finger, the English give two, now why is that do you suppose?'

'Because the English bowmen at Agincourt caused such havoc, the French threatened to cut off their fingers if they captured them and the English stood there and gave them the old two fingers, the ones they used to draw their bowstrings. Index and middle, okay? But we're not here for a history lesson. Oh, yes we are, aren't we? The story of Thornton King and his dealings with the Princess Spitskaya,' and, in a pastiche of Gilbert and Sullivan he suddenly burst into song. "*When assassinating duties must be done, must be done, then a model's lot is not a happy one, happy one.*"' There was a smattering of applause and wide grins from the next table. Thornton took a small bow. Taps looked embarrassed.

'Don't give up the day job, Thornton.'

'Unfortunately, old chap, I don't seem to have one, not at the moment anyway.'

He had been surveying the scenery while all this was going on and was rewarded by an enchanting smile from a table not too far distant. He smiled back. She turned away for a second but then looked back and, lowering her eyes, smiled again. She was sitting by herself. The signals were unmistakable as she looked up again and away again and back again.

Duncan Devonport-Fawcett was talking but Thornton didn't hear a word or any of the other noises round and about, and the French do not talk quietly. Physical attraction had turned him stone deaf. Eventually Taps realised it and tapped his companion on the arm. Thornton turned to look at him.

'You haven't heard a word I've said, have you?'

'Sorry, Taps, you're quite right. I haven't. What were you saying?'

'What has caught your attention anyway?'

'I spy with my little eye, something beginning with ...' He tapped his mouth with a forefinger. There were various aspects of the young lady he could put an initial to, the letter T being predominant. Taps, twisting in his chair, peered over his shoulder to see what Thornton was looking at. He turned back again.

'Okay, I get the picture, but this was supposed to be sort of a business meeting, Thornton.' He had taken out his notebook and pen and sat ready for action, 'and business before pleasure as they say.'

'Not today, Taps, old man, not today. Holly and I came here for a pleasant get away from it all treat and ever since we arrived we've been up to our necks in all sorts of shenanigans that initially had absolutely nothing whatsoever to do with us. Today I am taking that promised break so, if you will excuse me? The meeting is temporarily adjourned,' with which he got up and weaved his way across to the young lady's table. Taps watched him go just as two cups of coffee arrived.

'Bonjour!' Thornton said, pointing to a chair. 'May I?'

'Please do, m'sieur,' she cooed, her voice bringing goose bumps to Thornton's arms despite the warmth of the morning. He sat.

'Thornton's the name,' he said, extending his hand, which she took. He admired her long slender fingers. No rings. No high gloss vibrantly coloured nail varnish, though beautifully manicured and polished. He liked that. Do I kiss her hand, he wondered? Did they still do that sort of thing on the *Continong*? Better not, not at first meeting and not being properly introduced.

'Lovely day,' he said.

'You are English,' she responded, a dimple suddenly appearing on either cheek. There was just the trace of an accent.

'How do you know that?'

'The weather of course. You English cannot start a conversation without mentioning the weather.'

'Yes, well, like the poor, it's always with us, isn't it?'

'I am poor.'

'Are you?' He sounded really surprised which was hardly surprising as she seemed the very model of haute couture and the scent that radiated from her, making him slightly dizzy, was most certainly exclusive. 'You certainly don't look it and, if you are, I have absolutely no objection to you being always with us. If the day is lovely, you make it even lovelier.'

'How very gallant, m'sieur,' she said with a laugh.

'Oh, and by the way, you haven't told me your name.'

'Monique.'

'Monique,' he murmured, totally captivated and oh, that mouth of cherry cream never far away, as Mister Firbank would have put it; except that in Mister Firbank's case the much desired mouth of cherry cream that was never far away belonged to one of Cardinal Pirelli's choirboys, not to a young lady of Provençe.

It was at this point that a cup of cappuccino was placed in front of him; another was put down to one side and Taps said as he sat down, 'Thornton, how about introducing me to the young lady.'

*****

Holly stepped back into the house and for the first time took a good look around the room. There were two doors in the back wall, one of which led to the bedroom she had occupied, the other obviously to the rest of the house. Between them, fixed to the wall, was a gun rack holding a couple of hunting rifles and the shotgun back in its place. Along the bottom were a number of small drawers possibly for holding ammunition.

On the chimney wall naturally there was a large blackened open fireplace with a thick oak mantel that by now, after years of use, was probably as hard as concrete and above which rows of corncobs had been strung out to dry. To one side of it hung an assortment of calendars and a letter rack affixed to the wall and stuffed with old bills and receipts, mostly from local tradesman. On the other side was a large old-fashioned wall clock in an ornate wooden frame and with quite a pronounced tick.

The plain wooden table and its accompanying dining chairs sat in the centre and against the wall opposite the fireplace there stood a heavy nineteenth century sideboard on top of which various family treasures were displayed, a badly cracked Limoges plate, a pair of brass shell casings from the first world war holding artificial flowers and in pride of place, centre and under a glass dome, an ornate gilded metal frame of flowers, clusters of leaves, and butterflies with, in the middle, sepia photographs of the old couple's wedding of so many years ago.

On either side was a large black and white religious picture under glass, each showing a benign looking guardian angel watching over two children, obviously little brother and sister about to step hand in hand into danger. In the first picture they were about to walk over a cliff were it were not for the angel's outstretched hand and, in the second they were about to tread on a serpent, already showing its fangs. Obviously these kids never looked where they were putting their feet. One day the angels were going to get fed up and fly back to heaven leaving the kids to tread on something nasty like a venomous toad or a big black scorpion.

Laurent appeared carrying a tray on which stood a dented tin teapot, milk jug, sugar bowl, assorted cups and saucers and small plates and Madame Malherbe followed close behind with a second tray on which was a jar of conserve, knives, and a plate of warm bread, the scent of which reached Holly who suddenly realised just how ravenous she was. Laurent stood holding his tray and grinning at her until Madame Malherbe placed her tray on the table and took his from him. Then, with a nod of her head, she indicated for Holly to sit and, putting down the tray, prepared to pour the tea. She held up the milk jug and looked at Holly who nodded. She next held up the sugar bowl and looked at Holly again. Holly shook her head. Using her apron to hold the hot handle, she lifted the teapot, poured, and passed the cup to Holly who thanked her in French. Up till now she had been wondering whether the old lady was capable of speech or not.

'Ah!' Madame Malherbe shouted at a somewhat startled captive almost making her spill her tea, 'M'amselle speaks French?'

'Certainly,' Holly replied, taking her first sip of tea and eyeing the bread hungrily. A side plate was passed to her together with a knife, and the bread and conserve were placed within reach. Holly picked up her knife and dived in. She was beginning to wonder where her kidnappers had got to when they strolled in obviously in time for breakfast and greeting her affably with a number of Bonjours. This is getting more and more ridiculous she thought. Kidnappers simply are not supposed to behave in this way. Any minute now and the mad hatter will arrive to join us at the table and, as if on cue, Laurent senior appeared, still minus his teeth. Without a word Laurent Junior produced them from his lumberjack check shirt pockets; upper dentures from the left, lower from the right. 'You leave them in the chicken run,' he said.

Laurent Senior was furious as he wiped them off and stuffed them in his mouth. His idiot son could at least have called him outside to pass them over instead of doing it in front of their young lady guest. What kind of manners was that?

Holly decided the best thing she could do was concentrate on her breakfast and to say nothing unless directly addressed. She had obviously been lured into a lunatic asylum. Did the Marquis de Sade not have a chateau somewhere close by?

'No coffee, maman?' Marcel queried. 'You know I can't stand the taste of tea. Terrible wishy-washy English beverage.'

'Indian.' Holly said and bit her lip, but then decided to continue. She might as well be as mad as anyone else. 'Unless it comes from China of course, green tea that is, or from what used to be called Ceylon. Can't think what it's called these days. They're all changing their names aren't they? Oh, and of course the Japanese are very fond of it too.'

Having listened to all this without understanding a word as Holly had reverted to speaking in English, the old girl nodded, hauled herself to her feet, placing her wrinkled knuckles on the table top and using it as leverage, before she schlepped off towards what Holly presumed would be the kitchen.

'Coffee for me too if you please!' Alphonse shouted after her, helping himself to a plate, knife, and a hunk of bread.

Marcel turned to Holly. 'Well, Miss Day,' he said, 'I hope you slept well.'

Holly nearly choked on her mouthful of tea but fortunately managed to stop it going down the wrong way or exiting onto the table. She turned to face Marcel.

'That is the most ridiculous question ever put to me,' she growled. 'Did I sleep well indeed! What do you think after whatever it was you gave me? And you're not very good at it I might tell you. Do I look like a dartboard? I am going to have a bruise the size of this plate.' She indicated the one in front of her.

'Sorry.'

'So you should be. Now, tell me, what is all this about?'

'We need to talk to Thornton King.'

'So? Go talk to him. What's stopping you? Could I have another cup of tea please?'

'We don't know where he is.'

'Oh, is that all? Thank you.' She accepted the cup of tea Laurent had stood up to pour for her and was now handing over with a shy smile and a gracious little bow. 'Well, if you must know, he is at the *Pensione Garibaldi* in Nice. I mean, that is where he is staying. If you don't find him there he'll be out gallivanting, chasing a piece of skirt more than likely, as is his wont.'

'Gallivanting? Piece of skirt? Wont?'

'That's what the lady said.' She dipped a hunk of bread in her teacup, something she would never dream of doing at home. 'Why do you want to talk to him anyway?'

'We want to know where the ... where the ... '

'Come on, man, spit it out. Cat got your tongue?'

'Where the diamonds are.'

Holly stared at Marcel for a long moment and then broke into a peal of laughter. Marcel, stony-faced, watched her until she calmed down and wiped the tears from her eyes. She hadn't even tasted her tea-soaked bread, a great soggy chunk of which now fell back into the teacup and had to be fished out with a spoon.

'What, may I ask, m'amselle, do you find so amusing?'

'Thornton, no more than I, has absolutely no idea whatsoever where the diamonds are, if they really exist that is.'

'What do you mean, if they really exist?'

'What I say. We are only assuming they exist. We could have put two and two together and got five.'

'Oh, they exist all right. The Beloved Leader ...' Once again he stopped himself. Holly was suddenly very interested.

'Go on?' she said.

'Go on what?'

'With what you were going to say.'

'No, I wasn't going to say anything.'

'Yes you were, the Beloved Leader you said.'

'A slip of the tongue.'

A huge slip of the tongue, Holly thought, holding her teacup in both hands in front of her face and thinking hard, soggy bread now on plate grown cold and forgotten. So now we know what this is all about but why should these men believe Thornton would have any idea where the diamonds could be?

'I tell you what,' she said, putting down her cup. 'I'll come with you and we will all go and talk to Thornton. How about that?'

It was Marcel's turn to laugh. 'You think I'm crazy?' He asked. 'You are here and here you stay in case Mister King decides not to talk. Once he knows we have got you and we inform him of what we can do to you, he will come clean that's for sure. You know? The marvellous thing about a farm is that there are plenty of implements lying around that are most useful for something other than agriculture, if you get my meaning.'

'A mean meaning if ever there was one,' Holly said. So that is what all this is about, she thought. These guys have gone around the twist to such an extent they've tied themselves in a knot of Gordian dimensions. And, unfortunately for them, neither is an Alexander.

Maman returned with two cups of coffee. Laurent Junior was picking his nose and surveying the results on his fingers. Laurent Senior had fallen fast asleep.

******

'Do you mind if I smoke?' Monique asked.

'As long as you don't catch fire,' Thornton replied. 'Ha ha ha! That one's got whiskers on it as well.'

'Pardon?'

'Skip it. Well, are you going to smoke or aren't you? Because, if you're not, let's go at it again. I'm ready.'

'Oooh la la!'

'Oh, come off it! French girls don't really say that do they? Except in movies and fantasy land of course.'

'Pardon?'

'Pardon?'

'You are teasing me.'

'Not at the moment but I soon will be.'

'What I meant by oooh la la was, I was always made to believe English gentlemen were not, you know, how shall I say it? Very sexy, except maybe with each other. La vice Anglais?'

'Fairy tales,' Thornton said. 'Whoops! Wrong expression.' He cupped a breast in his hand and blew on her neck, following it up by a lick that somehow got transferred to her ear and loved it when she shivered and squealed.

'Ready or not, here I come!' He yodelled, moving a leg over but was stopped in mid-movement.

'No, wait. Let us just lie still for a moment and talk.'

Thornton flopped back on the pillows.

There was silence for a while and then, 'What do you want to talk about?' he asked, turning his head to her.

'You of course.' She raised herself slightly, supporting her head with one crooked arm and a fist on her cheek and kissed him gently on the mouth then slid a finger of her other hand over his lips. He took the tip of the finger in his mouth and was about to suck on it when it was withdrawn. She turned away to scrabble for her cigarettes on the bedside cabinet. He ran his fingers down her back in the small of which was the softest blonde down. She shivered again, accompanying it with a pretended purr. Thornton realised the fun and games were over.

There was going to be no retake.

She sat up in the bed, lighting her cigarette and pulling up her knees, wrapping her arms around them. The gate had not only been definitely shut, it was locked to boot. She turned her head slightly to look at him again.

'Would you like a drink?' she asked.

'I don't think so.'

He sat up in turn, got up and leant down to pick up his underpants off the floor. He slipped them on, turned, and stood stock-still, hardly able to believe his eyes.

She was still in bed, still with her knees drawn up, but she was levelling an old Luger in his direction.

'You're going to shoot me? My performance wasn't that bad, was it?'

'Your performance?'

'You really have absolutely no sense of humour do you? Are you what the French call a femme fatale? Well tell me, you blast away with that old thing and here I am on the floor spurting blood in all directions, how are you going to get rid of the body?'

'Friends.'

'Friends in need are friends indeed. What is all this about anyway?'

'Diamonds, Mr King, diamonds.'

CHAPTER 11

Watched by curious neighbours, a pair of uniformed policemen knocked on the door of Marcel's apartment but there was no answer and, when they tried it, were surprised to find it unlocked. In response to a gentle push the door swung open. They were obviously not going to find anyone or anything in there though, just in case, both had a hand on their weapon in its holster.

Nino had flown the coop having decided the sooner he was on his way back to Italy the better. He had made a thorough search of the apartment and finally found a stash of francs hidden beneath a pile of carefully folded linen in a drawer. Nino knew there had to be something there. Marcel never folded a shirt let alone a sheet and the careful layout was a dead giveaway. It was more than enough to see him on his way and keep him until something else turned up back in Naples, possibly a rich American tourist of either sex. He wanted nothing more to do with Marcel, Alphonse, Beloved Leaders, mad Englishmen, diamonds, or anything connected with them. He wondered how he could have allowed himself to get involved with them in the first place. Ah, of course, that old vice human beings would never be free of, greed. There was also, of course, the dream of never having to worry about money again, of living a life of luxury with all the trappings untold riches can bring. That is why people gamble. That is why people buy lottery tickets, play the pools, always hoping for the big one that always seem to be won by someone else and usually the most undeserving in the opinion of the losers, and Marcel was such a con man making him believe it would all happen.

On the way to the railway station he stopped off at a tabac to get himself a pack of cigarettes for the journey. The tobacconist accepted his note, held it up to the light and Nino ended up in a police station. The francs were forgeries. He should have known.

******

Rita had blissfully shampooed and bubble-bathed away all the

192

grubbiness of the previous twenty-four or so hours. Had it been only twenty-four? Maybe a little longer but, whatever, it seemed like a lifetime and now, basking in the limelight and the midday sun, she was tucking into a splendid brunch, pink champagne courtesy of the house, surrounded by flashlights and journalists all firing questions at her in quick succession. She had never before been such a centre of attention.

Reg sat at the table with her as proud as if he had himself experienced the events she was describing. Once again, if only as the detective inspector husband, he would be in all the papers. There must have been a major reason for the abduction of his wife but, when queried, he assumed an air of secretiveness and said he wasn't prepared to divulge police business. He would think up something plausible by the time they got home. The full story, embellished slightly more with each telling, would ultimately be revealed and then there would follow serial rights, probably in *The Daily Mail*, and possibly a teleplay or even a book. He wondered what kind of an advance a publisher might be prepared to offer. Perhaps they would be bidding for the rights, such would be their interest now that the Venables were celebrities and a newly acquired agent could probably demand quite a hefty advance if he struck whilst the iron was hot.

Earlier in their suite when she had recovered sufficiently to tell him what had happened and what the man had said, leaving out any mention of Holly, he point-blank refused to believe it had all been a mistake. No, there was something far far deeper lying behind it, of that he was certain.

Right now she was finding it difficult to concentrate on her food and answer questions at the same time, not because her mouth was constantly full but mainly because she had no answers anyway to the most overriding queries. She had already given a description of her kidnappers to the police and a description of the apartment in which she was held but who was it who kidnapped her? She didn't know. Where was this apartment to which she was taken? She didn't know. Who rescued her? She didn't know.

What she was very sure of was she did not want this circus to come to an end. She was a celebrity; a newsworthy person for the first and probably the only time in her life, and she wanted the whole world to know it. The fact that by the following week the whole world would probably have forgotten it was beside the point.

Inspector Gaston Leroux arrived and pulled focus much to Rita's dismay. He was, as far as he was concerned anyway, a central part of this story as it was all taking place on his patch. It would be up to him to solve the mystery of Mrs Venables' abduction and he felt he was well on the way to doing just that. He believed the apartment to which she had been taken was in Marseilles and he had men checking it out right at this very minute. The time it took, according to what Mrs Venables had told him, for her return to Beaulieu-sur-Mer meant that it was some distance away and Marseilles would seem to fit the bill. Also he already had at least one suspect in mind.

'Could you name him?'

Leroux turned to search out the person who had asked this question and noticed a fair rather boyish journalist with notebook and pen at the ready. He pursed his lips and shook his head. No, he was afraid he wasn't ready to name names though he would like to know the name of the enquirer.

'Duncan Devonport-Fawcett,' Taps told him.

'And you are with what publication?'

But before Taps could answer there were at least five more questions hurled rapid fire at the inspector and Rita went back to concentrating on her brunch.

******

Meanwhile back at the Malherbe farm, Holly had gone out shooting with Laurent. That is, Laurent, with a bandolier of cartridges over his shoulder was carrying the shotgun and letting off the occasional pop whenever he saw something move, but eventually he reloaded, handed the gun to Holly and was about to explain how to use it when she told him not to worry, she grew up with guns and, to prove it, immediately fired off one barrel and brought down a poor inoffensive dove flying by. Just happened to fly in the wrong place at the wrong time. Laurent was impressed. He put the warm lifeless little body in his hunting bag but took it out again for a second look just to make sure she had actually done what he thought he saw her do. He shook his head, not in disapproval, but in admiration. The bird went back in his bag but it really wasn't worth keeping, riddled as it was with shot. Laurent was beginning to wish he had brought out one of the rifles so they could go on shooting together. He gave her a shy smile and indicated she should

194

keep the gun for a while.

The fact that they were out hunting together at all was not something Marcel and Alphonse approved of but there was no arguing with Laurent once he made up his mind to something, not if you intended to remain unbloodied and all of a piece and, after a startled reaction at Laurent's original suggestion, it was with a quiet despair they had watched the pair slope off into the wood.

'What do we do now?' Alphonse wanted to know.

'Nothing,' Marcel snarled. 'Maybe he'll shoot her.'

'What good will that do?'

'It will get her off our backs. She's more trouble than she's worth. Whose crazy idea was this anyway?'

'Yours.'

'No it wasn't, it was Nino's. That stupid Italian! I could kill him.'

They were even more startled at the pair's return when they saw Holly carrying the gun open and correct under one arm and helping Laurent to walk, holding onto him with the other. Actually there was no need for her to hold him up at all. He was quite capable of walking by himself but he was thoroughly enjoying the experience. It wasn't every day of the week, month, or year, or lifetime for that matter, that Laurent had a beautiful woman he could cling to.

'Diable!' Marcel hissed. '*She* has shot *him*!'

As they got closer the two men standing by the cottage door could see Laurent's trouser leg was badly ripped and he was bleeding quite profusely from a gash in his calf.

'Sanglier,' he said, matter of factly, as they moved on into the house. 'Holly shot her,' he went on, looking over his shoulder. 'It would be a sow. They're the most dangerous, though I didn't notice any little ones about. I didn't even see her until too late.'

Marcel and Alphonse followed the wounded and his assistant into the house and watched as she sat him by the table, turned to them and said, 'I need something for a tourniquet.'

Madame Malherbe had come out of the kitchen and, seeing blood dripping quite liberally all over the floor, screamed and sat abruptly in another chair. She was carrying a tea towel that Holly immediately took from her to use as her tourniquet. Having tied it tightly around Laurent's thigh, twisted with the aid of a large spoon the blood flow decreased quite dramatically and Holly examined the wound.

'I didn't see it coming.' Laurent started to explain to his audience what had happened. Laurent Senior had now joined the group. 'And I didn't hear it. That damned pig got me before I could move. Holly was standing a long way off. Lucky she had the gun. Do you know what she did? She called to that pig. She actually called and the damned thing left me, turned and went for her. She shot it right between the eyes. We must go back and collect it. There is a lot of meat there. Maman, you can make fromage du tete if you look out for the pellets. Marcel you can take some back to Marseilles with you. Holly saved me from a real mauling I can tell you.'

He gazed adoringly at her. In his eyes she was obviously a combination of Joan of Arc, Saint Bernadette, Saint Francis of Assisi and that doctor fellow who talked to the animals.

'Yes, well that's all very well but this wound needs stitches and you need a tetanus shot,' the miracle worker said.

'Tetanus shot? What for?'

'Tetanus of course.'

'Pah! And it doesn't need stitches. Just bandage it up.'

'Well, have you got any antiseptic in the house?'

'Disinfectant.' Madame Malherbe spoke for the first time, having recovered from her initial shock. 'We've got sheep-dip. It's for ticks.'

'I know what it's for. I suppose a mild solution will do the trick. My father has always believed the old fashioned remedies were best. He maintains there's nothing like horse liniment for a strain or a sprain, and camphor oil or Friar's balsam for the chest. And I will need clean cloths to bathe the wound as well as something for a bandage.'

Madame Malherbe schlepped off to see to Holly's requirements. What a wonderful wife she would make for her Laurent. She didn't give a fig for Marcel. He was a rogue, a scallywag and beyond redemption. Any woman who considered marrying him would have to be out of her senses.

In Laurent's eyes Holly had now assumed the mantle of Florence Nightingale adding to the virtues of those already on the list. Marcel looked on and listened aghast.

'Out in the country, dark, wild animals, nervous women, what could be better? Huh! She's like a duck in water. Wait till I see that Nino. I'll grind him till his bones creak.'

******

Sitting in his cell Nino had rather similar thoughts. 'If I ever see that Marcel again and I've got my knife with me I'll rip him from arsehole to breakfast time!' It never occurred to him he wouldn't be in his current predicament if he hadn't lifted Marcel's stash of forged francs in the first place.

******

'Déjà vu,' Thornton said.

'What?'

'I seem to remember having been in exactly this position once before: fairly recently in fact, only that time I wasn't exactly down to my underpants and it was a whistling kettle that saved my life.'

She didn't know what the hell he was talking about and she was quite startled when he did the totally unexpected, slipped off his underpants, tossed them nonchalantly over his shoulder and climbed back into bed. She leapt out the other side and stepped back a couple of paces, still pointing the gun in his direction. He didn't actually lie down again or even sit. He knelt and pulled the bedclothes up to his chest. Standing there naked she looked beautiful and vulnerable despite the gun in her hand. He smiled at her. She frowned back.

'What do you think you're doing?' She asked, making the mistake of stepping forward again, thus being within easy reach.

'Waiting for you to shoot me,' was his reply.

'You are one crazy Englishman!' she said.

'Not at all. I'm just making it a little more difficult for you, that's all.'

'How? Difficult?'

'Well, shooting me on the floor which, I have noticed, is beautifully polished marble, you would be able to mop up the blood fairly easily, even though the marble is white and, if there were to be any irremovable stains, a rug could cover them. But shooting me in bed is another matter entirely. The blood would not only saturate the bedclothes, it would seep through to the mattress and possibly the base of the bed itself. Don't forget there are about eight pints of the stuff and you would find it impossible to get rid off. And, by the way,' he glanced towards the door, 'I do believe your expected friend has arrived.'

Despite the fact she wasn't expecting anybody, she couldn't help but turn to look and was the immediate target of a fairly heavy bolster flung with considerable force and followed by a leaping naked Englishman. Fortunately the gun did not go off but she put up quite a struggle until he managed to wrest it from her, send it spinning across the marble floor, pinned her down by the wrists and straddled her.

'Right, so that I don't have to go to all the trouble of handing you over to the police, illegal possession of a firearm would probably be the first charge, attempted murder the second: first question, are you or are you not expecting help to arrive?'

She shook her head.

'Good. I didn't think you were. I also didn't believe for one moment that you intended to shoot me. What were you going to do when it came to question time and you were faced with a bleeding corpse?' He let go her wrists and rolled off her, got up and held out his hands to lift her up. This was no kung fu lady like the previous one who would put a foot in his midriff and have him over her shoulders in a jiffy. As he expected she meekly took his hands and went to sit on the bed, looking for the cigarette she had previously lit but hadn't smoked. It was a length of ash in the tray and a filter tip on the wrong side. She put the filter back in the ashtray, took another cigarette from the packet and lit that, taking a deep and satisfying draw. She was finding it difficult to stop trembling and looked at her hands, fascinated. It wasn't just the exertion expended on the wrestling match but the fact that this man who she hardly knew other than intimately could have in the circumstances been truly vicious. It was the very first time she had pulled the gun on anyone and she had not known what to expect.

Thornton meanwhile had trotted around to the other side of the bed and started to get dressed, finally sitting on the edge to put on his shoes and socks.

'Now, young lady,' he said, half turning and resting one hand on the bed, 'you weren't really intending to shoot me were you? It was all a silly gesture really if information is seriously what you are after, but what is all this nonsense about diamonds?'

'It isn't nonsense. He told me all about it.'

'He? Who is this he?'

She remained silent, pulling on her cigarette.

'It wouldn't be this so-called Beloved Leader, would it? Every time I think of that stupid title I want to laugh.'

'No. It was someone who represents him.'

'Here? In Nice?'

She nodded.

'What does he look like?'

'I don't know. He gave me instructions by telephone.' She hoped he wouldn't pick up on this lie as she relived her meeting with him in the café the previous night.

Thornton indeed wasn't too sure about it but decided he couldn't prove otherwise so he might as well take her word for it.

'I suppose he gave you the gun by telephone as well.'

'Don't be stupid. It belonged to my father. He got it during the war. He was in the resistance and he got it from a captured German officer. I keep it because … '

'Because?'

'In my profession one cannot be too careful. There are crazy dangerous people about. Kinky people with kinky ideas. Girls get hurt. It happens but I don't want it to happen to me.'

'Your profession, huh?' He sat for a while and thought. The first thing to do when he got back to England would be to have a blood test. You never can tell in the wise words of a certain Mr Shaw. He stood up, leaned across the bed and kissed her gently on the shoulder. 'Do I leave the money on the mantelpiece?'

'Mantelpiece? What mantelpiece? Where do you see a mantelpiece?'

'It's an old joke.'

'Oh.'

'Is there anything more you can tell me?' he asked. She shook her head. 'Au revoir then,' he said.

She remained still until she heard the door close behind him then she turned to look. She would never be forgiven for being so inept but what was she to do? It was hardly in her usual line of work. He had left a bundle of francs on the bed.

'I didn't want that,' she said quietly to herself, 'not from you.'

And she started to cry.

******

It was Rita's turn to pour over the photograph albums. This was not nearly as much fun as the earlier jamboree, in fact no fun at all once she had perved over a couple of handsome mug shots, faces whose beauty not even scars or the police photographer could ruin.

Strange to think they could belong to vicious hardened criminals when one always thinks of hardened criminals as having faces that would scare the horses.

She didn't like being in the police station. She didn't like the look of the place or the smell of it and she hadn't seen a live person (as opposed to the pictures) who she could fantasize over. Wearily she turned another page, heaved a sigh and shook her head. No no no, always no, not a recognizable face to be seen. She closed the book and was passed another. Reg sat beside her to give encouragement but she had been at it a long time and was really beginning to droop. What a way to spend your very first visit overseas, and to somewhere as romantic as the French Riviera, playground of the rich and famous, the movers and shakers, the world's glitterati. True she had been literally swept off her feet but hardly in the nicest possible way and if that Italian hadn't been so ... she shuddered at the thought.

There hadn't been a single hour when she was able to walk the streets, stroll on the beach, visit a museum, see the sights, or go shopping and all the fame in the world was not making up for the tedium of the moment. Reg of course was used to police stations. They were part and parcel of his *métier* as it were. The only good thing that had come out of it was her emotional reunion with her husband. They had even, after all these years, indulged in a bit of you know what and, much to her surprise, she actually enjoyed it although he was a bit short on practice and it was rather like the rooster saying to the hen, this won't hurt, darling, did it? When they get home she would have to take him in hand as it were, maybe show him some of her magazines. He surely must have got over all this anti-vice business by now; he was only a few years off retirement and how was he going to spend his retirement years? Growing vegetables? Mowing the lawn? It was after all the Age of Aquarius and everything was supposed, if not standing up to be counted, at least to be hanging out.

She sighed again. She would never again get a chance for a little innocent or even not so innocent wandering that was for sure, so it was Reg or nothing and a little of Reg she supposed was better than a little of nothing. She turned the last page, closed the book and looked at her husband with that look that said I simply cannot take any more of this. He patted her hand, nodded, and got up.

'Shall we see if the artist can do a reasonable sketch?' he said. He

200

was definitely in police in action mode.

'Oh. Reg!' she whined, 'Do we have to?'

Now she felt she couldn't wait to get home, only hoping the house hadn't been ransacked in their absence. She had heard such terrible stories of what burglars could do to a house given the run of the place. She shuddered at the thought.

In Leroux's office Nino was being interrogated but keeping a tight lip.

'So where did you get this counterfeit stuff?' Leroux asked, holding up a note and squinting at it. The sight of his eyes being crossed was slightly comical but Nino resisted the urge to laugh, permitting himself only the slightest of smiles.

'Found it,' he said.

'You found a whole valise full of counterfeit money? It just dropped from the skies I suppose or you stumbled on it as you were innocently walking along the street.'

Nino shrugged. 'Something like that,' he said.

'Of course it never occurred to you that it could have been lost property and your citizen's duty was to report it to the police.'

'Never entered my mind.'

'No of course not, and look at the trouble it's got you into. Surprised you thought you could get away with it. Looks pretty amateurish to me.' He dropped the note back in the valise on his desk and, zipping it up, held it out to Mathieu who took it. 'Have that photographed, money separate, mark it up and bag it,' Leroux ordered and Mathieu left the office to do that. Leroux opened Nino's passport and studied it.

'Hmn, how long have you been in France?' He asked.

'I come and go.'

'Yes. The problem with this new common market business, nobody seems to be really bothering with borders any more so that passports are not stamped and we can lose track of people like you, but I promise you this, you won't have any use for this because you won't be leaving again for quite a long time as you will be a guest of the French government. Isn't that nice? On second thoughts, I don't suppose this is fake as well. No? Now then …' He passed half a dozen ten by eight glossies over the desk. '… do you recognise these?'

'No. Should I?'

'You should. Don't ring a bell at all?' Nino shook his head. 'You sure you don't want to change your mind before your dabs are found all over the place?'

'Okay, so I know it.'

'When were you last there?'

Nino shrugged and looked up at the ceiling, thinking hard, trying to remember.

'Come off it,' Leroux said, unimpressed with the pantomime. Over a long career he had had too many dealings with villains. 'You were there until this morning. You got out just before the police arrived.' He suddenly broke into English as he thought of something witty to say. 'In the nick of time before you were nicked,' and chortled to himself while Nino looked thoroughly bemused.

'Inspector, as your guest I don't suppose it is possible for you to offer me a cigarette?'

'I would if I were in a generous mood but I'm not.'

Mathieu returned accompanied by agent Gerrard. Leroux indicated Nino with a dismissive wave of his hand. 'See to it our guest here gives you his statement and then is made comfortable.'

Nino rose from his chair. There was no need to order him to do so. He knew the score. The three of them left the office. Leroux, seeing his Gauloise packet was empty and tossing it in the waste paper bin, reached out to help himself to one of Mathieu's Gitanes and was about to light it when there was a scream from the corridor that had him all fingers and thumbs with cigarettes flying in one direction, lighter in another. He rose hastily to his feet and made for the door.

'It's him!' the voice screamed. 'It's him!'

Leroux arrived in the corridor to find Rita pointing the quivering finger of accusation at Nino standing between the two policemen, about to be led away. Nino shrugged and gave his broadest smile to date and blew Rita a mocking kiss at which, much to everyone's discomfort, she shrieked even louder. Once you are face to face with your accuser and there is no denying the truth you might as well face up to it. It was as good as being caught in flagrante delicto. Once in court, a guilty plea and a begging grovelling repentance could ultimately play in his favour and reduce a sentence considerably. The law could be terribly gullible.

Leroux shooed the prisoner and his guards away with impatient brushes of both hands and, once they had gone, turned to Rita and said, 'Mrs Venables, Inspector Venables will you step into my office please?' He moved to one side to usher them through the door, then followed them, shutting the door behind him. 'Please, take a seat.'

'Oh, the devil, the devil!' Rita said, still quivering with righteous indignation as she sat in the chair Leroux pushed in beneath her plump behind before moving around to his side of the desk.

'There, there, please do not distress yourself, Mrs Venables,' he said. 'Can I get you something? A glass of water perhaps.'

Rita, now momentarily beyond speech, shook her head. Reg sat down beside her and took her hand. He was getting used to once again assuming the mantle of the solicitous husband.

'So, am I to assume this is one of the men who kidnapped you?'

Rita nodded.

'And this ...' He indicated the photographs still lying on the desk facing her, '... is where they held you?'

Rita took one look at the photographs and just managed to control the scream that threatened to rise in her throat.

'Yes, yes, that is the place! Look, that's the bedroom at the back where I slept. Oh, I will never forget it. Never! It will haunt my dreams forever.' She was being just a little too woman's romantic novel and Leroux wasn't taken in by that either. Reg thought what a brave little soul his wife was and wondered why he had never noticed it before as he sympathetically gave her hand a couple of gentle pats.

'The apartment belongs to a man by the name of Marcel Malherbe. Does that ring a bell with you, Mrs Venables?'

'I'm not sure.'

'We haven't been able to trace him as yet but, when we do get him, which we will, would you be able to recognise him?'

'Of course.'

'What about the third man? Can you remember his name?'

'Yes, I can actually. I did hear it mentioned, only his first name of course, it's Alphonse. I don't think he's French, not French French if you know what I mean.'

'You mean he's possibly an immigrant?'

'Something like that.'

'Hmn ... ' There was a long pause before Leroux finally said, 'Mrs Venables, Reg, would it be possible for you to stay in France a day or two longer to attend an identity parade? I will arrange it as quickly as I can.'

Rita turned to give her husband a quizzical look.

'Of course we can, old chap,' Reg said. 'Only too glad to help out a colleague.' He had preened a little in having his French opposite number use his Christian name, which was exactly what his French opposite number anticipated. 'It will do us good to relax for a couple of days, apart from the identity parade that is, before returning to Blighty.'

'Blighty?'

'Oh, sorry. Of course. Another name for England. From World War Two I believe. Maybe earlier. Maybe one. Maybe the Boer War, or could be the Crimea even. I'm not too sure.'

'Be that as it may, thank you. I will make sure the department contributes something towards your expenses.' He rose to his feet. 'Now, you go back to the hotel, Mrs Venables, and have a good rest. After all you have been through that is exactly what you need.' Having found his way to the door to usher them out, as she paused in front of him he took Rita's hand and kissed it. This time she quivered with delight. There was still some old-fashioned romance in the world.

******

With the conventions over and most of the delegates on their way home, cars were once more available and Thornton's credit on his Card stretched just far enough for him to hire the smallest at a special rate for the day.

His first port of call naturally was the Metropole as he still hadn't been able to contact Holly and he wanted to try and discover what had happened to her, and whether there was any news of Rita.

He parked the car and started for the hotel when he heard a whistle and a come hither 'pssst!' He stopped, looked around, and saw Luigi advancing towards him. He was not in his hotel uniform but wearing skin tight faded jeans, a casual shirt and bum-freezer jacket. The inevitable cigarette was hanging from his mouth but was removed and flicked away with a slightly theatrical gesture.

'Meester Keeng,' the boy addressed him with a smile. 'I hava somting for you.'

Thornton waited, saying nothing.

'Please, my Eenglish no so good but I hava thees.' He held out a shred of paper.

After a moment's hesitation, Thornton took it. What kind of a con was he being fed now? He glanced at the writing and saw it was evidently a car registration number. He looked up, raising an enquiring eyebrow.

'You are looking for Miss Day, no?'

Thornton nodded.

'She no 'ere.'

'Where is she?'

'She gone.'

'Well obviously if she's not here then she's gone but where has she gone to?'

'She gone weeth two men, to how it is called? A farm.' He made this sound as sinister as he was able.

'A farm!' Thornton's surprised reaction caused his voice to rise virtually an octave.

'Si, vero. I keeda you never, m'sieur.' Luigi was beginning to get his languages mixed up. 'I see 'er go. Two men in that car ...' He tapped the piece of paper, 'and Mees Day ina Mercedes up their behind.'

'I don't think that is quite the English expression you want, Luigi. What you mean is, she followed them in the Mercedes, yes?'

'Up their backside, yes.'

'Okay, let's carry on from there. Did they know she was following them?'

'Si, vraiment! They do so like thees weeth their lights,' he opened and closed flat fingers held together over thumb of one hand, like a duck opening and closing its beak, 'two times and she ... '

'Followed them.'

'S'right.'

'To a farm.'

Luigi nodded.

'How do you know they went to a farm?'

Luigi tapped the side of his nose. Thornton wasn't quite sure what this gesture was meant to convey except that Luigi was a sly little bird.

'What time was all this?'

'Night time. Maybe three o'clock?'

'Okay, so what do you think it was all about?'

Luigi shrugged.

'You must have thought something funny was going on or you wouldn't have scribbled down the number.' He waved the piece of paper virtually under Luigi's nose. 'Why haven't you been to the police?

Luigi gave his right hand a goodly number of vigorous horizontal shakes from the wrist and blew out hard meaning Thornton should surely be aware that people like he did not go to the police under any circumstances except ... He looked around to see if there was anybody about and then, in order to lower his voice, drew closer to Thornton. 'I tella you a secret. You no tella no one, hokay?'

It was Thornton's turn to nod.

'I have a special fren. He one big time policeman. I ask heem for favours. I ask heem about that.' He tapped the paper. 'He fine out every-theeng for me. A very big special favour, you unnerstan'?'

'Not really.'

'My fren ...' Luigi hesitated, waggled his head and bared his teeth held tightly together which meant something really important was being held back behind this enamel barrier. He wanted to let it out but he didn't know how Thornton would take it, he being an Englishman and Englishman usually being so uptight about these matters over which most Latins were so casual. Eventually he decided in for a penny in for a pound, or the Italian equivalent thereof.

'My policeman fren he ... 'ow I say thees? ... he have the hots for my beautiful young Sicilian body.' The word beautiful was almost sung; in fact the whole statement could have been a line from a Neapolitan folk song. He watched Thornton's face anxiously but there was no discernible reaction. 'You unnerstan' what I am saying?'

'Of course I do. But what about you? Do you give him your beautiful young Sicilian body?'

'I make promise.'

'I see. Keeping him on tenterhooks are you? Milking it for all you're worth.'

'Donna be stoopido, Meester Keeng. You milka da cow, you milka da goat, you no milka ...'

'Yes, well, you can stop right there, you've made your point. So your special friend has given you all the details regarding the ownership of this particular car. You don't want to inform any other policeman but you have kept the information for me. Why?'

'I 'ave a love for Miss Holly Day.'

This time there was a reaction from Thornton. He suppressed his inclination to laugh, or even smile. 'You're lusting after her beautiful nubile young English body, are you?'

Luigi looked a trifle embarrassed but continued bravely on. 'I no want somtheeng bad 'appen to 'er.'

'I see. Well I feel the same way, old chum, so what do you suggest we do about it?'

'You 'ave car. I take you there.'

'Listen, Luigi, I don't know what your real game is, that is if you have one, but I am highly suspicious of your motives. I don't believe playing the knight-errant is one of them so just give me directions and I will go on my own thank you very much.'

Luigi didn't understand most of this but he got the "on my own" bit. 'No no! not possible! You no fine it. Ees far away! I take you there.'

'It's likely to be dangerous. She may have followed two men in a car but who knows how many there may be at the other end?'

'No matter, I come with you. Better two of us than one.'

Thornton gave in. 'Have it your own way,' he said and had started to make for the car, Luigi following, when he suddenly stopped and Luigi practically ran into him.

'Sorry,' he apologised, looking sheepish, as though Thornton might think he had done it for an immoral purpose.

'Before we go, I don't suppose you have any news of Mrs Venables.'

'Ah yes! She fine. No problem. She back in 'otel.'

'Really? When did this happen?'

'Long time back. Come on, let's go, let's go!'

'What about your duties at the hotel?'

'I no work today. We go now?'

'Okay.' They reached the car. Thornton slipped into the driving seat; Luigi dashed around to the passenger side and was in like a flash before the key was even in the ignition just in case Thornton had the stupid idea of leaving him behind.

Probably finding conversation too much of a bind, he remained silent except for turning out to be a more than adequate navigator but then, even in not very good English, it didn't take much to say turn left, turn right, go straight. It was almost dark by the time they reached the track leading to the farm and Thornton stopped the car some distance from the house.

'We walk now,' he said.

'Hokay!' was the cheery reply. Luigi obviously had no idea of the possible seriousness of the situation and Thornton shook his head in despair.

'I don't suppose you would like to stay by the car,' he suggested. Luigi shook his head.

'No, I didn't think so. Come on then, let's see how the land lies.'

******

The way the land lay was that Holly was enjoying a family supper. A large fire hissed and crackled in the fireplace, the flames casting interesting shadows across the room lit also by the warm glow of oil lamps, there being one of the region's frequent power cuts. Holly thought it was delightfully cosy and did not want the electricity restored, it was all so dreamlike. With the smell of the lamps and the fire, the warmth of the room, the food and the wine, she already felt quite drowsy and was looking forward to sleeping in that gorgeous old bed; downy mattress, downy duvet, and downy pillows. She could imagine herself just sinking into it all, practically disappearing. She wondered if someone had thought to empty the chamber pot. Who in their right mind wanted to go back to civilisation?

To be practical, she really should head back to Nice so that people who might be worried about her could stop worrying, but it was all too much trouble. It was dark, she didn't know the way, and she was in no fit state to drive anyway. She poured a little more wine into her almost empty glass. This had been the strangest kidnapping in the history of that awful phenomenon.

Laurent Senior, at the head of the table, had already dozed off, his head falling forward onto his chest and jerking up every now and again as he regained semi-consciousness for a moment, clacking his teeth a couple of times before dozing off again. One never knew between jerks whether he had died or not. Madame Malherbe with a hunk of bread was wiping up the last of the sauce on her plate and Laurent Junior sat holding his wine glass and gazing at Holly with adoring eyes until, suddenly, he got to his feet, walked over to the gun rack and, taking down the shotgun, went out through the back door. Holly didn't think too much of it. Maybe a fox had got into the chicken run or Pan was playing his pipes in the goat shed and Laurent had gone out to hush him up, something bucolic like that. This wine was evidently pretty powerful stuff.

*****

Thornton and Luigi were both surprised as they cautiously approached the house to see the Mercedes standing in majesty all on its own and no sign whatsoever of the Peugeot.

'I stay here. I guard this car,' Luigi whispered as they reached the car.

Thornton thought this rather weird after all the boy's earlier protestations and wondered from whom he was going to guard the car. Would he put up a struggle if the two men jumped him? Or would he flee for his life? Probably the latter but, if that was what he wanted to do; Thornton was not going to argue about it. He went forward on his own, crouching low, and on reaching the house itself and bent almost double, he peered through the nearest window and remained transfixed at the sight of Holly, obviously completely at home and enjoying a meal en famille.

How many in the room? Three including Holly: an old gentleman who looked asleep and an ancient crone who looked ninety-nine but was wide awake. She was going bald, sported a couple of interesting warts, a pretty impressive moustache and obviously enjoyed her food the way she was lapping it up. He was stumped as to what his next move should be but it was decided for him when he felt the barrels of the shotgun poke him in his side just under the ribs and that hurt. He stood up straight and wasn't going to argue but raised his hands over his head then, urged on by the prodding, now in the small of his back, he opened the door and entered the house.

'Hello, Thornton,' Holly said as though he were an expected guest. 'It's all right, Laurent, this is an old friend.'

Laurent lowered the shotgun and glowered at Thornton who smiled sweetly back. Madame Malherbe rose from the table, wiped her moustache with a napkin and went to fetch cutlery and a plate to lay another place. Laurent Senior snored loudly and got cuffed by his wife in passing, which produced a bout of snorting, grunting, lip smacking and teeth clacking followed, more or less, by silence. Laurent put the gun back in the rack and resumed his seat.

'Pull up a chair, Thornton and try some of this delicious wild pig. It's absolutely scrumptious. I shot it this afternoon. How did you find me?'

'Holly, what on earth do you think you're doing?'

'Oh, do sit down, Thornton and stop looking so grumpy. You

209

didn't answer my question. How did you find me?'

'Luigi brought me.'

'Luigi? Who he?'

'Are you drunk, Holly?'

'A trifle pissed, darling. Why?'

'Why what?'

'Why do you ask?'

'For one thing, I don't recollect you ever calling me darling before. For another you've gone squinty-eyed. It's quite sexy actually. You remember Luigi, one of the boys from the hotel.'

'Oh, that Luigi! The one with no hips. I can't imagine how his pants defy the law of gravity and don't end up around his ankles.'

'Oh, so you have noticed him then. I should imagine they end up round his ankles fairly frequently.'

'Well, how did he know where I was?'

'It's a long story, Holly. Thank you.' This was to Madame Malherbe who had slapped a heaped plate down in front of him. 'Smells delicious.'

'And where is Luigi at this moment?'

'Guarding the Mercedes.'

'Guarding the Mercedes from what?'

'Have no idea. What has happened to the men who abducted you?'

'They've fled, done a bunk. Eat your food, Thornton.'

He picked up his knife and fork and stabbed at the hunk of meat in front of him, transferring a fairly large portion to his mouth. Holly was right. It was tender and delicious.

'Done a bunk? What do you mean by done a bunk?'

'Exactly what I say and don't talk with your mouth full. When they realised they had made a slight error of judgment and had two of us to cope with, they took to their heels. Rather they got into their battered old jalopy and disappeared in a cloud of dust. By now they must be well on their way to Marseilles which, I am led to believe, is their home patch. I don't suppose you remember passing a battered old Peugeot on your way here?' Thornton shook his head. 'No, didn't think you would. Long gone, long gone.'

******

The battered old Peugeot sputtered and ground to a halt just the other side of Nice. Marcel looked down at the fuel gauge and started to bash his hands against the steering wheel before laying his head on them and closing his eyes.

'Merde!' He yelled. 'This is all we don't need.'

'Not really,' Alphonse said. 'What we really don't need is what has just pulled up behind us.'

Marcel lifted his head and looked in his rear view mirror just as the first policeman was out of the squad car and walking towards them.

******

'Why did they bring you here in the first place?' Thornton asked.

'Well, the leader of this little gang of idiots is one by the name of Marcel Malherbe…' Madame Malherbe snorted so loudly at the sound of her son's name she nearly caused Thornton to choke on his food. '… And this is his ancestral home. Here is his father.' She pointed to Laurent Senior. 'Here is his mother, and this is his big brother.' She smiled at Laurent who grinned back.

'I presume when you mentioned two of us you were referring to yourself and big brother here, right?'

'Exactement.'

'Exactement!' Laurent Senior murmured, waking up long enough to scratch himself beneath an armpit before falling asleep again.

'In fact, if Al Capone himself had threatened me, Laurent would have had his balls for cat meat.'

'What a delightful expression.'

'It was Laurent's own.'

'And Al Capone is dead.'

'A figure of speech, Thornton, don't be so literal.'

'So the pair not wishing to have their you know whats turned into cat food skedaddled.'

'Fast.' Holly added for emphasis. 'There's something else though. While they were here, one of them let slip the word "beloved"'.

'His beloved?'

'No. I believe he was going to continue with "leader" but stopped. I tried to get him to go on but he closed up like a crab's arse.'

'Your use of the English idiom is excruciating at the moment, Holly, but then I suppose it can't be helped, considering the company you're keeping.'

'Huh! There is absolutely nothing wrong with the company I am keeping, thank you very much,' Holly fumed. 'Only the ones that have left and good riddance except for the fact one of them could have told us more about this Beloved Leader person who is obviously lurking hereabouts, and I have a jolly good idea who it is. I should have got Laurent to work him over, brother or no brother. Why didn't I think of it at the time? Ah, well, too late now.'

Thornton had been so taken with this information he hadn't noticed Madame had slapped another huge portion of pig on his plate, which he regarded with something like horror. True he had thoroughly enjoyed the first helping but this was too much. He had nowhere to put it. He looked towards Holly for help.

'Eat it, Thornton, or Laurent might shoot you, or worse, for insulting his mother's cooking.' She gave Laurent another smile and he nodded happily in return, though not understanding a word that had been said.

Thornton was by now looking so desperate Holly took pity on him. 'I tell you what,' she said, 'I will explain to Madame Malherbe that we have a friend outside who would really appreciate that plate of food,' and she proceeded to do just that in her quite passable French. Madame Malherbe rose and picked up the plate but Holly stopped her with, 'Let Laurent take it,' and then, to Thornton, 'That will give Luigi something to think about.'

It certainly did. Luigi saw Laurent coming and nearly had a laundry problem as he hurriedly ducked behind the Mercedes.

'Hey, kid!' Laurent called, shining a torch on the plate. 'Come on out. I have some food for you.'

Luigi's head appeared but nothing more for a while until Laurent shone the torch again and Luigi could see he appeared to be telling the truth. The fact that he had spent quite a long time without eating while waiting for Thornton to put in an appearance and was rather hungry did help matters, although he still tended to be suspicious and a tad jittery.

He stood up, moved around the car, cautiously approached Laurent and extended his hand to take the plate, keeping his beautiful young Sicilian body at a distance just in case he had to make a run for it. Laurent stood watching him for a while then turned and went back to the house where Thornton was being a little short with Holly.

'Come on, Holly,' he urged, 'we have to be getting back to Nice.

We simply can't dillydally here any longer, cosy and charming though it may be.'

'Yes, I suppose you're right.' She sighed and got unsteadily to her feet.

'Good grief!' Thornton exclaimed. 'What on earth are you wearing?'

'Oh,' said Holly, looking down at herself, 'this is a little outfit I borrowed from Rita. Tres chic, non? Is there any news of Rita by the way?'

'Yes. Luigi informs me she is safe and well back at the hotel and most probably bending everybody's ears recounting her adventure.'

'You can be most unkind when you want, Thornton. She's probably flat on her back, totally traumatised and sedated.'

Actually the lady in question was in the middle of packing and wondering which of the hotel staff had stolen her tracksuit. There would have to be a complaint to the management, an apology and compensation demanded.

'Right then.' Holly turned to Madame Malherbe. 'Madame, I am afraid we must leave you. It would appear the police in their hundreds are this very minute scouring the countryside for me and I would hate for them to come nosing around in this delightful and unspoilt corner of the woods, so ...'

'Comment?'

Holly checked, frowning and pulling back her head, and realised she had been speaking in English. Such fluency was impossible in her passable French but she tried hard to translate and a gracious Madame Malherbe got the gist of it and, in return, prayed that Holly might one day honour the family with a return visit, they had enjoyed her company so much, and perhaps she would like to take some of the pig away with her, an offer she graciously declined.

'Well don't wake M'sieur Malherbe,' Holly added. 'Just tell him I said au revoir.' Then to Thornton, 'He probably won't even remember I was here.'

She gave Laurent Junior a kiss on both cheeks and he responded by kissing her hands while the tears welled up. She also gave Madame Malherbe the three-cheeks Serbian kiss, being careful to avoid the moustache that could still hold a smidgeon of gravy. Then she sashayed to the door followed by Thornton who turned just before his exit to beam all round while uttering his thanks and saying his bon nuit, with a wave of his hand.

Once outside the cool air seemed to have an immediate revitalising effect on Holly who sobered up enough to walk to the cars unaided and now, full of joie de vivre, 'Ciao, Luigi!' She cried, 'Come sta?'

'Bene grazie, principessa.'

'Hear that, Thornton? I'm a princess.'

'Never denied the fact, old girl.'

'Right, how are we going to manage this?' She queried.

Luigi put his empty plate down on a convenient tree stump and, denied the use of a serviette, plucked a handful of grass to wipe the grease from his fingers.

'Do you drive, Luigi?' Thornton asked him.

'Of course,' said with a hint of scorn. Ridiculous question. He had been driving since the age of nine.

'Okay. You take the Mercedes ...'

'Yes, sir!' He replied with suspicious alacrity, sounding like an eager American marine. Thornton was beginning to wonder if the beautiful young Sicilian body was somehow beautifully bonded to the body of this car. '... we will take the hire car,' he finished lamely. There was a problem though. Where were the Merc's keys?

'No problem,' Luigi said and was about to hot-wire it when Thornton felt a tap on the shoulder and there stood Laurent with the keys.

'Thank you,' Thornton said. They drove in silence for a while, each brooding over their recent experience and perhaps wondering what was next in store. Luigi's taillights had long disappeared.

'I hope he doesn't smash up Jean Pierre's car,' Holly finally broke the silence.

'Is that his name? Jean Pierre? I never thought to ask.'

'So what have you been doing with yourself, Thornton, in my unexpected absence?'

'Well, I was supposed to meet Taps this morning ...'

'Taps? What on earth for? Thornton he makes my flesh crawl.'

'He wanted to interview me about the Spitskaya affair. Said he didn't think poor old Reg gave him the truth, the whole truth, and nothing but the truth.'

'But you didn't meet him?'

'Well, yes, I did as a matter of fact, for about five minutes, then I put him off.'

'Why? No don't tell me. A woman.'

'Hmn.'

'Was she fun?'

'Yes, until she pulled a gun on me.'

Holly laughed. 'What gives with you, Thornton, that all your dates pull guns on you?'

'They must be subconsciously aware of my secret desires.'

'Pull the other one. You don't have any secret desires or, if you do, I don't want to even think about what they could be. You are too patently obvious, Thornton King. Seriously though, why did this lady pull a gun on you?'

'One guess.'

Holly thought for all of two seconds. 'Diamonds,' she said.

'Diamonds. Which brings me to my next question. What on earth got into you that you went traipsing all around the countryside following two unknown men to God knows where in the middle of the night?'

'A tearful phone call from Rita,' Holly started to explain, 'saying how she had been kidnapped but they were letting her go and would I come and fetch her? I have to admit the whole idea seemed pretty preposterous but she went on to say instructions were waiting for me at reception. They were and I followed them. I did at one point try to gain the upper hand but that Marcel stuck a needle in me and that was that. They must have used the same trick to take Rita. Their reason for taking me, they said, was to get to you. If you were made aware I was being held and nasty things were being done to me with various agricultural implements you would spill the beans about the diamonds.'

'There are no beans to spill,' Thornton said. 'No diamonds either. Where on earth can they be? That is always presuming our hunches are right and they do actually exist.'

'Oh, they exist all right. I am quite sure of that,' Holly said. 'Why else this latest escapade? My big question is who is it that's after them? It can't be Marcel and his buddies. They're small fry. There's a bigger shark lurking in these waters. And by the way, how did your Luigi know where I was?'

'My Luigi?' Thornton chuckled 'He's certainly not my Luigi but he has what he calls a "special fren" who has the hots for his beautiful young Sicilian body and who is evidently a policeman, middle-aged, married, and deep in the closet I should imagine. He got the information that way.'

'I hope he didn't have to lose his cherry to get it.'

'Dear Holly, Luigi lost his cherry a long long, time ago but not to his special fren who he is evidently keeping on a string, poor man. I hope not for too long because one day the string might snap and Luigi could find himself on the end of a large debt to pay to a legal beagle. But why should I worry? That's his lookout.'

'All right then, riddle me this. Why should Luigi go to all this trouble in the first place? What is it to him?'

'He says it's because he doesn't want anything bad to happen to you. He has a love for you, he says.'

'You've got to be kidding.'

'Not at all. He's a hot blooded young Italian and you are a very attractive … princess.'

'Well this princess …' She laid her head on his shoulder '… is going to need a good night's sleep or she's going to turn into a great big blousy frog by morning.'

'Wrong. It's the prince who's the frog. But before you doze off, if you're going to doze off, back there you said you had a jolly good idea who the beloved leader might be. Care to elucidate?'

'Certainly. It's Taps.'

Thornton laughed so hard he nearly went off the road.

'What's so funny?'

'Taps? Of all people, Taps? You honestly expect me to believe that little upper class fancy pants twit could … I mean, Holly! … Use your nous. An organisation like the Army of the Righteous, a huge cult following.'

'I don't believe he runs it on his own. I never said that. I said he is the head, figurehead if you like. I believe all that has been happening here these last few days is down to him. The diamonds were meant for his organisation and he wants them, Thornton. That is why he is here and that is what all this is about. Just think of the times and places he has unexpectedly turned up, looking for a story always his excuse.'

'Taps …' Thornton chuckled. 'Woman's intuition again, huh? If it is anybody it's likely to be Hamish.'

'Hamish! Why Hamish?'

'That fake Scots accent is a dead giveaway. He's no more a Scot than I am and he really is a man of mystery.'

'Want to take a bet, Thornton?'

'Sure, why not? I can't lose.'

CHAPTER 12

The honorary princess had finished her packing and was settling the bill when Jean Pierre arrived to drive her into Nice to pick up Thornton, and then take them on to the airport. This arrangement was so that she could pay him for the use of and he could collect his car.

'Bonjour, m'amselle.'

She gave a little start as she hadn't heard his approach and, until he spoke, was unaware of his existence at her elbow.

'Ah, Jean Pierre! Bonjour.'

Charles acknowledged his brother-in-law with a brief nod then turned his attention back to Holly as he handed over the itemised account.

'Travellers' cheques?' Holly asked.

'Perfectly acceptable, Miss Day. Thank you.'

'Are these yours?' Jean Pierre asked, indicating Holly's bags. 'I will take them out to the car. You have the key?' He held out his hand, palm uppermost.

'Oh, don't worry,' she said as she handed him the keys. 'Luigi can take them. That's what he's paid for I guess.' She laughed. 'And I haven't tipped him anyway.'

'There will be no need for that, Miss Day,' Charles said in his haughtiest voice accompanied by a loud sniff. 'One of the other boys will take your bags.' He flat handed the bell with a little too much force, making it sound to Holly, or so she imagined, twice as loud as usual. 'I am sorry to say Luigi is no longer with us.'

'You've given him the push?' Holly sounded quite startled which, indeed was what she was. Had it something to do with her and Thornton? Were they responsible in some way for landing the boy in trouble?'

'No, he was not given the push, as you put it. Miss Day. He has simply disappeared. Packed his things and gone. Over night. The third person to disappear in as many days. Tch! I really shouldn't be telling you this, Miss Day, hotel business you know, but the strange thing is he didn't even collect his wages, a whole month's worth of wages and, even if that is small cheese to you, to a boy like Luigi it is big money. So explain that if you can. Perhaps he thinks we will send it on to him. Huh! And he needn't come back here when he feels like it begging for his job either.' Another guest was requiring Charles's attention. 'Excuse me, Miss Day. May I wish you bon voyage?'

'Yes, thank you,' Holly responded. "Quelle bloody peculiar," she thought.

******

Thornton was waiting impatiently at the *Pensione Garibaldi* as the old Mercedes pulled up, Jean Pierre leapt out, opened the boot and filled it with Thornton's luggage as it was passed to him, then he returned to the driver's seat as Thornton sat himself in the back.

'Morning, Holly,' he greeted her cheerfully, 'or should I say quark quark?'

'Quark quark?'

'Isn't that the noise frogs make? I'm not really very good at impersonations. Was always hopeless at charades, a real party pooper.'

'Do I look a mess?' She sounded worried.

'Not at all,' he replied. 'You look ravishing as usual. Did you say your fond farewells to your lover?'

'Who?'

'Luigi, the police officer's incipient paramour, if not yours.'

'Didn't see him.'

'What? He wasn't standing there, hand outstretched?'

'No. Evidently he's disappeared.'

'Oh dear.' Thornton thought for a moment and then theorised. 'Those goons who kidnapped you and Rita have taken him and are beating the shit out of him or worse for interfering in their plans.'

'He never interfered. All he did was bring you to me and anyway that was after the two goons who kidnapped me had given up and fled.'

'Well, could be they believe he snitched on them to the cops, something like that.' Satisfied with his deductions, Thornton leaned back; arms stretched wide along the top of the seat, and admired the passing scenery.

******

Jean Pierre eased his lanky body out of the car and bustled around to the back to open the boot and take out the luggage. He wondered if, when he hired out the car, he had told Holly the lock on the boot was defective and the boot was not secure. It didn't really matter anyway as they had never used it.

Apart from all the shopping bags there was Holly's case and vanity box, Thornton's bargain suitcase and last of all another case just like it, smothered in labels for the hotel in Beaulieu-sur-Mer. For a long moment Thornton and Holly stared at it in almost total disbelief and then looked at each other while Jean Pierre looked first at one then the other then down to the suitcase and back to the pair, wondering what was going on. Should he have warned them about the lock? Thornton finally spoke.

'Just a minute,' he said, 'where did that come from?'

'What?'

'That suitcase. Where did it come from?'

Jean Pierre shrugged. 'It was already in the car. I thought one of you must have put it there. It matches this other one, see?'

'Of course I can see!' Thornton almost yelled. Jean Pierre took a step back, startled by the vehemence in Thornton's voice. 'Open it up! Open it up!' Thornton barked and then, impatiently, 'Here, give it to me!'

Without waiting even for Jean Pierre's reaction, Thornton picked up the case, laid it on the floor of the boot and flicked it open. The case contained various garments, some unwashed, which he pulled out and scattered about willy-nilly until he came to what he already expected to find, a false bottom that had been pulled away, carelessly replaced and, in a creased corner of which, lay one small overlooked uncut diamond. He turned to Holly.

'No wonder the little bugger has disappeared and not bothered about his wages,' he said, holding up the stone between forefinger and thumb. 'I wouldn't know how many were in there or what they're worth but our little Luigi has scarpered with the bloody lot.'

Jean Pierre was totally confused. He took the diamond from Thornton and examined it. It didn't look much really, could have been a sliver of dusty glass or a tiny piece of mastic for all he knew. Though, had he tried to bite it, it would have probably broken a couple of teeth. He handed it back. Holly was laughing.

'What are you laughing about?' Thornton's expression was grim.

'They've been in the boot of the Mercedes all this time, ever since the case mysteriously disappeared,' She explained. 'No wonder Luigi wanted to guard the car. No wonder he was delighted to drive it back to the hotel last night. It gave him time to clear them out before we arrived at a more leisurely pace. He must have put the case in there when he first removed it from the hotel, believing it to be the safest place for it, or hopefully the last place anyone would think of looking, and you don't find it funny that everybody's been running around in circles searching for it when it's been right under everyone's noses the whole time? We've been merrily driving around the countryside to all intents and purposes sitting on top of a case full of diamonds and you don't find that funny?'

'Funny or not,' Thornton growled, 'we have to get them back.'

'Oh, yes? First of all, why do we have to get them back? They are nothing to do with us.'

'Yes they are,' he contradicted her. 'Rita was kidnapped, you were kidnapped and Reg didn't get to make his speech.'

'Probably just as well,' she said.

'Excusez mois,' Jean Pierre butted in, as he really wasn't sure about exactly what was going on. 'I hope the car was useful for you but I have to go to my work and I would very much appreciate it if you could pay me now.'

'Of course,' Holly said, rummaging in her handbag, 'how much do I owe you?'

Jean Pierre named his price, which to Holly's delight was what they had originally agreed and wasn't nearly as much as she thought it would ultimately be once the original quote was conveniently forgotten. She had enough francs in her bag to pay him and handed it over.

'Thank you so much, Jean Pierre. Don't know what we would have done without it and it's still got about half a tank I would reckon.'

He thanked her profusely with a number of small bows and, having pocketed his francs, extended his hand again to wish them both bon voyage before he turned away to put the scattered clothes back in the last case and take it out of the boot, but Thornton stopped him.

'Hold it just a minute please, Jean Pierre, we haven't decided what to do about this.'

'Thornton!' Holly sounded more than just a little exasperated. 'Even if you believe the diamonds have something to do with us, which I don't, not for one minute, the chances of tracing Luigi and getting them back I should think are pretty remote and we have a plane to catch so why don't you just give up the whole idea?'

'I'm not thinking only of Luigi. I'm thinking of whomever it is these diamonds were meant for. Whoever it is who organised the junior branch of the local mafia to do the kidnappings. Someone, Taps, Hamish, or someone else who we don't yet know, wanted these stones very badly and I for one want to know who it is. Seriously now, don't you?'

Holly considered this for a moment and then nodded.

'Right,' Thornton said, 'First thing is a phone call. Jean Pierre can you do us one last favour please? On your way to work could you drop that suitcase off at the police station? Ask for inspector Leroux and say I sent you. There's a good chap and thank you very much.'

Jean Pierre, still confused and not knowing if he were letting himself in for something, refrained from saying the police station was in the opposite direction to his work and resigned himself to being even later. Obviously this was an important police matter and that would be his excuse with the boss. He closed the boot and moved around to climb into the driving seat, looking in his rear view mirror to give a backhanded wave as he drove off.

'Come on, Holly,' Thornton ordered, heading for *Departures*, 'quick phone call to make.'

Charles answered the phone and was most surprised to hear Thornton announce himself.

'Yes, Mister King, and what may I do for you?'

'Charles, when you engaged Luigi to work at the hotel, did you get a home address for him?'

'But of course.'

'Can you give it to me?'

'May I enquire as to why you want it, Mister King?'

'Okay, I'll tell you. We've found the case that had the diamonds in it. The diamonds are gone and so has master Luigi. Put two and two together.'

'I see.' Charles was as bland as ever. 'Well, Mister King, I could give you the address he gave us but who is to say if it is correct?'

'Yes, there is that,' Thornton agreed. 'I guess if he were up to any hanky-panky at all, let alone having all his birthdays come at once in discovering a cache of diamonds, he would hardly tell you where to find him.'

'I can tell you however, I remember without looking it up, the address is in Palermo.'

'That's close enough. Thank you, Charles, and au revoir.'

He put down the receiver and turned to Holly standing beside him to pass on the news.

'You intend we should go to Palermo,' was her reaction, not a question but a statement of fact.

'Of course. Somehow we have to get there fast and head him off before he gets to his bolthole wherever that may be.'

'He could already be there.'

'My instinct tells me not. He probably took the train and is still on his way. If we get there first ... Holly, I don't suppose your credit card would stretch to a helicopter would it?'

'Thornton! Are you totally out of your mind? Helicopters cost a fortune.'

'I'm talking about hiring it, not buying it.'

'Hiring it costs a fortune, four figures an hour and no, my credit card does not stretch that far so forget it.'

'You're not being a very game bird this morning, Holly. Ah! Here is just the man we want.'

Holly turned her head to look in the same direction as Thornton, to see Taps approaching with bags and baggage.

'What did I tell you, Thornton? Always turning up when not expected,' she whispered.

'Nonsense! He's got a plane to catch just as we have, but where is the brawny Scot?' Then, even before greetings could be exchanged, Thornton plunged right in. 'Taps, old boy! How are you? Where's Hamish?'

'I have absolutely no idea. Hamish likes to go a wandering so he could be anywhere. Fortunately I am not my photographer brother's keeper and I have to admit I am always glad when he's not dogging my footsteps. As I say, he could be anywhere. He could even have gone off to Italy for all I know.'

If Thornton had been a character in a cartoon a light bulb would have been lit up over his head, or the word *idea* in a balloon.

'Palermo!' He said. 'I knew I was right all along. The man's gone to Palermo with Luigi.'

'Sicily?'

'You know another Palermo? Unless there are one or two in the United States of course but I doubt he would have gone there.'

'Don't talk nonsense, Thornton. Why on earth would he want to go to Palermo?'

'Listen, Taps, do you think you could afford to hire a helicopter?'

Duncan Devonport-Fawcett stared at Thornton for a long moment and then drawled in his most upper class cut glass voice, 'Thornton, my dear, are you under the influence or have you merely gone totally bonkers?'

'That is what I asked him,' Holly scowled, though whether the scowl was for Taps or for Thornton, nobody could be too sure.

'We've found the diamonds.' Thornton said.

There was the longest pause in theatrical history before Taps could find enough voice to croak, 'What did you say?'

'That is, we know where they are going to be and we have to get there first before our quarry goes to ground.'

'And where might that there be?'

'Palermo.'

'And who is it who has them?'

'Hamish and Luigi. So how about it? Can you afford a helicopter or not?'

'Not. Unfortunately but most definitely not.'

'But your magazine could.' This was from Holly who wasn't too sure the "most definitely" was truly definite. Her distrust of Taps was growing by the minute and she was now intrigued to see how far this would go. He turned to her. 'Maybe Thornton's not so crazy after all,' she continued. 'Think of the story. Worth its weight in ... diamonds?'

'Where do we find a helicopter?'

'Where else but at an airport?'

'Pity we won't have a photographer handy to cover the big moment? Never mind,' Thornton continued, 'you can have two stories for the price of one because I can give you our version of the Spitskaya affair on the way.'

******

Inspector Gaston Leroux looked down at the suitcase on his desk as though it had miraculously materialised which, in a way, it had. He looked up at Jean Pierre standing in front of him.

'In the boot of your car?' He said. 'Incredible!' He turned to Mathieu. 'Let's have those two idiots back in here,' he ordered.

'They're going to shit themselves when they see this.' He turned back to Jean Pierre. 'Then I need to go to Beaulieu to ask your brother in law a lot of questions and everything, as the English say, will be in the bag.'

******

'I hate helicopters,' Holly shouted above the clatter. 'They scare me to death.'

'I'm not too fond ...' Thornton struggled against the racket and gave up. He moved closer to Holly so he could talk directly into an ear without having to shout. 'I'm slipping up, Holly. I should have thought to ask Charles for Luigi's surname. If we miss him ...'

'Never mind. If necessary you can telephone again when we get to Palermo, and, if Jean Pierre has delivered the suitcase, I am sure Inspector Leroux will be enthusiastically hotfooting it all over the place. It won't be long before he knows as much as we do, and if he has associates in Italy, which I am sure he does have, especially after the other night, we probably won't be the only ones looking for the errant Luigi.'

'Hmn ...' Thornton settled back in his seat and eyed Taps sitting opposite who seemed a million miles away. It was strange he thought but, before leaving Nice, Taps had gone off to the toilets saying he wanted to change and had returned wearing his heavy winter overcoat. Now what did he want to do that for? Thornton thought. They were heading further south where it was going to be even warmer than the Riviera. Couldn't he have waited till they got back to England? Maybe he thought he was going to freeze to death in the helicopter.

He thought about the Spitskaya story. There was no way he was going to be able to relate it over this noise, not without totally losing his voice, so once again it would have to wait. He wondered why Taps looked so preoccupied. Maybe he hated flying. Maybe, like Holly he was terrified of helicopters. Maybe he was going to be sick. Actually it was none of these things. He was thinking of diamonds, and Thornton was beginning to wonder if he was going to lose his bet.

******

Luigi sat gazing out of the window as the train made its way towards Reggio Calabria; then it would be the ferry and the final stretch to Palermo where he would have to change trains to take him to his own village and home.

He imagined the joyous reception he would receive from the family, his mother would never stop crying and forcing food on him he had got so skinny, and he smiled at the thought. His battered holdall that had contained all his worldly possessions when he signed on to work in the hotel was on the empty seat beside him and on the floor between his legs was a large brown paper carrier bag full of oranges. He glanced down at it and then looked up at the mother and her little girl sitting opposite. The child smiled at him and, smiling back, he dipped his hand in the bag and produced an orange to offer her. She grew suddenly shy and didn't want to take it until the mother, smiling, gave her an encouraging nudge at which she stepped across, took the proffered fruit and fled back to the safety of her mother's side. Luigi laughed out loud. He had never been happier than at this moment. Maybe he wouldn't have been had he realised someone was on the same train, keeping a beady eye on him whilst himself going unnoticed.

******

Holly and Taps stood waiting by the concourse; Thornton at the far end of the platform so they had it covered both ways. It had been Holly's suggestion they split up. Although they attracted a couple of cursory glances, nobody seemed particularly interested in their presence, no official *jobs worth* poked his nose in, demanding to know what they were up to, so they waited. Discreet enquiries had assured them there was no way Luigi could have arrived before them and the train he would most likely be on was due any minute, that is if Thornton's surmise was correct and he had indeed caught the train. They could of course be on the wrong track altogether.

'What do you think?' Holly asked in order to break the moody silence.

Taps turned his head slightly at the sound of the voice but then looked away, making no answer, his hands deep in his overcoat pockets. Holly gave a shrug and peered down the platform to where she could see Thornton at the far end and the train just putting in an appearance dead on time.

'Well,' she said, more to herself than anything else, and thinking of Luigi being on the train with the diamonds, 'we shall soon know one way or another.'

The train pulled to a shuddering stop, doors were flung open with much banging and loud Italian voices filling the air as passengers disembarked. The train had not been over full but there were enough people to mask Holly and Taps as Luigi, smiling to himself, made his way up the platform.

He was only a few feet away when he saw them and stood stock-still, unable to move, such was the shock.

They started towards him against the flow and it was then that he recovered enough to turn and flee on legs like jelly, only to be confronted by Thornton coming the other way. Luigi turned back again. What was he to do? A train stood on either side, one waiting to depart, one in which he had just arrived. It would seem he was well and truly trapped. Taps and Holly were almost on him when Taps stopped and held out his hand.

'Give me the bag, Luigi.'

'What for you want the bag?' Luigi's trembling voice was almost falsetto. 'Ees oranges! You no want oranges!'

'Absolutely not true. It so happens I'm in the market for oranges right now so give me the bag.'

Holly and Thornton seemed to have been hypnotised into standing almost motionless, watching and listening to this exchange, a situation that changed remarkably quickly as Taps suddenly withdrew his hands from his pockets to reveal in his right hand a snub nose Colt twenty-two.

'Give me the bag, Luigi!' Taps yelled and Luigi screamed and finally did have a laundry problem soiling his beautiful young Sicilian body. Thornton just had time to think, "so that's why the overcoat" but was too far away to do anything. Holly however, standing beside him, was quick off the mark and brought the side of her hand down hard on Taps' wrist. Duncan Devonport-Fawcett felt the paralysing blow the full length of his arm and the gun clattered to the floor from nerveless fingers just as he reached out with his other hand and tried to grab the bag. No longer menaced by the gun, Luigi was having none of it. He turned and thought to dart nimbly passed Thornton when he was suddenly menaced by a fourth figure that had stepped from the train with the wicked looking skein dhu in his hand.

A few curious Italians stopped to look in wonder at this kilted figure that had brought Luigi to a full stop and it was Hamish who now grabbed the bag but Luigi resisted and pulled back. The bag even under ordinary circumstances would never have stood the tug of war but as a couple of oranges had split and wet the paper with their juice, it naturally ripped in half, sending oranges and diamonds rolling and scattering across the platform.

It seemed for a moment or two that the world had come to a full stop, and then pandemonium broke out as those passengers, alerted by Luigi's scream and who had paused to see what was going on, were suddenly on their hands and knees scrabbling for diamonds while others came rushing onto the platform to join them. The doors of the waiting train, whose passengers so far had merely been spectators leaning out of windows, intrigued by an obvious incident, flung open the doors and couldn't wait to join in the melee. They even came from the cafeteria and pandemonium ensued during which both Taps and Luigi tried discreetly to disappear only to fall into the waiting hands of a number of carabinieri. The policemen, despite constantly blowing on their whistles and dealing out a few loosely aimed truncheon blows, realised they had no chance of putting an end to the mayhem. Fortunately no loss of life was sustained but there were any number of badly grazed knees, trodden on knuckles, heavy bruising, swellings, torn clothes, sprains, friends of many years standing who would never talk to each other again, train schedules disrupted, and giant headlines all over the world as mementoes of this incredible day.

The riot squad had to be called out to eventually restore order in Palermo railway station.

******

Rita was in such a state the first thing she did on reaching home was head straight for the kitchen where, without even removing her hat, she set too to clean the gas cooker with vigorous rubs, using copious amounts of Vim on a soft scourer. She took a peek into the oven but decided that was too much and she wouldn't attempt it right at that moment. Her nerves having settled somewhat, she heaved a huge sigh and, drying her hands, set out to explore the house, ascertaining nothing untoward like a ransacking had occurred during their absence. Apart from being cold and smelling a little of damp everything was in order even though Reg had told little porkies when he said he had locked the bathroom window. Fortunately no opportunistic burglar could have passed by to notice it.

Although Charles, for the hotel, had apologised profusely about the theft of her favourite tracksuit and promised recompense should it not come to light, (she would be delightfully surprised in a couple of weeks time to have it delivered through the post, dry cleaned and with a note of apology from Holly) she was also depressed by the fact that, after all she had been through, there were no reporters at the airport in Nice to mark her departure or at Heathrow to interview her on her arrival. True, Inspector Leroux had graced them with his presence to say adieu and to thank them for helping him nick three minor criminal figures on very serious charges which should see them happily banged up for a long time to come but the fact remained, and a quick glance at a number of front pages as they passed W.H Smiths at Heathrow proved it to be only too true; her story was already old hat and the news of the moment was the woman who had brought forth quins after in vitro fertilisation.

'Serve her right,' Reg growled darkly, 'interfering with nature. Never did any good. The bloody world's over populated anyway.'

He was in the dining room going through the bills that had landed on the mat since their departure, a couple of which just had to be wrong and would have to be queried, which didn't make his mood any lighter. He too was naturally disappointed at their being wiped off the front page and was wondering what kind of a story he could concoct to regale them with at the station before the "Reg" jokes started to fly thick and fast behind his back. He was sure they would and wondered if he might get in first and divert them in Roper's direction. He wasn't aware that Constable Roper was still at Heathrow and dating a girl named Blodwen Hughes much to the disappointment of a young man named Mike.

Having removed her hat, Rita returned to the kitchen to start on the dishes in the sink. The kids would be home for Christmas and she didn't want them coming in to a less than pristine house. It would not set a good example so, even though she felt sure they wouldn't notice anyway, it was on with the pinny; spit and polish was the order of the day, well polish anyway.

At least she had managed to do some last minute shopping before leaving France: a new pipe and a bottle of calvados for Reg, a pair of minuscule swimming trunks for Robin, he didn't have very much to hide anyway, and a bikini for the blossoming daughter. Rita wasn't too sure this was really such a good idea as she had perpetual nightmares of said daughter becoming another statistic in the teenage pregnancy and single mother stakes and the bikini might give the wrong boy the right ideas or the right boy the wrong idea. Still, it was done now and she was sure the girl would take heed of motherly warnings and look stunning in it. And for herself, a touch of extravagance she felt she richly deserved, *Chanel No 5*.

Reg took the cases upstairs, laid them on the bed and started to unpack. One of the first things he came across were the folded, much fingered, slightly soiled pages of the speech that never was. He sat on the bed and looked at it. It was an awe-inspiring document but fate had decreed it would never see the light of day. Such a pity really. He would keep it safe anyway. Just in case ...

******

'Thank you, Holly, for my quiet, restful break,' Thornton said, 'I really enjoyed it. Hate to think I will have to go back to the office tomorrow. Well, don't really have to but feel I should I suppose. Wonder how Norris's boys have been getting on with the flat. Well, we'll soon find out. I'm pleased they upgraded us, aren't you? These seats are so much more comfortable than cattle class and so much more room to stretch one's long legs, but then we are the flavour of the moment. So it was the Honourable Duncan Devonport-Fawcett all along who was the Beloved Leader and you win the bet. As for my thinking it was Hamish, well I said he was a man of mystery didn't I? But CIA? That I didn't figure, not for a minute so there's a turn up for the books. I said he wasn't a genuine Scot though, didn't I? He said he'd been keeping tabs on Taps for quite a while evidently. Bully for him being able to rescue Rita like that. Said he found the phone number of Marcel's apartment in Taps' hotel desk. He made Rita promise to keep his identity secret for a while which, surprise surprise, she actually managed to do. Now the whole Army of the Righteous cult thing is dead in the water I suppose; unless they can come up with another charismatic leader, though I hardly think of Taps as being that. Must have been all the mumbo jumbo around him. I'll never tell him our version of the Spitskaya story now, not if he's locked up in an Italian or a French prison, or maybe the Scrubs, charged with organising kidnappings if nothing else. Holly, are you listening to me?'

But Holly was fast asleep.

'Ah, well.' Thornton sighed and reached for the in-flight magazine.

It was getting on for four in the morning when Holly dropped him off with a breezy 'ciao bambino!' and drove away. Lugging his shopping bags and suitcase, he entered the lift and pressed the button for his floor.

Arriving there, Thornton marched full of excited expectation towards his brand new front door. He couldn't wait to see what the boys had done with the flat. He heard the lift doors close behind him as he stood admiring the gleaming paintwork and then, 'Oh, shit!' he said. 'I don't have a bloody key,' and broke into uncontrollable laughter.

Dead On Time

By Glyn Jones

After being made redundant from MI5 Thornton King is trying to make ends meet as a private eye. With the aid of Miss Holly Day, and under the watchful eye of Princess Spitskaya, he enters the glamorous world of fashion, as Rear Admirals, Drug Barons, Arms Dealers, Film Stars all come to a sticky end in this romp of a comedy thriller.

The only link Thornton has to go on is the fact that all the men before they died were last seen in the presence of a beautiful girl, but each eyewitness testifies differently; that it was a blonde, brunette or raven haired girl. Is it the same girl or is there more than one strikingly beautiful murderer on the loose?

Thornton & Holly finally track down the killers to a modelling school, a cover for a school of assassins run by the Princess, where the students end of term graduation depends on their ability to do the job. But not all the students have taken their final exams!

Who will be the last to graduate? Will Holly make the grade? Is it for Thornton to hand out the diplomas?

Murder, mystery and mayhem wrapped up in beautiful but lethal packages take you on a roller coaster ride until the final chapter when all is revealed!

The perfect model for a murder!

Dead On Target

A Further Thornton King Adventure

By Glyn Jones

Convinced her uncle was murdered rather than the veridt of suicide, Rory Pemberton employs the services of Thornton King to unravel the mystery where Chief Inspector Venabales and the London police department failed.

Thornton, calls on his unoffical sidekick Holly and together, they investigate the rather strange goings on in Epping forest and an archery club that is somehow linked to a firm of city stockbrokers!

Be warned, if you go into the woods today you mightn't come out alive!

Read on for an extract……..

Available
March 2010

Chapter One

Thornton had a client. He was at his desk busily sorting through a mound of invoices and dividing them into neat piles of urgent, not so urgent, not nearly so urgent and bloody hell, if I don't pay this by tomorrow I'm in deepest shit, when there was a knock on the door and she followed it up by entering without waiting for a response. It was a miracle she had made it up the narrow wooden nineteenth century staircase in this almost condemned building, or didn't bring the doorjamb into the room with her, dry rot and all, but she was obviously used to manoeuvring her way through, onto, up, down, around, into, and out of tight spaces.

Thornton honestly believed himself under any circumstance to be a cool customer and he didn't mean to show surprise but his eyes opened very wide at the sight of her, probably a reaction she was quite used to because she didn't seem to be unduly affected by it. To put it bluntly she was huge, enormous, gigantic, three Amazons all rolled into one. She had more meat on her than a Sumo wrestler, and a Victorian lady novelist (of either sex) would have rated her at a million shekels or more in any Sultan's harem. At a cannibal feast, Thornton thought, she would have satisfied the appetites of forty covers; that is if they had a pot big enough to cook her in. Alternatively she could always have been spit-roasted.

Her name was Aurora Margarita Pemberton, known to her friends as Rory she informed him, proffering an all encompassing fist. Of course at school she was nicknamed "Amp" and when a teacher questioned this as being short for "Ample" with a real adult concern regarding bullying by those in her charge, the rejoinder with wide innocent eyes was, "Oh, no, Miss! It's because she's so full of life, Miss. It's short for "Ampere", miss because she's so electrifying. A real spark she is, miss, honest," which was a load of old codswallop if ever there was but invariably raised a giggle and settled the matter. Rory of course knew different but didn't seem to mind, Amy for amiable could have been her middle name.

'How do you do?' Thornton responded wondering if he was ever going to get his hand back and feeling mightily embarrassed that neither of his two rickety second-hand chairs seemed large enough to encase her bulk; and they could hardly conduct an interview standing up. There was also the distinct potential, if she did decide to sit down, of splintering wood and an unfortunate, ungainly, and undignified collapse with the possibility of damages both physical (current) and legal (future) that, considering the unpaid bills on his desk, would be catastrophic. Admittedly he had a diamond in his pocket but he didn't want to get rid of that until he was really in trouble, that is the bailiffs were battering down his door. He believed they could strip him of all his possessions bar his bed and the tools of his trade, but tools of his trade had he none, unless an ancient Smith Corona typewriter that had seen better days, was missing the letter F and badly needed servicing, could be considered a tool worth talking about.

There was also a further worry, the fact that the office temperature seemed to be hovering just a mite above zero, as was pretty obvious by the fact it was almost lunchtime and Thornton was still in his overcoat and you could see his breath as he exhaled. Freezing cold would increase the danger of painful injury. Bones, no matter how well padded, become brittle in freezing conditions.

'Miss Pemberton ...'

'Rory,' she corrected him with a smile.

'Oh yes, of course, Rory. I presume you have come seeking my assistance in some confidential matter and I am sorry to say, thoughtless of me not to collect some on my way in, but I have run out of shillings for the meter and as it would hardly be conducive to an intelligent conversation with chattering teeth, quivering lips, and frozen fingers ...' He paused momentarily to wonder what frozen fingers had to do with it...'and considering the hour of the day,' he looked at his watch, 'may I suggest we move on to enjoy the warmth of my local which is situated conveniently just around the corner. Well nearly,' he added as an afterthought, as around the corner was a good two blocks away, and why was he uttering these entirely unnatural and stilted phrases? Perhaps it was because Miss Pemberton with any luck was going to be his very first genuine client and he badly wanted to impress. But not being himself was not going to impress except badly and he mentally kicked himself for being an ass. Part of his problem could be put down to the fact that she was a most impressive young lady and not just because of her size. She quite obviously never had to or never would have to put shillings in a meter. Her couture was of the highest quality, the string of pearls nestling on the pale blue angora was of the finest, her accessories the most expensive Bond Street could provide, her manner the surest, and everything was in the best of all possible taste. This was ex-Swiss finishing school and no mistake and, were it still in existence, she would have been a debutante making her curtsy at Buck House, no argument.

'That's a jolly good idea,' Rory quickly agreed to his suggestion of moving out as the chill was already beginning to seep into her bones. She could feel her teeth beginning to chatter and her chilblains to itch. She had been quite warm on entering the building as the cab that deposited her on the doorstep had been well heated.

'Will we need an umbrella?' Thornton asked as he reached for his hat lying next to the tea tray on top of the filing cabinet. His coat stand, having lost one of its three legs was leaning against the wall in danger of falling over at any moment.

'I think not,' she replied. 'Clear blue skies when I came in, which is probably why it is so cold.'

Thornton had the distinct impression there was an adjective missing before the word cold. He was certainly glad though not to have to share his umbrella. Old it might be, well used against England's inclement weather, a little on the shabby and faded side but still the best there was from James Smith of New Oxford Street, hardly large enough though to accommodate the two of them and, in playing the gallant, sure as God made little apples as his mother would say, he would be the one whose shoulder was rained upon.

'Shall we go then?' He put on one of his meant to be charming smiles, which sometimes turned out to be more of a lopsided smirk, but she responded to it in kindly fashion as he held the door open for her.

'Thank you,' she said as she squeezed her way through at an oblique angle. Good, he thought, by the very nature of her gracious acknowledgement she was obviously not one of the how dare you treat me like a helpless little woman when I am as good as you are sort, and the whiff of her very pleasant and obviously expensive perfume as she passed by seemed to reassure him that neither was she one of the burn the bra ladies who, though he hadn't actually come into contact with any of them he usually, because of television coverage, associated them with greasy anoraks and sou'westers, marching in teeming rain and, he was quite certain, the smell of wet and camping stoves from stopping now and again to brew tea in blackened billycans. Thornton did have a sneaky admiration for them though, at the same time, he wondered how anyone with brains could imagine their actions had the slightest effect on stuffed shirt politicians and world affairs. The bomb was exploded, the moving hand moves on, the clock does not go backwards and you cannot practically alter history, only in history books.

Thornton had distinctly old-fashioned, pre-women's lib ideas. He liked his ladies to be feminine, even ladies as large as Rory, and why not indeed? He had no objection to a girl being joli laid. Often that was sexier, more attractive than a vapid plastic pin up with everything the right size, shape, colour, and all in the right place, and he sometimes wondered if there were some homoerotic tendencies lurking somewhere in his nature when he found himself wistfully dreaming of the twenties when the girls had bobbed hair, flat chests, and called each other chaps. Thornton was definitely not into boobs. Pin-ups could boast them but large boobs were off the menu: small was the order of the day: petite, just enough to cup in the hand and why, he wondered, were humans beings the only mammals to develop breasts before lactation? Oh, yes, he knew all about sexual symbols and all that but it did seem a trifle odd if nothing else. Come to think of it though, (as he followed her down the corridor) did Rory actually wear a bra? And did she have them especially made in some East End or Far East sweatshop where questions as to size, reinforcement, and broken industrial sewing machine needles wouldn't necessarily come into it? But he was really letting his imagination run away with him.

*****

Some time previous to Thornton and Rory's coming together, in the boardroom of an office suite, this one in the heart of the city almost within spitting distance of St. Paul's: elegantly panelled, redolent of polish, old leather, and stale cigar smoke; an emergency meeting had been hurriedly called to discuss what seemed an almost intractable problem and the problem, as it turned out, was Aurora Pemberton.

Word had got about that she was dissatisfied with the police investigation, undertaken by Detective Inspector Reg Venables and his squad, and dissatisfied more particularly with the coroner's resulting verdict of suicide while the balance of the mind etcetera;

238

and she was seeking help in unravelling the mystery of her uncle's strange death.

'Evidently word has it,' the chairman, Sir Peter Wheeler, known as "Wheeler Dealer Peter", a man of lean but impressive stature, steely determination and very little principle, if any, barked once everyone had settled down around the table, 'she's after getting a private detective to look into her guardian's unfortunate death so I would appreciate suggestions please as to what we do about it.'

'Bump her off,' was the first laconic response after a short silence.

'Be serious, Trevor, old boy. How do you suggest we do that? And you don't think it would look highly suspicious coming so soon after Sir Roger's unfortunate demise?'

'Not at all actually,' a cut glass voice broke in. 'She commits suicide because she just cannot accept her beloved guardian's death. Poor little thing ... '

'Little?' queried a voice from lower down the table followed by a general all round sniggering.

'I was referring to her femininity and emotional state. She was, after all, very fond of him.'

'And he of her,' another voice added, a remark that caused a further bout of chuckling.

'Now don't be like that please, Jack. Rumours, nothing but rumours.'

'Well he was an eccentric old bird, Sir Roger Pemberton, and we all know about the proclivities of certain bachelor uncles with their nephews and nieces, don't we? So who knows what took his fancy?'

'If he were still alive he could sue you for those remarks.'

'Just as well he's dead then,' another voice piped up.

'Look,' the chairman butted in beginning to show signs of irritability and before they could all start voicing an opinion, 'we are not here to discuss the sex life of the late Sir Roger Pemberton, real or imagined, but what we are going to do about his ward who is going to be, stating it quite plainly, a right pain in the arse, or worse. Maurice, we haven't heard from you. Any suggestions?'

'Yes,' Maurice drawled. 'Run her over.'

'What?'

'Run her over, old boy.'

Wheeler Dealer bridled a little at being addressed as "old boy", a somewhat undignified and uncalled for way of addressing the chairman of the board, major shareholder and guiding light of an old established company he had more than once pulled safely through the most difficult of times.

'She'd make a splendid target you have to admit,' Maurice continued, unabashed by the change of expression on Sir Peter's face. 'Couldn't hardly miss her, could you?'

'Right. Fine. Yes. Anybody second the motion? I take it, Maurice, you are volunteering to undertake, if you'll pardon the rather doleful expression, no pun intended, this course of action?'

'Certainly not. I never drive. Chauffeur does it all for me. And I certainly wouldn't direct him to knock her over. Think of the damage to the car. A tiny scratch on a Rolls costs an absolute mint to cover up don't you know and the insurance premiums would rocket. No, it needs someone who's never taken a driving test, is therefore without a licence, uninsured, preferably behind the wheel of a stolen vehicle and who won't mind, for a fee of course, going down in the Scrubs or Wandsworth for a spell on a driving without due care and attention charge and causing death by misadventure or whatever the current legal jargon is. With the way things are going these days it probably won't be more than a slap on the wrist anyway and an admonition not to be a naughty boy and never to do it again.' Maurice was obviously one of the hang 'em, flog 'em or lock 'em up and throw away the key brigade though of course it would never apply to himself or any of his own.

'And where do you suggest we find this person?'

'Oh, there're plenty around. If you were to ask me there's psychopaths virtually on every street corner these days. Turn over a stone and you'll find one. I put it down to the goggle box disturbing weak brains, not just because of the programmes you understand but I'm sure the rays have a terrible effect on brain cells. Addles them completely in my opinion. Never watch the damn thing myself.'

Sir Peter coughed to stop the flow.

'Yes, well just put out the word and, if there is a large enough reward, they'll come running.' Maurice looked around the table, well satisfied with his input.

'And what if he botches it? What if she isn't killed but only injured?'

'It will have put the frighteners on her, won't it? She'll know we've got her in our sights and she had better behave or else.' He waved an admonishing finger as though Rory were in front of him to take notice.

'We had hoped for that before with her uncle, if you remember, which unfortunately is why we are here at the moment.'

There was a silence whilst the board members ruminated on this. Obviously it was a plan with faults and they did not take kindly to plans that weren't considered a hundred percent foolproof, as if such a thing even existed. Many a dictator has ended his life wondering exactly where his plans went wrong. The first thing to worry about with this particular plan was that the person hired could blab and they'd all be well and truly up shit creek without a paddle. They had imagined their plan regarding Sir Roger to be foolproof and had just been painfully reminded by their chairman that it had most definitely gone wrong and they had been lucky in that the day of the inquest the coroner had missed his breakfast, had a terrible journey from East Croyden, standing all the way, was hungry enough to eat a horse and wanted his lunch. They hadn't reckoned on Miss Aurora's interference after the event though. Man proposes, God disposes, though in this case it seemed Miss Pemberton was going to do the disposing unless a solid means was found to dispose of her first.

'Why don't we just buy her off?' someone suggested.

The chairman glared down the table at the member who had come up with this one. Obviously the man was brain-dead. How did he ever get elected to the board? The sooner he was dispatched the better. He could turn out to be a distinct liability.

'Sir Roger might have been amusing himself with his test tubes and what have you down at the docks or wherever,' the chairman sneered, 'but he hardly died penniless and Miss Pemberton I believe is his sole heir. With what had you in mind to pay her off?' Sir Peter's glare became almost unbearable and in its light the miscreant shrivelled visibly. But worse was to come; everyone turned to look at the unfortunate who had opened his big mouth and the man blushed scarlet, recognising his stupidity if not his temerity, but he was fairly new to this game and consequently unaware of its pitfalls. His name was Wilkins, known from bathroom observations as "Wee Willy", and Wee Willy realised he was now in a dangerous situation.

'I do beg the board's pardon,' he whined, almost wondering if going down on his knees would help. 'I wasn't thinking clearly.'

'You weren't thinking at all,' the chairman snarled, showing nicotine-stained teeth that gave his dentist nightmares twice a year.

Wilkins, starting to sweat profusely, and cowered in his chair to which the seat of his pants was beginning to stick rather uncomfortably but, fortunately, attention was diverted when another voice in self-assured tones piped up with, 'Why not let her go ahead and have her private detective?'

All heads swivelled in the speaker's direction. 'But let's just make sure the person she chooses is a complete nincompoop who couldn't detect his way from his bedroom to the bathroom, remember why he went or find what he's looking for when he got there, so that eventually she gives up in disgust or is just too damn tired of the whole thing and pays him off with nothing accomplished.'

All heads now turned in the direction of the chairman for his reaction.

'Ye-es,' the chairman drawled, stroking his goatee as a sign of his own deep thought, (the beard he fondly believed gave him an air of distinction, a bit like one or two members of royalty who sported small amounts of facial hair) 'and who points her in the right direction? I mean in the direction of a private eye who is such a totally hopeless case?'

'I do.'

'You are acquainted with Miss Pemberton?'

'She has ... how shall I put this? She has made it quite clear she has an interest in me ... as a man, you understand.'

There were murmurs; growls, and grunts of masculine comprehension during which someone trickled out a silent fart and hoped it wouldn't be noticed.

'Naturally that interest is not returned.'

Naturally. Miss Pemberton was hardly likely to ever grace a *Pirelli* calendar. More murmurs growls and grunts accompanied by the lighting of a number of Corona Coronas, possibly to help disguise the fart that had made its silent way across the table.

'I mean!' He looked around. Would he, with his known and acknowledged reputation as a lady-killer, be interested in someone so ... so ... unsvelte?

Nods and sly glances were added to the murmurs, growls, grunts, and the blowing out of clouds of blue smoke. Even Wilkins, wanting to be part of this male bonding, gave a sickly grin, in memory of his recent faux pas, his stomach still churning over, the seat of his trousers now firmly stuck with sweat to his leather chair, his wee willy practically non-existent and his scrotum totally retracted and tight as a drum.

'We understand, Mike,' the chairman said with a knowing

smile, revealing his yellow fangs. 'Do you know of someone you can recommend her to?'

Mike nodded. 'I know just the man,' he said.

'Then I am sure we can leave the suggested procedure in your capable hands? Would anyone like to propose the motion that Mike proceeds as planned?'

'Proposed.' A hand went up.

'Seconded.' Another hand went up.

'The motion is passed.'

There were gales of laughter at the double entendre before they moved on to any other business.

******

'So then, who was it recommended me to you?' Thornton asked.

'Does it matter?'

'I suppose not,' as he lifted his mug, 'idle curiosity really,' and took in a mouthful of bitter.

'Mike Aliff.'

Thornton nearly choked on his beer. Coughing and spluttering he put down his mug so fast he almost sent it toppling sideway to spill a fair amount in her direction across the small dimpled pewter tabletop before he recovered it. He hoped none had splashed over her or that could be the end of a beautiful and rewarding relationship before it even got started.

'I'm sorry,' he spluttered, adding unnecessarily, 'accident.' He started to get to his feet. 'I'll get a cloth.'

'Don't worry,' Rory said, 'no damage done. Sit down.'

He sat down.

'Why the melodramatic reaction?' she asked.

'Mike Aliff recommended you come to me?'

'That's what I said.'

Thornton shook his head, frowning. 'Why?'

'Because he says you're the best, that's why.'

'There's madness in his method I warrant you, as that old geyser Polonius would have said, and I remember someone else saying that to me not so long ago, those very words in fact, and it nearly led to my early demise. What is he up to I wonder?'

'I don't believe he's up to anything except that he … well … this is a bit tricky …'

'Then let me say it for you, he's been trying, using an American expression I heard, to jump your bones.'

'There you are, you see. He's right. You are good.'

'Not at all. I just happen to be aware of the man's priapic nature. Who could miss it? If he saw a field of daffodils he would still walk about in a cloud of masturbatory fantasy. He's the kind of man who spent all his pay visiting brothels and buying dirty pictures in Port Said during the war. I'm also well aware that he'll maintain all the attraction comes from your side, that way when he's rebuffed his ego won't suffer any damage. What a toad. No, that's most unfair on the poor old toad. Well, well, well.' Thornton shook his head.

'What?'

'There's something very fishy about this. Mike Aliff and I … well … this is a bit tricky…'

'Then let me say it for you, you hate his guts.'

'Normally I'm not the hating type but yes, though I'm sure I don't hate his guts half as much as he hates mine you're dead on target.'

'Hmn.'

'Have I said something wrong?'

'You know why I've come to see you.'

'As I said, I can only presume it's to do with the death of Sir Roger Pemberton, yes?'

'What do you know about it?'

'Only what I read in the papers, saw on the news. Oh!'

'Yes.' She looked down and ran a finger around the rim of her glass before looking back at him. She was obviously holding in the tears and Thornton could have bitten his lip for being so crass. She had remarkably deep blue eyes. 'So you know what killed him.'

'Yes. I'm so sorry. That was a bit off-colour, that remark about being dead on … yes, well.'

The barman approached their table with a damp not too clean looking cloth and gave the surface a quick wipe down before turning to go.

'Thank you,' Rory said, looking up with a beaming smile.

'What's your name?' Thornton asked.

'Ross.'

'Irish?'

'Yes.'

'What happened to Sean?'

'Sean?'

'The last one who was here.'

Ross shrugged, shook his head, and continued on his way back to the bar.

'This pub seems to have a new barman every other week. What happens to them all?'

'They go back to the Emerald Isle,' she said and then, after a pause, 'or to a better class of pub.'

'Yes, I agree, it is a bit dingy, but it's handy.'

They were both somewhat grateful for Ross's appearance that had given Rory time to recover and Thornton time to think of a better way of phrasing things in future.

'Do you believe it could have been suicide? As you know, that was the coroner's verdict. Do you believe it?'

'I couldn't possibly commit myself on that one unless I saw the police findings and the coroner's report, and analyse how he came to that conclusion.'

'No, Thornton ... I may call you Thornton?'

'Of course.'

'You don't need the police report, or the coroner's. I've given it a great deal of thought and I simply cannot believe anyone, least of all my guardian, would commit suicide with a crossbow bolt. If you're going to stab yourself in the heart or anywhere else for that matter with a sharp instrument you use a kitchen knife. There are plenty of large sharp knives in our kitchen where he was supposed to have killed himself. Why a crossbow bolt? No, I cannot imagine for one moment a man like my uncle who, by the way, was rather squeamish when it came to pain, would stand there thrusting a thing like a crossbow bolt under his ribs. His pain threshold was so low removing the tiniest splinter from a finger made him react as though it were major surgery without an anaesthetic.'

'Removing a splinter from a finger, or anywhere else for that matter, can be extremely painful,' Thornton contradicted her.

'Maybe for you men. It's a well known fact that women can stand much more pain but, to get back to what happened, I simply can't see him pushing the thing up at an angle. Surely, if he did use it, he would have pushed it straight in?'

'An angle?'

'Yes, according to the autopsy the thing went in from below the ribs and moved upwards. Maybe it was an accident. You know of course that he was a very important scientist with a top secret naval

research establishment, as a long shot … damn it, now it's my turn …'
She stopped and Thornton waited for her to regain her composure.
'I believe there is an old Chinese proverb,' she murmured, 'that says
we will always talk of feet in front of a cripple.'

'There's another Chinese proverb which goes, "I complained
because I had no shoes until I saw a man who had no feet."'

She gave a wan little smile and took a sip of her Martini Rosso
before going on. 'Could he have been conducting an experiment in
ballistics that went wrong do you think? After all the power of steam
was discovered in a kitchen.'

'Was the crossbow still there when you found him? I believe it
was you who discovered …'

'Yes,' she nodded, 'on the floor just outside the pantry door but
quite a way from his body, or the body was lying quite a way from it,
and there was nothing attached to the bow that could have been used
as a trigger so he didn't use it to shoot himself. No, accident is out as
well which leaves only one alternative, murder. That should have
been the coroner's verdict, murder by person or persons unknown.'
There was another pause and then, 'So, will you take the job?'

'Of course.'

'In that case, if we're going to continue our discussion, may I
suggest we move on to somewhere more congenial for a spot of
lunch? The snacks in here don't look all that exciting, do they?'

'I don't know,' Thornton said, 'they serve a good scampi in the
basket.' He was partial to a bit of scampi but Rory was already out of
her seat and on her way. He looked at Ross, busy wiping glasses and
Ross gave a nod. Thornton gave a wave and followed his new client
to the door.

******

François saw them enter and rushed across the restaurant to greet
them. Admittedly he didn't have far to travel, *L'eminence Grise* not
being the *Savoy* or the *Ritz*, and he didn't actually pant, jump up and
down, or roll on his back and pee himself with excitement, but his
effusiveness gave all the indications of a puppy whose mistress had
gone to the corner shop for a bottle of milk or a packet of fags and
had been away seemingly for months.

'Miss Pemberton, how delightful! How wonderful! How unexpected!'

'I know, François. Naughty of me just to drop in like this,' she almost simpered in girlie fashion, 'but you might just possibly be able to squeeze me in somewhere?'

It would be a tight squeeze whichever way you looked at it but he would manage it somehow. His waiters were adept at manoeuvring between tables seemingly no more than a couple of feet apart. The whole restaurant, packed with diners, though no one fortunately waiting for a table, seemed to be in mid-air fork suspension mode as they concentrated on just how easy it was going to be for François to squeeze in Aurora and her escort. One bean-pole unmannerly woman with teeth and a rather scraggy neck, staring hard at Aurora, giggled loudly and received in return a withering glare from Thornton, which unfortunately made her giggle even more. Aurora though seemed oblivious to it as they made their way to the small table François had brought out of hiding for just this sort of occasion and which was being busily set by one of the minions who greeted Aurora with many a smile and a bow. She was obviously a very popular patron, probably a generous tipper.

François, having placed a chair to seat Rory, now seemed to recognise for the first time that she had a companion and, remembering the previous visit Thornton had made to his august establishment, pulled himself up slightly and with rather a fixed smile said, 'And you, Mister King. Very nice to see you again.' He was not going to admit that the incident during Thornton's previous visit, if incident it could be called, had made his restaurant the most talked about, written about and the *in* place to dine so that it was booked solid for months, especially after Duncan Devonport-Fawcett wrote it all up in the glossy magazine that hired him. Despite its popularity François didn't allow standards to drop but, if anything, grew even more imaginative in his culinary inventions and, being a good businessman as well as a cordon bleu chef, he did use the opportunity to discreetly raise his prices. Not that his well-heeled clientele would have noticed and, with inflation what it was, prices were rising all the time anyway.

He allowed Thornton to pull in his own chair and seat himself whilst he held Aurora's napkin high and dramatically flipped it open before laying it across her lap whilst Thornton dramatically flipped open and laid down his own.

'And how have you been keeping, François?' Thornton enquired with an engaging smile.

'Very well, thank you, Mister King. Very well.' He managed to go so far as to turn over both their wine glasses though his attitude was still just a little on the frosty side as though it was all Thornton's fault that old Shoggi had snuffed it in so undignified a fashion in his establishment and that he had lost an excellent customer with the demise of the Princess Spitskaya.

'What do you recommend today, François?' Rory asked and, before he could reply, 'What do you fancy, Thornton?' She opened her menu.

Thornton, who was only too aware of François' prices even before they were raised, was a little hesitant in replying.

'Lunch is on me,' Rory said as if reading his thoughts. 'Don't hold back though personally I am going to have something ever so light.'

'On a day like this?' François was horrified. 'Mais non! No no no! Forgive me, my dear Miss Pemberton, but on a day like this you need something to keep out the cold. May I recommend the stuffed fillet of sole? Or perhaps the Paupiettes de veau Perigourdine. The veal is so tender it melts in the mouth.'

'Sold. How about you, Thornton?'

'I'll take the same.' He closed his own menu without even having looked at it and held it up for the maitre to take.

'Bon.' François whisked the menus out of their hands and was gone.

'He's forgotten something,' Thornton murmured.

'What would that be?'

'The wine?' He leaned forward to whisper.

'Oh, no, he knows exactly what wine to bring. Oh, I'm sorry! You're my guest and I didn't even think to ask you what you would like. How remiss of me.'

'Absolutely no problem,' Thornton said gallantly. 'I'm not a great connoisseur, I'll knock back whatever plonk comes along.'

It was her turn to lean forward across the table as far as she was able. 'Whisper it who dares,' she said, 'but the truth is, I prefer Italian wines to the French. Il vino amabile, and you will have noticed François' wine list is all French he's such a patriot. So he keeps a bottle or two of my favourites just for me but you will see when the waiter brings it the label will be well hidden. The other problem I have is I suffer a terrible feeling of guilt whenever I order veal. Those poor little things to be born to such a short and sad life. Human beings really are monsters. I find it hard to believe those farmers who raise them and those butchers who slaughter them can sleep peacefully in their beds of a night. And their poor mothers, the calves' mothers I mean, not the butchers'. How they must suffer having their babies taken away from them so young.'

Thornton was finding it a little difficult to believe he was actually hearing this but he chipped in with, 'I wouldn't let your conscience bother you too much, Aurora ...'

'Rory.' She smiled sweetly and raised an admonishing finger.

'Rory. After all nature is even more cruel, red in tooth and claw as the saying has it. Eat or be eaten. One of those sweet little calves probably wouldn't last three minutes in the wild before being torn to pieces. I can never understand vegetarians who use the cruelty to animals argument as their reason for not eating meat. If, like me, they had first-hand experience of African wildlife they would realise how much more cruel nature is. Even those little circus charmers, the chimpanzees occasionally feel the need for meat and in a pack can hunt down and tear to pieces a screaming terrified monkey.'

Rory shuddered visibly at the thought and laid a spread of chubby fingers on her pearls just as their waiter appeared with the wine, the label discreetly hidden by the napkin.

'Perhaps we should have had a white,' Rory said, the wine being the colour of blood, 'Of course we should have had a white! Who on earth drinks red wine with veal? Take it away, take it away!' Her voice had risen somewhat and she was making shooing gestures with both hands.

'What does it matter?' Thornton asked. 'The only good wine is the wine you like.'

The giggler started up again only now the giggle turned into the kind of laugh that requires a huge noisy adenoidal intake of breath between each guffaw. It was a bit like the braying of an ass, which was more than likely appropriate. Her companion looked rather embarrassed. If he was her husband, Thornton thought, casting a mean look in their direction, she was heading for a divorce and how on earth did he get to marry her in the first place? If they weren't married she would not be asked to lunch ever again. He decided they had to be brother and sister and the brother was performing a fraternal duty. She was down from the country for the day and as soon as he had seen her on the train and on her way home, he would rush into the nearest bar for a good stiff drink. How else to explain it? She was noticeably no oil painting, what with the teeth and the flat chest that was most definitely not sexy, so maybe her reaction to Rory was some sort of transference, a defence mechanism.

'Is something wrong?' François was immediately beside the table.

'Oh, François, you've sent a red wine instead of a white. Now that is not like you to defy convention.'

François leaned closer so that he could lower his voice almost to a whisper.

'Miss Pemberton, it is with much regret I have to inform you, at the moment I have no Italian whites in the restaurant. If I had known you were coming ... I will send someone out for a bottle immediately. What would be your preference?'

'Oh, never mind.' And then to the waiter still hovering, bottle in hand. 'Pour.' An imperious gesture nearly knocked over a wine glass, rescued by François in the nick of time just as the food arrived.

For someone who felt so dreadfully sorry for the poor calves, Rory tucked into her veal with abandon and the fact that a red rather than a white accompanied it didn't seem to diminish her enjoyment one iota. For a while, between mouthfuls, she babbled away about nothing in particular, mainly complaints about London, how it was getting filthier and noisier by the day, the traffic was appalling, crime was rampant and there were so many immigrants you could stand in Leicester Square all day and play spot the Englishman. If you came up with more than six you would be lucky. Air travel had a good deal to answer for. It was only when she had demolished the food that she returned to the matter in hand.

'So, Thornton, how long have you been practicing?'

Thornton's fork was halfway to his mouth and remained there as he raised his eyes to meet hers. Practicing? Practicing? What a strange word to use. Do private eyes practice? Doctors have a practice, dentists practice, you reluctantly practice playing the piano or the violin when you're a kid and your parents are wasting their hard earned money paying for the lessons, but a private detective? He had never thought about it. He lowered his fork, mouthful still on it. Was this to be the beginning of the end? He could figuratively see those pound notes floating out the door before they even had a chance to talk money.

'It depends,' he prevaricated, 'on exactly what your definition is of practice.'

'My definition of practice,' she said, obviously a bit peeved at the prevarication, 'is exactly what the word means. How long have you been a private detective?'

'Not very long.' He might as well be truthful. It will out in the end.

'And just how long is not very long?'

'Maybe a year? Maybe a bit longer?' He took another mouthful of food. He might as well finish it up before she finished with him and François was right, the veal really did melt in the mouth.

'And in that time you have earned a reputation for being the best in your field?'

'Not exactly.'

'And what exactly does not exactly mean?' She was obviously growing even more irritated and poured herself another glass of wine, splashing a few blood red drops on the snowy white linen.

'Look, what has Mike told you about me?'

'He couldn't praise your capabilities highly enough but he didn't exactly go into detail.' The word exactly was heavily accentuated.

'No, he wouldn't. Well, Rory, if you want my full CV I'm afraid you simply can't have it because it is virtually all top secret and filed away in the catacombs of Whitehall labelled not to be opened for fifty years, or something like that.'

'Really?' She was intrigued. 'Why is that?'

'Let's put it this way, if I were to write a book on my activities, the department would slap an immediate ban on it and I would probably be gaoled. National security and all that.'

'But you can whisper it to me, can't you? After all I am employing you.'

He shook his head and put an index finger to his lips. She was hooked, but she wasn't going to admit it.

'Thornton,' she said, sounding the essence of patience, 'I know you come highly recommended but when I make a purchase in Harrods, despite the fact the store has a reputation for quality second to none and will always make an exchange should you not be completely satisfied, I do like to see what I am buying in the first place. Now you really are going to have to tell me just a little about yourself.'

Thornton heaved a sigh, reached in his pocket and withdrew a small stone he placed on the table in front of her plate. She looked at it for a while before picking it up.

'And what may this be exactly?' She turned it over between forefinger and thumb, held it up to the light, rolled it in the palm of her hand.

'That, my dear Rory, is an uncut diamond.'

Rory sniffed.

'I promise you. It may not look much at the moment but, cut, it could well be worth something like two thousand, maybe two and a half.' He had absolutely no idea of a diamond's value.

She put the stone back on the table.

'Really. And why are you showing it to me?'

'Did you ever hear of a cult, an organisation, called The Army of The Righteous?'

'I seem to recollect seeing some TV footage about it. Seemed a pretty harmless bit of foolishness to me. Just a collection of hippies carrying on in typical hippy fashion though the fashion for beads, bracelets, long hair, smoking pot, playing with crystals, taking LSD, and letting it all hang out as they say must surely end soon, if it hasn't already.'

'Not harmless at all, Rory, highly subversive in fact and consequently dangerous.' He had lowered his voice now to almost a whisper, there seemed to be an awful lot of whispering going on at this luncheon, so that she had to lean forward to catch what he was saying. It was even less easy for her, the edge of the table pressing on a full stomach. The braying ass's ears would develop a stitch or pop their gristle if they endeavoured to stretch any further as Thornton went on. 'Their leader had negotiated with an international thief, a South African I believe, I bumped into him very briefly and purely by accident at Heathrow Airport, strange little man, for the delivery of a whole sack full of these precious little beauties. We don't know what the final objective was if and when they were cashed in, what the funds where going to be used for, but even the CIA were anxious as to exactly what they were about and had put a man onto it. Well, I beat the CIA to it, thwarted the organisation's exchequer and their schemes by tracking the diamonds from the south of France to Sicily.'

'Why Sicily?'

'There was a young Italian involved, no more than a kid really, went by the name of Luigi. He suddenly upped and skedaddled one night with the diamonds so I figured, as he was Sicilian, Sicily was naturally where he would be heading. Maybe he wouldn't do anything with the diamonds immediately but gradually, in small drops, he could try to sell them in Messina where they deal in precious metals, gold, silver, and also of course diamonds, hoping not too many questions would be asked. So colleagues and myself hired a helicopter and got there first, waited for him at Palermo railway station. We'd tipped off the Italian police of course and he was nabbed as he got off the train. Not only that but they also arrested the organisation's leader who was obviously there to collect.'

'What happened to them?'

'They're both in jail in Italy as far as I know.'

'Sounds like James Bond,' Rory whispered, slightly awestruck.

Beneath the table Thornton crossed the fingers of one hand and hoped his story, which wasn't exactly the truth, the whole truth, and nothing but the truth, didn't have too many holes in it but words once issued cannot be reclaimed. Hopefully she would forget the awkward details.

'Well,' he said, slightly self-deprecatingly, 'I was on Her Majesty's Secret Service.' He had seen the latest Bond movie only the week before.

It would seemed she hadn't noticed any holes in his story. She picked up the stone once more and turned it over in her fingers.

'You tell me this is worth between two and two and a half thousand pounds?'

'Maybe even more. I'm not a diamond merchant and I've not been to Hatton garden to have it valued so I couldn't say exactly but I don't think I'm too far off the mark.'

'What are you doing with it?'

Of all the questions she could have asked this was the one he had been dreading. He cleared his throat.

'Well, Rory, I have to admit here to a small misdemeanour. I kept this one as a sort of souvenir and something to put aside for that proverbial rainy day.'

'You mean you stole it.' She was looking him straight in the eye but he never flinched.

'Mea culpa. I'm afraid the temptation was too great and there were so many who would miss one small stone? Nobody. One teensy weensy diamond.' Thornton shrugged and finished his last forkful of food. 'After all,' he added, 'nobody knows just how many diamonds there were in the first place. I believe the original thief died of a heart attack at Heathrow airport but even he probably didn't know.' He conveniently forgot to tell her they spilled from a wet carrier bag that split. It had contained oranges to cover the diamonds and were rolling with the stones all over the station platform creating a minor riot.

'Where did the diamonds come from originally?'

'Hazarding a guess and knowing what I know about that part of the world I would say Sierra Leone.'

'And how did they get from Heathrow to the south of France?'

'In a suitcase with a false bottom.'

'And you suspected they were there? How clever of you.'

Thornton didn't contradict her but merely smiled modestly.

Aurora seemed fascinated and lost in thought as she fiddled with the stone. She pursed her lips and narrowed her eyelids.

'I tell you what, Thornton,' she said finally, looking up at him, 'I will give you a cheque for a thousand pounds now and, if you solve the case, a further thousand and a half plus all expenses. In the meantime I will keep this piece of stolen property and, if you don't come up with the goods as they say, well, it won't have been a dead loss would it?' You will have made a thousand at least, plus expenses, and I will have this stone cut into a very nice ring for me. She held it up to the light between thumb and forefinger as if she could already see its sparkling facets.

Lady Haw Haw was so totally fascinated her lower jaw was practically on the table. She couldn't take her eyes off them and her companion, first glancing around to see who else might be looking, coughed to remind her she was being just a wee bit obvious and whatever transaction was going on, it was no business of hers.

She turned back to look at him and whispered, 'I'm fascinated,' so that the whole restaurant could hear. He looked around again, smiling apologetically to the world in general. What a worm. She couldn't wait to tell her friends in the country what curious people she had come across in the big city.

'If you do solve the case,' Rory continued, 'to show my eternal gratitude, the stone will be returned to you and you will have made handsomely out of it, right? I might even take the trouble of having it cut for you, as an extra present. Agreed?'

Thornton had the feeling that somewhere down the line he was being done but he wasn't too sure, maths was never his forte, neither was logic which is a bit of a drawback for a private detective but the thought of that thousand pound cheque up front (wouldn't his supercilious bank manager raise his bushy eyebrows in surprise?) made him nod in agreement and she slipped the stone into her handbag just as François appeared once more to enquire as to whether or not they would like a dessert.

They decided on a chocolate, orange, and hazelnut mousse and, to round off the meal, coffee, accompanied by parfait amour for Rory, she obviously had a very sweet tooth, and a fine cognac for Thornton. He never could resist it. He rolled the balloon in his cupped fingers and sniffed the bouquet. He couldn't help feeling that, like coffee, sometimes the aroma was better than the taste but he lifted the glass to his mouth, took a sip and, as always, almost sighed with the physical pleasure of it, decided there and then he had better start practicing to be a detective.

'My turn to ask questions,' he said.

'Fire away.' She took a sip of her own sweet mauve liqueur.

'Right. Enemies.'

'What?'

'Did Sir Roger have any enemies that you are aware of?'

Rory shook her head. 'He simply was not the kind of man to make enemies. A milder, kinder gentleman would be hard to find.'

'Hmn ... still waters run deep as the old saying has it.'

'Thornton, all he was interested in really, as far as I am aware, was his work, and I know nothing about that because, like yours used to be, it's a secret world, isn't it?'

'What do you do with yourself, Rory?'

'I beg your pardon!'

'Do you have a job? An occupation? Are you, as they say, in gainful employment?'

'Does this have any bearing on the case?'

'It helps to know exactly what the domestic set-up was. For example, do you have a nine to five, which means leaving the flat all day? Or do you have a job that takes in night shifts?'

'I don't have a job at all unless you call voluntary work for charity a job and that takes up a great deal of my time, fund raising, organising, travelling, both here and abroad. Yes, come to think of it, it is a full time job but I love it and I wouldn't do anything else.'

'Any help around the flat?'

'There's a daily, Mrs McIvor, a truly harmless old biddy. Well, not exactly old, middle-aged rather I suppose, she just gives the impression of being old.'

'You trust her?'

'Oh, completely! She's an absolute poppet.'

'So was Lizzie Borden.'

'Who?'

'Lizzie Borden, a supposedly completely inoffensive young lady in Massachusetts who allegedly murdered her parents with an axe. There was a rhyme written about it, "Lizzie Borden took an axe and gave her father forty whacks. When she saw what she had done she gave her mother forty-one." Maybe it was the other way round, mother first followed by father. Can't remember where I first heard that.'

'What happened to her?'

'Nothing was proved and she lived to a ripe old age in the very house where it happened. Isn't that macabre? Do you think the ghosts of her parents haunted the place? "Lizzie, dear Lizzie, why did you do it?" There is always the question of motive you see, and what possible motive could Lizzie, a demure and dutiful daughter living quietly in small town America, have had to murder her inoffensive old parents? Like Jack The Ripper, another mystery, another unsolved case. This Miss McIvor of yours … '

'Mrs.'

'Mrs. Married? Divorced? A widow?'

'I believe she has what she calls "her old man" who goes by the name of Jimmy, originally from Glasgow.'

'Do we know what he does for a living?'

'He's a mini-cab driver. I know that because he drops her off and picks her up every day and she's mentioned it, and I've seen him once or twice.'

'Capable of violence do you think?'

'I doubt it very much. Looking at him I wonder he has the strength to turn the steering wheel he's such a weed.'

'He doesn't have to be a muscular giant to be strong or dangerous. Dynamite, as they say, comes in small packages.'

'You're full of other people's sayings, aren't you?'

'Aren't we all? Have you ever used his cab?'

'No.' Rory raised an eyebrow to indicate she wouldn't be seen dead in a mini-cab.

'The night you came home and found your uncle, where had you been?'

'Thornton, I've already given the police all this information. It really isn't going to help you.'

'Maybe, maybe not. All right, let's move on. Mistresses.'

'No.'

'Gay?'

'No.'

'No sex life at all?'

'Whatever he did to relieve himself sexually I know nothing about it. He never married. There are no dirty magazines in the flat, straight or otherwise, no sex toys. The police went through it with a fine tooth comb. Certainly being shot in the chest by a crossbow bolt could hardly be in the nature of a masochistic sexual game gone wrong.'

There was an audible gasp from the Haw Haw's table and both Rory and Thornton turned to look. Thornton leaned back in his chair.

'If we had two more chairs placed at this table would you care to come over and join in the conversation?'

The male companion was absolutely horrified. His mouth started to quiver and it took a while for him to find his voice.

'I b ... beg your p ... pardon?'

'And so you should.' Thornton turned from him to her. 'Did your mother never tell you it is rude to listen in to other people's conversations?'

'I think we had better leave,' the companion said, rising. By now the whole restaurant had ears flapping fit to start a windstorm and all eyes were on Lady Haw Haw.

Blushing with embarrassment she got up, threw Thornton what she thought was a contemptuous glance though it seemed in fact as though she was about to burst into tears, and they made for the door, there to wait by the desk for their bill. In their haste they had even forgotten to leave a tip and such was their state they would no doubt forget to leave one whilst paying. Out of sheer embarrassment they would not be returning to the Grise for a long time.

'The only reason I am pursuing this line of questioning,' Thornton said, turning back to Rory and wishing he didn't sound quite like Reg Venables, 'is because if he picked up a piece of rent or rough trade ... '

'I told you, there was never anything like that.' She sounded rather annoyed but he went on regardless.

'Seeing as to how he would be considered a security risk he would more than likely keep it a secret from you and everyone else and rough trade can get very rough.'

'Forget it, Thornton. You're barking up the wrong tree. My God, we're full of the platitudes today, are we not?'

'All right then, what about foreign visitors, foreign correspondence? Could he have been blackmailed by a foreign power because of his work?'

'I suppose it's possible but he gave no signs of distress or being under any sort of pressure. Not to me he didn't. No, wait! The last week or so he did seem a little more preoccupied than usual but I just put it down to absentmindedness.'

'I'll check with one of my colleagues in the department.'

'Mike Aliff?'

'Certainly not Mike Aliff. No, I was thinking of my friend Holly, Holly Day.'

'Oh, yes, Mike mentioned her. If I recall he referred to her as that snooty stuck-up bitch.'

'He would,' Thornton chuckled. 'But snooty would have been enough. Stuck up is sheer tautology. Another question. How come there was a crossbow in the flat anyway?'

'Some time ago archery was my uncle's hobby, both longbow and crossbow. He wasn't into competition or anything like that, a bit too old for that sort of caper, but he took it up as a form of exercise. At one time he was quite serious about it and an excellent shot I am informed on good authority but I believe he hadn't pursued it for a while. That is except for a month or so ago when he said he had been invited to take part in a challenge match.'

'Neighbours.'

'What neighbours?'

'You live in a block of flats, you have neighbours.'

'Once upon a time people had neighbours but it was a long time ago, Thornton. During the war there were neighbours. Out in the country there used to be neighbours but even out in the country these days you're unlikely to have any because the cottage next to yours has been bought by city types as a second home and you never get to know them. They roll up on a Friday night in their Landrover or any other make of four wheel drive gas guzzler, and their labradors their green wellies and before you can say hello across the hedge it's Sunday night and they're shooting back to their jobs in the city. They don't even use the local store but bring everything they need with them. Here now we have the sound of television sets. I wouldn't know any of our neighbours as you call them if I passed them in the street. That's the way it is today. Today neighbours are a scarcity. Today there is the sound of teevees, usually too loud and, in the summer, cheap music blaring out through open windows without a thought for other people. I suppose in a way we were partly to blame that we don't know anybody in the building. Sir Roger was hardly the gregarious type and I didn't exactly knock on doors. Isn't it sad?'

'Presumably the police questioned the people living in the building?'

'And got nothing. No one saw anything, no one heard anything, only their TV sets.'

'Then I had better start looking in other directions.'

'Yes, Thornton, you better had.'

www.ingramcontent.com/pod-product-compliance
Lightning Source LLC
Chambersburg PA
CBHW021956170626
46808CB00001B/180